BAILEY'S ROAD

B. G. SIMPSON

ISBN 979-8-89504-460-5 (softcover)
ISBN 979-8-89504-461-2 (hardcover)
ISBN 979-8-89504-462-9 (ebook)

This book is a work of fiction. Names, characters, places, and incidents are the product of the author's imagination or are used fictitiously. Any resemblance to actual locales, events, or persons, living or dead, is purely coincidental.

Cover art generated at www.designer.microsoft.com

Printed in the United States of America.

CHAPTER 1

The Evening Run

The distance down a dim-lit dark dusty road was too far for the eye to see, not for the faint hearted to go aloft on foot. The sweat ran down tanned leathery skin in the heat of the evening twilight. Step-by-step, breath-by-breath. On the trail, the warm muggy air was calling him out, like it was a part of him, knowing every movement thought out. The pain was real in body making the evening run invigorating. The noise of feet hitting the pavement set a rhythm to every step, heart pounding, head clear of stress, and the day's worries done—left behind on this dusty road, pushed by the pain, driven in the dark by the evening noise of crickets, dogs barking in the background. Ahead was this fence separating all from crossing the border of Mexico. Small shack house's dotted the side of the hill. Noise of nightlife could be heard faintly in the distance. The turn to the beach and seven miles back was the order of the night. Down the turn facing west a mile and half from the ocean, hitting the last turn, a pocket of air became cold cooling sweat beaten brow.

The fence was intriguing, worn from time, and battered by use and weather. The ocean breeze was now pushing against body causing more work to stay in rhythm. The smell of the salted sea could be felt on lips and burning skin, yet the need to push on kept propelling, kept willing all strength forward in anticipation of the next step. The road ended soon, and nothing was left but sand, uneven terrain, and wind hitting faces of awkward and unbalanced processions. To the left over the fence could be seen off in the distance the bullring of Tijuana, Mexico as small tack lights surrounded the top. The unknown runner glanced slightly to notice the bullring, just to make sure its usual place, and viewing the right path of a continued run. The ocean waves could be heard echoing in the distance, the runner became fleet of feet, knowing there was cool water to quench the heat pressing him, completing him, moving him, in the direction of this unknown water source. The muscles of legs felt the sting, gently cooled as it splashed over wanting body—like hot coals dipped in frigid waters.

No thoughts of the tough day gone by, pumped full of vigor of a fast-paced life, feeling the burn of physicality, in that moment, in that present time of life. At its best when experienced height of exuberance. The physical drain covered all adversities. Today was the best day of his life for that moment, for that experience. Internalizing everything—the ocean sounds, the coldness of the water, the darkness of the night, and the dim lighting of the moon on the ocean's waves. Knowing that crossing the water inlet, while being close to the border of Mexico, would always surprise, not knowing the current being stronger than usual, enough to pull anyone out toward the oceans door. The challenge was swimming past its doorway, taking the living breath and remaining strength from weary limbs as payment against the rage of gathering waves, power out of control, passing the limits of human experiences. Muscles tensing, confidence fading, darkness overwhelming. Yet the brisk event would take all to the end of despair. This was living, no boredom, no anxiety, while a pure will of adrenaline moved of passion, pressing him forward of the night. The water moved with tides, pulling at an angle, not sure the leading journey taken of direction. Looking to view the sand from the other side. Feeling the distance still out of reach, already spent, already drained of hidden energy, with several miles to go when the run continued before reaching the final goal.

Something brushed up against plummeting legs while pushing into the muck of drifting tides. Plunging sporadically to avoid anything else that might be swimming in the oceans waves. The beating of heart slammed against chest in a rhythm not thought possible. *Come on you can do it,* was the thought. All muscles were at the brink of needing rest. Feeling the other side of the water inlet under feet through movement of a sandy bottom. Gaining confidence, coming to comprehend the pace was set, conserving energy to pull weary body upon the sandy shore. Lying there in the comfort of a moon-lit-night, feeling strength slowly coming back to limbs gone weary. Thinking about the race coming up ahead, in another week. *Why did I ever get into such an exhausting sport?* Was the thought, but then remembering it wasn't by chance, or by some unfit superiority in the back of one's mind, it was destiny driving him by some insane melodramatic way of living. A gift seen past the lines of despair.

Young in his prime, ready to walk any line of competition—a young man of reason, a young man of in-depth common sense. Standing on my feet, gazing past the scribbled lines of darkness, past the long barriers of coastline stretched endlessly toward the sea. A leaning slender silhouette, muscular frame, blond hair, and brown eyes that pierced through the unknown of night, seeing beyond limits of human eyes so carefully made. Vision was the weighing factor driving him to succeed. The vision to go the extra mile. Bailey was his name, not a name of honor or royalty, but of a plebian character, a heart for the people. A young man that was full of heart and integrity, driven to accomplish anything. Never limiting abilities. Being game short of fame for a new challenge, no limits beyond human realities. Tender in spirit, shown in innocents to fragile confidentialities, no mischievous actions, a peacemaker in softly spoken manner. Holding life to a gentler side of given opinions, standing to the challenges when presented. A man of honor and courage, which looked beyond what the human heart could envision, and looked for a better way, on any given better day of history, to find a pathway leading toward victory. Standing at the beginning of life trying to find direction, finding his path or journey leading to purpose, along with present day responsibilities.

As time moved on, Bailey had developed an insatiable love for running, not knowing this passion or gift would teach him about the germane process of life. This would eventually fuel emotions, for those things yet to come to be burned in memory.

November 18th, 1975… was Bailey's birthday, soon to turn seventeen. That weekend, before all was said and done, challenging others in a race against one of the toughest schools in the valley. The butterflies, at that present moment began to kick in, when thinking about the task ahead. This was a normal procedure that would take form before each race came to a climax. Bailey understood the pain and misery were all a part of the journey, a part of the harmony constantly facing him, soon to leave behind marks of meeting certain goals.

Coming back to reality, Bailey continued the run on the beach, hard sand using the moon lighting the pathway that lay ahead. Regaining strength, propelling, moving forward, an inscrutable creature cutting new avenues in secrets unrevealed in water, wind, and sand. The dark of night faced and knowing of others stirring. In the distance, seeing beach houses coming up on the right and the Imperial Beach Pier farther off to the left. A beach campfire was blazing in the brilliance of an evening fire ring, as the light of the fire pulled him in the direction of where he needed to go, a bug zapper pulling in the biggest bugs, a utopia of bug heaven, giving a mark to shoot towards. Holding running shoes in his right hand, picking up speed, and drawing closer to people around the fire ring. Passing the ring, noticing quickly six people sitting around in the comforts of cooler breezes telling stories of old past realities. An older gentleman says, "Hi," and Bailey acknowledged by a raise of left hand. Too out of breath to speak, running past the fire ring up off the beach toward an ending street, just passed the sand and crashing waves behind, eluded by darkness that had quickly caught up to him, unrevealing secrets of another time had dropped in—giving no further vision toward another day marked of history. Stopping to sit on a telephone pole that lay as a street blocker to keep cars off the beach. Then got back up and continued his run in the mystery of the night. Home was still four and a half miles away on cemented sidewalks moving in the rhythm of the streets, as these land markers pulled in the direction of small patches of light strung across the valley of tangled track houses and sounds of the night air that breathed with life—as life like no other crept in silent movements of a bustling rural city. Bailey lived in the suburbs of San Diego County—a rich community of staggered growth of a booming economy. Reaching a familiar street after running through the neighborhood, and seeing the porchlight on, and the familiar number at the side of the house, as the air in lungs moved him in a rhythm of the night's long run of familiarity. Looking up after getting closer, seeing the seven-hundred-block written in black script. Happy to make it home in one piece.

CHAPTER 2

The Race

Bailey stood at the starting line in ocean blue tank top and shorts shimmering in the mid-afternoon sun, as early tendrils of sweat started to make its way down his face. Face was set in a stupor of hidden strength rising on the edge of inner character. Twenty-five young men leaned *in* waiting for the sound of the gun before lunging from a sudden jolt. Bailey learned at an early age how to clear mind of any future unknown, without fear, without being thrown off by the anticipation, relaxed, drawing from inner strength, living only that fleet second, a span of time, not confused by the weary drama of, what if? The gun popped a loud and deafening noise into the ears of the cluster of young men causing them to move quickly down a long-paved road toward an old country house. The course was hilly with sharp hair pin turns that Bailey was well familiar with, running this path over a hundred times. The boys called it Suicide Hill, a course not taken lightly. Bailey jumped out of the start with three other boys, all taking the lead, like horses propelled by pure will of inward beauty. Calm and collected, conserving energy for the hills to come. As they near the old country house, Bailey exploded down a long-rugged path off to the left, leaving the others only to follow. Jagged and slippery, the trail became single file, focused strength became the only needed attribute to sustain each runner on the hidden trail. By now, Bailey was flying sure footed knowing the course's every dip and curve. Gliding over the rough areas to keep from falling at such a high speed. This trail was not made for this type of footwork, but somehow the course was chosen for the cross-country team.

Bailey glanced over left shoulder to make sure having a sustainable lead, surprising to see Joe from a competing school was right behind. Short, dark haired young man with muscular legs and biceps. Grooming parents started running with him at a very young age of four years old, knowing youth of earlier training gave him an edge over most others that would challenge. Yet for some reason, Joe knew Bailey was somehow different than the ordinary boy who tread this valley and forged these trails unknown. He was an inspiration for others to follow after, and today wasn't any different than usual, because Bailey had set the pace and tone of this race much earlier. Prepared and prepped and ready to go, Joe started feeling it in his legs, when first hitting that monster of a hill jetting up before them. Suicide was just as its name proclaimed, a suicide's mission was from the get-go, and Joe accepted the rules of engagement. Knowing the familiar pain of training, and Bailey would almost kill to win this race at even the cost of passing out once at the finish line. Bailey reminded Joe of an earlier famed runner referred to as Prefontaine. A college jock from Oregon that broke every college distance mark in the state and then some. The only person he knew who would be faster was a boy named Steve Scott that later in life broke the sub-four-minute mile over four hundred times in his career to follow. Joe thought Bailey to be like this type of runner, who was really bad at losing to local boys, who would spur the local headlines from such runners if ever beaten. Yet Joe knew Bailey had that same type of irritating agenda, unsettling of mind, once on that starting line. Knowing he was in for a ride, and Bailey didn't take to heart someone winning on his own familiar field of battle. Joe knew what it would take to beat Bailey at his own race and if anyone could make that accomplishment, it was Joe. Bailey picked up his pace using the downhill turns to eat up the distance. Breathing deeply, keeping his rhythm and body relaxed as much as possible. At the halfway point Joe was five steps behind, making stride-for-stride with no words said, just an empty head to conserve energy. Bailey and Joe were the only two left of present-day history, keeping up this pace since the beginning of this race, stride-for-stride running for victory at a very quick pace. Hearts were put on the line, who would be quicker, who'd win the prize? Bailey knew to beat Joe; he would need a considerable lead. Joe had a final kick that was too much for most to handle, and Bailey wasn't about to experience it first-hand.

Down at the lowest end of the course stood this mountainous hill called Suicide, it was a match for the human heart. Bailey spent his whole summer training on hills such as this. He was prepared for this challenge. His calves were enlarged from workouts that became over demanding of muscles. Focusing, knowing of the pain that was up ahead.

At the bottom of this macabre quake of wonder, Joe was closing in on Bailey's feet. Hearing the patter of Joe's shoes right behind. Keeping his mind empty, no thoughts of disillusionment, no psyche-out. A man on a mission, with a mission on his mind.

Keeping his head down, pushing up the mountain as an untamed lion attacking its prey. Not thinking of Suicide Hill and its massive existence. Only focusing on the run, itself, with competition closing in behind. The mission, conquering the mountain that stood in the way. No pain was too severe to endure, no heat was too depleting, just a constant propelling forward, up this massive hill, a force pulling him toward an end.

Bailey flew up Suicide leaning into the monstrosity as expert to this macabre hill. Hidden strength became as companion. Climbing Suicide, greeting a long-lost friend waiting at the top. Looking over his left shoulder, no Joe to be seen, taking off in a sprint with half a mile to go. Feeling victory in his veins, no letting up, no slowing down, just an all-out sprint back down this road where first starting. Not looking behind, Bailey felt Joe to be close by, quiet—serene, slowly catching up while eluding his competition of purpose, trying to slip on by unnoticed without being caught. Yet boy wonder was soon to blunder, as Bailey knew quite well his competitions cursory way of winning. Bailey's father and the crowd could be heard screaming at the top of their lungs, "Come on Bailey, he's right on your heels!"

Bailey was pumped for the end, lengthening stride with stride in the direction of finish line, as the crowd set the stage of this near end accomplishment. There were about 150 people jammed close to the red tape taking up every inch of space, egging the two runners to the finish, visualizing fire was the chase. Bailey's lungs were about to burst yet no thoughts were on ever failing, only on the race itself—no Joe was going to psyche him out today, no smoke of illusions to float by like mist to confuse, no politicians giving greetings at the end, just the inward satisfaction of winning. Bailey felt exuberant about being chased and watched by the many. People were now jumping up and down on the paved road. No other runners could be seen on the last quarter mile stretch—just Bailey and Joe fighting for that finish line, knowing the only prize was to race another day. Twenty-five feet to go, Bailey reached down inside that hidden place where the seeds of faith grow, in a place where courage lays and blooms like flowers in open sunshine, where the sounds of chaos all around are lost in the distance of space covered up by courage and joy and goodness, where the sweat and pain are ignored, where sycophantic energy takes over, blanking out the crowd, blanking out the noise, anticipation of the taste of victory drawing near, while Bailey made that final surge across the tape in that circle of friends and family patting him on the back—encouragement given on this fast track. Bailey could taste its beauty like it was soaked up through his skin. Looking up then smiling in the direction of Joe. Thinking he had a much longer lead but remembering at the last moment his father reminded him of Joe's unforgiving kick. Bailey's lungs were about to burst, not having the training from youth, the way Joe had from his parents. Yet Joe was standing up straight, calmly congratulating Bailey's accomplishment, while Bailey was crouched in the throw-up position. Death felt close, a reminder of his competition was unmoved by the experience. Bailey didn't care. He savored this victory knowing there would be other days for retribution, as seen by the look that crossed the other boy's face.

Bailey's coach said, "I thought he had you for a minute, but you held him at bay, good race." This was to prove different when track came up the next spring when he had to face Joe. He became his most enduring competitor on the track. He had this incredible kick that usually burned most of the competition. Bailey had profound respect for Joe and his running ability. Yet Joe never beat Bailey on his cross-country course the whole time he had to compete against him in high school, but now it was a different story on the track.

Somehow wasting time running in circle's wasn't Bailey's first love. The open road was more to his liking, adjusting to his environment was the challenge that he liked facing. He had no vision of wasting time running around a track like a treadmill belt that never ended. He liked facing the trails of the unknown, no complete sight of the oncoming trail, no preplanned strategy to overcome, just pure relaxed flight through the air.

CHAPTER 3

Colorado Bound

The evening was close to an end. It had been a long day, a treacherous year for this young man from a coastal city. No more congratulations, no more pats on the back. Young Bailey's family moved inland out of state and left him behind to fend for his own. In the big city, looking for answers to life's questions, no home left to go to, just his insatiable drive left, his enduring heart, and calming spirit. Now nineteen, only a youth to the many, but had this incurable desire for life and adventure. After communicating with his aunt, he decided to drive across country and start over. This town might bring new meaning to life—or a new direction that would reach to the stars not hanging too far off in distant places, where his mind takes to wander from time-to-time. It was early April. The flowers had started to bloom early. Many trees had fresh leaves growing on their branches. The air was crisp with the great wonder that spring brings with it a fresh start. Bailey was not sure of his future or what was to become of him. Jumping up early that morning to try and conquer this mammoth mountain rising to the sky behind his aunt's house.

Aunty and uncle lived in the hilly community on the west side of Colorado Springs. Bailey's uncle had built three houses on this street and had rebuilt two other homes to accommodate a growing family. They owned ten acres of land up on the hillside. It was a beautiful area with lush greenery surrounding the base of the mountains, sitting on the top of a mesa seeing the city in the distance. They set their roots here when they first got married and never left. They were destined to live a lifetime of love and happiness together. They had four boys who were rambunctious from the very start of life, always willing to challenge anyone and everyone they would meet with a competing heart. There was Rin, Johnny, Spike, and Holden—Holden a young man that was adopted when he was noticeably young. He was accepted just like he was born into the family. As far as anyone else was concerned he was just an awkward egg that hatched a little late in season. Rin was the athletic one, who became really good at rock climbing, and got so good he would take people on mountain climbing tours on the backside of the 'Garden of the Gods,' a serene, beautiful, back drop of incredible red rock mountains that went up about 3,000 feet. Spike, the book worm, who spent all his time in school, always dreamed of being a doctor and fell short a couple of times but kept trying. Failure had taught him about that wayward form of humble pie, he wouldn't give up no matter how long the journey was to take. Johnny was more into eateries of the fine art of the culinary kitchen. Becoming engaged to this handsomely smart girl and married her. She was beyond beautiful and had stolen a good portion of the boy's heart, and love had chased him across the street to live in one of dads houses. A fresh cup of coffee was just a door away, into his mother's backyard, up the stairs, and into the usual kitchen. They had breakfast together every morning before a new day would get started. Dreaming, like all young boys dream of becoming that man which won his family's approval, gleaming boisterously back to the kitchen to get seconds of coffee. Wearing a few pounds on looking a bit less than moderate. Eventually becoming a culinary chef and spent many a day in the kitchen. Life was good and full of plentiful rewards of a married man's life. Later on, ending up working for a famous culinary eatery. Holden became a famous D.J. in Denver for a radio broadcast station that played rock and roll music. He was a good man and married this beautiful young lady that had common interests. Bailey's uncle retired as a fire chef with the local Fire Department after thirty years of service. Rin and father would build elaborate kitchens as a business in an 80 by 40 old-red-rustic-barn behind the main house and sell them once or twice a year to pass the time away of earlier retirement. Bailey's uncle also had milking goats, a small egg ranch, and a couple of mules up on the hillside. Frequently going up to the chicken coop early in the morning and getting fresh eggs and milking one of the goats. Bailey got a job at a local taco shop in town part-time and decided to go to the church on top of the hill. It was a large church with beautiful stained-glass windows in the back balcony that rose 25 feet in the air. And life was complete at the moment. It was about as normal as it ever could be.

So off to the mountains Bailey went on his first short run of this new spring season, just to familiarize young useful lungs to a new reality. Driving his Custom Supreme Oldsmobile and headed for the park at the bottom of this mammoth mountain in front. There were running trails all over the hills below, starting at 6,700 feet going all the way up to about 12,500 feet. He decided to start light on his first day not being accustomed to high elevation. Months to come, Bailey had talked to some of the locals and was told about a marathon that they would put on in June. Being asked if interested in competing. Telling them he would think about it and let them know. Before the marathon, there were some shorter runs that would help improve his racing skills, before making a commitment to a more difficult event. Deciding to do a couple of those easier races first before considering running a marathon. Then seeing where this would take him.

Back at the house, Bailey was able to stay and live in his aunt and uncle's basement. It was the same size as the house—about 1200 square feet. There was an L-shaped couch, a big screen TV, and a coffee table in the middle of a front room, with a bedroom off in a corner, and laundry room close to the stairs. Sunlight would pore through the windows at certain times of the day, sometimes waking him quite early. His aunt would come down to do laundry from time to time, but besides that he was mostly alone.

Moving on, Bailey's uncle's mother had three children besides him. Uncle Ron's younger sister had a daughter that took a liking to Bailey—

on several occasions this soft-spoken mountain girl kept showing up at the house on short notice asking for the thin wiry boy. She was a very sensible girl with big brown eyes, and a petite frame that caught him staring. She usually radiated a smile that would light up the room. Being around him quite frequently holding herself to a way of softer speaking, holding back a bit, not to give away her Tom-boyish ways of sometimes taking over. From time to time, she'd glance his way when he wasn't looking. She had just finished high school the year before, and wasn't much too dating boys to frequently, being the youngest after five brothers had come before her. Yet somehow Bailey knew she'd show an interest, always showing up at the perfect times. Come over to help to do dishes, and once to do laundry. Showing a great appeal for the young man in his quiet stirrings, of a young boy with heart. Betty before had better days of finding things to do, usually not hanging around boys was never on her list to do. She would stay home most of the time helping her grandmother with chores or taking care of her brothers children. Bailey caught on quickly, he had a secret admirer. His heart told him that they might be a good match for each other and having her around he began to see how sweet and lovable she was. Yet with time he would get to know her. She was attractive with a keen sense of awareness of their strange attraction to each other. Dropping anything to be with Bailey to spend a few moments exchanging stares, to drop a smile or bat her eyes trying to catch him glaring. Somehow, he talked her into going to a few of his races to take pictures—being only an excuse from the get-go. One evening, Bailey was eating dinner in the basement front room watching TV as Betty came down. She was dressed up to kill any staggering hearts laying wasted to the side, while trying to catch him with shaky hands not knowing what to do with them. He could smell her perfume right away, which drew his interest. She sat down next to him, as his heart began to beat a little stranger. He was lost in her eyes for the moment as she looked at him with a giddy expression, trying to impress, trying to unhinge this boy of shaky awkward moments. She looked at the TV quickly to bat his stare away, like all girls play these silly games. Trying to impress but keeping him abreast of her real intensions of laying her hands on him. The light was coming through the window, early evening, not a cloud in the sky as it lit up her face. His heart began to pound. *What the heck is wrong with me?* He thought. *Why am I feeling this way?*

Bailey took a long soft look at Betty as she pretended not to take notice. He then decided in his awkward way to reach over and gently brush his lips against her cheek. Well, Betty had other plans and as Bailey was moving toward her, she turned as their lips met. Caught by surprise the boy was shaking more than grandma's old 57 Ford. He couldn't say any words as mounting fright developed. They were clumsily eye-to-eye while Bailey felt heat from his face run in all directions. Betty grabbed Bailey by the back of the neck like a big cat grabbing her cub. She reeled him *in* like she just caught an influential person. She laid a lip-lock on him that would have smothered the furriest of cuddly animals. He couldn't let go if he tried. Breathing was his main concern after about ten seconds. The lack of experience in this area caused him to fight for air. To conclude, Betty loosened her death grip on Bailey as he continued a crimson face. Developing a loss for words with only being a half a second from passing out beyond the limits of damaging brain cells. Betty looked over in astonishment then asked if he were okay.

He replied, "I think so?" He said, "Is that a new way of making out?" Then he realized that was the wrong thing to say, continued in his awkward way.

Betty stood up abruptly with a disgusted look, "I wasn't making out with you, you big dork!" As she ran up the stairs and left without a word said to anyone else.

The days to come went by quickly now that Bailey was working. With his long runs, early morning, or late afternoon, plus his work schedule kept him busy. Time eluded him quickly for a young man of constant challenges, yet somehow spending time with his aunt and uncle. Now and then, Betty would still come over and say hi, but no lip-lock advances were made by her. She realized that wasn't one of Bailey's thrilling moments of specialties, even though he was attracted to her strange sense of awareness. Not inclined to put himself in another situation where lacking experience.

A few days ahead, Bailey had a ten-mile race coming up that weekend and wasn't sure if Betty was still willing to go for moral support, or if nothing else, to take a few pictures of the lanky boy treading down some dusty trail. Getting up that morning to do the usual bit of getting ready, for a new day of adventure. Each new race would cause the butterflies to kick up in his stomach. Trying vigorously to rid his mind of the race coming up through the 'Garden of the Gods,' yet couldn't quite shake the pre-race jitters. As Bailey walked up the stairs, seeing his aunt sitting in a kitchen chair with one leg crossed, smoking a cigarette, and talking to Betty from across the table. Wearing bright red lipstick, her shiny shoulder length brown hair combed perfectly, white shorts with a colorful checkered blouse. Suddenly, seeing Bailey plodding up the stairs with a lost-little-boy-look pasted on his face as their eyes met. Surprised, he gave a raised eyebrow to that effect in her general direction.

"Oh, hi Betty! How are you?" Like he was reading a script from a play and almost missed his lines, "Are you still going with me to the race?"

Betty expressed a fading smile…"Of course. I'm looking forward in getting out of the house. Besides, if I just stay home my grandmother is sure to put me to work."

Bailey acknowledged with a shaky smile, "Yeah, my mother used to do that to me every weekend that I was home." The odd couple returned pleasantries with aunty, for about two or three minutes while she wished Bailey well in his race to come. They both say their goodbyes and Betty and Bailey jet out the side door towards the car. Walking closely behind, the boy noticed her cute little bouncing figure of delight, and soon he'd forget about pre-race jitters. This was the perfect diversion of pending race hype. Bailey hurries to open Betty's door. She smiled apprehensively as she slid in the seat. He viewed her clearing the door and walked around to get in. The doors were closed, and soon seatbelts clicked, and a few minor adjustments done, and they were quickly on their way. Betty turned with a determined mindset, "Okay, we're off." She softly said.

Bailey turned to look in his rearview mirror as he began to back out of his aunt's long driveway. He could smell something soft and fragrant. It caused his heart to stir. His mind began to wander to that smothering first kiss. He wished he hadn't stumbled so awkwardly for first impressions, and Betty could tell he was a tad nervous by the unpolished expression glazed across his face. She showed the same nervous tension as her perfume drifted in the air. She had brought a disposable camera that was resting in her lap. The red fingernail polish she wore matched her blouse and lipstick. Her face looked lit up like a Christmas ornament. Bailey dismissed it with an amusing acknowledgment. Then he decided to pay her a complement.

"I like that fragrance." Betty smiled with a nervous twitch, but then returned,

"Thank you."

The trip to the *Garden of the Gods* was only five miles away. Bailey could see the sky jetting up with Pike's Peak in the background toward the heavens. It was a beautiful sight, one worth seeing. This was a place of rolling hills with green contouring pine-trees and red-rock mountains as the backdrop. As soon as they arrived, Bailey sought out the registration table to get his number and a map of the open course.

To Bailey's surprise, there were over 3,000 people in this race. At first, he considered this to be only a small hick town, or a backwoods race. Boy was he wrong. There were TV cameras and people from the local sports network stations setting up their equipment before the start of the race. Back in the day, if the sports networks showed up it usually was a big event. Bailey was a *no* name just short of fame. He wasn't one to know of local traditions, not really the *Prefontaine* of the decade. He had character and finesse, and he might have had a high tolerance to pain but lacked the macho experience. Betty, on the other hand, was the lone girl with five brothers as siblings. A harsh natured girl from her tough Tomboy ways taught by her brothers, even though she was showing Bailey a gentler side, she wasn't about to let anyone roll over her newfound experiences. He respected her and found more value in her friendship than trying to push their relationship to an emotional level he wasn't quite ready for. He thought having her along was a pleasant experience. Knowing Betty was in his corner gave him a little added confidence he needed to get over the edge. In a few minutes, the race was about to start, with runners stretching and jogging up and down a quarter mile piece of road at the mouth of the starting point.

The butterflies began to come back again. Bailey did some stretching and took a few deep breaths as he tried to relax. He looked over at her from a distance of twenty feet and noticed this strange look in her eyes.

She looked back and smiled sheepishly, as if thinking of something outside the box of normal thinking, something sneaky. Betty surprised him by walking quickly over, without giving much thought and laid the biggest kiss right on his mouth. Surprised but bitten, he'd been pulled off his feet. This was all it would take to fuel a fire under the teenaged boy's emotions. His heart began to soar. He was flying high, staying dry, and getting ready to let lose. He looked back and noticed that gentle smile sparkling in her eyes before the starting gun caused him to shudder. A massive mob of runners jolt forward from all corners of the world as a ringing was left in Bailey's left ear.

CHAPTER 4

Ten Miles of Hills

This race was custom made for Bailey's style of running. He had no idea what was ahead of him since he didn't really have time to actually go over the course. Instinct had to take over as he grooved into the flow of warm bodies. This was one of the most grueling courses in the country. That's the reason it got so much recognition from TV and sports networks. Bailey couldn't have hand-picked a course any better; its turns and dynamics were familiar to his feet that had *Suicide Hill* written in the script. He had been training in the high elevation now for two and half months as his young body began to adjust to the quickly thinning air. It took a while before he could filter through all the front-runners. He could actually run a pace to keep a rhythm with which he was comfortable. The air felt light on his lungs as he pushed himself past each runner. This was a slow methodical procession that began taking on extreme focus. It had been a while since he had put his body in a race that demanded his absolute best. His legs sensed the familiar natural height pumped into his system.

His mind wandered from reality. He was not thinking of the pain that existed in his frame. The sun was coming up over the top of the mountain quite early. The air still chilled by the morning dew on the ground. The smell of pine trees was drifting in his path.

He had no idea how far back he was from the runners in the front. His focus was the run itself, not worried about the pack of twenty runners that lay ahead. He knew in his heart that if he started too strong, he wouldn't last through the whole race. This race was much longer than he was used to.

Bailey remembered in his training days with his coach, recalled training that started with his mind and heart in sequence to a perfect rhythm, as given strength for the miles to come.

At every mile, there was a timer person calling out times for each mile, and drink stations with water in small paper cups or Gatorade. Bailey came into mile four at 17:00, a little bit slow for his usual pace. This heightened his adrenaline to pick up his pace, as the slower pace conserved his energy for the hills to come. Bailey was never considered normal compared to the average teenager, he one of a kind, who'd take down any road of mystery without a second thought, sometimes getting *in* over his head—like swimming in the ocean to reach the other side. He didn't drink any water until mile four, because he'd spent the previous evening hydrating.

The sun began to heat up his body, and sweat began to form on his chest, arms, and at the outside lines of his face. Grasping, he'd just finished a set of about four long hills. He smiled inwardly. And then the course flattened out, giving his legs a chance to rest, he kept his mind relaxed, and body poised for the next set of hills. The course was in a pattern of two miles, flat at first but then climbed three thousand feet on two miles of road and finished with four miles up hill. It was one of the most physically challenging courses a runner could try to endure.

Bailey started on the steep downhills almost midway, remembered the course back home where he had to glide over the rough parts to keep from falling. He could see no runners in front of him, and none behind. His composure remained intact along twisting mountainous roads that lay ahead. He was a seasoned distance runner, breathing in a rhythm that felt comfortable, his tanned frame absorbing every bump and twist. He was a well-tuned engine.

His mind pushed him beyond normal human limits, emptying out all his thoughts, no cares of the world, just him and the road seeking a mutual bond together. Like time stood still for this lone runner experiencing this peaceful bliss. No schedules to keep, no deadlines of school papers, no stress of life's inconsistencies. Bailey became one with the road, the surrounding trees, and the wind rushing through them, the sounds of nature and the quiet peace that comes from losing oneself in the distance, a deafening silence that rose above common development. He had peace in his own psyche with a heartbeat set to a rhythm that felt comfortable. He was in a place that could only be experienced when the mind and body pass beyond human limits, a place where control was left in a rhythm of his mind and heart beating in sequence.

Coming around the corner of mile six Bailey saw a cluster of seven runners all still intact with each other. Blowing by the two mile downhill he ran a 4:02 and 4:03 mile pace prospectively, and easily caught up to the group of men. He looked stoically forward to this enormous mountain that lay ahead, grabbed two cups of water from the station, poured one over his head, and quickly downed the other before surging on up this unfamiliar path.

The cluster of runners soon to come began to break-up slowly, as the hills took their toll on each runner's power and ability to withstand pain—an inward struggle of mind over matter. Bailey remembered his extreme hill training from days gone by and leaned into the mountain like it was a long-lost friend. He took deep breaths, stayed in tune with his body, and found a relaxed pace that felt okay to his head. The water had worked its magic by rejuvenating him and allowing him to focus. He passed the next three runners at the beginning of the next set of steep twisting hills. They tested his endurance, pulled at his muscles, and gave no pity in return.

Bailey thought himself back into that peaceful place. A place where no pain was allowed, no thoughts are experienced, where people don't exist. This fantasy world that kept him one, complete, serene—his secret dwelling place where his mind would wonder, not held to the conditions of the road in front. This dreamland of his propelled him beyond the reality of normal existence, where only heroes find their way through the light of day where others dare not follow.

He quickly overtook two more runners at mile eight, without acknowledging that they were a part of the same road. Bailey continued forward, ever pushing, ever plotting his footsteps, to a place where victory held others to a higher standard. For the ordinary man who walked this earth would never experience such bliss. It was a place where leaders of a hollowed-out heart lived—a place where the ordinary man would never go. It was a place for a dreamer, a back door schemer, being chased by the wind.

Bailey's calves started to tighten up a little from surging forward. He dropped his pace for the next half-mile just to get the lactic acid production to slow down in his legs. Something he learned from his old coach from back home on a better day of training.

He could see two more runners about one hundred feet ahead. He began to dig in again, pushing, leaning into this monster of a road. The sweat ran down his face into his eyes burning from the salty moisture. Bailey wiped it from his eyes with his tank top. He saw a cameraman, giving orders to his crew filming the runners as they went by. One of the TV crewmembers yelled at Bailey, "What's your name? I need to tell my boss!"

Bailey's throat was so dry he couldn't say the words.

Back at the end of the race, word was given to the local sports network that some unknown runner was surging forward who gained on the only runner in front. Mile nine was only two-hundred feet ahead, and Bailey was only forty feet from the leader. With only one mile ahead, he could see a crowd of people at mile nine, some young lady shouting at Bailey. "Hurry you're in Second' place!"

Bailey began to shudder at the thought, *what me…second place?*

He knew what he had to do now that he was gaining on the leader… just keep his composure, his head down, his rhythm sure and steady. As he plotted ahead, he noticed the mountain showed no mercy on those few who tried to conquer her unforgiving dimensions. The burning of the legs, the lack of air for his lungs was all part of the mountain's foreplay, her sting, and the pure combative form of her nature.

Bailey understood that to tame this mountain, he had to put no limit on his ability to surge forward. He had only ten feet from the lead runner with only half a mile to go and all up hill. The familiar footsteps of the runner in front of Bailey began to take form. *Was it Joe? Could it be? That ever so familiar short, dark haired, muscular figure of Bailey's past...it was Joe.* It had to be Joe from Bailey's past days in high school. He was his competition. Bailey had heard the stories of Joe going on to make a name for himself nationally on the running track, but he had no idea that his long-lost competitor would be in such a race, so far from home, in a town that wasn't famous for such previous events.

Bailey knew if the course stayed on an uphill swing he had a better chance at beating Joe, based on past events; but could he do the same now that Joe was a little more seasoned, better trained, and in the best shape of his life?

Bailey could see what looked like the finish line about a quarter of a mile ahead, crowds of people yelling in the distance, the sun bearing down on both runners, and neither runner showed any hint of letting up their grueling pace. Bailey surged past Joe getting a ten-foot lead on him while still trying to extend the gap between them. He leaned hard into the hill, emptied out his mind of all that was around him. No voices could be heard, all pain was gone—just he and the road were one, of the same mind, of the same heart.

Joe began his kick with one hundred yards to go, shooting him forward like he had wings on his feet. His focus on the monster of a mountain as well as Bailey, aware of Joe's unforgiving kick Bailey delivered the best performance of his life, his calves on fire, his lungs about to burst—both runners neck-to-neck, neither relinquishing his will... twenty-five feet...it was an all-out sprint...both young men pumping their arms vehemently, five feet to go as Bailey leaned forward with his long frame just to nose out Joe at the tape.

Ready to collapse Bailey bent forward gasping for air, as did Joe. The crowd gathered around the two, one of the coaches yelled, "Get back, and let them have some space!"

One of the sports reporters walked up to the two young men with his microphone, cameraman with the equipment, *talking to his camera like a visual audience of thousands of people witnessing this great feat.* And they were.

"What is your name young man?" The commentator asked with a big smile on his face.

"Bailey, ah…Bailey Simms," Bailey whispered out.

"We had trouble locating your stats from the registration table. We couldn't find out who you were." The commentator said.

Bailey didn't know it, but he had just broken the course record that was held by someone he had never heard of from twelve years earlier, his time was twenty-eight seconds faster than the previous course record. Suddenly, remembering he'd forgotten all about his admiring side kick Betty, who'd come with him from earlier that day. She couldn't get through the crowds of people until about twenty minutes later.

Bailey was camera shy, only nineteen years old, and in his worst of conditions—being sweating, a bit on the smelling side, and unwilling to know how to act. And still wet behind the ears as his father would say. He was not there for glory or prestige, he was only there to face the challenge of the mountain, to spend some time with nature, and to get a tad of attention from his friend named Betty.

She finally caught up to him. The look on her face said it all. She looked like a ghost showing this puzzled stare in her eyes. She asked Bailey straightway. "Who are you? You're not some famous guy that's trying to keep a low profile or something—are you?"

Bailey looked a bit surprised and confused about the rapid questions. "Well, no. I had a good day that's all. I had my 'Wheaties,'" while showing a grimacing smile as he was still winded.

A couple of businessmen in suits approached Bailey while he was talking to Betty as they asked *who* his sponsors were or his manager's name. Bailey wasn't quite sure what they were talking about and said from continued confusion, "What?" the businessmen look at each other with a surprise of laugher.

"I guess, Bailey's new to the runner's world," one of them said.

The one businessman pulled Bailey off to the side and told him about the excellent job he did that day. He was impressed with his efforts. He also gave Bailey his business card and told him to call next week sometime to talk about further races up ahead. There was a famous coach he wanted to introduce Bailey too named Carlson Reynolds. Bailey said he would stay connected and let him know what was going on in his life.

As he started to walk to his car a young man approached him from afar to ask, "Hey sir, where're going?"

Bailey turned suddenly by the quick inquiry. "Excuse me?" Bailey said.

The young man showed a peculiar expression on his face, "Sir the awards ceremony starts in ten minutes. Are you coming?"

With raised eyebrow Bailey said, "Oh, I guess. I forgot."

Betty looked at Bailey surprised herself, she repeatedly told him.

"Awards ceremony?"

"Yes, it wouldn't be right if the winner of the race didn't show up, would it?"

Bailey smiled before saying, "Well I guess not."

The young man escorted Bailey to a dozen chairs behind a podium where an old friend, Joe was already seated. "Dude, you did well," Exclaimed Joe. "Your kick has improved so much since the last time we competed. I didn't know you were in the race." Joe replied confused about the finish. He shook Bailey's hand as he patted him on the back.

Bailey responded, "Well, you could have easily won yourself Joe, you were right there also. Anyhow I'm glad it's over. Those were some killer hills."

Bailey took a seat next to him. The master of ceremonies came to the podium and congratulated several runners—the top five of each category, to be exact. Each winner received a trophy and the runner who placed first received a check for $15,000. and a nice trophy. Bailey's eyes got as big as saucers, not emotionally ready to receive such a prize. Also, included was a gift certificate for five hundred dollars for runner's apparel and a subscription to a runner's magazine for two years.

Bailey received his awards along with the others, thanked everybody for a great race in a beautiful landscape of red rock mountains, talked to a few people toward the end of the awards ceremony, and then left with Betty.

CHAPTER 5

Summer Storm

It was close to evening. Betty and Bailey had spent most of the day together after the race. She said her goodbyes from the side porch of his aunt's house. He leaned down and gave her a slight hug while thanking her for giving of her time. Betty smiled, showing a concentric glint of pleasure in her eyes. She reached up and kissed him on the cheek, and then left him standing there on the porch.

He was exhausted from his bout with the mountain. Every muscle ached in his lower extremities, but it wasn't anything a hot bath and a few aspirins couldn't fix.

Bailey went to bed around eight o'clock that evening. As soon as his head hit the pillow, he was asleep. It was a well-deserved slumber after conquering that giant of a race. He didn't move a muscle all night. He was in a deep, dreamless, sleep that only accompanied extreme exhaustion.

Betty walked the three blocks up around the back of Bijon Street where Bailey's aunt and uncle lived, to head home. There was still enough light left to guide her down the streets, so the roads looked familiar from before, as she'd taken this route so many times over. She had no idea what to think of the things that had transpired that day, or what would happen to Bailey's life if he were offered some type of scholarship that would pull him far away from her and this quaint small town. She kept it to herself and never mentioned the outcome of the race with her grandmother. Her heart couldn't handle any type of rejection right now, not when she had tried so hard to be friends with Bailey so quickly. She didn't want to hold on to the faint hope that they might not ever be together someday, not with everybody else pulling at his shirttail. She was convinced that the best maneuver was to let him go for now, before there could be any real hurt between them.

This young lady's intuition was sometimes far more sensible than a young man's of her age. She knew in her heart she was starting to fall for him. She was scared, scared for all the wrong reasons was her thought. Her heart begun to hurt, and she didn't want to experience what she believed was ahead in the weeks to come. She lay in her soft warm bed, facing the wall, water splashing on the back of her eyes when shortly after she fell asleep.

The temperature that night dropped to twenty degrees. The wind picked up to thirty to forty miles per hour as it began to snow. Betty stirred from her sleep. Shivering, she got out of bed to get another blanket and looked out her bedroom window. The sight from her window offered a peek into a frozen wasteland that she'd never seen so dramatically. Her thoughts came rapidly, before she could fully comprehend what was happening. *Wait a minute.* She thought. *This is June. It can't be snowing. It doesn't snow in June. What's going on? This is summer.* But sure enough, snow was coming down, and as the night progressed it began to come down harder, so hard she couldn't believe what she was seeing.

The national weather station saw a cold front moving in over the Rocky Mountains, but they had no idea what it was bringing with it, or if this phenomena would stay local. The last time the temperatures dropped this low was back in February. Something was definitely not right. Betty's grandmother woke up because she was chilled beyond any normal condition as her hands started to hurt. This usually only occurred in freezing weather, and she would have flare-ups of arthritis.

She went into the bathroom to get a tube of medicated ointment from the medicine cabinet to rub on her tender hands, when she noticed the white flakes hitting her bathroom window. She opened her window and took notice. The snow was coming down in silent blind flurries of a time she'd only remember of youth.

No wonder my arthritis is acting up. It's snowing and colder than the dickens. She thought. She shut the window, hurried to the front room, and turned on the TV to seek out any information from a local news station regarding the obvious weather anomaly.

The local weather station was sending out an emergency broadcast about the extreme cold front that was stalled throughout the Midwest, a storm that unrepentantly hit the area, but something else wasn't noticed by the local weathermen held in secret. The broadcast was warning people not to go outside of their homes because the massive volume of snow that this storm was dropping was most unexpected. Betty's grandmother began to worry about her house being covered up over the doors and windows, and of course her porch area. She walked to Betty's room and saw that the girl was already awake, staring out the window all wide-eye and wondering about the scene before her. She could see from her angle that the snow had already covered the car in the driveway. She tried to call the Morse residence from earlier when asked by her grandmother. Betty already knew Bailey's aunt and uncle were gone for the weekend to La Junta, Colorado to visit Uncle Ron's father. He was getting on in years and they were worried about him. He was in his nineties, and still working on the forty acres of land given to him by his youth. He was stubborn and set in his ways, according to Uncle Ron. They knew grandpa needed help that he couldn't offer, having his own ten acres to deal with, along with something else that Uncle Ron wasn't telling. Betty turned to her grandmother, with eyes wide. "What's going on Grandma? Why is it snowing in June?"

Her grandmother shook her head in a returned reply with worried expression glinting in her eyes, "I have no idea? I woke up because my arthritis was acting up, and this is what I woke up to."

Betty returned a disconcerting stare before saying, "I woke up because I was cold and noticed it then. What did the weather station say about it Grandma?"

"I'm not sure, honey. I don't think they know what to think about it either. They mentioned that NASA was looking into the storm patterns that were hitting this area. But something's going on that they aren't telling. I could only imagine what those political sharks are doing to our community. It's all just so confusing."

The snow was getting deeper, and Betty began to worry about getting out of the house before the snow became too high. One of Betty's older brothers had left his two kids with them for the summer, being in the military he was called abroad for active duty to Korea. Ryan was seven, and Mattie eight, too young to know any danger from the beautiful white snow covering their porch. Betty remembered that Uncle Ron had buried a bunker on the other side of the hill, full of supplies, long enough to last six months, she thought.

Bailey's cousins had two snowmobiles in the barn above the house, simply perfect for this present situation—if she could only get to them. Betty knew that if she could wake up Bailey and get to the snowmobiles, they could ride them back to her house and get everybody out before the snow became too deep. Her intentions were to act now while there was still time.

With the snow piling up so rapidly she knew they had to react quickly.

"Grandma…" She said. "I need to go wake up Bailey so he can help us! He's closer than anyone else. Uncle Ron's snowmobiles will help us get to a safer place. The bunker would be perfect, and room for all of us. Uncle Ron is sometimes a crazy old man, but he knows something that everyone else is blind to, and for some reason he has placed that bunker on the side of the hill buried in the property." Betty considered not waiting.

Grandma responded, "If you go out there now, then you are just as crazy as your Uncle Ron! You can't even see in front of your face! That would be the death of me if something happened to you! You're not going!" Grandmother shouted.

"But Grandma, I have too. I believe we would be worse off staying here. We don't have enough supplies or firewood to keep us warm."

Grandma considered her statement. "Oh honey, this is going to blow over by morning. You don't need to be out in that mess right now."

Betty didn't say any more to her Grandmother but started planning ahead what to do. She knew that Grandma was old-fashioned in some of her ideas. They weren't always for the best. Betty lit up the fireplace with some dried-out firewood she found in the basement, to bring some warmth to the old farmhouse. Grandma rocked in her custom-made rocking chair and fell asleep. Betty walked over and wrapped a blanket around her.

Then she had to make plans. Betty dressed up warm with some long underwear, her ski boots, gloves, and the winter pair of snowshoes that her grandfather had made for her when she was younger. They were an oversized pair that would strap to almost any size boot. She went down to the basement and retrieved a compass, a couple of flashlights, a first aid kit, a few bottles of water from the pantry, and left-over sandwiches from the day before. She got a buck knife from a kitchen drawer and the nine-millimeter handgun that grandfather left in the house with a full box of rounds and threw all the supplies in her backpack. She sat down and wrote her grandmother a note explaining where she was going and left one of two walkie-talkies on the kitchen table with the note. Before leaving, Betty looked at the compass for direction, mentally walking through each step before leaving the house. She left the house quickly and quietly, so as to not disturb the others. She trudged up the street through the quickly rising snow in the direction too Bailey's place of residence. The snow was very deep already. Even with the snowshoes on she was sinking six inches, but without them she would sink two feet deep or more.

She was glad that her grandfather was the type of man that was overly cautious and prepared for everything. It was dark and the air was very cold. The sting of the cold burned at her face. She was starting to have second thoughts about this being a mistake. Betty could barely see anything in front of her. And the cold was the type of cold that sunk to her bones. She was already freezing, and she'd only left ten minutes ago. Her hands showed the first signs by shaking, and her mind quickly wondered back to Bailey's race. She had to be strong like her brothers had taught her, like Bailey showed from the day before. That warrior spirit she'd seen in that skinny boy pushed past the elements of pain. She could do this, she just had to believe and keep going, not give up, not give in to this unbearable cold. And the wind frequently pushed her back in the opposite direction, causing her to drift to the left.

She quickly turned on the flashlight to see if it would help any, but to her dismay not much could be made out from the light on either— everything was blinding white in the fading strength of a snowy night. The snow was coming down too heavily. There was no identifying anything. This was chaos. It was all a white blur in this now depleting world of confusion. Betty recalled the directions from her house to the Morse house. She had walked it so many times. As a blind person's point of view, who familiarized themselves with their surroundings and become accustomed to each step taken. They had memorized every detail of their steps, to try and not trip up or make a wrong move, so she wouldn't go in the wrong direction. She had to keep her head. The thought of not making it crossed her mind for just a second, but she then pushed it out of her head quickly while she continued prodding into the misery of the storm.

She'd been walking for quite some time when she heard a voice in the darkness, faint and weak. Ten more steps and she saw the small frame in front of her. A little girl around twelve years of age that played down the street seemed to be stuck in the snow. She was bundled up but had no snowshoes on. Betty bent down to help her up and quickly asked,

"Are you alright?"

"Yes!" the little girl gasped for air. "My parents never came home last night. They got stuck in the snowstorm. I was trying to get from my house to Billy's, but I got stuck!"

Betty looked around and saw nothing or no one to help her, understanding she needed her help. "Okay, you can come with me. Jump on my back and I'll carry you to my Uncle Ron's house."

The little girl didn't hesitate, "Okay." She said while shivering from the building with wind and frozen flakes. The snow and wind, combined with the burden of the little girl on her back were draining Betty, but she knew the little girl didn't stand a chance without her. Betty sensed the hill they were climbing was the one up above Bijon St. She knew that they were close to her uncle's house, only one more block to go, if she could just hold on. She was out of breath, and her face stung something fierce, but she didn't dare let the little girl down until they reached her uncle's house. The chills had begun to set in, and the wind kept pushing her to try and keep her from moving forward, yet she pushed on. Her arms started cramping from carrying the small frame of legs and limbs, and Betty's strength was pushed to its very limits. Thinking about the race that Bailey had been through the previous day inspired her to keep moving forward, not let the pain stop her progression of getting to Uncle Ron's property. She had to do it.

She was a real trooper, remembering her brothers, and how they were always tough on her, helping her to become stronger. Sometimes there were tears, but her brothers kept on her, kept pushing her to be better. They taught her self-defense, how to use a gun, and made her get up to do pushups with them every morning. This training gave her the confidence she needed to get back to her uncle's place, a place of safety, where Bailey would be. Only this one life lay in the balance of her toughness. To save this little girl's life was worth all the torture that her brothers had bestowed upon her from her earlier years.

Betty sensed Bijon Street by the slant of the landscape. The upward climb was going to tire her further, but once the street leveled out, she knew she would only have a few more feet to go. She strained her eyes trying to make out the mailboxes that would guide her to the right house. She remembered that her Uncle Ron's house was the third one on the right. She stretched her arms, as a blind person might in an unfamiliar environment. She tried to feel out where she thought the mailboxes would be. Soon, her hands grasped the frozen metal of the first mailbox. A brightening smile graced her lips in the blinding fury.

She counted in her head how many steps it took her to get to the next mailbox. She remembered that her aunt had told her if there was ever an emergency, she would keep a key on the top ledge above the door in the side entrance of the house. Betty noticed only three steps on the side entrance of the house when there were usually six, comprehending that three of the steps were buried beneath this white mirage. She set the little girl down on the top step with great relief in her arms and reached for the key. *Oh great. It's there.* Betty thought. No signs of the window of a lower level below because they were covered by snow. Bailey would never hear her banging on the door. She unlocked the door and let the little girl and herself into the house. She closed the door behind them. Auntie's little dog, a Chihuahua named Cuddles, came up the stairs from the basement, barking at this sudden intrusion. Who would come and break this barrier of comfort in space, without letting her know? Betty thought, she reached down to grab the little nerve ball of teeth and tail then smiled, but the little dog jumped to her side avoiding contact of human hands frozen from the white wonderland outside, being unrecognizable of any normal world she'd ever seen. The small dog was sleeping with Bailey. She barked further to get their attention, then sat down and wagged her tail. She looked up with beady eyes and shook, as if unaware of the maelstrom conditions facing them. Who would come in her house of safety at this dreadful hour—was the look seen of her body language?

Betty took off her snowshoes, jacket, gloves, and boots. She ran down the stairs and over to the far side of the basement, while Cuddles followed behind barking after her. It was about 6:00 A.M. already. Bailey was still fast asleep, snoozing in the cold chills of slumbering sleepy heads lost in dreamland of memories and uneasiness. Betty turned on the light, and the pinned-up anxiety burst from her lungs as she yelled. "Bailey, get up! We have an emergency!" Bailey startled awake from Betty's rude entrance, sat up in bed, groggy, confused, and still showing signs of pain from the day before.

"Where…ah…what's going on princess? I mean Betty."

She showed Bailey a quirky smile and rolled her eyes, and then gave him a blank unblinking stare. "Yes…dork-man," she said in a sarcastic manner. "We're having a snowstorm in the worst of ways, and it's burying all the houses in the valley! I need your help! We need to reach my grandmother and my brother's kids before they get buried alive! Pronto mister hotshot, it's time to see what you're really made of."

Bailey rubbed his eyes, and jumped to his feet, aware he was standing in his boxer shorts. He looked at Betty and told her to turn around. With a grin and a sigh, she stated. "Don't even go there. I have five brothers. You don't have anything I haven't already seen. Besides," she said, "I haven't had such pleasure."

Bailey looked offended. "That's not funny," he squealed out, "I'm not here for your entertainment." Betty covered her mouth suddenly to hold back a giggle. She cut it short though and replied, "We need to hurry because time is of essence."

Bailey flashed a hesitant stare in Betty's direction. "Sure thing, I'm hurrying." He replied. While he got dressed Betty continued to tell him about the snowmobiles that Uncle Ron had in the barn just above the house.

"Before we start them. We need to check gas and oil. Have you ever driven a snowmobile?"

Bailey still with the inquisitive stare said, "I'm from southern California. Do I look like I know how to drive a snow mobile?"

Betty batted her eyes, "You dork. It's really simple. You turn the left handle like a motorcycle. You don't need to lean into curves. It will turn naturally. There are no brakes. You just let off the gas by letting off pressure on the grip." Betty showed hesitation, but then batted her eyes at the uncooperative boy. "Follow behind me so you don't drift off into deep snow. I'll keep you out of trouble. Got it?"

Bailey replied with his continued awkward stare. "Yeah…I got it!"

Then Betty remembered about the twelve-year-old upstairs. "Oh… by the way, I found a neighbor's kid on the way. She's upstairs waiting for us. She is buried in the snow. I mean she's okay now, but I saved her from a snowy grave." Then Betty explained that they would leave her behind for now with Cuddles, so they could get the others. Betty remembered she had the walkie-talkie and heard it squawk. She heard static at first, but then an older voice came over on the speaker. Betty pushed the call button. "Grandma, is that you?"

A worried voice replied. "Yes dear, it's me. I've been worried sick about you! Where in the hell did you go?" Betty had never heard her grandmother swear before and realized how badly she scared her by taking off without a word. Feeling guilty, Betty said,

"Sorry Grandma. Don't worry about me. I made it to Uncle Ron's. Bailey and I are coming to get you and the little ones. How deep is the snow around the house?"

Grandma glanced out the window with a worried look. "It's halfway up the porch, dear. The snow is still coming down strong. I don't think you and Bailey should attempt coming here. It's too dangerous."

Betty pursed her lips at the corners as she wondered how far she would take this. "I'm coming anyhow, Grandma. I'm not leaving you guys behind. I have Jackie with me from the down the street. She was stuck in the snow too." Betty released the button on the microphone and waited for her Grandmother to respond. There was a pause. Betty showing impatience said, "Grandma, are you there?"

Grandma finally responded, "Yes, I'm here. I don't think you and Bailey are going to be able to dig us out without shovels." Grandma's statement made a light go on in the back of Betty's head.

Betty quickly responded, "Don't worry Grandma we'll get you guys out somehow. Anyhow, …I got to go before the snow gets any worse!"

Grandma seemed a little hesitant about cutting the conversation off, "Okay dear, but keep your walkie-talkie on so I can call, if I need too."

Betty released the button and put the squawk box away. She looked at Bailey and remembered her uncle kept all the boys ski suits in the basement in an old cedar chest and boots in the corner closet. She found the chest. There were gloves, a couple of ski masks, and two heavy-duty jackets. Betty walked over to a dresser in Bailey's room. She pulled open the bottom drawer and found an old pair of long underwear. She handed them to Bailey.

"Here, put these on. You can thank me later."

Bailey eye-balled Betty with concerning stares, "Whatever." While Bailey's getting dressed in limited privacy. Betty planned for their trip. She started looking for keys to the barn and snowmobiles. Above the washer, along the wall she found a small rack with different sets of keys and spotted the snowmobile keys hung on hooks above. She looked back at the rack and found the keys to the barn also. She snatched the keys up and yelled for Bailey. "Let's go before we run out of time!"

Bailey gestured that he was ready with a salute to the forehead. Betty suggested that he was still a dork by rolling her eyes. They both ran up the basement stairs and almost ran into Jackie. Surprised, Betty informed her. "Jackie, please stay here until we return to get you. You'll be safer here for a while, plus we don't have enough room coming back. We'll be back soon." Betty picked up the small rodent with mousy ears and wagging tail. "Here, Cuddles will keep you company." Betty reached over and turned the thermostat on, to heat up the house. Jackie nodded in understanding and gave Betty a hug. Quickly, Bailey and Betty were shooting out the door toward the barn in the mystery of this white wonderland blinding them at every corner.

It was a good three-hundred feet to the top of the hill before the barn came into view. A foot of snow was sticking on the slanted roof already as seen in the distance. The barn was forty feet wide and eighty feet long with a loft in the top. Bailey noticed the wear-and-tear of its many years. Uncle Ron kept tools for making his kitchens in there. Over $50,000 worth of equipment, a tractor, garden tools, a sit-down lawnmower, and the two snowmobiles that Betty was after. They got to the side barn door and unlocked it. Bailey pushed the snow back by the force of the door. They were only able to open the door enough to squeeze through. Betty shot a stare across the barn at Bailey.

"Hey, check in the corner for the gas can. I'll look in the tanks to see if they need any."

Bailey walked to the corner and saw what looked like a five-gallon tank of fuel. He picked it up and shook it. It was about halfway full. He yelled across the barn. "Is there a funnel?"

Betty turned her eyes looking above him. "Up on the shelf above you," She yelled back.

Bailey saw the red plastic funnel she was referring to lying upside down on the first shelf above him. "Cool." He replied.

Grabbing the can and funnel he hurriedly walked over to the snowmobiles to check the tanks. He saw Betty had already removed the center twist plugs from the top, ready for Bailey's steady hands of approval. He sat the funnel over the first tank as Betty held it in place. He picked up the heavy can and began to pour. The strong vapors of gasoline hit their faces and caused her to pull back while he sloshed the heavy liquid.

Betty yelled out, "Don't pour so fast…the tanks don't hold that much!"

Bailey threw a hard stare. "Alright already…just tell me when."

She went back to concentrating on not overfilling the tanks, and then yelled.

"Okay…slow down!"

Bailey topped off the first tank and moved to the other. Shortly, both were filled, and Betty returned both plugs. She turned the choke on midway and tried to kick-start the first machine. She waited for a few seconds and popped the clutch into neutral as she pushed the starter to see if it would start, but it didn't. She looked over at this strange boy with a meddlesome stare. "Try the other machine…you don't have to wait for me."

Bailey had enough of her barking orders. She reminded him of a Tomboy he once knew at school. He brushed her off and went to the other machine. Bailey didn't say a word, only rolled his eyes. He mimicked everything she did to try and start the snowmobile; except he turned off the choke. It started up right away with a loud thrumming. Betty got an exasperated look in her eyes.

"You got lucky, dork."

Bailey gave her a look of *shut up or you can do this by yourself.* He smiled transparently when she flinted her eyes. "Okay, smarty-pants—you can give it a try." He took the grips out of her hand and leaned into the machine like he had its number. He shook the machine back and forth, and turned the choke off on the first snowmobile, sensing it was flooded. The first snowmobile then started right-up. Betty brushed her hair back with the back of her hand as she looked away to other things she might need for this little adventure. She grabbed a fold-up shovel hanging on the left side wall from amongst other tools. She stuffed the bigger end into her backpack, and then grabbed a screwdriver and a hammer. Bailey saw her pull the big doors of the barn inward. Betty took the lead by driving the first snowmobile up past the doors. A rush of frigid air and snow hit their faces. After being inside the barn for a while they both apprehended it was freezing outside. Bailey drove the second machine up on the icy snow. Betty went back and locked everything up. Noticing right away outside the snow never let up. Within a few minutes they were off, sliding down the first hill of Uncle Ron's property.

The wind cut at their faces as they made the first turn while pushing ice and snow to the sides had permeating their senses. Betty took the lead. She was worried about her grandmother and the two little ones. Her expression was one of a blank stare. She had begun to grasp the snow had changed the landscape exceptionally to the point she wasn't quite sure which way to go. She began to focus on memory, instead of what lay before her. Then she thought *where the slant was. Where did it go?* Her bottom lip moved with a bit of emotion. "Oh yes…it's there." She whispered under her breath.

The trees were her guide, her way through this white blur of oblivion. A sixth sense began to point the way to Grandma's house. They made the turn up on Bijon Street. With the rush of the wind, it felt like dry ice burning their skin. Bailey sucked in brittle air that put a chill down his spine. This was madness. Further ahead, they made the left uphill turn below the church with stained glass windows. Not a soul was stirring in this wasteland left behind of a once lively world. The landscape had been changed into a world unfamiliar to the eye for sight or the mind to envision. Bailey kept on her tail so not to slip up from an unknown dip or hill up ahead. From the top of the hill, they both were amazed by the buried landscape. *How could so much snow drop so quickly?* Bailey thought. Betty was more than concerned about their situation. How was she going to find her house now, in this white mirage lost in this abnormally blinding obscurity?

Bailey pulled up next to Betty. His expression was of shock. "Betty…can you find it?" She wasn't sure what to say, yet only nodded. He wondered if she had everything worked out. She took off down the second long hill. She tried to remember how the trees looked on each street. This was definitely an odd way of finding one's way home. She hoped they were okay. Betty shot past a familiar tree and quickly looked back. She recognized from so many times passing by. Her house was only one block more if she could only remember where the house was. She pulled up to the front of what used to be her house, but where was it? She recognized the tree, but where were the windows? From the right side of the house, she signaled for Bailey to come over by pointing a finger in the direction of a covering up the window that only showed the very top of the window frame. Betty began to panic.

"They're in there Bailey…you have to get them out!" Betty was in tears. Bailey jumped off the snowmobile and reached for the shovel sticking out of Betty's backpack. He started digging right away. Betty broke out the walkie-talkie.

"Grandma, are you there!" Static noise came over the speaker. The snow was shooting sideways in this frozen land of the forgotten. Grandma came over the speaker.

"Yes Betty, I'm here…we're, okay? Can you see us?" Bailey tapped on what looked like the bathroom window. Mrs. Morse almost dropped her walkie-talkie from hearing the noise of Bailey's tapping. "Oh dear," She said startled while almost dropping the squawk-box.

Betty yelled into the speaker, "Grandma, go to the bathroom window…Bailey's there…get the kids ready…we have to leave!" Grandma's hands began to shake. She didn't know what direction to turn. Betty felt a frozen tear stick to the back of one of her eyelids. Bailey didn't wait. He pulled off the screen and shimmied like a snake down into the tub.

He saw Mattie first. She looked like she had been crying. He grabbed her first without a moment's notice. She showed a sparkle of hope with thumbs up when she saw Bailey's silhouette reflected off the bathroom window. Ryan came second. Bailey pushed him up quickly through the open window. Betty grabbed his hands and pulled him through. He saw Mrs. Morse and knew she wasn't going to fit through the small opening. He looked back up through the opening. He yelled at Betty. "I have to break the window to get your grandmother out!" The snow continued to fall like ice. Grandma was already bundled. Bailey looked into her elderly eyes, and wondered how this freezing weather was going to affect her for the long three blocks. "Do you have a ladder?" He asked.

"Downstairs in the basement up against the hot water heater," Grandma said.

Bailey responded, "Okay…I'll be back." He ran down the hall and found the door to the basement, ran quickly to the bottom, and saw the ladder, grabbed it, and returned within a few seconds. He looked at Mrs. Morse and said, "Granny…I have to break the window out on the left."

Grandma showed a stiff countenance for calling her Granny, and not by her proper name. "Well, young man, I insist you call me Linda or Mrs. Morse thank you very much…I'm not this person you call Granny by any means, mind your manners son, or you might be feeling the back of my hand across your head!"

Bailey showed an embarrassing flash of bad memories. "Don't get vicious Mrs. Morse. I'm just a boy trying to get along in life as you can see. I'm only trying to save time, even though we have never been properly introduced. We've limited time to save ourselves Mrs. Morse, I mean Linda." Bailey realized his words had twisted his way of thinking. He wasn't sure how to address Mrs. Morse in an emergency situation. He'd just met her.

Mrs. Morse snubbed her nose at the boy with the awkward words and stifling behavior and said, "And who needs to be saved young man?"

Bailey, being dim-witted from freezing weather, and being rolled out of bed at an indecent hour stammered through his words of edification, "I believe all of us Mrs. Morse, if we don't hurry. I mean no one really knows how bad it's going to get out there."

Mrs. Morse finished with introductions before returning, "Well, I'm ready when you are, young man." Bailey stood at the ladder and swung the shovel toward the glass window. It shattered in a rain of broken glass in the bottom of the tub and across the ladder. He grabbed the bathroom rug and threw it up over the windowpane so Mrs. Morse wouldn't get cut on any of the broken pieces he'd missed. He brushed the broken pieces off the best he could and signaled for Mrs. Morse to step toward the ladder.

She widened her eyes with no lack of words. "Yes, I know the procedure, young man. I've done this once or twice in a lifetime." Bailey knew he couldn't win against her.

Betty reached down and pulled while Bailey pushed. Bailey got more than his feel of squishy tissue. Considering the circumstances, Mrs. Morse brushed off the physical contact as if a trifle inconvenience. She had just remembered.

"Oh Bailey," she yelled back down the window. "Could you get my medications? They're lying on my bed. My rooms the second door on the left."

Bailey shrugged his shoulders and ran back to get the forgotten pills of the crazy old bat with the cantankerous disposition. Bailey was back soon and out the window. Without thinking, he grabbed Ryan and slung him over the front of the snow mobile and Mattie behind. Grandma rode with Betty. Bailey looked at both children and said,

"Hold on you two…this might leave a few stains in your undies." Both children looked at each other and smiled. Betty led the way and Bailey quickly followed closely behind.

Ryan started screaming. Whoopee…!" This is fun! Can you go faster?"

Both children, not thinking about the cold, clung to Bailey like they were his two young lion cubs waiting for their father's guiding hand.

The snow was hitting their faces in a freezing blaze of frozen nettles. Ryan didn't care, he kept screaming like he was on his favorite circus ride. Bailey caught air over several hills of hidden wonder as they shot forward into the drifting snow. This world was not the same world they had left the day before. It was a world pushed back into an ice age of distant histories of an age long forgotten, a time when dinosaurs use to roam this great valley, when at one time they were the dominant species to roam this land leaving their footprints behind in history.

When scrambling for the keys earlier, Betty had forgotten to get the key to the bunker. She slid off the snowmobile and shot for Uncle Ron's house.

She jetted past Jackie and Cuddles and skidded to the basement floor. She looked above the washer but saw nothing was there. *Where was the key?* She thought. She had forgotten that her Uncle Ron had a small keepsake box on the top of his dresser. She ran up the stairs remembering Uncle Ron's bedroom was shared with auntie. In the confusion of Betty pounding up the stairs, Cuddles started barking. Once in his room, she saw the box where her uncle had left it out in the open where she had figured it to be. She pried it open, yet nothing was there, "What's going on, no key?" She whispered. Then she had remembered that all secret little boxes usually held a hidden section. She found it in a drawer of a lower end. Betty snatched up the key and slid it into her front pocket. She shot out of the room in the direction of the front door and stopped to give Jackie a little half hug and then said, "We're coming back for you in a little while." Betty blew a kiss her way and headed back out the door in the freezing cold where the others were covered with snowflakes. Betty got back on the snowmobile and shot up the hill as Bailey followed after.

From a short distance, the doorway to the bunker stood out with earthen colors, yet the snow brought it to life by being surrounded with the brilliance of white. The snow made the door stand out like a bull's-eye. Betty remembered Uncle Ron showing her the hidden doorway during the summer months from before. It was different with this changed landscape of whiteness. The doorway to the bunker had an over extended eve that blocked snow from covering its darker features. She saw the bunker's muddy colors from a short distance of fifty feet. She parked the snowmobile next to a familiar tree with low hanging branches covered by heavy snow. After pushing out a huff of air, she turned and looked at Bailey.

"We're here…"

CHAPTER 6

The Bunker

They were all freezing by now. The younger kids were not used to all the snow that had fallen in such a brief period of time. They had blue lips and chattering teeth. They were giving Cuddles some competition in the shaking department. Betty walked up to the entrance with Bailey's help and pulled a familiar bush out of the way of a brownish roll-up door, thicker than any roll-up door Bailey had ever seen. Betty unlocked the door with the key she had in her pocket. She had just remembered that there was also a three number electronic tumbler lock that she had forgotten about. She turned in shock. "Bailey...I forgot it has a combination lock too. I don't know the numbers." Bailey stared pensively at the lock. His eyes suddenly blinked with discovery. "It's someone's birthday!" He belted out.

Betty wrinkled her forehead in frustration. "You don't have to shout. I'm standing right next to you..." This made the two younger kids smile. They were freezing and these two bickering was annoying. Grandma brushed them off like there were more important things to worry about than flaring emotions from over exposure of the elements.

Ryan showed quivering blue lips, and in a blaze of excitement said, "Come on…Betty…its cold out here!"

Betty turned with an indignant scowl. "Hush already…so I can think!" She had no idea whose birthday to start with, after trying her uncle's, then her aunt's, several of Grandpa's kids, nothing seemed to work.

Ryan yelled in the background while dancing up and down, "Ahh… phooey…I gotta pee!"

Then Bailey had an idea. "Who's the last grandchild on your grandmother's side of the family?"

Betty turned with widened eyes. "Well, I Am." mentioned Betty, "I guess it's worth a try." She put her birthday date into the keypad… They both looked at each other in surprise as the electronic tumbler popped open. Betty pushed a button on the side of the keypad, and the steel door began to roll up. The storage container, turned bunker, was like one from a railroad train, about sixty feet long and ten feet wide. Betty hit the button to quickly close the door behind, leaving them in the dark. They were all shaking trying to warm their bones. Grandma sat to ward off a dizzy spell. Betty reached for a lantern she'd seen at the last minute and turned it on. Uncle Ron had made a beautiful fortress out of an old steel container. He had special bunkbeds on the backside of the left far corner that stacked three high. Bailey counted three sets of three, enough for nine people. That was enough side rail beds for Uncle Ron's whole family. It had the appeal of a real apartment. It didn't have any windows, which meant no ocean or city views, but still quite appealing. The smaller kids had their mouths open. Bailey and Betty started focusing on details, to find evidence of food or water or anything of importance. After several minutes of looking, they'd come to realize there was nothing to eat.

Bailey stated, "No canned foods. Not even military rations. That's a little odd. What was Uncle Ron thinking?" Bailey turned in disappointment. And then he noticed something strange about the back part of the bunker. It looked uneven. To the point it caused him to slant his head and look at it sideways. He had learned from a wise old father that the most valuable things in life were usually hard to find, difficult to figure out, and hidden in the most unlikely places.

Betty pulled her backpack off remembering she had food and water on reserve as she hauled out sandwiches and water for Ryan and Mattie. Betty looked down and realized this jaunt had taken quite a bit out of the old woman. She was seated in a desk chair looking at the ground. Betty shot her eyes back at the odd-looking boy staring at the back part of the bunker. "What'd you find?" Betty said from an air of wonder. The boy of blunders with the prying stare whipped his head back around.

"I don't know…something's wrong with this wall…its uneven…do you have a flashlight?" The unknown runner was all consumed with the wall, considering he'd found something most revealing, comprehending that dead men tell no tales of hidden secrets. He put his hand out for Betty. His full attention was absorbed by this peculiar predicament as the mystery of the wall was about to unfold. Betty waited for him to turn his eyes back to her before tossing the awkward boy a flashlight. Ryan tried to talk with his mouth full of left-over tuna and cheese sandwiches.

"Where's all the food Betty?" He mumbled. She turned her eyes to the small boy dancing in a rhythm of no patience and small bladders.

"I don't know squirt. That's something we haven't figured out yet." Betty said.

Bailey recognized an old C.B. radio on the top shelf of a storage rack about halfway down the bunker on the right side of another wall. He turned to look at Betty.

"Do you know how to use the C. B.?"

"Yes, I do, but do you see any electrical outlets around to plug into?"

"No, but wasn't that an electronic tumbler on the combination lock outside the door?" Bailey shot back.

Betty's face lit up with a giddy acknowledgment. "I believe your right Mister hotshot. Good thinking…I guess you're not the dork I thought you were after all." Grandma couldn't believe these two were actually friends.

"Not so funny." Bailey announced. "I'll check the corners for clues, if any. Betty, can you see if there is a plug for that C.B. radio, and Mrs. Morse could you tend to the kids while we look for clues?"

"Okay Bailey," Blasted Mrs. Morse. "Who died and put you in charge?"

Bailey turned with a puzzled expression. "Sorry Mrs. Morse, I do apologize, if I sound like I'm barking orders. I'm only concerned about our situation. With everybody pitching in and knowing what needs to be done, we have a better chance of survival."

Mrs. Morse looked at the boy with a concerned air of disapproval. "Young man, you're right. You and my granddaughter did save us from a snowy grave."

Bailey did show a diminutive smile and went back to what he was doing. Suddenly, Bailey could see ridges that stood out on the center of what looked like a hidden door. He clicked the flashlight on to get a better look. Placing his hand against the wall he could feel air blowing under the ridge. Half-way up this uneven ridge he felt for a lever or any indication this might be a way to another compartment. *How peculiar*, he thought, *a handle?* Bailey's fingers wrapped around a dependent lever that he might have found on an old Chevy truck. He pushed it down and heard a click. To his surprise, this outlandish looking door popped open and swung toward the inside of the bunker. Bailey whipped his head back around to view the others.

"Hey guys…look at this!" Bailey embellished. "There's something back here…leading down a long dark tunnel?" He couldn't see but blackness before him yet smelled a heavy damp metallic coldness rushing by. It sent a chill down his spine. *What was this? And what was Uncle Ron in too?* Bailey slipped the flashlight back and forth on the tunnel walls, left side then right. A motion-sensor-light flipped on when he crossed the threshold of the doorway. With the sensor-light pointing the way, Bailey could see a fuse-box off to the right of the tunnel wall. He walked over to the panel and opened a hinged grey metal door and flipped on a breaker. The whole tunnel lights up all the way down this uncharted dimly lit road. He saw it disappear ahead into the darkness. Betty came to the doorway with an expression of *oh my God*. This was something new. Lights were hung about twelve feet apart all the way down this long mysterious road, but leading to who knows where? And parked off to the right side of the road was this red four by four truck standing high up off the ground. Bailey's mouth flew open. The truck was perfectly modified with off-road capabilities in mind. It had a lift-kit with over-sized tires, plus a snorkel exhaust system connected to the front—an all-terrain heavy-duty vehicle. They were both still in shock. "What the heck," Bailey responded. He turned his head around to look at Betty. "Is this Uncle Ron's insane idea of the end of the world? I don't get it?" Betty showed a hesitant stare end route to the giant man-cave full of secrets. She raised an eyebrow in a puzzling acknowledgment.

"Hey, Uncle Ron was always talking about preparing for the end of the world. I didn't think he would go this far." The truck was any young boy's dream of unrealized potential. Betty saw Bailey staring with his mouth hinged open seeing him drooling. This caused her eyes to roll to the side, all boys were delirious about such toys. The odd couple didn't stop there. They started walking in the direction of the center road to the end. And then, one-hundred feet later something else brought them to attention, masked across their vision. "What's this?" Betty asked, "Another fantasy for old men turned into boys?"

Bailey moved his eyes in the direction of this so-called station wagon, parked to the left side of the road. This was a perfectly reconditioned black hearse, with shiny chrome bumpers and all the trimmings. Bailey reached to his right of the driver side and tried the door. The door popped open to reveal the most alarming details of personified perfections. The hearse was a dream fulfilled, with the most beautiful black leather seating made for that year and model. A slide window separated the back tinted dark black. They looked to reflect the soundproof renditions of days of yesteryear. You couldn't see anything through them because of the darkness of color.

"You want to look in the back?" asked Bailey.

"I thought you would never ask." Betty stated sarcastically. They both head for the back of the hearse. The back door popped open showing vivid lights of hidden treasures. Upon closer inspection, the black hearse revealed not only phantom flames done in black cherry-red glittered paint, but also skulls that were noticeable only when the flashlight played over the body of the car. The back was not what they expected either. The lighting had been customized to track lights along the top of the roof of the car. Black velvet draped from the center outward to the corners, like the netting of a canopy bed, with the tails coming down to the corners. Uncle Ron had taken out the rollers in the floor, which allowed other material to be slid in and out other than caskets. It was a solid floor. The carpet that covered the floor had the deep red-purple look of deoxygenated blood weaved into intricate patterns of purple lines running through it into spider-web patterns. To the side was a beautiful seat made of shiny cherry-wood in the shape of a casket but made for seating. The seats back was done in bright red velvet that had the same appeal of the freshly painted oxygenated blood as the front.

"Do you want to look any further?" Betty laughed.

"No. I'll leave that for the morbid people in the family, thank you very much." Then Bailey walked back up to the front of the hearse. He sat in the driver's side seat and noticed that the keys were in the ignition. Betty closed the back of the hearse before walking back up to the driver side.

"Why would Uncle Ron leave the keys in the car?" Bailey asked.

"He had an issue with auntie losing keys." Betty said. "Auntie was always misplacing hers. I'm guessing this was one way of not losing the keys."

Bailey looking beyond the hearse knowing this mysterious road was here for a reason, a reason they would soon find out. A mystery lay at their very doorstep. He got up out of the seat before closing the door to the hearse.

"Let's see what else is in this tunnel before we go back to the bunker." Bailey used a raised voice because of distance. The couple left the hearse behind in the dark and started walking toward the inky blackness ahead. Once at the end, they noticed that the tunnel continued around another long dark corner. Bailey looked behind him. The bunker looked small from how far they had walked. He had figured there was another exit besides the bunker way. There was no explanation of how the vehicles got inside. That mystery was still to be solved in some distant future. He had figured Uncle Ron had left some secrets behind that no one else knew of, how else would he have gotten the truck and hearse in the tunnel?

Bailey and Betty could feel air rushing by from the lower end of this mysterious road. He noticed right away a large tanker on the left side of the bending corner with a spout hanging out of the end. He could smell gasoline vapors and pulled back. The tanker was full. Bailey turned to look at Betty. "Uncle Ron pulled the vehicles and tanker in before he put the bunker in place. It only makes sense." He showed an air of curiosity when seeing the darkness ahead. "Wow…I wonder what's down at the end of that road?"

Betty shook her head. "I don't know?" She stated. "Let's get back to check on the others. We'll continue this tour later." Bailey nodded an approval as they turned back around to walk where they had come from. He flicked the flashing-light accidentally across Betty's face. The curious teenaged male ego noticed a smug of dirt on this difficult girl's forehead. Showing a nervous twitch toward the girl with more than attractive dimensions, with curls and curves and moistened red lipstick, and the mystery of an abrasive attitude was extra, as boys are often attracted to the outside of a cookie before tasting some of the inward beauty, as scorpions often sting before you know what stung you. Bailey was no different. Without thinking, he pulled her to a complete stop with his right hand. Betty, wondering what this strange looking boy was about to do. He reached up to wipe the smug of dirt away. Betty could feel his warm breath across her face. It made her smile as they both felt compelled to get closer. She noticed he had sleepy crumbs in the corners of his eyes. She blinked to draw focus remembering how rudely she chased the boy out of bed earlier that morning. It made her smile. She stated her thinking.

"Hey, you have," she pointed toward his eyes. "You've got sleepy crumbs in your eyes." She finished saying. The boy of bashful beginnings was embarrassed and tried to give excuses for his lack of physical hygiene.

"Oh, after that long race yesterday I was in a sleep-like-coma." His bottom lip twitched.

"I'm still a little sore in my calves. Those hills were a killer!" He was a bit off the subject.

Betty put her hand over her lips to hold off a giggle, and then decided to reward him by saying, "I was really proud of you. I kept telling people that you were with me. I was more than astonished that you were that good. Why didn't you say anything?"

Bailey was confused about why she would complement him in their current situation.

"Why would I say anything about being a good runner? My being a good runner has nothing to do with our present situation." The confused boy said.

Betty developed a hurtful look. "Well, I didn't really mean it the way it came out. I was only making conversation."

Then Bailey felt stupid. "I'm sorry…you were fine, I came across to strong…it's just our situation is different than yesterday, and I'm worried about the rest of the family."

Betty batted her eyes as she reached over to take his hand. The lost boy of unrelenting facts tried to make up for first impressions of weeks gone by. He pulled her close and gently kissed her. Betty resisted taking the lead and gave Bailey a chance to redeem himself. Soft lips and warm comforting quivers made Bailey's heart thump hard against his chest, like Roger-the-Rabbit. Finally, Betty moved in closer and wrapped her arms around his neck.

Grandma, in the distance, yelled her echoing voice in the heat of battle.

"What the tarnation is going on around here! Here we are at the end of the world and you two are all kissy faced!" Grandma gave Bailey the look of death, as if she were the grandmaster at the local Kung Fu studio and exclaimed. "Get your filthy lips off my granddaughter, you overgrown child molester!"

Betty pulled away from Bailey embarrassed with a little half quivering grimace. "Oh grandma, don't get your attitude in a twist! You know I like him. It was just a kiss!"

Bailey, too surprised, backed away from Betty like grandma was going to smack him.

Grandma continued to yell at them. "You two lovebirds need to come here…wait till you see what my son put into the bunker's floor… its quite the discovery!" Grandma walked behind Betty to keep the two of them separated. They slowly walked in ahead of her to check out her latest detection. Ryan couldn't be seen, but Mattie was standing just inside the entrance with a silly smile on her face while eating something that looked like a cookie.

Bailey, trying to break Grandma's stares away from him by the unwarranted kiss to her granddaughter asked Mattie a silly question. "What ya munchkin on squirt?"

Annoyed and being cut from the same rock as Betty she stated, "It's a cookie retard. What does it look like?"

Betty standing up for her latest heartthrob said, "Watch it munchkin or I'll make you cry!" Betty turned to look at her grandmother and said,

"Grandma, the little witch is riding her broom again!" Betty barked out.

Her grandmother rolled her elderly eyes at her granddaughter. "Oh, Betty don't go overboard, at least she's not screaming and crying because the world's ending." Her grandmother explained. "If this is the worst of her performances it's an acceptable loss." Grandma shook her head.

Betty fit-to-be-tied continued her performance of vengeance. "I'm going to make it the end of her world if she doesn't watch her tongue!" Mattie stuck her tongue out at Betty behind grandma's back.

Betty's face scowled a crimson red. "Alright you little witch, wait till grandma's not around. You'll be singing a different tune when it's just you and me!"

Grandma shot a dismembering stare back at the two girls. "Now stop it, the both of you! You act like your sisters!" Grandma turned and looked at Bailey as to include him in on this little family tussle. "Those two will be the death of me." She said.

Bailey confused responded, "There's a hearse station-wagon at the other end of the tunnel?" Thinking of what was still in the dark behind them. "It's behind us on that road."

Grandma spoke wondering if Bailey was referring to her future departure from this earth. She wrinkled her forehead and widened her eyes. "Well, young man, I'm not going to kick the bucket today, but it might be in the near future."

Bailey attempted the same look of confusion. "I meant what you said about the girls, reminded me of the old hearse that Betty and I found on the side of the road. It doesn't end there. The road continues."

"What?" Grandma said, being confused about the topic at hand.

"We'll show you later," replied Bailey, knowing he took the subject too far.

The conversation ended when Ryan poked his head up out of a hole in the floor. Bailey looked down beneath him. He saw a steel ladder reaching for the bottom of a secret place. With eyes widened he turned to glance at Betty. "Come on…let's take a look."

Bailey reached down and pulled Ryan up out of the hole in the floor. He noticed it was some type of storage area. He went first, and Betty followed after. Below were storage racks full of can goods, and packaged food packed in rows off racks full of enough for an army. The couple saw a refrigerator, and a stove. This was the makings of a fully stocked kitchen. A smile broke out on Betty's face. Off in the far-left corner Bailey noticed a door, to another room? He walked to the corner and opened the door. Inside lay a big beautifully decorated bedroom, with double sided sinks with master bath and a two-sided water treatment system shower, with a full-length vanity mirror, and a king size poster-bed centered in the room. Betty perked her lips and raised an eyebrow. She wasn't impressed. It all had Uncle Ron's touch in each piece of furniture. It was his usual signature. Betty had remembered when Uncle Ron was always gone up over the hill with the boys till late at night, always kept auntie worried. She motioned with her eyes when seeing the ladder.

"Uncle Ron almost thought of everything, except how Grandma's going to get down this ladder?"

Bailey looked at her like he should answer, so he said, "I don't know? We'll think of something."

CHAPTER 7

Tunnel's Secret

Bailey looked at Betty with an unsettling expression. "We need to find out what's in the rest of that tunnel." Bailey showed an expression of hurry. "Bring that pack of yours. Put some supplies with food and water. Oh, and bring that gun of yours and the knife."

Grandma, hearing the whole commotion of carrying weapons exploded. "What gun? What knife? Heavens-to-Betsy, what are you two kids getting into?"

Bailey returned. "Relax Mrs. Morse. It's only for safety precautions. We don't know what we'll run into. It's only a little added protection, just in case."

Grandma still suggested worry. "Well, you'd better be careful, and don't forget to keep that safety on so you don't shoot yourself in the foot."

Betty rolled her eyes. "Grandma I'm well aware of how to use a gun. My brothers made sure of that." Betty loaded up her backpack with some goodies, the fold up shovel, and a few bottles of water with the knife placed in a sheath on her belt. She put the gun in the back of her jeans like she was some bad girl in a mystery movie. Betty glanced over to her sidekick. He placed his hand in the air expecting a high-five. She accommodated Bailey with a slam of palms.

"Ouch!" she said, "watch the tender mittens tough guy! I'm not made of steel!"

Bailey developed a smirk of acknowledgement, "Oh sorry sweets, I got a little excited."

Betty wondered what boy-wonder would say next. "You dork."

"Why do you always call me that?" Bailey asked.

Betty shook her head. "Do I have to hit you in the head with a sledgehammer for you to know why?"

Bailey laughed. "No...I guess not...come on sweets, let's go before it gets too late."

As they were leaving the bunker, they said their goodbyes to Betty's grandmother, Ryan, and Mattie. Betty handed a walkie-talkie to her grandmother, hoping she wouldn't worry. "Keep it on until we get back." Betty said.

Grandma raised her eyebrows. "Yes honey, I will. The both of you need to be careful. I'll see if that old C.B. radio works while you're gone."

Betty whipped her head back around. "Good idea Grandma. Let us know if you're able to contact anyone." Bailey's eyes were set on the bright red truck. He turned to look at Betty who was just coming out the back door of the bunker. He stopped in his tracks and said, "Boy that sure is a nice truck." She turned and knew what he was thinking. The oversized tires made it look bigger than the trucks actual size.

"Let me guess," she teased. "You want to take the truck?"

Bailey pushed a smile out on the corners of his mouth. "If you wouldn't mind, besides we don't know how far this road goes—do we?" Betty showed a glistening sparkle in her eyes. Bailey reached over to check the driver side door. He met with success and climbed aboard. She ran around to the other side and threw her backpack up on the seat. Then slid up on the seat and closed the door. He reached for the ignition and started the truck. It roared to life. Vibrations of power echoed off the walls. Concerned about being careful Bailey stated,

"Don't worry I'll take it easy." Betty felt nervous by borrowing Uncle Ron's truck. The bashful boy across the dash began to smile, "I could have used one of these back home." Being in a playful mood he looked over his right shoulder. "So, this is a date?" He insisted.

Betty crinkled her nose. "No…not really…only with dinner and a movie is it a date."

A smile broke out on Bailey's face. "I'm the only guy in the tunnel that would go out with you. I think you're stuck with me."

Betty scrunched her face. "Oh please!" She mimics sticking her finger down her throat in a mock performance. Bailey lost the smile and revved the engine. He put the truck into drive and did an upturn down the road. The road ahead took them into the mystery of the dark. He took one last look in the rear-view mirror. An unexplainable queasiness weighed heavy on his mind. Something about this road didn't feel right. Bailey sensed something strange was about to happen, but he didn't know what.

Betty looked over and noticed his stare had changed from a giddy boy, to a serious man on a mission. "Are you, okay?"

He seemed uncertain to answer. Without turning to look at her he said, "I'm fine…just this whole day has been kind of strange."

Betty's eyes flickered with surprise. "What do you mean?"

He flashed his eyes toward Betty then back down the road leading to who knows where. "I don't know…too many things have gone wrong." A flash of memories of the last six hours crossed Betty's mind. She knew Bailey was on to something but couldn't explain the day's circumstances either. Rounding the next corner, the truck slid into the turn.

"Sorry…didn't plan the turn right."

Betty's eyes widened. "Keep your eyes on the road dork. Don't crash my Uncle's truck!"

Bailey developed an exasperated expression. *This girl with the attitude needs to take it easy.* He thought. The young man of concerns flicked his high beams on and ignored her last comment. As he drove past the first right turn, motion sensor lights came on down the tunnel. Bailey being confused about the sudden lights asked, "Should we just keep going?"

Betty raised an eyebrow, "Unless you want to walk…"

He changed the subject. "So, you think Uncle Ron knew about this road? As you can tell, someone put lots of money into this road, and who knows where it goes or who put it here?"

Betty glanced over at the eccentric boy with a puzzling look.

"Oh, you mean like the government or something?"

"Well yes…who else would go through all the trouble and money?"

"I don't see any black suits hanging around doing ominous things, do you?" Betty barked out.

Bailey shook his head and kept driving. He began to notice his speed was creeping up a bit above forty. Not wanting to hit a wall he slowed down. After a while, he became mesmerized by the blurring of lights swishing by. The tunnel went forever. Two miles later the tunnel veered a different direction. Betty saw the compass move southeast. A close call on a corner wall caused Betty to close her eyes.

"That was close." Bailey said with a flash of his eyes.

"Yes, I know. Where the heck are we going?" Betty belted out.

"Don't ask me…I just the driver."

"Bailey, be careful. I'm afraid of what might be ahead."

He looked over at the girl of mystery, wondering if he got in over his head. She had an anxious look in her eyes, constant dangers, extreme weather, and unsettling personalities full of friction, what else was in store?

Bailey thought he would entertain her with meaningless conversation. "You know, fear is just a frame of mind. If you don't give in to the fear, you can usually stay calm."

Betty looked over at wonder-boy and speculated where he was going with his statement. With a smirk pasted across her face Betty said, "So what do you suggest?"

Bailey looked confused, "Like with running…you can't just sit hiding in a cold dark hole. You have to take chances."

Betty got that dork look on her face again. "Well Mr. Philosopher where else can we be? We're traveling down a cold dark hole right now— you're such a dork!" Bailey was done trying to impress a girl who obviously was smarter than the average high-school graduate.

Suddenly, Betty sucked in air and screamed causing Bailey to slam on his brakes.

"What?" Bailey shouted with a tone of exasperation.

Betty was holding her hand over her mouth. "We have to go back!" Betty was fanning the air with bent wrist and fingers straight.

This caused Bailey's smile to grow. "Go back...go back where?"

Betty wrinkled her forehead. "I forgot about Jackie at Uncle Ron's house...and Cuddles!" Betty reached for the walkie-talkie and shot a concerning stare. She could imagine Bailey driving Ms. Daisy and she had lost her way. Suddenly, looking at Bailey and asked, "Do you think my grandmother will be mad?"

"I don't know...call her and ask?"

Betty twisted her lips to the side. "A big help you are."

He waited for Betty to make the call before turning around. Static could be heard on the squawk-box. She pushed the receiver button down and yelled into the speaker.

"Grandma...please pick up!" She waited for a few seconds before repeating the call.

"Grandma...this is Betty please pick up...over."

A small voice came over the speaker. "This is Ryan. You guys are in big trouble. You forgot about Jackie and Cuddles at Uncle Ron's house."

Betty responded with water splashing on the back of her eyes. "I know Ryan. Tell Grandma I'm so sorry!" It sounded like Betty was about to cry. Bailey felt bad that Jackie had never crossed his mind. Betty continued her words of remorse. "She trusted me. I let her down. I feel like such a fool. Bailey and I are turning around to get her."

The sassy seven-year-olds voice came back over the speaker. "Why'd you want to do that? She's already here at the bunker."

Betty turned to look at Bailey with shock. "What?"

"She's here." Ryan repeated.

Betty focused her eyes. "Ryan, tell her I'm so sorry for being such an idiot!"

Ryan smiled and said, "Yeah, she already knows you're an idiot."

Grandma grabbed the walkie-talkie from the sassy seven-year-olds hand. She wrinkled her old face which was already far into the wrinkled stage and gave Ryan the look of death. Ryan backed up like a stork standing among alligators. Grandma's voice came over the speaker.

"Betty it's your grandmother. Jackie's fine…she's with us, and auntie's little dog."

Betty let out a slow breath of air while pointing Bailey to the open road. She had paused so long Grandma had to repeat herself.

"Betty, are you still there?"

"Yes Grandma, we're still driving southeast." Betty was looking at a compass that her uncle had mounted on the dash. *Boy, Uncle Ron thought of everything.* She thought.

"Are you guys still in the tunnel?" Grandma asked.

"Yes Grandma, it's a long dark road going downhill. I'm a little scared. Bailey and I think we should continue. This might be an old access tunnel that the government built for emergencies."

"Well honey, stay in touch with me every half hour or so, so I know you're okay. Jackie said the snow is getting worse. It was an unbearable cold. She said the wind is blowing something fierce."

Betty thought of the mousy little rodent with wagging tail that was considered family.

"How's Cuddles doing?"

"She's fine. A little overwhelmed like the rest of us—that's all."

"Okay Grandma, I'll talk to you later."

"Okay honey, bye for now."

Betty turned off the receiver to conserve the battery. She turned to look in the back seat. At first, she saw the first aid kit under the seat, then the jackets and two pair of gloves. She found two ski masks and two pair of snowshoes under the seat that were an adjustable pair. She turned around to look at Bailey. "I'm glad Uncle Ron is a little crazy, because if he wasn't, we would probably be dead by now."

"Hey Betty." Bailey asked. "Why hasn't the government told the public about this extreme change in the weather, which seems to be more than life-threatening.?" Betty considered his statement.

"I don't know. They thought it would create an extreme panic throughout the communities causing looting, mass hysteria, death, and mayhem. You know…the end of the world type of stuff."

Bailey looked over at Betty like she hit the nail right on the head. "Don't scare me like that. There has to be a logical, non-violent answer to this situation?"

Betty's face turned serious as she stared out of the truck window. She then turned her gaze back at Bailey. "Think about it...I mean our situation. If you were in charge of everything, and there was nothing you could do to change something that would alter the face of the world, would you tell everybody or keep it to yourself?"

Bailey reflected an image of worry. "Then what would they do?"

"Absolutely nothing, because as soon as they tell everybody in the world two thirds of the population is going to die in a deep freeze, they wouldn't survive two minutes outside of their own front door."

Bailey expressed a reluctant nod. "Don't you think that's exaggerating a bit?"

Betty's eyes flickered from memory. "That's the whole reason why Uncle Ron placed the bunker down here in the first place. He knew something that no one else knew, including his boys, because if they would have told anyone, they would be at the bunker right now."

Unexpectedly, Betty jerked sideways and grabbed her walkie-talkie. She turned the noise box on and waited to hear the static. "Grandma pick up, this is Betty...over." A few seconds went by before Grandma's voice is heard over the speaker.

"Yes dear, what's going on?"

Betty's face turned serious. "Grandma, listen to me. Please listen very carefully." Grandma could hear Betty's voice waver with emotion. Betty continued her emotional outpouring of brooding sentiment. "Bailey and I believe you guys could be in great danger." There's a pause so she could gather her thoughts. "Please take me seriously."

Betty let go of the button for a minute and looked at Bailey. "I want you guys to get in the basement of the bunker. Place the rug over the top of the entrance perfectly to cover the hidden door. Don't make a lot of noise. If Uncle Ron gets to the bunker with auntie, they'll know the combination to the lock. What I'm worried about is if other people follow them. They will or could force their way in, which could end in tragedy. Please do that for me. Okay Grandma?"

Grandma's hands shook as she thought of the implication. She pushed the button on the speaker again. "Yes honey. Do you really think it will get that bad?"

"I don't know Grandma, but it's better to be safer than sorrier."

"Yes…your right, honey. We'll do that." Grandma laid the two little ones and Jackie down for a nap. She had to wake them to get them below. Grandma put the walkie-talkie down for a minute. She shook both children a wake. With a finger pressed against her lips and whispered in a muffled voice. "You have to hide in the bottom bedroom." She said. Ryan felt a surge of fright and started to cry. Grandma reached down and covered his mouth. "Shhhh…" She whispered in the lowest voice she could go. "Now just do as I say. Ryan, listen to Grandma. Quit your crying."

Ryan looked up past tears. "What's going on Grandma? Why'd you wake us?"

Grandma continued to hush him. "Shhhh…I said be quiet. If I have to tell you again, I'll spank you. Do you understand?"

Ryan nodded his understanding at the elderly woman with quivering lips and widened eyes. Jackie raised her head from the top bunk. "What's goin on? Where is everybody?"

Ryan glanced at the top bunk and shushed Jackie like he was helping Grandma. He whispers aloud. "Be quiet…there are frozen people outside trying to get in."

This brought Jackie wide awake. "What frozen people?" Jackie said at full volume.

Grandma shushed Jackie and signaled the children to the uncovered hole in the floor. She whispered into Jackie's ear. "Take these two, and little Cuddles downstairs and hide in the bedroom. Please don't talk, don't fight. No obnoxious sounds," that made Ryan giggle because it reminded him of his farts. The little girls only smiled.

Then Grandma said, "Now go!"

The three children scurried down the ladder whispering giggles of playful secrets in the dimly lit room. The younger ones saw it as a game, but Grandma was full of worry.

She quickly covered the opening after blowing a kiss in their direction. Grandma knew she couldn't climb down the ladder with her withered hands. They shook nervously as she stood in the dark. Water built on the back of her eyes. She covered the entrance with the rug after securing a top plate over the hole in the floor, a perfect disguise of deception. Nothing looked out of place. "There now, they'll be okay."

Grandma whispered in the dark, but anxiety laced every inch of her frame.

Betty returned her gaze down the long undulating road ahead. It seemed endless, the lights still coming on as they advanced. Both Bailey and Betty could see different colored lights ahead. There was red and green mostly pointing the way. It gave them a target to shoot for. Betty rolled down her window and let the cold damp air hit her face. Something else left a strange scent in the air, but what was it? As they drew near to these bright green and red lights, they could see the road spread out into an open gap between a bridge and the other side where two huge gates of steel separating them from something strange. They were held open for a reason, yet no one was around to show any interest. Just Bailey and Betty sitting in the truck, staring up at this ominous find as if they'd left earth for another place to an altered experience from another time. Their curiosity perked. Ahead, the dark revealed something obvious hidden on an exacerbated scale. Both young people sat with their mouths hinged open. No lights were lit beyond a certain point so the impeding glare of darkness to come was still a mystery. Only a few twinkles of blue lights like seen on an airport runway showed past the darkness to come. Someone had planned and built all this for a reason, a reason beyond the thinking of two young people who sat in awe.

Bailey started to cross over the bridge, slowly. The butterflies began to kick-up in his stomach. What was this place? And why were they the ones to find it? Everything on this little excursion had been a mystery so far. Bailey's adrenaline pumped through his veins. It caused his senses to be heightened. He felt compared to a fly on the wall staring out into the world with a thousand sets of eyes in miniature form, yet nothing lined up to his way of thinking. They were just sitting on the edge of the truck seat waiting for a signal that the world was about to end.

Bailey started to sweat from the visual. Betty was feeling something similar, except she said, "Oh my God…I have to throw-up!" She looked at Bailey as exasperation took over her face. With that said, Bailey leaned over the passenger side of the door, and opened it just in time for Betty to projectile vomit ten feet out.

"I guess you weren't kidding." Bailey said without thinking straight.

Betty gave him a crippling stare. He continued his caustic remarks. "So, I take it you don't deal with stress very well?" He looked at her dumbfounded and said, "Just breathe Betty!" With hand gestures of pushing in air.

Betty had enough of his obvious ignorance. "Shut-up dork. Mr. Philosopher. I'm car sick. You retard! I've been sick ever since we started this little joy ride." Betty rolled her fists like she wanted to punch something. Bailey backed off considering it might be him. A protruding vein was sticking out in Betty's forehead. She looked back at him like he was a Moron without serving a purpose accept to make people mad.

"No more B.S.! Just get us there already and stop your delusional comments!"

Bailey wisped his hand across his forehead and whispered under his breath.

"Well, so much for a freaking date." Bailey thought for a moment. *What got her all worked up? I was just trying to help.* He thought about what Betty had said *so* verbally. It was so strange to him he started to laugh. Betty developed a misinforming look in her eyes as she continued to lean overturning her head sideways, viewing this misaligned male of an attractive nature full of bizarre stupidities.

"What's so funny?" Betty asked with a continued scowl of indifference.

"Well," Bailey insisted, "you called me by every name except by my real name, and this is our first date in the local tunnel dear." After a brief pause, Bailey epitomized his reasoning. "I've had better."

Betty thought it through and started to laugh too, but "oh no..." more bile followed, as she continued dry heaving with a cantankerous noise.

Bailey turned his head away and scrunched his nose. He saw green spiraling down off her lips like drool. He covered his mouth and nose and tried not to think about the visual. And then he thought to reach over and pull napkins out of the glovebox. Then a light turned on in his head. "Ghetto paper," he said, with a smile while handing her a hand full.

Betty looked up between rounds of wrenching stomach flexion. She gave him an obtrusive stare. "What?"

"Ghetto paper...you know the paper that people collect from all the different fast-food eateries out there—I mean in the real world. You save it and stuff it in your glovebox for occasions like these when there are no paper towels or napkins around."

Betty looked around this giant cave to make sure they were alone, and she was actually hearing this. She held her building rage as Bailey continued to prove a dismal point. "I'm glad Uncle Ron thinks like me. He saved all this paper."

Betty's face broke out with a smile…well a smile. Still wiping vulgar bile from her lips, she said, "Are you a Moron?" Betty continued her words of revenge for Bailey showing a lack of maturity. "I didn't see any fast-food restaurants in the tunnel dear, on our way down to the local massive bridge!" Betty began to roll on the ground, not from pain but Bailey's frame of mind. Between laughs she waved him off with her hand. "Stop…" She said between cackles of laughter. "I'm going to pee!"

Bailey, frustrated by her lack of moral support, kept going on his little rampage of nervousness. He looked at Betty like she was pushing her luck. "That's why I like running so much by myself. I don't have to depend on someone else to be successful at it. It's me and the road with no drama."

This untied the lace that was holding Betty from exploding. "You think I'm drama?"

Bailey's face turned pink in frustration from bi-polar conditions. "That's not what I meant," He said, with an elevated heartbeat showing in his head. "I mean people in general…what I mean, are those people who spend their whole life making bad or wrong decisions for themselves and their families! You misunderstood me." Bailey barked out.

Betty continued the hard stare. "Well, it looks like you're going to get your wish, Mr. Philosopher. Most of the people that you want to avoid are gone." Betty's anger turned into a hurtful stare. Bailey had an *Oh my God* look on his face and felt like running in a direction she could not follow. Then he decided to finish her off. "You know, there are pills for what you have."

That's the final limit. Betty stormed off into the darkness past the giant gates—a world beyond any known hope. Bailey got nervous all of sudden and thought, *where is she going—now who's the smart one?*

He grabbed a flashlight and chased after her. Betty being quicker to the draw lost him in the dark…

CHAPTER 8

Deadline

Bailey flicked the flashlight on. Betty was already climbing stairs in the distance. He could see a set of elevators up ahead about three-hundred feet past the metal stairs, which went up six flights. The elevator had blue lights lighting the way to the right, a place hidden just beyond the corners of the stairwell. Thinking he'd be able to beat her to the top. He thought knowingly that the stairs would drain her, especially after all that stomach wrenching spasms. He pushed the elevator button. He heard the mechanics of the elevator moving from top to bottom. He glanced back over his shoulder and looked up toward the stairs. After adjusting to the dark, Bailey could see a sparkle of light coming from Betty's earring. He knew she was there. The elevator opened and the boy of bashful beginnings entered and pushed number six. The elevator lit up to accommodate. Within twenty seconds, Bailey reached the top. Coming out of the elevator the lights above shot on, the sight before his eyes was more than amazing. As soon as the doors opened, he started lumbering in the direction of the stairs that Betty was coming up on. Even Betty jerked from sudden surprise of illumination. At once he saw her coming up to the fifth level from below. This place was amazing. He was on the top floor of what looked like the inside of a giant stadium, except cave like—a horse-shoe shape. He felt like he was standing on top of the world. This made his heart flutter.

And seeing the beautiful Betty bouncing innocently toward him, his bottom lip began to quiver. Bailey knew somehow in the back of his mind that meeting her and getting to know her was something destined. It was by no accident. Betty saw the uncooperative boy in the distance coming her way as she maintained her hurtful stare. She could tell by the flash of his eyes that he was sorry to have ever opened his mouth in the first place. He waited until she got to the top floor as he hung his head in a sensitive gesture of sorrow. Betty was sorry too. Besides, he was just a silly boy trying to draw attention, and he did help save her grandmother and those kids that he didn't even know. Her eyes indicated that she was willing to forgive if they were willing to put these differences behind them. Betty tried to say she was sorry, but Bailey stopped abruptly and moved in quickly and stole a kiss, hearts pounding, lips soft and warm, his tenderness grabbed her and drew her in. He was so irritating at times, but now, like this…she melted in his arms, warm bodies set afire. Finally, Bailey loosened his grip on her, and stood back gazing at her with a sense of tenderness. Betty was speechless, spellbound, and the terrible things she was going to say to him seemed to disappear. Bailey reached up and pushed a curl of hair away from her eyes. Her lungs were moving her chest so passionately, she held her breath in to keep him from watching her. Her face had flushed a brighter shade of pink, and the difficulty in breathing had to stop. It was embarrassing. Bailey could see by the long straight line in her neck as she turned her head held an elevated heartbeat. It made him smile. And to make it even worse, the boy with the small brain leaned in for the kill. He reached down and kissed her again. Betty, feeling she was losing control sucked in air, and then pushed this weird boy at arm's length. She then whispered gentle words of breathlessness, "okay…you're forgiven…but I just want you to understand me."

Bailey showed sensitive comprehension by a sparkle of hope in his eyes. "That's all I want too." He said. Sensing this moment, a changing factor of direction, he decided to change the subject. "Do you still have the water and food in your backpack?"

Betty wanting to accommodate this strange boy that caused her heart to do flip-flops, "Yes I do." Then she finished by saying, "I have four bottles of water, some homemade sandwiches and a box of cookies, and some apples and two bananas."

The kiss kept flashing through Betty's mind as she felt something for this eccentric boy not felt for others. She knew she was hooked. No going back. Bailey reached down and brushed the top of her fingers with the back of his hand. A chill crawled up her arm and prickled her arm hair. She pulled away. She didn't understand why this abnormal boy made her chest heave and her heart to stir like it was about to explode. Bailey gave her a few feet of distance between them. With a graceful smile he looked down at her feet and then back up into her eyes. He knew by her expression he'd stolen her words and set her aflame. Something sparkled between them. Then Betty remembered throwing up and put her hand to her face in astonishment. "Oh God..." she said. "My breath must be God-awful...sorry," she giggle while wiping at her mouth.

Bailey brushed off her embarrassment and went on to another conversation, trying to cover her disapproval of bad tastes and uncomfortable stares. Bailey remarks were gentle waves of comfort. "Let's find a place to eat lunch and rest for a while." Then he finished. "We have lots of exploring to do later."

Betty developed this giddy expression like she felt love in the air. He reached over and tenderly took her hand. He could feel she was still shaking. Not sure if he caused this or her to be sick, keeping that hidden from words. Suddenly, from an unknown source, a loud voice came over a speaker, "T-minus two hours and forty-five minutes." They looked at each other with an air of surprise, over in the distance, above the two larger super-gates, hung a huge digital clock showing a countdown.

Bailey pulled Betty's hand toward the elevator. "Look...we've got to go!" Both sensing these giant gates were about to close, less than three hours from now. Betty thought of those left behind.

She yelled over a siren going off, "Bailey...the others...!"

His eyes turned serious "I know...call your Grandmother...they need to know!"

Betty swung her backpack around as they entered the elevator. Bailey pushed the lobby button while Betty turned the squawk-box back on. They heard the static as she made the call. "Grandma…this is Betty are you there?" She waited for a minute hoping her grandmother would pick up soon, and then repeated the call. Finally, her grandmother answered.

A scratchy old voice came over the speaker. "Yes, dear this is Grandma…what's going on?" Grandma said with a touch of nervous tension.

"Listen Grandma…please…we're at the entrance of what looks like a giant conservatory or atrium. This place…it's a major size cave of some sort, it was meant for the end. You have only two hours…" Betty looked up at that giant digital clock before finishing, "And forty-three minutes to get here."

Bailey whipped his eyes in Betty's direction and knew what she was thinking. There was a reason they were here. The couple comprehended there wasn't enough time to go there and back. Bailey, right away thought of the hearse. Betty let go of the receiver and waited for a reply.

Betty's Grandmother finally responded. "I know something major is happening. We found a radio and have been listening to the news. It's awful out there!" Her Grandmother said while letting go of the receiver.

Betty looked at Bailey with a disconcerting stare. "What should they do?"

He looked up at the clock, "They should come to us. Load up with as much supplies as they can within a few minutes and get here before these gates close."

Betty sensed he was right, so she continued to tell her grandmother Bailey's plan. "Listen Grandma, please do this for me. Get the kids and yourself into the hearse and drive here. It won't take but an hour or less. Carry as many of the supplies as you can and put them in the back of the hearse. Just get here as soon as you can!" Betty let go of the receiver as she bit her lip with a worried look of wonder in her eyes.

Grandmother answered a few seconds later. "Oh honey, I don't know the way, and it's so dark down that road."

Betty became insistent. "Grandma, listen please. Do this for the children. You don't have much time. The road is clear. You only have to make a couple of turns. Most of the way will have lights. Please do this!" Betty said with emotion scratching the back of her throat.

Grandma returned, "Okay dear, if you say so." Yet grandmother's heart began to pound with anxiety. Their conversation was disconnected, and grandmother's sense of urgency kicked in. She uncovered the trap door in the floor and yelled for the kids.

"Mattie…Ryan…Jackie…get up here now!" Grandma thought to draw their attention quicker by putting two fingers in her mouth to whistle. She blew so hard her front teeth dislodged and fell to the ground. She whispered, "Oh poo." Grandma reached down and picked up her teeth, brushed them off and put them back into a mouth. She then yelled down the hole once more. "Hello…" Grandma yelled, "Don't make me come and get you!"

Ryan came out of the room yawning and putting his hand over his mouth while stretching. He squinted with one eye open. "What's the racket for Grandma?"

Grandma yelled even more. "Get the others…we've got to go!" Grandma showed a smug expression while reaching up to get dirt out of her mouth from dislodged teeth.

Ryan was jolted awake by Grandma's yelling. He sensed adventure. He poked his head back into the room mimicking his Grandmother in his own sort of way. "Hey…tards…we've got to go!"

Jackie shot up off the bed like someone turned on a loud stereo. Mattie blinked her eyes open, and Cuddles started barking and waging her tail. Momentarily, the kids were climbing up the ladder and Grandma was spouting orders of coherence. The battle of survival was on. Grandma was trying to gather supplies of most importance. The three rattled children looked at the old woman who was set aflame with emotion.

Ryan, not being shy by any discovery said, "Where're we going?"

Breaking Grandma's train of thought she looked up. "We have to take that dag-gum-road in the dark."

Ryan wisped a stare at his older sister. "I'll get the food." Ryan embellished.

His Grandmother displayed a distressed stare, and she is full of elderly anxiety said, "We've got to go!"

All three children scattered in three different directions grabbing for food, clothes, water, and other necessities. Ryan looked out past the bunker doorway and saw the truck was gone.

Ryan belted out. "Where's the ride Grandma?" Grandma raised her head and looked into the distant low-lying shadows and pointed at the hearse. Ryan turned his head with an inquisitive stare. "But Grandma...that's for dead people?" Mattie released a giggle. Abruptly, their Grandmother looked back as they were closing in on the hearse.

"Where's that little rodent?"

Jackie with eyes widened said, "Oh...we left her in the room downstairs."

The old woman cast the girl a withering stare. "Well, go get her... she won't survive down there on her own!"

Jackie jogged back to the bunker and was back in three minutes, breathing hard, holding the little fur-ball of teeth, tail, and nerves. The Chihuahua was shaking like Grandma's old spin-cycled wash-machine. Her tongue was rolled out panting, comparable to a red-miniature-carpet. A little whine broke to the surface from the poor pooch's mouth. Jackie held her tight. Grandma yelled out while opening the driver side door. "Someone needs to ride in the back!"

Ryan, with his disgruntled attitude said, "You ride in the back Grandma, you know some dead people, we don't!"

Grandma showed a smug look of indifference. Ryan insisted, "But grandma! That's for dead people!" Ryan's Grandmother looked up as the color rose in her cheeks and shot a heated glare at the nonconforming youth.

"Don't give me any lip munchkin! I have to drive this abomination down that road!" Ryan looked confused at Grandma's explanation. "You know...that road there yonder...Bailey's Road...the one in front of you!"

Ryan noticed his grandmother's temper was flaring, but he also sensed she had her hands full too. He backed off as Jackie came to the rescue. "Mrs. Morse...don't worry...we can all sit up front. I'll hold one of the smaller kids on my lap...there's room. Besides this is an older model...the seats are longer than newer cars."

Grandma didn't expound on Jackie's comment. She leaned forward and pried open the door. Then the old woman remarked. "Okay, suit yourself, but no complaining about anything while I'm driving. Chatter makes me nervous."

"Okay, we won't say a peep." Jackie replied as she showed her fingers pulling a zipper across her lips. Ryan smiled and grabbed her hand like they were all well acquainted. Mrs. Morse started the death mobile as the children piled into the hearse, snug, tight, and ready to go. As the engine started Mrs. Morse yelled out, "Thank my son for good mechanics!" Off they go down the path, with Grandma heavy on the pedal. "Hold on… we're leaving town and we ain't going to Kansas!" Mrs. Morse saw the lights come on in front of her as she moved ahead in the dark. "Well, well, the good Lord is lighting our path." She said.

Ryan developed a look of terror in his eyes. "Grandma…you're scaring us children with your crazy driving!"

Grandma shot a searing stare across the dash. "Zip-it junior. I might lose my concentration and hit a wall!" Ryan sat back in his seat and closed his eyes. Grandma trucked on down the road, leaving their old lives behind.

Bailey and Betty took the elevator to the bottom of the atrium and walk past the gates. They get into the truck and drive to the other side of the long, massive bridge of safety. They get out of the truck, sat down at the end as Betty dangled her feet over the edge. Bailey looked over the railing, down into the abyss. Betty reached over and poked him in the ribs. Bailey flinched so hard he grabbed for the railing. He whipped his head to the side with a heated glare. "Don't do that! I'm afraid of heights!"

Betty leaned over the rail without a stir of emotion and spit over the side. She watched it disappear into the darkness. "I wonder what's down there." Betty said.

Bailey reached over and grabbed her arm. "Hey…don't do that…it's not funny. You could fall."

She broke out with a smile. "I'm not afraid of heights silly. My cousin used to take me rock climbing all the time—it's nothing to really think about. I grew up in these mountains, and I know my way around them without all the hang-ups you city folk seem to carry."

He ignored her comment and sat down next to her, opened up a bottle of water and chugged it, gasped for air, then took a huge bite out of the first sandwich.

She raised an eyebrow. "Hungry…are you?"

He nodded. "Haven't eaten since yesterday," made other plans." A smile broke out across his lips.

Betty got the gist of his playful stare. And reached up and ran her fingers through his hair like he was already family. Bailey batted his eyelashes in a wanting stare, leaned over and kissed her on the forehead while leaving a touch of peanut butter behind from his breath. She took advantage of this opportunity and pecked his lips. He tasted like peanut-butter and a hint of jam. It brought memories back of good-old-schooldays. That was one of the easiest sandwiches to fix, and she had gotten plenty of them. She began to think about their present situation.

Betty took a long look below before commenting, "You know…if this is a place of refuge, where is everybody?" Bailey surprised by her quick assumption. "Nobody showing up for the big show is kind of strange."

Bailey raised an eyebrow knowing she was on to something. "Their timing was off by a few days…you know…sudden panic, they won't see their families anymore. They left all at once." Then he looked at her. "You would have gotten the same idea. Go spend the last few days you have left on earth with family, and **bam**…they were too late coming back. They were stuck because the weather hit all of a sudden, you know… it's not like we've got the best weathermen in the area. These hills behind us are the great Rocky Mountains. Stranger things have happened than pending severe weather. Anything's possible."

Betty considered his statement before turning her head to stare down into the gap between the gates and the other side of the road, while the darkness below left an eerie prickly feeling on the back of her neck. Quite suddenly, she got this crazy idea and reached for her backpack. Betty pulled a glow stick out and snapped the end of it and watched it light up. She shook it to a bright green color. She looked at Bailey and said, "I'm going to count. Tell me when this hits the bottom." Bailey remembered seeing this done on a rock-climbing program. The idea was that for every second that clicked by an object would fall an average of 32.2 feet per second. Betty continued. "We can figure out how deep this canyon is without having to physically measure it." Betty dropped the glow stick and started counting. Bailey watched the glowing color drop like a rock, bouncing and spinning as it slowly reached for the bottom. He yelled stop when Betty hit eleven seconds on her watch. She tried to figure it out in her head. Suddenly, she looked up at Bailey with caution. "354 feet…that's the depth."

Bailey looked down and shook his head. "Wow…that's a long way."

"Yeah…it sure is."

Bailey looked up reviewing the tunnel they had come from earlier. A mystery was all he could think. He asked with an air of curiosity. "How long do you think this tunnel and road have been here? Do you think it's a way to get people in or out?"

Betty stared at the odd boy with his questioning. She wanted to make sure he was focused on her words before answering. She stared at the tunnel from where they were seated. She didn't say a word for a while, as if trying to absorb its secrets as seen in her eyes. She had memories of the past like she knew of a connection to another day not mentioned of history. Betty explained what she held in the back of her mind.

"About five years ago. I heard Uncle Ron and auntie arguing about some government men that came to pay Uncle Ron a visit. They were trying to buy the piece of land up over the hill. For sentimental reasons Uncle Ron didn't want to sell. Auntie thought something was going on to be more than strange, but Uncle Ron kept something from her, something peculiarly off, something not said, is my guess. The only thing that I knew for sure was they had offered him a lot of money, from what auntie revealed later—but something was missing from this odd story. I'm sure he never mentioned the tunnel to her, because he knew she would just probably worry, and tell the wrong people, so he kept it to himself."

Bailey looked at her and asked. "Do you think this tunnel is the reason why the government wanted to buy his land?"

Betty raised an eyebrow. "It has to be." Betty replied, "There's no other explanation for them wanting it. It had to be blind luck that Uncle Ron dug so perfectly in front of their tunnel, like he was destined to get this abstract idea to dig, to find a place of safety for his family to dig in, but instead ran into something most unexpected."

Bailey's facial expressions perked. "And what would that be?"

"Uncle Ron said once…something I overheard that the land above the barn was always caving in up over the hill. Uncle Ron had his suspicions that there was something down below, something held in secret from everyone." Betty finished her thought. "He knew their plan a long time ago. How else could he have gotten the truck and hearse plus that tanker inside the tunnel? He had to put them in first before the bunker. It only makes sense. The government had planned this event five years ago or longer—who knows? Then if Uncle Ron didn't sell, they would have just taken the land over anyway—in the end. You know how the government is, if they want it bad enough, they just take it. Holding back until needed…you understand…a low profile at first, not start any trouble; or get their names in the paper. They thought old men with stubborn dispositions could easily have an accident, poor old man disappearing beneath rock and dirt—a cave in, then the government scheming their way into the property." Bailey had a serious stare in his eyes. Betty explained further. "Someone was smart. I should have known those government men were up to no good." Betty then looked at her watch understanding they were running out of time. Her Grandmother still wasn't here. She jumped to her feet. "It's almost been two hours since calling Grandma." She said.

Bailey swung his eyes back in her direction. "Call her back. They had a problem?"

She reached over to her backpack and grabbed the walkie-talkie lying on the top. They could hear static. "Kids, Grandma…please come in, over." Betty waited a few seconds before she heard Ryan's little voice come over the speaker.

"Ten four Big Betty. What do you want?" His little voice squelched on the speaker.

"Where are you guys? You should have been here by now."

"I know," reported Ryan, "but Grandma had a little accident." Then Ryan yelled, "Hey, I can see green and red lights flashing ahead. What is that?"

"You're getting closer to us Ryan, just keep Grandma coming towards the flashing lights!" Betty yelled.

"Ten four Big Betty, we're on our way!"

Little Ryan's puzzled betty C.B. talk. She wondered what was up. Turning to look at Bailey, and then the timer above. They still had plenty of time to get to the gates. Ten minutes had gone by before Ryan called back.

"Calling Big Betty, calling Big Betty. Houston, we have a problem!"

Betty grabbed the walkie-talkie. "What's the problem munchkin?"

"Grandma broke our ride, and we've got to walk from here!"

Betty could sense a small cry of alarm in her nephew's voice. "Oh no…!" Betty exclaimed. She shot a brazen glare at Bailey.

"I know. I'm on it!" He said. He quickly jumped to his feet and headed for the truck. Betty shot up to follow.

"Wait a minute…" She said, "I'm going with you!"

He smiled with an assertive sense in his walk. When looking across the dash, he said. "Buckle up sweetheart…you gotta hold on tight, this could get bumpy." Bailey slammed the truck into four-wheel-drive and pealed out into a one-hundred-and-eighty-degree turn jetting up the tunnel, burning rubber and screeching tires, like the police were chasing him.

Betty grabbed the handle above her head to keep from banging against the glass. She saw that competitive stare in this strange boy's eyes—something she saw the other day. A killer instinct rose in him set afire.

Betty reflected her worry. "I hope they're okay!" Betty sighed. She was also worried about the clock. "How much time do we have left?"

"Only about thirty minutes or less, give or take a minute. Bailey's eyes were focused on the road ahead as he shot up the tunnel with burning blazes of exhaust-pipes and permeating fumes. He could see billows of smoke up ahead. A twisting mass of confusion caused him to slow down. The hearse could be partially seen in the distance, a smashed-up wreck, broken and bleeding fluids. The children came out behind billows of smoke coughing and sputtering, leaning over in suffocating conditions.

"Where's Grandma?" Betty yelled. She was tumbling out of the truck behind Bailey.

Ryan leaning over trying to get his breath coughed out. "Something's wrong with Grandma! She's not moving." Ryan gasped. "She's stuck. We couldn't get her out. Her door jammed up!"

Betty grabbed little Ryan and pulled him further away from the smoke. Betty looked over her shoulder and screamed at Bailey. "Bailey, get my Grandmother out of that burning car!"

He didn't wait. Lunging into the burning flames and caustic smoke. He noticed right away that the driver side door was jammed, and all scrunched up. He had to reach for Mrs. Morse from the passenger side. Flames shot up past the engine. The heat burned at his face. Bailey saw Betty's Grandmother unconscious or worse trapped behind the seatbelt. Trying to free her, but the seatbelt wouldn't budge. It was no use. He yelled for Betty in the black acidic smoke.

"Betty…I need your knife!" Bailey's eyes and throat were burning from the gasoline flames. His eyes swollen with tears. He yelled again. "Betty, I need your knife!"

Betty swung her head around and heard the cry. She pulled the knife from her sheath and charged her way through smoke and flames. Bailey took the sharp hunting knife. He cut the belt loose, which had Mrs. Mores entrapped. The young couple carried Mrs. Morse across the road to the awaiting truck. Jackie held the back door open as they slid her in. Mrs. Morse was lifeless. After laying her across the back seat Bailey headed for the front of the truck with eyes set to tense emotions.

"Get in!" He yelled, "We don't have much time!"

The children piled in. Betty stayed in the back with her grandmother. Bailey reversed the truck about two hundred feet before he spun the tires out and did a 180 degree turn back the other way, squelching tires, and sliding sideways. The hearse exploded, sending heat and rumbling friction toward them with fiery. The children started screaming. Bailey was full throttle on the foot peddle, putting distance between them and the fire as it raged in their direction. They could feel the heat hit the truck, almost lifting it up off the ground. Bailey pushed the truck harder. The children were crying. Betty moved to cover her grandmother's head.

Bailey showed a look of rage in his eyes, determined, moving his eyes sporadically back and forth, focused on gaining more ground, yet keeping control of this monster of a truck. Its power showed through as Bailey pushed it past normal limits of control. His heart was pounding, hands were shaking. His blood moved like a base drum in his head. Sweat dripped down the back of his neck.

The explosion put an incredible amount of pressure on the tunnel's internal structure, and it began to collapse where the hearse was and forward. Bailey yelled out, "Hold on you guys!" Looking in his rear-view mirror, he saw the flames gaining ground as they shot out of the tunnel getting air beneath them. The truck slammed down hard and skid sideways taking the bridge on a very tight corner. Betty concerned about her grandmother with tears in her eyes engulfed her every nerve. Fear gripped the children as they saw the looming gap between the bridge and what lay below. The eerie cavern behind was a mystery of hollow blackness that took them to the next level.

Betty squealed. "Hurry Bailey...we don't have much time!"

Bailey flashed his eyes in the rear-view mirror. "I know!" still pushing the speed past limits of safety.

Ryan began to pray in a mock way. "Oh God please help Bailey be the best driver in the whole wide world right now, please, please..." He repeated his prayer a couple of times. The flight of the truck flew up over the bridge as they heard the intercom in the background, "T minus ten, nine..." The distance between where the truck was at and the entrance to the gates was a good five-hundred feet.

The voice over the speaker continued, "Five, four..."

Bailey pushed the truck harder. He said, "Hold on!" The girls were screaming...Ryan started crying.

"Two, one..."

Betty insisted. "Bailey!"

Bailey's face flushed with emotion. "I know!"

The intercom continued, "Closing in process. Please stand back away from the doors!" The massive gates started closing. No one else in sight. Bailey was still about a hundred feet from the gates. His heart hammered against his ribs. Sweat beaded on his forehead, unblinking eyes set in determination.

Betty squealed when she saw how close they were. "Hurry Bailey, you've got to hurry!" His face quivered with tension. There was only about twelve feet left before the doors were totally shut. The truck rocketed in the direction of the small gap left immeasurable inches. They were at maximum speed. One hundred miles per hour. The truck crossed the opening with an inch on both sides of where the mirrors stuck out. Bailey slammed on the brakes and slid the truck sideways for fifty feet until it came to a complete stop. The massive doors were sealed and shut. There was no going back.

CHAPTER 9

The Garden

Bailey got out of the truck. The back side door flew open where Betty was sitting. She was immersed in tears while holding her grandmother's head in her lap. The distortion of her face displayed an unrelenting message. "She's gone Bailey. She gave her life for the children. My grandmother's a hero. Don't you get it?" Bailey was confused about Betty's frame of mind. *What, Hero?* He thought. *None of this chaos was heroic. This was madness.* Pain etched Betty's every word. Her eyes were pools of tears as she considered her grandmother's demise. Betty looked down at the others from the elevated truck's back seat.

The two little ones were crying. Jackie showed a remorseful glare. Ryan stared at his grandmother; sullen faced, not wanting to believe she was really gone. Larger-than-life tears began to make their way down his little face. He belted out.

"Sorry Grandma! I didn't mean to give you a tough time. Please come back!" He showed a painfully remorseful stare from watery eyes. "It's not fair...she was good to us!" Ryan yelled. Then the small boy collapsed to the ground. Bailey reached for him by putting an arm around his shoulder in comfort. He sat holding Ryan in his arms of warmth, speechless, thinking of the painful memories of their grandmother's end. Bailey looked up across this endless ground of cement that gapped a distance of a good five-hundred yards before revealing a clear path to the edge of a park-like-setting. It was beautiful in a bizarre sort of way. Bailey's curiosity was perked from the flickers of color up ahead. Leaving Betty's grandmother prostrated on the seat, and the others there, Bailey got up and started walking in the direction of floral colors in patterns of blue, red and yellows. The smell of healthy plant life pulled him to keep walking. The children stayed behind to reminisce about such a great woman's passing. Betty rocked back and forth while holding her grandmother's head.

The walk would do Bailey good. Tension tightened the muscles in his neck and back. A redounded feeling of remorse began to tear apart this small family by a world turned upside down. Why was this happening? And why was the weight of the world left on the shoulders of a bunch of kids—who most of the time still needed the guiding hands of adults to point them in the right direction. They were now on their own, buried inside the depths of this mountain, hidden in secret, with the entire world left behind. And Betty's grandmother didn't ask to have a bunch of kids thrown into her lap. She just took on the responsibility because they were kin. Life had presented an unplanned circumstance, and these children were left to fend for themselves.

Bailey looked above. Water dripped from overhead off the points of stalactites and stalagmites. Ribbons of rock swirled above their heads and reached down the cave walls. The Atrium had its own lighting that wasn't affected by the crash. He began to look around the giant cave with growing interest and grasped it was totally protected from the outside world. Even the temperature seemed regulated to perfection. There was a lot of money put into someone's efforts, a perfect plan remitting purpose. A flashing glint of wonder crossed Bailey's mind.

After about fifteen minutes of putting distance between him and this new little family, he went back after surveying the area. He signaled for everyone to get back in the truck as he pulled closer to this odd-looking park. It was what he had pictured before in the distance, gentle trees, the sounds of running water from some unknown place not made out yet, and that same peacefulness that he'd felt from before. This place was amazing. Bailey got out of the truck and walked to the center of this breathtaking vision of greenery. He began to absorb this place of a peaceful setting. It was strange but different—like paradise, a Garden-of-Eden, trees of fruitful delights with twisting vines of foliage, the smells of vibrant plant-life making itself known. Bailey felt a melancholy peacefulness drifting in the air. Artificial sunlight balanced with a perfect amount of heat and light. How could trees and grass and flowers grow without the help of the sun? Bailey remembered the shovel in Betty's backpack. He knew that they would have to dig a grave for her grandmother, yet that had to be in Betty's nudging. Right now, she was in a time of fractured moments. The children were still crying, and Betty looked up beneath swollen eyes and unsettling emotions. She was like an open book showing pages of her own life of personal history.

Venting from remorseful endings Betty said, "She was a mother to me growing up. We were close." Another sob escaped from Betty's lips. "I never knew my mother as much as Grandma. My mother died when I was only four years old. I mostly remember Grandma being there for my brothers and me." This caused her to look at Bailey with a sense of worry. "I hope they're okay and somewhere safe."

A puzzled look crossed Bailey's face. He knew anyone out there for more than but a few days without food, without water or supplies were in a hopeless situation. For a second, Bailey thought he could go rescue people, but then he remembered the tunnel had collapsed behind them. Then he looked to these young children and considered their chances. *Who was he kidding?* He thought. *They were just kids.*

It was a disheartening and devastating fact of nature that this storm outside, in the world above, was not temporary. It was a deadly force to be reckoned with, and ice-age condition that wasn't going away, facing them head on. Despair without triumph, pain without comfort, Bailey was at a loss. He identified a fresh start was what laid on the road ahead of them—everyone else gone of the Earth, a global extinction, this was all still fresh and unbelievable.

Betty looked past the truck seeing the garden area and asked the children to go pick flowers for their grandmother. She began to share about her family with Bailey alone. This was a time of venting her emotions, clearing her conscious, reminiscing memories.

"You know, my dad was in the military. He was in the war back when I was about eight years old. That's when he was killed in action." Betty paused for a second and looked up into Bailey's eye. He brushed the hair away from her face. "I never wanted anyone to feel sorry for my brothers and me. We still had family around. It's different when you lose both your parents. It just leaves a big empty hole inside you. My grandmother tried to fill that spot. She was good to us. We had our aunt's and uncle's, with my cousins around, but the emptiness was something that couldn't be totally filled. It was tough because I didn't really know my mother. I don't remember a lot about her because I was too young. And then, losing my father was harder. I had to rely upon my brothers a lot more than before. They weren't so good at parenting themselves. They had their own problems to deal with besides, what was already missing. Without mom and dad around, setting the example, they felt the emptiness too. The boys were much older. I was born six years later, after my youngest brother was born, so I didn't really fit into their adult lives. I was like one of their own kids, not a sister. Grandma was the one I made a connection with, not the boys. They had moved out and had their own families to deal with before I hit adolescence. I had to find my own place in life. It was through my grandmother that I was able to do that. She was a lot like mother. Well, at least from what father had told me—before he died. Grandmother always talked like my mother was too good for this world. She said that's why God took her away. Grandma used to say mother was stubborn, opinionated, and optimistic about everything. Well, anyhow, that's what the older ones used to say." Betty's eyes sparkled with a moment of hope. "Grandma had to make up for two parents that were gone. She had to be strong for all of us kids. She didn't ask for the job. It was thrown into her lap. We were like stray puppy's found in the bushes." This made Bailey's eyes to glisten with a sparkle of light. Betty's bottom lip quivered when she saw the building emotions in Bailey's face. A tear rolled off her cheek. An unimaginable gentle breeze blew her hair back. She sucked in air and held her breath. Betty's face lit up like her Grandmother was still hovering over the top of her body. Then the feeling was gone. Betty's faced twitched as the rush of air faded in the distance.

Understanding, Bailey reached down and put his arms around her in comfort.

"I'm sorry for your loss," He said. Bailey looked up and saw the children coming back from a grove of trees. Jackie was first, Mattie was second, and Ryan was lagging way behind pulling at what looked like his zipper. This caused Bailey to smile. He was assuming something got watered. Betty pulled the children in and began to explain quietly the process of death, and how they needed to bury their grandmother. Ryan turned around and looked back at the area they had come from, with quiet gentle trees standing in the distance. His looked to be full of many unanswered questions. He pulled at his zipper again. Jackie gave a peculiar glare like she knew of some secret. Once Bailey had heard Betty talk about burying her grandmother, he grabbed the shovel from Betty's backpack and headed for the trees. A tear ran down Bailey's face. This reminded him when he had lost his brother.

In the back of his mind, Bailey knew this small band of misfits had a purpose since they had been thrown into the mix of what was left. This place almost felt like it was calling out to him. It made him feel at home, even though he had no connection to this place yet. Something hung in the air that made Bailey feel at peace. There was history to be made, and somehow, he knew this was going to be their permanent home, far away from the turmoil's of life from above. This was the place he and the other four needed to be, a habitation of safety and warmth. Bailey reminisced about days gone by. He hadn't really paid attention to how far he had gone past the others. He felt the knots in his neck and back beginning to untwine. The quietness of this place overwhelmed his senses. He heard a bird chirping in a tree above him, gentle and sweet, busy carrying her catch to her small nest of waiting hatchlings.

Suddenly, he knew where he was standing was the perfect place for Betty's grandmother. He knew from his own firsthand experiences this would be a place long remembered. It made him smile as another tear trickled down his face. He sensed their loss. This beautiful big Oak tree in front of him was imposing and strong yet surrounded by soft and gentle flowers with an assortment of colors. Honey suckle fragrance tickled his nose as he took the shovel and began to dig.

Bailey had found the perfect place for Mrs. Morse to find eternal rest. He dug a deep rectangle of a hole, shovel at a time, one foot two feet—three then four. He stopped for a second to catch his breath. Another tear escaped down his cheek. Sweat began to run down his neck and back after about fifteen minutes of digging. He looked behind him and saw Ryan standing in the distance. He had followed him and knew of his purpose. He saw Bailey as a man striving toward defining reasons. Bailey went back to digging. His watery eyes blinded his vision to not seeing clearly. He stopped to wipe his face, adding moistened dirt to his soiled surroundings. Bailey took off his shirt. He had muscles reflecting from an unnatural light. Pretty soon, he was standing shoulder deep in the darkness below him and light from above. Ryan slowly walked over and looked down at his grandmother's grave. The smell of moistened earth hit his nostrils. His bottom lip moved with emotion, he wiped at his face. Bailey offered him a bleak smile and put his hand out to help the little boy down inside this grave. Ryan took the shovel from him and started to dig. He looked up at this strange looking man. *How'd he know what I needed?* Ryan thought. Wanting to know what Bailey was thinking. Ryan removed his shirt too, to mimic Bailey. He scooped the dirt and brought it up to his shoulder. Bailey helped him toss it to the side. Somehow, this strange young man knew the affections of a small boy held in the tender part of his heart for his grandmother had to be shown in a physical way. He wiped his eyes as he dug, tears mixed with watered moistened earth. When they were done, Bailey noticed sweat running down the small boy's face. He felt a glint of satisfaction in Ryan's effort. Bailey climbed up out of this unwanted grave, and then reached down to pull Ryan up with shovel in hand. They walked back to where the girls where. Bailey shirtless like Ryan, dirty, grubby, with a remorseful stare, he rested his arm across the small boy's shoulders. Betty looked up and saw the connection.

They took the truck on sodden soil where they had dug this unwanted grave. Betty saw the pile of earth in the distance. She covered her mouth sensing this to be the end—her time with Grandmother was over. Bailey jumped down into this unwanted grave as the others slowly interred Grandma's body into the darkness. Bailey got up out of the hole in silence. Tears were flowing, eyes blurred by the vision of death. Betty reached around her neck and removed a necklace that Grandma had bought her for her sixteenth birthday. She bent down and dropped it on her grandmother's chest. Then she stood back up. Sickened with grief over this great woman's passing, and yet relieved that she was to stay with them in their hearts forever. Betty blew a kiss toward the grave. Ryan and Mattie wrapped around her like they were her own children. She said from memory what lay in her heart.

"Thank you, Grandma, for your eternal love and unconditional ways bestowed upon me and my brothers—Ryan and Mattie are thankful for you too. I now show my love and undying respect for you, and your irreplaceable dedication that you've given to me and my brothers over the years. I will always have good memories of you. I'll never forget your heroism you showed this day to save Ryan, Mattie, and our friend Jackie. Amen."

Bailey began filling in the hole with dirt. Their tears showered the ground like rain that made things grow. He finished filling the grave. The children and Betty lined her place of rest with flowers. The garden had given to them a place for Grandmother to rest.

CHAPTER 10

Control Center

Bailey and the children knelt down next to the grave, reflecting their respects in a moment of silent prayer. They closed their eyes in a consoling remembrance of their grandmother. After a moment, Bailey got up and Ryan and Mattie walked a few feet away, giving Betty more time alone at the graveside. He whispered to the children to let Betty have time alone and reached for them on top of their heads. He then quietly informed Betty that he wanted to take the children with him to the top of the sixth floor. Something he remembered seeing up there earlier that drew his attention, based on the fact that it was getting later as the day rolled on, they were limited in time.

"We have to find a place to rest for the night, and food." Bailey said. Betty looked up and nodded without saying a word, still encumbered by great emotion. She put her hand atop Bailey's letting him know she was staying for just a while longer. Jackie remained knitted to her side. "It's something I have to check out." He insisted. She displayed a forced smile and suggested by the look in her eyes that it would fine.

The two younger ones walked with Bailey toward the truck. His stomach was growling from hunger. He sensed the children had to be famished. He felt drained of energy from the race the day before. His only connection left was with the young, bereaved girl and the three children—not to leave out that little rodent with teeth and tail. He got out of the truck and turned back to look at the children. "Come on Ryan and Mattie, We've got exploring to do." Showing them a bit of excitement. The two children followed him to the elevator, curious about where Bailey was taking them. The elevator opened up and the three got inside. Ryan looked up and reached over to take Bailey's hand. Mattie mimicked his motions. The two children soon forgot about the sadness that was with them just an hour before. Ryan looked up at the buttons for the different floors and noticed Bailey had pushed the top floor, number six. Bailey looked down and observed the walkie-talkie still in Ryan's grasp. It was his last remaining connection to the old woman now departed. Bailey smiled before saying, "I'm glad you brought that with you," not thinking ahead, he appreciated that Ryan had his best interests at heart, even though it was unintentional.

Ryan was the first to ask a question. "Where are we going to stay?"

"I don't quite know yet squirt. We have to explore a little to find a place." Bailey replied, "That's what we're doing right now. We need to find a place to sleep." Ryan, with curious eyes, reached up wearing a red baseball cap and scratched his top lip with his index finger. From the opposite side, Mattie reached up and tapped Bailey on the arm, still thinking about the garden.

"Is Betty, okay?" Bailey surprised to hear her voice looking down.

"I think so honey. She just needs a little time with her grandmother." The elevator opened and the three of them walked down the hall. Ryan ran to the edge and looked over the top, separated by a four-foot shiny cemented safety wall. He looked down into the opening below. The atrium spread-out before him, it made him pull back. Ryan's eyes bugged out.

"Wow," he said. "That's a long way down!" Ryan was imagining tumbling to the bottom at the speed of a fast-moving train. It made him feel a little woozy. "Don't want to fall," He said aloud. "That would leave some stains like grandma's old leaky Ford."

Mattie looked at him and giggled then said, "And possibly in your undies."

Ryan widened his eyes from the visual, and then scrunched his nose. "You probably have poop stains in you undies."

Mattie gave him a sour look and moved her eyes toward Bailey so he would defend her, before replying, "You're the only one that wears streakers. I've seen Grandma throw your undies out."

"Not so!" Ryan yelled.

"Is too…" She yelled back.

Bailey separated the two. "Now stop your fighting. Both of you know we won't survive two minutes if you two don't quit."

The two children scowled at each other, and finally Mattie turned around and acted like he wasn't there. Bailey turned to look down a hallway with aggregate doors in a half-circled walkway. The shape of a horseshoe, giving Bailey a feeling of an oblique visual of downhill progress. Six different doors to the left with different name plates were placed on each door. There was the general conference room, and heads of state, computer programming room, and…oh yes, a bathroom for ladies and one for gentlemen. And the door that interested Bailey was the Tower-Control-Center door just up ahead—the last door down the hall to the left. After reaching this last door, Bailey turned the knob and walked into a long room with white and black checkered tiled floors and a soft glowing white ceiling. The room was about a hundred feet long and thirty feet wide. It was full of computers. But there was only two that were still on. They were both in the far-right corner hidden from view. Bailey started walking toward them. Ryan held knitted to his side, but Mattie lagged behind drawn by other things in the room. To Bailey, it looked more like a weather station than anything that would be used by the government from a military perspective. The two computer monitors that were still on were showing a weather system with bright reds and oranges mixed together, and blues and greens all representing various stages of severe weather conditions. He remembered learning to read such maps when his dad had taught him how to fly a plane. It didn't look good from what he could tell. Curiously, twenty feet ahead, Bailey saw a partially opened door to a small utility closet. He also saw something lying across the floor from its narrowing vision of pant-leg and white top-coat—*a lab-coat?* He thought. Then it dawned on him someone was unconscious lying on his side across the floor. Bailey looked at Ryan, who was still mesmerized by the floating screen of colors like the piped piper was pulling him in, except not with a flute but colors. Mattie was glaring at large graphs hung on the wall. It reminded her of arts and crafts at school, except a lot more complicated than stick images or green oak trees basking in the sun. These graphs and pictures seemed quite alarming. Bailey, from across the room, reeled the little mesmerized boy in.

"Hey look..." Bailey pointed toward the closet. Ryan opened his mouth in surprise and Mattie was still mesmerized by the graphs overhead.

Ryan pushed the door back with his foot, still looking down with his mouth open he said, "Is he dead?"

Bailey noticed the lab-coat moving up and down. "No...I don't think so?" Then Bailey saw the empty bottle lying next to this older-looking gentleman with long abstract white-graying hair and thick glasses. Bailey saw his name tag read Dr. EL. And below his name it said meteorologist. He was drunk off his feet and was sleeping it off in the closet. Bailey thought. *What was that about?*

Ryan reached down and picked up the empty bottle and said, "Dang...he drank the whole bottle! He's all buzzed-up." Ryan said it like he knew a lot about people getting drunk.

Bailey showed a hesitant grin realizing there might be some drinkers in his family-tree. Then the smell of rum, bad-breath, and closet farts hit him. Bailey pulled his head back in alarm. He said, "Holy sh..." and stopped himself when he realized the small boy of emulation was listening.

Ryan looked up at Bailey with a sour face. "Who pooped their pants? Was it Grandpa?" Ryan pointed a finger at the old man lying prone on the floor. Bailey didn't say anything, he only smiled. Ryan backed out of the closet to get fresh air. Bailey reached inside the man's pocket and pulled out a pen and paper and wrote the old man a note. Put the pen back and clipped the note to the man's white lab-coat. Ryan looked bored and was ready to move on.

Mattie came over and looked at Ryan like he did something wrong, expecting to cross her at any minute. Ryan gave her a corny glare. "Go in that closet...that old guy in there left you a present." Ryan looked up at Bailey like he was getting away with something. Bailey grabbed her before she crossed the threshold of the doorway.

"No...honey...Ryan's just messing around."

Ryan looked up at his befuddled sister and said, "He pooped his pants. Go ahead, get a big whiff!"

Mattie crinkled her nose at her brother as if she would throw up. She looked at her brother after turning red. "Shut up...you're retarded."

Bailey reached for Ryan and put his hand over his mouth. "Dude... please...you're making this worse...stop."

Ryan tried to remove Bailey's hand from his mouth. Ryan finally turned around, losing interest and saw a clock on the wall that looked familiar of something he would have seen at school. He turned to look at Bailey with pushed together eyebrows and wrinkled forehead. "Where's all the food at Bailey?"

"I don't know little man. We still have to find out."

Ryan reached down and pulled the walkie-talkie off his belt clip to call the others. Ryan's voice shot out over the speaker. "Betty come in... over." He repeated the call. "Betty, this is Ryan, come in over." Ryan was confused and forgot to let go of the button. "Oh sorry," He said.

A softer voice came over the speaker. "This is Jackie. What do you want?"

Ryan reflecting a scowl being against the girls. "Bailey needs to talk to Betty, please give her the walkie-talkie." Ryan belted out.

From the other side of the call Jackie handed the squawk-box to Betty. "Yes, what is it?" Betty said. Still a small amount of emotion left in her voice.

Ryan returned. "We've found someone here, some old man on the floor." Ryan looked up to Bailey to get his approval to continue. Bailey didn't move so Ryan continued. "He's some kind of doctor." Betty was beginning to pull her emotions away from her grandmother's grave. Bailey moved his hand up and clicked his fingers. Ryan didn't hesitate. He handed the squawk-box over.

"Hey…we need your help finding food and shelter. Are you almost ready?"

There was a long pause before Betty answered. "Yes, I'm ready. Why? What's up?"

"Can you meet us on the sixth floor?"

Still distraught by the loss of her grandmother she said, "Okay. We'll be there in about fifteen minutes." Betty didn't wait. She turned the walkie-talkie off and stood.

Bailey heard the walkie-talkie turn off and headed for the restroom outside, back down the hallway. In the mirror, Bailey saw dirt and grime covering his face and arms, neck and back. Ryan came shortly after. He met to look of exhaustion in their reflection of the mirror. Both with their shirts off, comparing them to stranded victims of 'Lord of the Flies" on a deserted island. Bailey dove for the sink and started giving himself a sink-bath and Ryan copied him.

Betty looked at Jackie with a hesitant stare. "Okay sport. I've got what we need, let's go." The younger of the two girls flashed her eyes at her new best friend.

Jackie showed a sparkle of light in her eyes just before saying, "Okay missy. I'm your sissy, and we're heaven bound." Both girls began to giggle at Jackie's little poem.

"Did you just make that up squirt?"

"Yeah, I guess so." Betty reached down and squeezed her, thankful for gaining a new friend. They crossed the courtyard of the atrium and headed for the elevator. Betty pushed the button and heard the elevator jerk downward. She reached over and pushed hair out of her younger friend's eyes. It was only a few seconds, and they were moving toward the top. There to greet them at the top was Mattie. Betty looked around and saw that she was by herself.

"Where'd the boy's go?"

Mattie looked behind her as if she had been alone the whole time. "Oh…they needed to clean-up before…you know, before we find a place."

Betty confused only nodded with a lack of understanding, figuring she would find out answers as they went along. A few minutes later the boys come strolling out of the bathroom. The girls took long hard looks at the boys as they exited, hopefully not to screw-up at any moment.

Bailey shouted accidentally at the young ladies. "Oh…who has to pee?"

Ryan, without thinking about just coming out of the bathroom said, "Not me…I peed on a tree."

The girls looked back at this overly zealous lad and Jackie said, "Well, we're built a little different than you squirt. We have a gentler side to us, sophisticated, lady-like. We don't go around peeing on trees like dogs."

Ryan looked up at Jackie like she had insulted him in the worst of ways. Ryan tried to defend himself. "I don't pee like a dog on trees. You do."

Betty grabbed him suddenly and knew Ryan was acting out, feeling a few things pushed to the bottom of the barrel. "Calm down little man. It was meant as a joke. I'm sure Jackie doesn't care that you peed on a tree. We have more important things to think about than this."

Mattie started giggling and Betty showed a smile. Ryan had a hurtful stare on his face, certain he'd been slapped. He tried to justify to Bailey why he peed on a tree. "I'm not a dog, and I normally don't pee on trees, I just had to go really bad…that's all." Ryan reflecting a scowl when looking at the girl's bathroom door.

Bailey gave him a lesson of how to treat the girls. "Don't take everything so personal little man. They're just girls. It's their job to give us a tough time. It's in their nature. The way to calm them down is to do something really nice for them. It's the only way to confuse them or throw them off track. They eventually get so confused they don't know how to react. So, in turn, they start to feel guilty about the way they treated you. They give up. Learn to play their games, squirt. You'll have to stay cool, not get hot-headed. Capriccio little man?"

Ryan put his hand up to slap Bailey's. "No problemo." Ryan raised both eyebrows.

"What's for dinner?" Ryan asked, "I could eat a whole bear, just heat him up and give me a fork and knife." Bailey shocked by the visual widened his eyes. Then both leaned against the wall waiting for the girls to show their presence. They came out of the bathroom one at a time, checking out the boys like late arrivals.

Betty started conversation. "So, what's on the evening's agenda?" Betty's face was fresh and clean like she did a quick makeover. Bailey smelled a touch of perfume and powder, and darker lines that once were there disappeared behind touches of make-up. Then answering her question of the evening, thrown off a bit of powder and perfume.

"We need to go exploring." Bailey replied. "We should split-up. You take the girls and I'll take Ryan." Ryan liked the sound of that. He had enough of looking at the girls. "We can cover more ground. Ryan and I will start at the bottom and you girls can start at the top. We'll meet in the middle."

"Sounds good," Betty said. She turned her eyes at the lad that acted out, sometimes showing a wayward tongue. She wanted Bailey's assurance that Ryan would be okay. "Be good," she said, when looking at Ryan. Betty leaned in and gave Bailey a peck on the cheek. Ryan lit up mimicking a black cat touched by a black candle, then showed fish-lips and pretended to give himself a hug.

Jackie exhibited a smug look across her face. "What's wrong...you in love with yourself?" Jackie sarcastically said. Ryan dropped the act and wanted to punch her. Bailey moved in and stopped him. He turned his view back to Betty while holding his hands in front of Ryan.

"Okay...now's a suitable time to go. See ya in about an hour." Bailey and Ryan headed for the elevators, as the girls disappeared down the hall.

CHAPTER 11

Exploration

The elevator opened up and the two young men got in and headed for the basement floor. Ryan glanced up at his new mentor and said, "I'd rather not be around those chumps anyhow—their troublemakers."

Bailey couldn't believe the attitude. "They're not chumps Ryan. Their just silly girls that want to have fun at our expense." Bailey paused before finishing. "Try and stay calm little man. We're all in this together."

The elevator came to the bottom floor as they got out of the left inside exit. The right side of the elevator led back into the Atrium, the left into a huge storage area of crates. The room was dark in cave like form lacking light, so Ryan reached to turn the light-switch on. To their surprise, this strange hidden warehouse was stacked from floor to ceiling with these wooden crates. *But what was in them?* Bailey thought. After thinking about it for a minute, this place might be of the military makings, or holding weapons of mass destruction.

This warehouse looked like a large indoor shopping mall for soldiers-of-fortune. The ceiling was about thirty feet high and went about eight-hundred-feet down one isle before coming to the end of the wall. Row after row of crates lined the racks full of stamped military red-labeled government seals painted on the sides in red. The rows had numbers on them, which followed a sequential pattern of logic or order. Toward the back, Bailey saw several forklifts on the floor, obviously for moving the crates from top to bottom. Ryan was curious about the crates too, but at the moment he was more concerned about finding food. The small boy of quick-to-make blunders saw no place to lay a weary head, or any hot bowl of soup turned in disappointment.

"When are we going to eat?" Like his new mentor would pull his next meal out of hat and be done with it. Bailey's face grew a smile.

"Let's try the next floor, maybe we'll have better luck." The two misguided youths turned around and headed back to the elevator. The door opened, they got in, and Bailey pushed number two. Ryan leaned on his mentor with anticipation. To their surprise, the elevator doors opened up to a large galley—a kitchen of their hearts content.

Ryan practically ran toward two big double doors and found a pantry full of delectable delights. "Food!" Ryan yelled. Bailey reached over and grabbed him from behind.

"Hold on little man." He turned Ryan around. "Call the girls and let them know what we've found." Ryan didn't hesitate. He flipped the light-switch on the top of the squawk box. It was one of those modified walkie-talkies with a light on the top like one of those famous Swiss-Army-Knives with extra gadgets. Bailey couldn't believe what he was seeing. A kitchen for captain and king, *how'd they rate?* The stainless-steel kitchen appliances shined reflecting showroom quality comparable to Whirlpool or LG. A large dining area was past the main galley through double doors, an inviting table that seats twelve. The latest decorations of dark walnut furnishings, chandeliers, and silver lined wine goblets, velvety seating, candelabras,' embroidered styled napkins, silvery utensils. From Bailey's point of view, this was upper-class surroundings of imposing artful design. He made his way back through double doors covering his face quickly from night blindness. Jackie's voice came on over the speaker right when Bailey crossed the thresh-hold of the galley door.

"What do you guys want?" Jackie said. She had this belated scowl pasted on her face, from what he could tell from her voice, thinking this little scoundrel was wasting her time. Ryan thought he'd light a fire beneath her. "We found dogfood for all you wolvers…"

Bailey grabbed the walkie-talkie out of Ryan's hand. He looked untrustingly at the awkwardly rude boy. "That's no way to score points with the ladies." Bailey said. He held the walkie-talkie above Ryan's head as the boy of unruly behavior tried to reach for it. "Stop Dude, don't make this worse than it is." Ryan still distorted by girls showing a lack of concern for boys of his youth. He had already turned red-faced and looked like he would pop from overheated emotions, yet Bailey, being a little older and a little wiser tried the positive approach.

"Hello Jackie, I'm sorry for Ryan's attitude, he will be dealt with, but we hit the jackpot. We found the kitchen, and the pantry is full of food. You ladies are more than welcome to meet us on the second level. We've desserts to eat and steaks to barbeque." A smile grew widely on Bailey's face. He reintegrated with words, "Hurry…before it's all gone." Ryan let out an untrusting sigh.

Betty's voice bellowed out past the speaker. "We found keys to the rooms to this enormous hotel, well, more like the Luxor suits in Vegas." There was a short pause before she continued. "There's an elevator on the fifth floor toward the back. It leads to four more floors above. The ninth is something special." Another pause and Bailey rolled his eyes while looking sheepishly at Ryan.

"The rooms look like they were built for the President and his staff in mind—not ordinary people like us. The penthouse suite over-looks this beautiful lagoon just past the garden."

Bailey wasn't sure what to think about that. He was only concerned about dinner at the moment and bringing them all together. Then he playfully showed a silly grin to Ryan while using his right hand imitating a duck quaking. That put a smile on Ryan's face, perceptive eyes seeing suggestive hands imitating too much chatter.

"Why don't you meet us for dinner?" Bailey asked.

From the other end, Betty smiled as if this was a personal invitation for her wanting heart. That unmannered kiss of a few hours back went through her head. It caused her heart to skip a beat. Bailey heard a change in her voice through softened words in gentle rhythms. He could feel her smiling on the other end.

"Hey…sure…we'll be right down." Betty responded. Jackie saw the giddy expression on her face like she was in love. The twelve-year-old rolled her eyes completing her expressions with an inquisitive stare.

"Why do you like him so much?"

Betty held up between two conversations, thinking she was losing her focus. She batted her eyes wistfully, concentrating, wrinkling her forehead, pulsing of words in mixed up rhythms, pauses of sentences— confusion, sudden breaths of silence. She dropped the giddy sparkle and wondered. "I don't know. He's sweet in a way, good looking. He saved us." Betty said the words trying to cover up her hidden meaning of love and her sudden memory of his frequent dorkiness. She looked at the twelve-year-old knowing she wouldn't understand off-balanced expressions of a silly girl's heart. She hadn't reached that stage of her life yet, still missing her soon to grow girlish feature and curving hips that quickly throw off the watchful eyes of the opposite sex.

A long pause before Bailey returned an answer. "Okay, if you say so. We can check that out later, but for now let's meet on the second floor of the galley."

Betty with a glint in her eyes said, "Okay, I'll see you in a few…" The line got disconnected. Betty couldn't finish. She knew the boy cut her off mid-stream. This made her lose the last little bit of dignity she had left and crossed an unhopeful frown toward Jackie.

Ryan went back to the double-door pantry looking for anything he could scarf down without much effort. Bailey grabbed him from behind. "Little man. I said wait. We're not animals you know. There's going to be rules to follow, so everything here lasts."

Ryan cast an unforgiving frown. "Why do I always have to give in first, the girls try to constantly cause problems? I found the food!" Ryan said it like Columbus discovering America with his little rooster tail in the back of his hat sticking out from the small space for adjustments. Ryan showed a small piece of strutting hair, with star-spangled expressions of the freckled face kind. Bailey saw it like Ryan was imitating an old dog marking his latest territory with a steady stream of warmness.

As a decisive point of unarmored words, Bailey had to put his foot down to calm the boy's relentless reasoning. "Listen Ryan and listen well.

We're all lucky to still be alive." Bailey focused with piercing eyes, in a firm voice. "I know you've had a lot on your plate today and losing your grandmother. Changes always have a way of stripping our minds of what we think to be important. Just hold on, have a little patience. Please don't act like you're the only one that's been damaged. *You* wanting to fight everybody can only make things worse. The girls feel the same sense of loss that you do."

This sparked a chord in the little boy's heart. Ryan started to cry. "I miss Grandma! Why'd she have to die?"

In Bailey's limited understanding of life and death he tried to explain the situation. "Life's not always fair little man. Think about all of those people outside right now that are out in the freezing cold, suffering, no food, no way to warm themselves." Then Bailey looked around. "Look at this place. You've got the wrong attitude. Look how lucky we are. We've survived the greatest event of the planet, and we're behind walls of safety and comfort. No one else has had that same type of luck, except us. Do you get me?" Bailey expressed a casting glare. Ryan hung his head with crocodile tears watering his face.

Bailey continued to explain his sense of reasoning. "Soon they will run out of food and supplies to keep them safe and warm. Where will they go? What will they do?"

Ryan looked up with blurred tears of vision. "I guess you're right, were in a better place than the people outside." More blubbery tears escape the young lads' eyes. Bailey put his arm around Ryan as the elevator before them opened up. Three young girls made their presence known. Betty had a hurtful stare in her eyes, but quickly lost it when she saw Ryan wailing remorseful tears in front of everyone. The girls remained quiet. While the small boy wiped at his eyes, pulled up his pants, and fanned a loud fart he laid in the girl's direction, everyone giggled. Bailey smiled as he shook his head. Ryan developed a hick look on his face like he was imitating one of his uncles. "Don't say I haven't ever shared anything with you." Betty looked at Bailey embarrassed for the hooligan child of ill-mannered boys.

"Sorry. He has no filter." Bailey shook his chin side-to-side and pushed Ryan's head away. "Dude, you're sleeping outside with Cuddles."

Quickly, Jackie had made the connection with their little dog taking off and not returning. She felt responsible since letting her down. With face flushed she barked worry. "Cuddles took off. I didn't see where she went. I lost track of her, and then forgot…" Jackie trailed off her words.

Betty glanced at her and said, "No worries. She can't go far. This whole place is enclosed. She'll show up sometime." To change the subject, Betty looked around and opened her mouth. "Wow! This is a big kitchen." The odd couple of replicating stares took the lead. They both walked into a large refrigerator about forty feet deep and thirty feet wide. She was impressed. The shelves were full of cheese and milk, cold cuts for sandwiches, pickles and parmesan, fruits and frijoles, vegetables, and vitamin water, from A to Z to *your kidding me, what are those?* Betty proclaimed silently. She saw that someone had thawed out some juicy T-bone steaks. There was fresh pasta salad, potatoes to bake, sour cream and chives. There was a whole wine rack attached to the back wall, displaying the best of vineyards across the globe. Betty was intrigued by the choices. She got this boorish stare with English accent. She implored the odd boy with the flamboyant personality to take heed of their dire situation, playing the role, to a tee. "Kind sir, will you be dining in this evening? Oh dear…" Betty put her nose in the air like royalty with bent wrist on her hip and the other hand to her forehead. A punitive chuckle came from Bailey's mouth. "Oh! And what shall I wear to the ball my faithful prince?" Betty patted him jokingly, hand on his chest, as her eyes widened set to sparkle.

"Let's take a look at the packages princess," Bailey rhetorically remarked. Betty leaned in and rested her head on his shoulder. He firmly grabbed her around the waist and swung her about. She slid down the front of him to steal another kiss.

Ryan walked in the middle of the kiss. "Yuck…I think I'm going to hurl." Ryan said while crinkling his nose. Betty mockingly smothered Ryan with unwanted kisses as if contagious, "Stop!" the small boy said. "You're giving me germs!" Then the others heard the noise and joined in the little romp of torture. Ryan started laughing because of the attention, yelling, "Stop! I'm going to catch some cooties! You're melting my brain!" Ryan laughed so hard he's unable to control his bodily functions. Hot brisk bleeding air escaped his lower extremities causing the girls to back off.

Jackie fanned the air, achieving a prudish flutter of the eyes, she said so sheepishly. "I see. So that was your problem young man?" A wave of laughter broke from the new family of friends, closeness, a bond, a trust in the making. This was a time of sharing, even in this weird and wacky sort of way. They were only separated by what lay beyond the walls of fortitude, hidden secrets held back until another day. Bailey and Betty round up the small band of misfits and made the most of the moment. They prepared a banquet that night of a grateful feast. Looking up at the clock, the time was late, a day they would always remember. The group hurried the night along, cleaned up the kitchen and put away everything in its proper place. The lights lay low for another night. They made their way to the penthouse.

The ninth-floor apartment was quite the treat from Bailey's point of view. He was tired, overworked, and ready for a nap. Betty made the children shower and head off to bed. The two girls had shared a room with nice-sized beds, a dresser in the middle separating the beds. Ryan had his own room with bunkbeds. He fell asleep as his weary head hit the pillow. Bailey, red-eyed and spent, knew he had to shower, snuck past Betty, and entered the bathroom. "Oh good…hot water." he said. A few minutes later he heard someone enter the bathroom. Mesmerized by soap in his eyes and hair he felt a tad of embarrassment. He heard the squeaking and closing of a door, a draft of drifting air, a flush of a toilet, and a gentle jolt of a glass door sliding open. He smelled perfume with sensing pleasures, soft features carefully measured. This delicate female had just entered his-own personal space. Bailey held his breath.

She softly said with words that surprised. "Hand me the scrub pad. I'll wash your back." Bailey sensed flushing of skin, small quivers of confinement, visualizing uneasiness of a physical nature. He reached passed steamy water and handed her the scrubber. She filled it with soap in their seductive situation. Bailey's heart began to pound. He, being a youthful boy of marinating thoughts realized his dire situation of mounding manipulation. Face-it, she was the ultimate challenge of female interventions, something he'd never imagined, he was afraid to open his eyes. Bailey kept his eyes closed as she washed his shoulders, back and legs. Life in its rarest of forms held no secrets.

Suddenly, in the shock of reality Bailey sensed she was not making this a physical encounter. She was hurting from losing the closest person she ever knew—her grandmother. Bailey slowly opened his eyes. His focus was on the gentle tears running from her eyes—reddening and swelling of tenderness.

She was in mourning. Betty was beautifully brave beyond bereavement. She missed her grandmother, and being close to Bailey at this time was sealing a bond that would last a lifetime. He held her close as the walls of confinement began to crumble.

CHAPTER 12

The First Day

It was in the morning that Bailey heard a child's voice in his ear. "Wake up, Mr. Sleepy head!" Ryan was staring over the top of him like he was an elongated puppy sniffing for leftovers. Bailey, startled from the invasion of close personal space pulled back his head to draw focus. He reached up to remove sleepy crumbs from his eyes. He turned his eyes toward the clock on a nightstand to connect time management with little boy's and agendas.

"Oh… Ryan. Good morning." Bailey said awkwardly.

Ryan gave him a hangdog look with quickly moving eyes left and right, compared to mechanisms of mayhem, pushing, and planning little moments of pain. "Hey dude!" Ryan stated, ignoring the greeting. "Everybody is downstairs already in the galley. We ate breakfast already." Ryan so vividly expressed. He wore evidence of breakfast, egg, and cheese on the corner of his mouth.

Bailey, showing signs of wanting solitude remarked, "Okay. I'm getting up. I'll be right down."

"Okay." Ryan squeaked out as the boy of curiosity walked back to the front door.

Bailey rolled himself out of bed, stood, and stretched with hands raised high, yawned, and headed for the bathroom. Quickly, he noticed a single bright purple tulip standing tall in a vase, a note of lipstick and memories written in the mirror. *Honey, I hope you slept well. I didn't want to disturb you, love Betty.* A trace of a smile broke across his face. Memories of mourning and emotional moments flickered in his head. Bailey looked into the mirror, past the writing. He saw this young lad, circles of sadness left darker lines under his eyes. Then the memories of this place flooded back. He pushed air from his lungs, slow and deep, another yawn, worry written in his eyes. He shook the feeling off and got dressed. Feeling the tightness in his legs from the race the day before, then memories of mayhem, grandma dying, losing little Cuddles, the strange drunk man in the closet, this place of secrets. Bailey drew in air then let it out slow as he made his way into the hall. Elevators moving up and down, silence before him, long dark tunnels, memories of cold and ice, snowmobiles flying, the hidden bunker, snow covering windows, now this. The elevator opened to the galley. A handful of kids and Betty greeted him. Through open elevator doors Bailey saw an older gentleman leaning forward with a bag of ice draped over the back of his neck. Betty, sliding in close with a warm embrace, her petite frame leaning *in* to meet him midway. His heart leaped with courage and confusion mixed as one. Eyes blinking, bottom lip quivering, the smell of perfume and sweet breath, like cuddling with puppies, memories of warm embraces, hearts leaping in response. She calmly pulled her fingers through her hair with a gentle sparkle in her eyes. This strange man from across the table finally looked up. He saw the sparkling connection of youth and young love. A quivering acknowledgement from the corner of his mouth. With outstretched hand the older gentleman said, "Hello, you must be Bailey...I'm Dr. EL."

Bailey reached his hand in greeting. "Hi, Dr. EL, how are you feeling this morning?" A blink of solitude flickered in his eyes, as not to reveal secrets or acceptance. "We saw you by pure accident in the Tower Control Room yesterday. Considering your condition, we thought it wise to let you sleep without disturbing you." Thinking, Dr. EL was in an emotional moment with the world ending, the last bit of normality spent alone in a closet in a drunken state. A hesitating stare of assumption, Bailey continued his thought. "We weren't sure why you were the only one left behind. What happened to everyone else?"

A blazing glint of remembrance crossed the doctor's mind. "I don't have family left behind. I was chosen to stay and keep watch on the weather monitors, but when the doors started closing, I knew it was too late, they couldn't get in because…" The doctor looked up over the rim of his glasses. "They didn't make it." A moment of pain etched in his eyes. The galley was quiet for a long time. Then the doctor broke the silence. "How'd you and your motley crew get into the mountain without clearance?"

"We didn't." Bailey responded. "My uncle dug a hole into the pathway of one of your tunnels years ago and placed a bunker in its path." Bailey said with a curious sparkle of light, "It was blind luck… you might say." He glanced at Betty, needing her assistance in telling this bizarre story of redemption. Still looking at her he said, "Betty had this preconceived premonition that being in the bunker was the best plan of safety. Well, until the weather became out of control. We had no idea how bad this event would be. We were a few of the lucky ones." The doctor considered the boy had become some type of hero in a way, left unsaid he looked up in silence. Then Bailey gave helpful information.

"I have a truck downstairs that my uncle left behind in the tunnel. We're lucky to have that too." Like Bailey was trying to score positive points with a doctor no less, three times his age. Dr. EL reflected a quickly fading smile. Bailey thought of the tunnel that collapsed.

"Dr. EL, is there another way out of the Atrium, without going through the main gates?"

Dr. EL with an unblinking stare. "Well, since you asked, yes there is, but not close by, the exit is at the other end of this compound, not too far, down another long tunnel." He explained.

"Could we use the tunnel to rescue people?"

Dr. EL showed an expression of surprise. "Not until these stormy conditions subside. You would only die out there like everybody else."

Bailey raised an eyebrow. "My Uncle Ron put special equipment on the truck to help with these alarming conditions."

Dr. EL still with an impending glare. "I don't recommend going outside," said the doctor as a repeated note of warning.

Bailey pushed the issue. "Wouldn't it be too late by then? Could anyone wait these storms out that long, without…?"

Bailey didn't finish. He saw the despairing look in the doctor's eyes. So, the doctor finished Bailey's sentence, "Without you dying out there? No." An impetuous glare set in his character.

Bailey sensed a fight if he continued, so he dropped the subject. He thought of family time. "I thought it would be a good change of pace for the kids and us…" He turned and viewed Betty from the side of his left shoulder, while including her into the mix of a trip to come, "to go on a little adventure hike, to see what's in this place."

A reassuring nod changed the doctor's mannerisms. "Well, if you don't mind a little cave-dust, I think you'll be fine, yet you might want to pack a lunch for the trip. The tour will take longer than you think." Dr. EL reached for his coffee cup, which was empty. Betty noticed his stare toward the cup and reached to pour more hot steaming hangover relief.

He brushed her off with a wave of his hand. "No thanks dear, but I'll take a thermos to go!" Betty had at an earlier time filled his thermos to the brim. It was time for the good doctor to move on. He stood and thanked the young lady that fixed him breakfast, had a repeat of greetings and then was gone. Bailey finally sat, and inhaled his breakfast, comparable to a vacuum slurping energy from a coffee cup and a plate of eggs, bacon, and toast. Then he looked at the others. "So, what's your pleasure?" He said with a silly expression. While trying hard to loosen the load of yesterday's close calls, without replaying their bitter memories. It was an obvious motion of events that would take time to heal. Everyone was still hungover with sadness. And oh yes, they had to find their little dog too.

In the lobby of the hotel, Betty had picked up a brochure showing different attractions of appeal that might interest the children. One being the Zoo down a central tunnel past the garden. She took the brochure and laid it in front of Bailey.

"What's this," he stated.

She smiled, as the day was already planned in her pretty little head. "The Zoo…it'll be fun!"

"We better find out if there's a Zookeeper, if not, we might have our hands full in taking care of the animals." Bailey responded back.

Ryan cast an evil glare at Jackie. "I hope there's no hungry Lions or Tigers, but if there is, maybe they'd like girl meat better than boy." Jackie shot a heated stare back at Ryan. Then the verbal scuffle began. Loading up, Jackie shot the little irritating idiot with both barrels.

"I know they definitely won't like messing with you because you stink!"

Ryan's face turned crimson. "That's how I keep them away, like a skunk does with that spray he has under his tail."

Jackie shot back. "That spray under your tail just means you're rotten to the core."

Ryan whipped around like he would punch her. "Who are you calling rotten!"

Betty stepped between them with a personal reminding grandmotherly scowl. "Now stop it the both of you!" Jackie rolled her eyes away from Ryan to Betty, and then to the ground.

"He started it. He's a little stink-turd if you ask me. He's always complaining and acting like a big baby!"

Ryan reached over and punched this unwanted guest in the stomach. Bailey grabbed him when Ryan circled for another blow. "Dude, really? You hit a girl!"

Jackie eyes bulged out in surprise. "See…" she said from the lack of air. "He's a little gangster!" Despite the hit, this made the adults and Mattie smile…well, not including Ryan, and his victim of circumstances, Jackie. Bailey showed no lack of reasoning and looked at Jackie. Knowing this would teach Ryan a lesson in humility.

"Okay, you get one free punch back at him, but not too hard."

Ryan developed a frightful stare, "What! She gets to hit me back?"

Bailey lowered his eyes and showed a concerning stare. "Well, yes, if you really want to know, since you think it's okay to do whatever you want."

Jackie didn't wait for Betty's approval. She reached back and let a hard blow fly to Ryan's mid-drift. He buckled in pain. Betty was appalled at her quick rebuttal of retribution. The blow, back at Ryan, had been so severe that Ryan lost his ability to breathe. Both Bailey and Betty were speechless. Everyone turned to glare at Jackie. She was sorry she did it, but it was too late. The damage was done, but this lesson was a difficult one to learn for this awkward ill-mannered boy, which guaranteed any future blunders would be well thought out before reacting so quickly in the heat of things. Jackie knew from her own firsthand experiences that this lesson of holding his tongue would never be forgotten, especially around a bit older girl who was used to defending her honor. A tear leaked out of Ryan's left eye, yet he remained quiet about this scuffle of differences with this well-informed little girl who was a head taller. Respect was a key issue burned in Ryan's head that day. He looked up at Bailey as if some hidden agenda were in the making. Lost battles of lessons learned, he wasn't telling, but Ryan wised-up that day, bit his tongue, swallowed his pride, gulped the tears back, and sensed with a moment of personal pride that all things of violence had consequences, and yes, words were hurting as much as blows to the stomach. Bailey felt bad that giving advice to another child to hit back to defend her honor, yet he knew Ryan would learn to take his punches in stride and would become a better boy and then a man in the process.

In the distance, Betty could see her grandmother's grave. Still the way they had left it, packed dirt swallowed up by the bed of flowers, remembered tender moments of loneliness without her grandmother. Betty didn't want to bring up yesterday's memories with more words. She only wanted to pay her respects for the moment and then move on. This part of her life was hard enough to deal with, and Bailey, from her point of view, had come into her life at just the right moment. Their soft romantic moments of kisses and breathless palpitations were all a part of growing-up and moving on. The world they were left in had its own personal image of what was part of this daunting life. They were left in the rubble of lost causes and detached memories.

CHAPTER 13

George's Jungle

She ran over to her grandmother's grave, knelt down before the mass of flowers and memories and fleeting prayers. She remembered Grandma when she was little, tickles and giggles, moments of tenderness, bedtime stories that stuck through the years. She was a young lady now growing up, set in a direction of an obscure life unknowing of a future and with this extraordinary boy with loving stares and obstinate movements. From her point of view, she needed her grandmother. She would know what to do. She had graduated with honors from the school of hard knocks. Shown by her bravery she considered her grandmother valedictorian, top of her class. She wouldn't have wasted a moment of her life pointing her in the wrong direction. Her advice was always given by placing her granddaughter's heart first, before her own. Betty knew what real love that day was. It was like her grandmother had expressed through the tides of life, live, and let live, but defend when necessary. Betty kissed the grave, dropped a few tears on the flowers that lay below, "Good-bye Grandma. I'll love you forever."

Betty got up, brushed off her clothes, and wiped the tears with the back of her hand. They waited patiently as Betty walked over. She pushed out a smile with a dim sparkle in her eyes. *She was ready,* she thought. Bailey reached over and took her hand. She leaned in on him and kissed his shoulder. Ryan kept quiet but showed a faltering note of misunderstanding. Jackie took Betty's other hand. In silence they walked through this mysterious garden, green foliage, rushing sounds of water, birds chirping overhead. Suddenly, Betty saw it first. *What was this place?* She thought. It was more than beautiful in the distance, remotely hidden, like an imagined paradise. In front was an enormous lagoon, deep, becoming, replicating a peaceful aura. Ryan ran toward the water's edge. Betty kicked her sandals off and dragged her foot through the water and kicked some on Bailey. It was cold and alarming, yet he took the playful punishment. He grabbed her hand and reeled her in, then kissed her neck. A shudder of prickly arm hair caused the water to bead on the surface.

Ryan giggled and said, "Huba, huba!"

Jackie turned and gave him a grimacing glare. Ryan ignored her. Bailey noticed Betty's backpack from the day before draped over her shoulder. He slid close to her and put his hands on the straps.

"Hey, is lunch in the backpack?" Bailey asked.

"Of course…" She returned with a growing smile. "I wouldn't forget about our little family." They walked together past trees and flowers, foliage of twisting greenery. They could smell the earth, hear the water flowing, and feel a gentle moisture tickling their noses. Jackie rubbed dark clean dirt between her toes. Bailey was holding his shoes in one hand. Ryan had tied his shoestrings together and draped his shoes over his left shoulder. Mattie was tiptoeing through pebbly rocks not to step wrong, fall, stub a toe, or scrap a knee. Ahead, everyone saw the dirt road. Mattie stopped to put her flip-flops back on. Bailey reached down after she had scurried into them, heaved her high and bent her small frame over his shoulder. She screamed with delight and held on. Ryan ran behind him like a stray puppy following his mom. Jackie crossed a thankful stare at Betty and knew they were so lucky at this moment, to still be here, to be alive. A teary sparkle in her eyes, she missed her parents, her little brother. She knew they were gone. A sad moment of memory caused her eyes to flutter. She knew she was saved for a reason, a reason she didn't understand yet, but it would come, and when it did, she would be ready.

In the forefront, they could see a waterfall cascading thirty feet high off a cliff from Bailey's left shoulder. They continued to walk around the right side of this lagoon. Something from the top of the waterfall was hidden behind, they couldn't see what, yet Bailey knew it was there. A floating platform lay in the distance of circulating water in the center of the lagoon, banishing water misting in the air. This reminded Bailey of Hawaii, the seven pools on Maui. Sparkling water gathered from tropical rains.

"Look Bailey!" Ryan squealed out with excitement. "We could swim over to the middle."

"Maybe we can come back later!" Bailey shouted atop the noise of waterfall cascading in the lagoon below. He was focused on this dirt road ahead. He could barely see three tunnels in the distance.

Betty turned to look for just a brief moment. "We'll take them swimming later, before dinner." Bailey cast a gentle smile her way and nodded. He turned back forward and saw something that looked similar to being a golf-cart. The sign was hanging over the tunnel that caused Bailey to raise an eyebrow, the large curved cursive writing said, *George's Jungle,* in green ivy color with a monkey standing on the side holding two hairy coconuts in his hands while showing teeth and gums. Bailey could only imagine what that meant. They were just golf-carts right, orange, and brown, with *George's Jungle* embossed on the side, nice hard-top covering of white, but no windows. Bailey figured no high-speed chases, flips through the air, nothing extreme or off roadish. These oversized golf-carts had their own appeal with big knobby tires. Similar to a Jurassic park setting, leaving this modified golf-cart for uncharted mysteries, not for the ordinary adventure drifting by.

The three tunnels were directly in front, dark, cold, and secretive. The one they wanted was in the middle. Betty matched up the picture on the brochure with the sign over the tunnel's entrance. "This is it." she said. Everyone climbed into one of the jungle looking golf-carts. Bailey unhooked the miniaturized all-terrain vehicle with its stiffer than usual seating, turned a key already in the ignition. He heard almost nothing but felt a slight vibration beneath them. He slipped her in gear and rolled her backwards about ten feet, before turning her in the direction of the tunnel.

"Electric." Bailey responded. Betty turned in question, not really concerned what type of vehicle they were in. She was glad they were all together, still in one piece.

A question arose from left field stopped Betty to ask. "Tomorrow, could we sit down with Dr. EL? And find out if there is a bulldozer to use, maybe we can clear the tunnel."

"We can also find out if Uncle Ron or any of the boys made it to the bunker." Bailey returned, still looking at her.

"Sure, we'll do all that we can to make a way back outside." Then Bailey steered the newly acquired family taxi in the direction of moving on. The air in the tunnel was cool and crisp. It gave Betty a chill. Lights above popped on as soon as they started moving past twenty feet. Betty had remembered auntie's little dog. She wondered where she had gone. She hoped to fine her. The tunnel was a good five-hundred feet long. A tropical setting met them on the other side. Bailey swung his view to look at the children. They had their mouths open. This was the ticket. Something to draw stressful attentions away from everyday life. Jackie had a giddy expression written in her eyes. She felt at home with the surroundings. The first structure they saw was massive gates of a gothic novelty, placed at the very edge of a tall stone wall, comparable to the walls of some great city of the past. This brought a chill in the air when thinking of such a past. Tropical bird calls could be heard at the tops of the trees. A big blue, red, and orange bird flew overhead. Ryan ducked like it was after him.

"Wow," he said. "Did you see that, Bird?" No one said anything, still mesmerized by what was in front. When Bailey got close to the gates, they automatically started opening. Someone knew they were coming. Pulling in past the gates as they closed behind. Ryan looked back feeling they might be trapped.

This was definitely a zoo, but no zoo they had ever seen. Some animals were hard to find, buried behind hidden structures, cages behind foliage and twisting climbing roads. An aviary was just ahead. Bailey drove around it looks at something strange up ahead. He could see what he thought to be a chubby little man, asleep, sitting on a chair, with three small monkeys in a cage making a mess all around him. He was pale, sweaty, and looked uncomfortable. He was trapped by what they could tell. And next to him was a familiar little dog waging her tail.

Jackie perked up when she saw their little dog. "There she is!" Jackie pointed toward the cage as thinking to be redeemed from putting down the little rodent from the day before, and then forgetting about her.

Ryan totally engrossed in another animal farther away. "Wow, look at that monkey!" Ryan belted out.

Confused, Jackie looked at him. "It's not a monkey squirt, it's a gorilla. He might be an ancestor, but definitely not a monkey. He's much bigger."

Ryan squealed like a little girl. "Can I play with him?"

Betty gave him a once over. "Squirt, calm down, they're dangerous, not something you want to pet, besides look in front of us. Cuddles, she'd been rescued." Betty focused on the little dog. She looked at her with a disapproving scowl. "You're a bad girl. You shouldn't have run off." Cuddles glanced at Betty with a nervous twitch with her tail tucked between her legs.

Suddenly, the chubby little man jerked awake. "Oh…hi you guys…I need help…if you don't mind…" still disoriented from being stirred awake.

Ryan, curious how this peculiar chubby little man got stuck behind bars, "How'd you get stuck in that cage?"

Chubby little man in the cage rolled his eyes. "I didn't plan to get stuck." He looked down at Cuddles. "It's her fault. She pushed the door shut. We've been stuck here since yesterday afternoon." Bailey saw the keys sitting on the ground next to a chair by a metal water bowl. He reached down and picked them up, still looking at the nerve twitching rodent as the chubby little man protested. "I should feed that mutt to the lions." Bailey ignored the comment, as he reached over and unlocked the cage door. Sensing his sudden release caused the chubby little man to blink in thankfulness. "Oh, I'm sorry. My name's George, please to meet you guys. Some people call me George of the jungle, but I've never liked the concept to well, thank you very much, just call me George."

Bailey reached over and shook hands as Betty did the same. "Pleased to meet you also," Betty said. She handed George a bottle of water. He obliges and chugged the twelve ounces to quench his thirst. Cuddles ran over to a close by water bowl and lapped up water lavishly like she'd just crossed the Sahara Dessert.

George gasped after finishing his water bottle and squeezed it crushed. "Ahh...thanks." He said, still with this lost look of curiosity of why only this little family was here and no one else. "Where is everyone?" George embellished. He reflected a flicker of doubt in his eyes. He looked in Bailey's eyes with a curious stare, knowing they were all just kids. Bailey wasn't sure what to tell this so-called zookeeper. His hesitation seemed too long, everyone remained silent, well, everyone except Ryan.

"Everyone's gone mister. Left behind in that snowstorm, or whatever it is. We're the only ones who made it past those large gates, us, and Dr. EL. He's back in the control center." Everyone turned to glance Ryan's way. Betty looked at him knowing he'd said enough. Ryan took a step back and clammed up knowing he'd spoken out of turn. George, still showing a tad of curiosity in his eyes, was dumbfounded why no one was talking.

"So, let me get this straight." George asked. "No one made it past the gates, except your little crew, and some Dr. EL that I haven't met yet?"

Bailey nodded. "Pretty much George, we're it."

The zookeeper expelled a troubling flicker of pain in his eyes. "But my family was left behind, and your little dog caused me to get stuck with these three." George turned to look briefly at the monkeys, and then at Cuddles. "How do I get out now to see my family?" George asked.

"You can't. Not at the moment. The weather has buried everything in the valley, we're lucky to be alive." Bailey reported.

George held back an emotional appeal of concern. He reached down and picked up Cuddles wondering if she really could understand. "Sorry girl. Somehow this was meant to be."

Betty reached into her backpack and pulled out a tuna sandwich and a small box of chocolate-chip cookies and an apple and handed the gift of the simple meal to the Zookeeper. George took the food thankfully. This would be his last meal and testament with trembling hands and beads of sweat. This band of misfits finished up with their introductions and invited George to dinner for later on that night. Jackie scooped up Cuddles and slipped her under her arm, treating her as a once lost family heirloom. They lumbered back to where they left the golf cart. George gave them a quick tour of the grounds. He explained about the up-keep and cleaning of cages and feeding the animals and taking care of them. Jackie seemed fascinated by the animals and George's punctual concern for those of the animal kingdom. She paid attention to every detail as if to be tested shortly after. Bailey saw the connection between the zookeeper and Jackie. It was a match made in heaven for comrades of the same mind.

After three hours of zoology 101, the group gathered and made their way back toward the garden. In the tunnel, Bailey could feel the ground beneath them trembling from something not yet known. He turned the wheel back and forth to avoid flipping the vehicle, and then it stopped.

CHAPTER 14

Eden

Bailey glanced over at Betty wondering what that was all about. She drew his focus away from the slight tremor by glancing at the distant waterfall. "Bailey, can we just take it easy for the rest of the day?" She asked, wondering if she needed his approval. "A nice swim in the local lagoon seems fitting before dinner." Betty exclaimed.

"Sure," he said while thinking, The stress of a lost little dog, meeting George, and feeling tremors without answers didn't make any sense at all, but taking a break did.

Without him noticing, Betty had prepared ahead of time, and so did the children. They were all wearing bathing suits under their clothes. This was the tough part for Ryan to do, keeping a secret among family members. Betty had told him to keep silent about the swim, so Bailey wouldn't say no or have an opportunity to change their minds. But to the misinformed boy it didn't matter. After plugging in the zoologist golf-cart, Ryan took off running in the direction of sounding water as the pitter-patter of little feet faded in the distance. Bailey indicated a curious expression in Betty's direction.

"What, Ryan already knows?" A sparkling glint of pleasure crossed her face. He saw her eyes move with a flicker of hope. From hearing the water up ahead, and by the smiles on the girl's faces, he knew.

Bailey exclaimed, "But I didn't bring…"

The girls were already stripping down to bathing suits, and he didn't have time to finish his sentence. They moved quickly to misting water in front of them. Wondering what was going on when seeing their plan being implemented. He was left in the dark about their little secret. He looked over at Betty, knowing he would easily sway, yet Betty didn't mention the water while holding back the surprise. Face it. They were kids who wanted to forget about all the terrible events that had faced them just recently. They wanted to feel normal for once before everything else began to change.

"For grandma," Ryan said, yelling above the noise, "she'd want us to have fun!" Bailey stripped down to black briefs that hugged him tight and dove in. Betty looked over at Mattie, who was feeling the water with her big toe. Uncertainty crossed her eyes.

"You remember how to swim, don't you girl?" Betty asked.

"Yes, but I'm not that good at it." Mattie said.

"Don't worry," Betty responded, "I'll stay with you. Besides, we're supposed to have fun…right?" Mattie showed a flicker of hope in her eyes by Betty's nudge of approval.

"Yes, I guess so. That's what grandma would want us to do—have fun."

Bailey popped up next to Betty startling her with a spray of cool-water and warm breath. She pushed him back under as she strained to keep him down. From underneath, Bailey could tell the water was deep, a lot deeper than he had figured from earlier. It was alluring to the senses. His spine tingled, his heart pumping from the chill, his skin crawling with goosebumps. His lips turned a light color of blue from the cold. He poked his head up out of the water and looked at the shoreline. He saw Ryan staring down into the water guessing something strange was holding him back. He had figured Ryan didn't see any steam rising so, guessing it must be cold. Mattie had finally splashed four feet off the shoreline with a scream, which splashed on Ryan.

He drew back with widened eyes, pulled his arms around his midsection. "Hey!" He said. "Watch it girl! You're splashing water on me!"

Mattie gave him a stupid glare. "How else you goin to get wet? Jump in, you big baby!" Ryan ignored her at first. He shied away from the water's edge. With a little more teasing from the girls though, he finally jumped in with a scream, and a splash offsetting his direction with a spin. Ryan couldn't believe how cold the water was. Quickly learning to force his body to relax a bit, with shaky limbs along with prickled arm hair. There was no other way to get in the water without showing sensitivity. And none of them were willing to even consider failure, after all the snow and ice they experienced. This was easy in comparison. There was no one around besides them to even care what they did this day. Ryan knew this would help him grow-up—and this was all part of his journey.

Betty revealed a pink bathing suit under her regular clothes. She glanced up for a minute to see if the boy of immoral behavior was paying attention. He was, but he turned away from her view when she looked in his direction. He dove back under and reached for the bottom with one breath. He could see the water had a certain flow to it, but determining depth was hard from viewing at the top. The lagoon was a man-made oddity of construction—deep contours gave the it more of a holding tank look than a pool. Bailey figured it was used for some type of habitat for mammals. Once acknowledged, he became alarmed. The water wasn't just for the purpose of swimming alone. It had the purpose of a habitat, but for what? Bailey couldn't reach the bottom and fell a few feet short of touching the color of cold blue when he had turned and headed for the surface. Believing it to be twenty-five to thirty feet deep and hadn't got sufficient air in his lungs. Feeling the pressure on his ears quickly resurfacing.

Betty, surprised by his sudden appearance, swam over with quivering lips. Ryan swam to meet them in the middle. From the middle of the Lagoon, they all noticed when looking down in the water, the platform floated independently from the bottom. Ryan was hesitant about swimming in deep water, feeling his size would hinder his ability to make it that far. Not knowing his limits of athletic ability, he held back.

"Hey…Bailey!" Ryan asked, "You think you could swim over to the platform in the center?" Ryan motioned with his eyes.

Bailey turned with one eye closed and nodded. "Sure, I'll check it out—be back in a minute." He dove under the water imagining a hunt for hidden treasure. Ryan, still a little unsure of his abilities, put a hand on Betty's shoulder. A few seconds later, he saw Bailey pop-up next to the platform.

"Dang," he said. "He's fast!" Bailey, in the distance, pulled himself up on the platform, laying there for a moment to catch his breath. After several minutes, he looked to the side and noticed three-black inner tubes tied to the end of freshly painted wooden planks glued together in a crisscross pattern forming a floating deck. Reaching down, he untied them quickly, then jumped back into the water. Bobbing on top he grabbed the first tube to bring himself up through the center. Then notice beneath him two dark figures moving toward him from the other side of the deeper end.

Bailey widened his eyes to get a clearer view. *They were dolphins.* He thought. Just then, they came up between him and the black inner tubes. Betty, and the children, looked across the lagoon in surprise. Bailey reached up and touched the first one nearest him, sensing they wanted to play, and these inner tubes were familiar items of choice.

Ryan yelled, "Look!" The chatter of mammals heard in the distance got everyone's attention. Bailey tied the three tubes together and held on. It was an automatic ride back to shore. The dolphins moved up between the children with a playful burst of energy, almost giving Ryan a heart-attack. Bailey untied the tubes and gave one to each of the children.

He floated next to Betty and leaned in on her while forming a silly expression of young love. Betty slid closer to Bailey to draw warmth from his body. A sudden soft kiss, a breath of warm air, a smile of tenderness as their arms touched. Betty's heart was pounding.

On the shoreline, Cuddles was barking sporadically.

Ryan slid up under one of the black inner tubes, his arms flaring over the sides. He touched the smoothness of the top of one of the dolphins. The mammal nudged him in surprise. Ryan revealed a slight giggle from somewhere inside his belly.

Then Bailey got an idea. "Want a ride around the platform and back?"

Betty wiped water away from her eyes. "Yeah…will they do that? I mean are they trained?"

Bailey glanced at the dolphins. "I think so. They brought me over here." He expelled a growing smile from the corners of his mouth.

He waved his hand while firing a high-pitched whistle to draw their attention. Both dolphins responded and came over. Well trained and ready for a ride. Bailey set Ryan and Mattie up with their own dolphin as he showed great confidence in their new friends. Each child laced through an inner tube for this strange tractor pull ride across the local lagoon. Bailey noticed the undecided stare on Ryan's face.

"When I tell you, grab a hold of the fin. They'll pull you through the water but hold on tight!" Ryan decided this was an abnormal idea and backed away from the challenge. Betty took his place and positioned herself for the water ride. Once signaled, Betty excitedly pointed as the two dolphins lunged toward the other side. Giggles and screams, bouncing before bedlam, the two girls zipped across the water, barely hanging on. Betty's tube flipped over twice, but she managed to mirror her accomplice. Mattie turned a pale color of white, yet she didn't let go. She closed her eyes and screamed. The dolphins hit the corners of the platform and went opposite directions around the corners from the other side. Mattie was nearly breathless when opening her eyes. She almost lost control when crossing the path of the other dolphin. Betty was coming from the opposite way. Screaming and yelling, laughing and almost crying while Cuddles barked up a storm. They moved with jet-stream preciseness, skimming the water's surface. Mattie lost her grip at the last second as her inner tube flipped over. She dove below and popped back up, Ryan, all wide-eyed watched the girl's smooth sailing of laughter and limbs. Bailey reached over and tried to coax Ryan to try it. Not wanting to be considered a big baby, he hesitantly gave in. Bailey would tag along for the ride by sowing his arm through Ryan's inner tube, as Jackie would take the other.

"On your mark…get set…go!" Betty whistled. The dolphins lunged forward in a playful manner, zipping and zooming along, then moving in rhythm. Ryan's head jerked back so hard he almost bit his tongue. They were off. Ryan's dolphin was a bit slower because Bailey had tagged along for the ride, but it didn't take long for him to catch-up. Bouncing and spinning, twirling, and gulping, Ryan looked like a ghost. He held on the best that he could, griping the inner tube while turning white. He crossed to one side and turned around the platform barely missing the corner, Bailey pulled him up from a couple of brisk dunks, like donuts in hot oil. Betty was laughing, Mattie was screaming, while Cuddles ran back and forth on an unabridged shoreline. Once home-free, Ryan bobbed a couple of times before pulling himself up out of the water. He gulped air sporadically to catch his breath. Then he looked back with this expression of terror.

"What's wrong?" Betty asked Ryan. He was pouting. He leaned over to vomit up small pockets of water. He didn't look happy from Betty's angle of understanding.

"You guys are a bunch of insane retards!" He said. "Why would you even allow me to do this?" Feeling he'd been tortured. Then Bailey realized the youthful boy was put together a little differently than the rest. Ryan lay on the shoreline mimicking an over-heated puppy. Getting his second wind. Feeling being run over by a herd of wild animals. Betty watched his stomach heaving in and out in silent gasps of terror.

Bailey looked back at Betty, "Hey, maybe we should get ready to go back—it's getting late, and the waters getting colder." Betty seconded his vote for leaving. Ryan didn't wait. He got up and grabbed his gear and started walking through the garden. It was a three-quarter mile walk back to the elevator at the other end of the compound. Bailey looked over and noticed Betty's swimsuit was fitting a bit snug. She saw him looking yet kept the vision of catching his view in silence. After remembering the shower scene, he turned a shade of pink and turned his head. Betty showed a transparent smile while getting dressed. She slipped a t-shirt back on over her wet bathing-suit and put on her tennis-shoes. With her backpack swinging over her left shoulder, she reached and gently took Bailey's hand, an infinitesimal glimmer of hope, a quivering smile of recognition, a tight squeeze to prod him along. The two little girls walked in front of the couple. Ryan twenty-five steps ahead of the girls. Bailey felt a moment of giddiness. A misting chill hit their backs from behind. Betty turned with a growing sparkle set in her eyes. She noticed Bailey wanting to be closer. Pulling Betty to a stop. She smiled and reached up gently to kiss him, playfully biting his bottom lip. He let go of her quickly when noticing the children turned to look. When walking again, Betty's hair whipped around and tickled his face with wet moisture. He felt the tender touch of her cold sliding fingers laced in his. She was hooked, and so was he. It was a mutual awkwardness from the children's view. Bailey affectionately reached to pull her close as they walked—there was a curious glare from Jackie, a prodding sigh from Ryan, Mattie not paying attention. They quickly caught up to the children at the end of the garden. Feeling the warmth of artificial heat and light starting to dry the water through soaked through clothes. The temperature, even though quite comfortable, put goose bumps on Betty's arms. The air was 65 degrees, acclimated by the conditions of the cave. Different from the world above. They were taking part in a world buried in hidden secrets. Unbalanced at the moment as it might seem, it was their journey. This place would become their new home. Making the best of it was all they could do for now.

Betty's thoughts of the previous days passed through her mind. She was worried. She felt this was a good day spent together, but would there be more like this to share? Then the thought came to her. "Bailey, the garden, where we buried my grandmother. Can we name it Eden? It will be our garden, where grandma lays…a place we hold sacred."

Bailey turned to look at her. He wondered about her statement and frame of mind, but said nothing, only nodded.

Betty wanted the world to feel normal again, even though knowing if it were, she wouldn't have this time with Bailey and the children as it was of present. It would be different. He would be some type of celebrity in his running career, at some promising college, making a name for himself among the elites, far away from here—away from her touch, and her heart. She needed him. Her hidden soul reached out to something he had that she didn't quite understand. She didn't know what it was, yet she knew apart from him that feeling would be gone. She loved him, was her thought. Even in this short span of time, as love goes, it kept her on her toes. This was her new beginning—having purpose in guiding these children and having new love in her life. With Bailey at her side. This was perfect. Dysfunctional in a weird sort of way, but doable. Any mountains to climb or valleys to cross didn't matter, as long as they shared this journey together, everything else would fall in line, was her thinking. They were moving on to a new beginning.

CHAPTER 15

Dr. EL's Plan

The small band of misfits found the elevator. Made their way to the fifth floor and walked hurriedly back toward the second set of elevators. They passed hundreds of boxes of clothes, jackets hanging on racks, boots, skiing equipment, all for winterizing warmth to be used for freezing weather. Obviously, the weather outside was expected in the worst of form. At least the government started to head in the right direction.

Someone was thinking ahead, Betty thought. She knew she was right about Uncle Ron and his premonition of the government having a plan. Someone other than ordinary people made major plans that didn't include the general population. They were lucky to be here. No one had counted them into their numbers, but for some strange reason they were the lucky ones. They got past the gates at the right time in the right place, even though they barely made it in.

Without saying a word, the group continued to walk down the hall of the ninth floor. Betty led the way. She abruptly stopped in front of a big over-sized exotic looking door. Yeah, this was the same room she had seen from before, was her thought, like a neon sign saying break me down the president is here. Betty used her key, but Ryan stepped in front of the doorway setting off an alarm. At the last moment Betty noticed some strange lights coming from the foyer. A motion sensor light above them kicked on and shot red streams of light all across the hall, thinking the Hope Diamond was being heavily guarded. *Of course, this would happen.* She thought. This was the presidency suite, nothing left to chance. Bailey knew with Ryan stepping through the beams of light had tripped the alarm. It was loud and annoying, heard throughout the whole compound. There had to be a way to shut it off, Bailey thought. The odd couple turned to look at each other for the answer. The flashing light led to the other end of the hall. A red courtesy phone flashed a red neon color over Bailey's right shoulder. He couldn't hear the phone, but he did see the flashing lights from the corner of his eye. Bailey ran over and picked up the courtesy phone.

A voice was heard on the other end. "Is that you Bailey?"

The familiar voice of Dr. EL heard earlier perked his attention, "sorry about that. Is there a way to turn it off?"

"Yes, there is. Is Betty standing there with you?" The doctor asked.

Bailey turned around to see a discontented scowl on her face with her arms folded in showing everybody her impatience. "Ah…yes, she's here, what's the secret?"

"Have her put her eye up across the eyehole of the door from the outside. It has a retina scanner. The president didn't trust anyone—not even his cabinet of advisors."

"Okay. I'll tell her, but will it work on her?"

"It should—she was the first in the room. It picks up heat signals from warm bodies, records temperature, body size and mass, if anything changes from the next time someone tries to cross the threshold. Well, you know the rest. The president has never been here, so it's programed to pick up the first heat signals it reads. I guess she's in charge."

Bailey didn't like the sound of that. He hung up. The alarm was so loud that he had to use sign language to the small figured frazzled girl. They were in the trenches with bombs going off all around, was the thought. Betty rolled her eyes and moved the door's eyehole back into her vision, then the alarm stopped. The beams of light disappeared.

Betty gazed at her partner in crime. "So why didn't it set the alarm off when I was here earlier?" Betty asked.

"It's for the Pres. Dear girl—not ordinaries like us. You were the first." With unblinking eyes homed in on Bailey, she crossed the threshold.

Ryan looked up at his mentor. "Sorry about that. I didn't know it was booby-trapped."

Bailey reached down and rubbed the top of Ryan's head. "Don't worry squirt, no harm, no foul." Beyond the entrance lay a large three-bedroom suite. The total square footage was about three thousand square feet. The children ran to separate bedrooms to get changed out of wet clothes. Of course, Ryan chose the bedroom decorated with the Colorado Rockies baseball team. The boy looked all bug-eyed. "Wow!"

Betty went room-to-room collecting wet clothes. She hung them on hangers over the 30-foot balcony out past a sliding glass door. Bailey smiled. The hanging of clothes reminded him of the ghetto. They were nine stories high above the atrium floor. No one seemed to care they had laundry hanging over the rails on the highest floor. This was the best view in the whole cave. A watchful tower for the President's suite. From the dining-room, Bailey came back in from the patio. Glancing over at the kitchen clock on the wall. It was just now three o'clock in the afternoon. Betty headed for the primary-bath as the kids went to doing their own set of necessities, brushing hair, changing into comfortable clothes, or wasting time playing video games, just taking a break from all the drama. The young couple decided to take a nap, not so much to be together, but to get a moment away from the kids. They were both drained from the events of the last few days. So much had happened, so many close calls. Betty's head was still spinning, and Bailey hadn't recovered fully from the race, or chasing after Betty's grandmother, getting past the gates, avoiding near accidents of crashing into walls. It had been a nightmare. Bailey changed into shorts and laid face down on the king-size bed. The pillow had a soft fragrant smell of perfume. Betty was in the bathroom, doing what girls do, as the naive boy of bashful behavior fell asleep. He dosed in the comfort of regaling memories for the aristocratic mind of gentle fabric softener of prickly sheets, with powdery puffed pillows and drifting dryness of a softer perfume smell long gone of any remittance while lingering in mind from a time well spent.

Betty dipped beneath hot water to warm her body. Once finished with her shower, she slipped out and put on a white bath robe that hung on the back of the bathroom door. She made her rounds to check on the children. Jackie was brushing little Mattie's hair, and Ryan was draped over his bed playing with a video game under shadows of a bunkbed. Everyone was absorbed in this free time of trivialness and relaxation. Betty told the girls to stay in the apartment, no wandering around, no getting into trouble, the same went for the little troublemaker next door.

She slipped into something more comfortable. Silky pajama's suited her fine. Coming out of the dressing room she saw Cuddle's at the door with a wagging tail of curiosity. She picked her up and scurried back into the girl's bedroom.

"Can you girls watch her while Bailey and I take a short nap before dinner?"

Jackie wondered about sleeping arrangements and young ladies with young men exhorting forceful kisses, so she just asked. "Where's Bailey?"

Betty saw the expression of curiosity glint from Jackie's eyes. Reinforcing her innocence of circumstance Betty said, "We're taking a nap, that's all." Betty's eyes fluttered a shy acknowledgment towards Jackie, her pretend sister of trust. Jackie showed a friendly nod and let it go. Betty handed her the mutt of shaking shivers. "Here you go." Then young Betty bounced back to their private abode of the bedroom and raised an eyebrow. Bailey was already snoring. Drooling and dribbling on softly formed pink pillows. This was annoying. Then Betty heard what sounded like a tightly well-tuned trumpet. She wrinkled her nose and held back a giggle. She reached for a pillow then left the room and took to the couch, sensing the boy of bashful beginnings was under a lot of pressure.

Ryan was bored within ten minutes and slipped out of his room to check on the others. Seeing Betty on the couch he went to check on his mentor in the master bedroom. Ryan crinkled a quirky sparkle of hope and crawled up next to him. Blowing in his ear, tickling his neck, nothing disturbed him. After staring at the ceiling for ten minutes, Ryan's eyes became heavy, and he fell asleep.

An hour and a half later Betty woke after falling off the couch. She got up sleepily to check on her prince, noticing Ryan had cuddled up next to him. She couldn't help but smile and grabbed a blanket from the closet and covered it up, sensing the small boy was starting to bond with the older of the two.

Betty made a call to George so they could plan dinner together, set the mood for the start of something special—she meant for first impressions on the whole group. She glanced at the clock and would meet him at six, according to the phone call, a plan of edible delights. She didn't want to disturb the boys knowing Bailey and the little unmannered troublemaker were weary from the week's unwanted drama.

Jackie came out of the bedroom to meet Betty's glance. Looking at her to meet a smile.

"What's going on?" She said.

"Want to help prepare dinner with George and me?" Betty asked.

Jackie showing a tad sparkle of delight. "Sure—what time is it?"

"It's only five-thirty, but we've got some preparing to do while the boys sleep."

Jackie sensed Betty was honest about not snuggling up to Bailey. He was in the primary-suite, and that odd little boy with unstable movements had cuddled up next to him. She saw a wrinkled blanket lying on the couch and knew.

Much later, Bailey woke in the darkness of the room. He would have been able to hear a pin drop if appropriate for the occasion. He even noticed Ryan was gone. Everyone had deserted him. Even though the room was cool a line of sweat rolled off his face. The heavy weight of worry laced his heart from all they had been through. A digital red light mirrored the time to be almost 7:00 p.m. Reminiscence flashes of vivid pictures of the last two days blurred through his mind. Bailey reached up and turned on the light. He slammed his head back down on the pillow, trying to gather his thoughts. Smells of soft pleasurable perfume came back to memory. He recalled seeing Betty with him in the shower. He felt a twinge of shame, yet he knew there to be none. She was grieving at the time, nothing meant by her forward productions of an emotional breakdown. Yet her physical finesse of closeness touched his heart. She was detached from losing her grandmother. She was different from girls he knew in high school. Then a banging on the front door pulled him from memories of tender moments and young girls making his heart stir.

Bailey got up and headed for the door. He saw Ryan from the eyehole. A scrunched-up nose, with curious eyes with a scratch and sniff like intelligence, he was just an inquisitive little boy trying to get by. Once the door opened, he looked up at Bailey like he had all the right answers for personal events that were about to happen, as youth doesn't always understand the path so easily taken.

"I'll be right out, squirt." Ryan didn't say anything. He let himself in and closed the door. He reached for a light while Bailey got dressed. Coming out of the room he saw this little inspector's glare was irritating. He viewed Ryan like he was the key ingredient for making gunpowder or plutonium. Attention was paid toward this small boy of irritations and unsettling mannerisms. Ryan remained quiet, trying to give his awakened mentor a chance to redeem himself for having Ryan dragged around the lagoon with those mammals of the water. Bailey looked down at the man-child, awkwardly wrinkled clothes, energy of a fresh new puppy. He closed the door behind them as they walked with geek-like gawkiness down the hall like two geeks trying to get along. Bailey put his hand on top of Ryan's head and pulled him close as a big brother might do.

"Are you okay squirt?"

Ryan continued the stare. "Yeah…Betty wanted me to check on you." Ryan rolled his eyes halfway up as he waited for Bailey to respond.

"I'm fine squirt. What's for dinner?"

"Don't know, but it's starting to smell really good in the kitchen."

Bailey remembered speaking to Dr. EL had to be a priority before more time escaped them. "That's good," he said without really paying attention. The elevator door opened up to the galley. The boys could hear singing from George entertaining little girls with laughs and giggles. Ryan looked at them with a hesitant frown. Bailey interrupted their little moment of song and celebration.

"Hey girls…George…when will dinner be ready?"

Betty with bashful enthusiasm showing a flint of flirting eyes responded, "In about an hour, why?"

"I wanted to see Dr. EL for a few minutes, if you don't mind." Ryan showed no interest in what Bailey was talking about. He seemed only interested in the smells developing in the galley. Mattie looked bored and reached up to take Bailey's hand. She smiled at him in his surprise. Bailey reached for an apple while handing it to Mattie, a small gift of sweetness. He glanced at Mattie. "Hi beautiful, how are you?"

With draping curls of thick red hair her eyes sparkled with light. "Can I go with you?" Mattie had asked. Bailey only nodded.

Betty's face and apron were powdered by flour with a smudge on her ear. With flirting conditions, she reached up with canoodling lips on Bailey's cheek. Warm breath and smells of the kitchen rolled off her like fine-wine perking ones palate. He saw and felt the sparkle of love in her expressions. Bailey reached for her ear, removing the touch of flour. She brushed her hair back with the back of her hand. Bailey kissed her on the forehead while offering George a hardy smile.

"We're off!" He said, with a feinting air of confidence.

Mattie polished the apple against her dress. They were quickly on their way up to the sixth floor. Mattie was an image of the perfect little girl of trust and curiosity as she looked up at Bailey with a smile. As all little girls liked to be noticed, she said. "So, who told you I was beautiful?"

Bailey surprised suddenly by her heart felt recognition, "I told myself angel...don't you think yourself beautiful?"

She thought about it for a second as the elevator opened up to the sixth floor. "Well, sometimes, but not now...not with everything all mixed up, and grandma gone. I don't feel so beautiful anymore."

Bailey considered her words and knew she was talking about her frame of mind, and not so much her outer appearance. He reached down and brushed her thick curling hair aside.

"Listen to me Mattie," Bailey paused as she turned her eyes toward him.

"No matter what happens to any of us you'll always be beautiful, just like Betty. You are here for a reason. I don't know what that might be yet, but I know someone thought it important enough to include you. That's why I think you're beautiful." She wrapped her arms around Bailey and started to cry.

"I didn't know being here was meant for me too, I'm sorry for not being supportive like Grandma would want me to be." Emotion splashed on the back of Bailey's eyes, yet he held it at bay. He didn't care to show tears to a little girl who saw him as a leader. He might have been seen as a replacement for a grandmother now gone, from her point of view, not wanting to spoil that—he remained quiet about the subject. Mattie brushed her tears away as she bit into the apple.

Bailey changed the subject. "How's the apple," He said.

Mattie held up the apple offering a bite just when they came close to the Tower Control Room door. Bailey bit the apple as if sharing a moment of gratitude. He hugged her with his right arm as he knocked with his left hand.

In the distance of knocking interruptions, Dr. EL raised an eyebrow. "Come in!" he said as Bailey opened the door and Mattie and he crossed the thresh-hold.

Dr. EL had this perplexed look at him after hanging up the phone. Bailey, showing hesitation, waited for the good doctor to clear his way of thinking. Then Bailey broke the moment of silence. "Can I help?" He asked.

Dr. EL looked over the top of gold rimmed glasses. "Well, I hope so, because you and your little crew could become the rescuers of people, as you'll find out later. But right now, we can't penetrate this freezing weather. It has hit the whole northern hemisphere in an unbelievably bad way. Look at these pressure readings here on my screen." Dr. EL pointed out with his pencil. "See the red and orange and yellow colors here and here, the mountains are covered in a thick layer of ice. It's over sixty feet thick or more. Even if we had the ways and means we couldn't get through."

Bailey nodded in understanding. "So, what do we do?"

"There's not much we can do but wait this extreme weather out." Dr. EL glanced at the boy who showed promise. "It doesn't look good for people out there. Most of the northern populations have tried to move south, according to the phone call I just had with the joint chief of staff—there's no getting around it, this mess is everywhere." A pause gave Bailey a moment to soak up his meaning. Then the doctor continued.

"The Joint Chief knows of your little clan, and that nobody else made it past the gates. Air Force one is flying south. Some place in the tropics with better conditions, he didn't tell me where."

Bailey saw the disappointment in Dr. EL's eyes. Then he got this off-the-wall idea.

"Sir...the tunnel left behind...do we have a way to fix it?"

Dr. EL turned his eyes with a flicker of hope. "Maybe, something left behind from our always overspending government."

Bailey's ears perked. "And what would that be?" He inquired.

Just a glint of a smile crossed the doctor's face. "A state of the art, all terrain twelve wheeled, water-proof JR-22 Q-Tank, built to bull-doze its way through anything. Lucky for us we're working indoors and not outside in that freezing weather climate."

Bailey went along with the doctors little proposal of delight. "Where would I find such a toy?" He exuded with a curious blink of an eye.

"I think in the sub-basement." The doctor said. "A place we haven't seen yet. We'll check it out later." Even Mattie showed an interest in this vivid explanation of some new expensive toy to push around the compound, which was created by the government left behind to lead them to other secrets still hidden.

"So, what else is in this warehouse?" Bailey said on a curious note.

Dr. EL developed a widening smile. "There's heavy military equipment that the good old U.S. of A. thought we might need to dig ourselves out of a deep freeze." Then DR. EL laughed with a chuckling response to misery and hope side-by-side. Bailey didn't see the humor in having to dig themselves out of the tunnels, and neither did little Mattie, who had just finished off her apple.

"I believe there's a level two below the main floor of the warehouse. Something the military thought they'd need to hide from those of a curious mind that might expose these secrets to the wrong people. Meaning they didn't want anyone finding out about their stash of military equipment."

The doctor went back to sharing about his limited knowledge of the Q-Tank. "It's like a large cockroach that can dig through anything with incredible results. It has a three-dimensional graphics card that is similar to a G1000 from the cockpit of an airplane, known as the Avionics as the debonair eyes of the sky. The G1000 is a type of monitoring system that keeps you aware of everything around you, so not to slip up or make any mistakes. It introduces pressure readings, geo-thermal expositions, leading temperatures of change, changes in the terrain, sudden pit falls, or warnings of wind conditions, unexpected weather anomalies not considered will pop up on the visual visor."

Bailey remembered getting his pilot's license at the early age of sixteen, and grinned from knowing the Piper plane he flew had a downgraded model of the G1000 and knew exactly what Dr. EL was suggesting.

"When can I get started?" Bailey asked with raised eyebrows of anticipation.

"Now just hold your horse's young man. You don't even know how to drive this new contraption, let alone understand the Q-Tank's technology."

Bailey's face showed a hint of perception. "Dr. EL, I know this will be easy to learn. I learned how to fly a plane a few years ago. It can't be much harder. There was an earlier model of this G1000 unit inside the cockpit of the airplane I flew. Lucky for you, I'm your man."

The doctor showed a glint of surprise. "Maybe you are the man." The doctor said,

"Because also below is a dozen or so plane kits in cold storage. You and your little crew can learn to put them together while waiting for the weather to turn."

Bailey astonished by the sudden Intel of information. "What's next?" He insisted.

"Well young man, first the Q-Tank, and then on to other items hidden below. I'm surprised at your age you've got a pilot's license. Lucky for me, you and your small band of misfits made the gate." Then the phone started ringing. Dr. EL quickly reached for it.

He looked back at Mattie and Bailey, suddenly stunted by the quick interruption. He hung up with an all-presuming smirk. "We have been summoned for dinner. Betty said bring an appetite." A smile broke out on the good doctor's face as he stood and escorted the two young people toward the door. Mattie, assuming that the doctor was all knowing at most areas of understanding, partially because of his age and also his education, decided to trust his judgment of adherence.

Mattie asked the informal doctor. "What's for dinner?"

The doctor showed an elusive face. "Don't know little one...it's a surprise." Down the hall into the elevator, they went. They ignored the chilly hallways with the gap from below, as they noticed the atrium went up pretty high, this was their world now. Dr. EL was known to be the grandfatherly type who had his way with words. And these young teenagers and children were caught in the balance of indubitable predicaments. They were on a road not made for weary travelers, but for those of finesse. His aged way of thinking began to worry him, with no certain future, no family, or friends, but as he was given this second chance of proving oneself, first, in overcoming his drunken loneliness, and now having purpose to lead this young dysfunctional family still impressionable, still young of heart. Dr. EL understood their situation, acknowledging Bailey facing adulthood, Ryan's adolescent way of thinking, and three young girls with incomplete hearts. He was dubious to know what they were facing up ahead. He now had a purpose of leadership, right in front of him, shaping young lives, giving direction. They were leaving a trail of darkness from a few days ago, and now set on a journey with epic proportions soon to follow, but nothing would be taken for granite—as he would have to advise them when needed. Dr. EL pondered their demise, their eternal commitments. This place of safety was a miracle in a wake of these miseries internalized cessations not understood, while others were left in the wake of severe weather from a quickly fading Earth. With clear blinking eyes he entered the elevator for the fiftieth time.

The galley doors opened to celebration and laughter. The three not knowing what was in the air, but for some apparent reason it was contagious. George had a unique way of entertaining. Betty was floured from head to toe. Ryan looked like the Pillsbury dough-boy, unbaked but smitten. Jackie was rolling in laughter as George stood over the oven with chef-hat and high emissions of comical conditions as a brother or uncle would be. They were just having a fun time. Then this overwhelming smell hit them. All pulled toward the essence of delight. George turned with raised eyebrows. Everyone pitched in to help. George started another joyful song of celebration, like he was Captain Jack Sparrow stealing back his ship. Ryan looked over at Bailey, missing out. They were all singing now, a song from long ago about silliness and insensible rhythms. It didn't make any sense at the moment, but nothing mattered, at least not at this point in their lives, as they shared, giggled, and laughed. Betty reached and pecked Bailey on the cheek. She reached for the door.

"I need to get cleaned up boys. Be back in a moment." Ryan took her hand and left with Betty.

Jackie and Bailey set the table in the next room with double doors of overly expensive ornaments, silvery settings, and embroidered napkins with specialty lit candles. This was a treat. Jackie's eyes sparkled when Bailey lit the last candle, George still putting things into their proper place of arrangement. Jackie went back into the kitchen to help George with placing their delicate hors d'oeuvres-of-delight in holding trays and bowls of mounding food. Steaming hot pleasures rose from the kitchen. Mattie's eyes got as big as saucers. Bailey had to suck-in drool to keep from slobbering on his shirt. George had this giddy look about him as if sharing with the best of company after so much pressure from before of the outside world. Living in their own little world now, away from the chaos.

Betty and Ryan made their way to the fifth-floor scooting toward the back of this unsearched warehouse of wares. Ryan had a giddy smile of remembrance on his face. She pushed powder from off his forehead. It tickled his nose to a crinkle. Betty was covered in flour knowing she needed a quick shower before going to dinner. She caught an idea from higher emissions that made her smile. "Hey squirt, want to make an impression?"

Ryan looked up as they got into the last set of elevators heading up. "What do you got in mind?" He looked at this lady of mystery as Betty reflected a sparkle in her eyes.

"We'll dress up, that's all. We'll make an impression and throw them off-balance."

Ryan grinned and nodded at the same time. "Okay, I'll dress up and keep them drooling," Ryan said as if controlling their future dealings with the people left in the galley was left up to him. Betty rolled her eyes. The elevator opened to the penthouse floor and the two moved down the hall.

Fifteen minutes later, Betty came out dressed in a little knock-out-number—a beautiful black dress that caused Ryan's lower jaw to drop, curves and feminine features standing out in the dress. She was attractively packaged in this tightly curved silky dress, soon an iteration to draw the boy's luring eyes. Ryan couldn't help but stare. She had fixed her hair, put on make-up, and smelled of something heavenly, while soft fragrances of long waving hair drifted in the air.

Ryan looked all bug-eyed and bamboozled. "You know all the guys are going to be looking at you tonight." Without a filter Ryan said, "I think you're over doing it a bit, don't you?"

Betty showed an exasperating stare. "Let's go munchkin before I change my mind about making an impression." Earrings and necklace with a matching bracelet, with tall black heels, she looked the picture of perfection. Ryan flared his nose as if she was a distraction. Betty wrinkled her forehead and pushed her lips to the side. "So, you think I over, did it?"

Little Ryan cast a glare of flaring eyebrows and knew he better beware. "No, not really, you're hot…that's all. Let them suffer," he said.

Betty shook her head with a flaring remittance of getting along. "Whatever…" while turning away in the direction of the penthouse door.

The elevator opened up to the galley as Betty and Ryan made it passed tempting smells in the kitchen. Betty bounced past double swinging doors catching everyone off guard while Ryan followed quietly after. All the men stood wondering why she'd gone to such trouble. Ryan saw everyone staring like she was Queen of the day, while dreaming of quickly picking a boatload of new male concubines to fill her harem.

"Well," Ryan said, "maybe I'll go put on a dress and make-up so you guys will notice me!" They all looked at the small boy of blunders then laughed. He would have cared, but the smells of enticing foods pulled his interests.

Betty retained a growing smile in her rebuttal to say, "You should have asked me sooner squirt. I would have hooked you up. I had a spare in the old closet." Everyone laughed.

Ryan lost interest and took a seat. George and Betty had prepared a feast fit for a king. Tenderly marinated, smothered in barbeque sauce, tempting copious of meat, pasta of perfection, white wines from the best of vineyards, baked potatoes, a divine salad made the way it was supposed to be. Don't forget about the peach cobbler basking in melted a la mode as choices could be.

The doctor was impressed. "You out did yourself," he said with smiling eyes and his bureaucratic and behooving stares.

They had a relaxed atmosphere of dining. Bailey and the boys cleaned up the mess. Betty put away leftovers. Everyone said their goodnights and would be soon off to bed, dreaming about this new world that was presented to them.

Dr. EL stopped Bailey in the hallway. He reminded him of their talk earlier. "Don't forget about our little discussion."

Bailey nodded. "No, I won't forget sir."

Then George asked kindly from a distance, "I might need a little help with the animals in the morning."

Jackie perked with excitement. "Oh, pick me! I'll be glad to help with the animals!" Then Jackie volunteered Mattie as her sidekick, who nodded in agreement.

George gave an eye-raising glint in support of the locals. "Thanks. I appreciate any help you girls can give. You're a life saver."

CHAPTER 16

Sub-Basement

Bailey got up early that morning. Thin-red-lines of the clock flashed 6:30. He reached for his pants and slid off the couch. Made his way to the primary-suit and then knocked.

"Betty…it's time to get up." Bailey said. "Dr. EL will be waiting for us at the breakfast table."

Betty blinked her eyes and rolled to her side. "Okay," she said, "I'm getting up." The two little girls were already up and gone to the local zoo as promised. Ryan heard the murmur of voices and slid from his bed. Sleepy times with more than usual long days made him want to stay within cozy-covers, but he also wanted to see this surprise of the government issued Q-Tank as well.

Betty knocked on Ryan's bathroom door. "Are you almost ready squirt?" Ryan spit toothpaste out to answer, "Yes, I'm almost ready." He mumbled. Betty could hear the gurgle of rinse and spit. Once ready, they all headed down into the warmth of the galley. Ryan could feel the crackle of swimmers toe and flinched.

"Ouch." He said, as he dragged himself into the elevator with pressured efforts. In the galley, sat the aged Dr. EL reading from a plastic schematic notebook of some sort. From Bailey's angle it looked important because he could tell the doctor was deep in thought. Betty made the mornings of introductions.

"Good morning Dr. EL. It's nice to see you got things started." His smile grew as if anticipation of his new arrivals, just on time and ready for a new day. What the young couple hadn't understood was that the good doctor was looking for these fancy little Q-Tanks in advance, *preparation meets opportunity,* was his thought. He glanced up at Bailey with an expression of concern.

"I hope you're ready to learn how to drive our latest invention." The doctor said.

"You mean the Q-Tank sir?"

"Yes, young man that's exactly what I mean." Dr. EL stated. "But it's been difficult to find. The Q-Tank is located on a sub-basement level 2, hidden from the usual drama of curious eyes." Bailey walked over to where DR. EL was seated and viewed at what he was pointing. "It's here Bailey. I'm not sure how to reach the bottom level yet. This is unfamiliar territory for all of us. My field of expertise doesn't usually require me to go to such levels to spy on what our government has left behind. I'm only required to attend to the weather station on the sixth floor of this facility, and not much more."

Not really paying attention, Bailey was thinking of the tunnel left behind that had collapsed. "Will this fix our little problem of the tunnel," Bailey asked. "I mean this modified Q-Tank?"

"Don't really know son. We won't know until we get down there and take a look and test out the equipment."

Bailey sat down at the table across from the doctor as he study the schematic a little bit more in detail. Betty had already served Bailey a cup of hot coffee and left over omelet from the skillet. She also packed a lunch for four and stuffed that inside her backpack, which she had used from the previous day. She also filled a thermos of coffee along with storing six bottles of water in the bottom. Ryan sat next to Bailey downing the omelet and drinking milk, like a tiny scurrying church mouse grabbing the last few crumbs of left over goodies. Once finished, the group quickly stood to make their way from the galley on the way to the basement level floor. Today would be an adventure of finding new toys for these discourteous boys.

Dr. EL walked into a quaint little office once on the Atrium level floor. Across the Atrium was the makes of a military storage unit full of wooden crates. All marked with the same type of government seal that Bailey had seen from before. Yet DR. EL wasn't interested in this level at the moment. He was interested in the floor below this one if he could just figure out how to get there.

"According to the schematic on page three there's a secret way to get on the lower sub-basement floor." He stated.

Bailey followed Dr. EL to the entrance of the office as he stood there and waited for him. In the office was a medium-sized desk sitting in the middle of the floor, with florescent lighting overhead that quickly blinked on. Several grey file cabinets lined in a row again the far side of the wall undisturbed, with maps and diagrams tacked against the wall in some type of orderly fashion. But strangely, there was a panel hidden behind the door not seen by the natural eye, yet the doctor knew it was there, hidden in the utmost unlikely of places. So, DR. EL reached around the door and noticed what the schematic had pictured, a metal hinged box placed perfectly inside the wall with a grey-handled twist lock connecting to a metal hinged door. He undid the lock, opened the panel while viewing two buttons like in an elevator for different floors, this one was grey in color with green numbers in the center. The first embossed lettering had L1 embossed in it, the second had L2. Dr. EL pushed L2 and quickly behind everyone they looked to see the room changing. From in front of the office, in the center of the large warehouse, everyone could see the floor starting to descend and drop below. Bailey and Dr. EL with Ryan and Betty jumped down onto the descending floor, surprised that this place of secrets were quickly to be exposed. There was a hydraulic lift of substantial size holding the weight of this substantial unit. Bailey figured that the power lift could hold a considerable amount of military equipment, which at the present time was revealing more hidden secrets below. Ryan had this silly adherence of discovery on his face considering this was really neat and cool. The floor was made of six-inch-thick solid gray plated steel and was thirty by thirty in diameter. Obviously, this whole room was of a military making, left behind by the government, and now left in the control of their hands. Now to Bailey this started to make sense.

From top to bottom, the large hydraulic lift came to stop at this lower level 2. It was about thirty feet below from where they had originally started. Once at the bottom, the lights slowly flickered on. Ryan had his mouth open. They were all speechless. The room looked like the inside of a giant air-craft-carrier filled with military vehicles of war, dump-trucks, and jeeps, and eighteen-wheelers, a dozen or so crated airplane kits, and a familiar looking thing that the good doctor was after, the new modified all-terrain JR-22 Q-Tank that he had seen in one of the many schematics. DR. EL looked down at the present schematic and seemed confused about what was before him. He almost couldn't believe it. Ryan was the first to come over to take a look.

The Q-Tank was a dream fulfilled, except something looked strange about it. Basically, being a modified tank turned bulldozer, yet had other functions too. The body was rough looking like a regular tank, but it had six wheels on each side. Instead of using a belt type system, which could damage roads or anything of a softer nature, this had tires, better traction, and better stability. It made for a quieter ride. The Q-Tank had an entrance in the top like a regular tank, but instead of having a mounted gun on the front it, it had a scoop bucket like that of a bulldozer. There were ten in all, which were camouflaged in a gray and white color fit for being hidden in the snow. Dr. EL suggested.

"Bailey, get in. You and Betty can try this new toy out and find out how much you can pick up on your own." Betty turned with a hesitation in her eyes as she looked back at Bailey, waiting for him to respond. He had this stupid impairment of discovery still keeping him stationary. He'd never driven a tank before, and this one didn't appear to have any windows. He scratched the back of his head replicating being in a trance like stupor. Dr. EL began to lose his patience. "Just get in the contraption and see if any of the gadgets make any sense." The doctor said.

Bailey rolled his eyes as he climbed up to the top of the first one available of this strange invention drawing his attention. A hatch opened from the top that looked extremely expensive. Once Bailey got in, Betty followed after. Tight and snug was the fit, only a two-seater. The little tank had buttons and gadgets all around. Like in a car, there was an adjustment handle to move the leg length for those of a taller influence. Bailey noticed right away two headsets. They looked like the helmets that airplane pilots would use for a SR71-blackbird. He had that experience one summer with his dad. Bailey was impressed, and giddy. A kid in a candy store scoring a hand-full of the best of sourballs. There was a computer monitoring screen built right into the headset with a hidden visual visor. Once the Q-Tank was turned on, all the buttons and switches lit up. It looked similar to the cockpit of an airplane in the dark at 14,000 feet since no light entered the little dozer. Bailey started turning on buttons and switches lighting the Q-Tank up, while Betty closed the hatch. He reached over and handed Betty her own helmet and said, "Here, put this on." Betty didn't argue. They both slid on the headgear as Bailey reached for the left side of the helmet and turned on a switch to the sound system. He reached over and turned Betty's on too. "Wow!" Bailey yelled into the microphone. Betty pulled the headset off with an aggrieving stare.

"Dude…really, don't yell! The speakers are turned all the way up!" He looked over at her with a slight transparent smile.

"Sorry, not used to the headgear yet," he said as he reached over to turn her volume switch back down. Betty saw a compact glovebox in front of her. She opened it and pulled out the instruction manual, the 'how to' of safety and instructional operations. She comprehended this to be in several languages as she flipped through it quickly. The English version was seen by flipping the little manual around and upside down, a 455-page second edition, according to the table of contents. On first impressions, the overqualified dirt-digger had a steering wheel on both sides like in the cockpit of an airplane. This made Bailey nervous because not too often the person sitting on the right side could make things exceedingly difficult for the main person on the left and considering what DR. EL had told Bailey from the day before, Betty was in charge. This didn't sit so well from his point of view. Furthermore, this miniature modified mud remover had three shift handles located in the dash between both steering wheels. This made Bailey think of this cartoon character that featured a two-headed Lama trying to make heads or tails of which direction to go, even all the more confusing. The Q-Tank had a brake and gas pedal like on a regular car except two sets as if they were in training. The instructor could take over at any minute, except this time it was the blind leading the blind. But the most alarming part was that it had no windows. Bailey distinctly remembered his airplane from training had windows. Betty looked confused about being in the dark too. Then he remarked. "I guess were flying IFR?"

Betty gave the impression of being left in the dark. "We're what?"

"We're flying Instrument Flight Rules sweets. No windows." He pointed toward the front of lacking windows. Betty showed a flint of worry in her eyes, not trusting her handy-dandy ground-pilot taking off down some distant road like a blind-man without directions, not even a white cane to give him a five-foot warning of what's ahead. Bailey had to learn to trust the G1000. It displayed a three-dimensional graphics similar to an X-Box, a difficult involvement but surreal. Betty wasn't sure she could trust an overconfident runner, who reminded her of a bobble-head, who'd at most leave a cloud of dust behind. He was new at this just like she was. Bailey pushed a button on the side of his headgear and the G1000 monitoring system came to life on the visual visor. A small screen moved at a ninety-degree angle in front of his eyes. He was plugged in like in the movie Tron. He could imagine, his sexy co-pilot in her zipped-up one-piece suit showing her curves of perfection. She, being Olivia Wilde, playing the part of Quorra taking a journey across cyber-space set to do battle on their light-cycles, except they were in a phone-booth size bulldozer taking pot-shots in the masked oblivion of the dark. This caused Bailey to smile from his overactive imagination. Betty saw her headgear blink on too, showing them both the layout of the room and the dimensions of movement. The images started blinking in different colored lights displayed in the visual visor. This was something they had to adjust too. It wasn't a video game. They didn't have second lives to give away or pal-up with another player to save themselves. They had to learn this for real without the mistakes that most video-gamers experience. That's the interesting dilemma that kids lacking experience don't understand about repetition, yes, in the video games you can just start over, but in everyday life it's not so easy. Bailey was daydreaming about another time. *Before you're ready,* Mother would say, *No bedroom*

babies or college dropouts. Mind your manners and eat your vegetables.
Remembering the hassled words of youth. Then coming back to reality.

The JR-22 Q-Tank was like being seated on the inside of a cockpit
of an airplane, every movement pushing you with purpose. Tuning his
way of thinking to the hard drive of a computer, each position moved
by mental accuracy, each reaction made through the headset of the visual
visor then connecting to the steering. This would take some getting use
too. Then Bailey cut in. "You see the blinking lights in your visual visor?"
Betty expressed a cheesy acknowledgment of comprehension.

"Yes dork…what do you think?" He knew he couldn't get by with
saying non-intelligent comments without the commitment of thinking
through his words before engaging his brain. He attempted to teach
Betty with his limited knowledge of earlier days from flying.

"You point or steer the Q-Tank with the video scope in the direction
you want it to go. Try to avoid the blinking red objects projected in front
of you." Betty shook her head while rolling her eyes.

"Tell me something I don't know."

Bailey looked concerned. "Can you be easy on me? I'm a little
nervous. It would help if you could give me a break. Some of this is
common sense, yet other things pertaining to hand and eye coordination
is a bit difficult." Betty turned her eyes toward Bailey with a different
frame of mind.

"Sorry, didn't mean to throw you off."

"You didn't throw me off. Your making me uncomfortable because
you know we're both new at this." Betty kept her cool knowing Bailey
was right. This wasn't a toy to be played with. They had to learn this, and
being a pain wasn't helping. He thought she had the same personality as
Ryan but knew it would only hurt her feelings to point that out.

Betty went back to reading the manual as he went back to teaching
his limited skills on the G1000. "This unit is modified from what I
learned three years ago. The intelligence used, and from the government's
point of view, sparing no expense to make this the best functioning
graphics as possible." He read the buttons on the left side of his steering
wheel recognizing that the Q-Tank was pressurized for depth, but the
depth of what? He saw an equalizing pressure gauge in the dash. "Betty,
can you look something up for me please? Check in the table of contents

for pressure readings for being in water." Betty turned her head to the left to catch his glance.

"What? You mean like we can go into water?"

"Yes, according to this gauge, the Q-Tank is built to go into water like a submarine, but I need to know how deep we can go." Betty began to flip through the manual like a good co-pilot would do in assisting the one on the left.

Bailey informed her. "I saw something like this on National Geographic's, you know, like that French oceanographer with the Television program."

Betty developed a slight sparkle in her eyes of her terse acknowledgment. "You mean Jacques Cousteau?"

"Yeah...that's the guy." Betty rolled her eyes.

"He started off as a Naval-Officer." She said. "He didn't become famous until later. He had all kinds of talents. He was an explorer, conservationist, filmmaker, innovator, scientist, photographer, author, and researcher who studied the sea in all forms. He didn't drive bulldozers on the bottom of the oceans floor though—that's for enigmatic nimrods like you."

"Whatever man, can you just please look it up? See if there's anything on pressure readings?" Bailey hardened his eyes, wondering if this compartment was going to seem really pressurized by the end of the day. Betty saw his expression and knew she wasn't scoring points.

"Yes, page 455, the last page." She read before saying another word, "A depth up to two-hundred feet. There should be a switch on the left side of the steering-wheel."

Bailey looked over to his left and saw the switch. Betty read silently. The Q-Tank automatically pressurized the cabin after turning on the switch. The tank had the ability to move each tire independently of each other for better traction. The hull was almost impenetrable. Betty relayed the information to the commander-and-chief. She thought him to be a little to bossy. As nerves flared and patience thinned, she continued reading. Bailey tried a more delicate conversation to swing her mood. "I could have used one of these back home."

Betty flared her nostrils when she thought of the bobble-head driving this contraption on the side-roads scaring the crap out of his neighbors.

Drawing focus, Betty thought it was time for her to pay attention and find out what this video-visor was all about. She saw rolling numbers to the left of the monitor.

"What's the numbers for?" She kept her eyes on this imaginary roadmap in front of her.

Bailey took a wild guess. "I think negative altitude for when the Q-Tank is under-water. The numbers on the right are pressure and density altitude readings, my best guess."

"And that means what in English?" Bailey's eyes widened.

"Ask Dr. EL when we're done. He's the weather genius. I'm only familiar with the basics." Bailey thought of trying to explain, but then decided she could be harsh.

The two looked through the visual visor with the vivid graphics of the G1000. They were trying to anticipate how to control the scoop while driving the tank at the same time. Then Bailey thought of something really stupid.

"Haven't you always wanted a job that you and your partner could share?"

She looked over and saw the same cornball grin again. "No, I'd end-up killing you by the end of the day." Bailey couldn't believe what he was hearing, but knew he set himself up for the fall. Then he pushed his conversation to the limit.

"Things would be different if the end of the world weren't so eminent. I'd be signing a Nike deal or headed off to college on the shirttails of some fancy school with clout. You would be barefoot and pregnant working on your sixth kid. Your husband would be the local T.V. repair man with the size 40-inch waste barking orders for his dinner while you're trying to wipe shot off dirty faces, and at the same time changing poopy diapers."

Betty should've been mad, but it made her smile instead. "Whose snotty kids are you talking about, yours?"

Bailey had a confused look on his face. The girl with the giggles didn't let him get away with anything. She put her hand over her mouth, and then she barked out a laugh.

"If you ever leave me barefoot and pregnant! I'll punch you in the face!"

Bailey raised an eyebrow deciding to talk of personal predicaments was too hot of an issue and not understanding a woman's heart kept him in the dark.

The two went back to trying their luck with the Q-Tanks limited movements with the manuals guidance. Suddenly, the boy of bashful beginnings thought of something cool. "We should take the Q-Tank out into the Atrium to get our feet wet."

Betty raised both eyebrows. "You're not thinking of driving this thing into the lagoon, are you?"

He blinked twice while trying to get her meaning. "Not go that far, just where I can lean on the gas pedal a bit, you know, to see what this baby can do." Bailey unbuckled his belt and reached for the hatch. He poked his head out from the top while sucking in air. He hadn't realized that they hadn't turned on any air flow from inside. He felt a little lightheaded. Betty felt the chilly air flow into the cab too, sensing they both were sucking in too much carbon dioxide. She reached down and turned on the air. He looked to get the good doctor's attention, and noticed Ryan and he were in deep conversation. Then DR. EL turned to notice the rising hatch.

"Excuse me Dr. EL! Could we take the Q-Tank outside in open space of the Atrium, I mean to open her up a bit?"

DR. EL folded his arms in front of him and placed a hand on his chin while thinking of the boy's proposal. He showed a slight flare with the wave of his hand knowing well this boy loved a good challenge. "Sure, if we can figure out how to open the next room above?"

Bailey hadn't even considered how to get the Q-Tank past the borders of level 1. It never occurred to him. "Drive it up onto the hydraulic lift. We'll find out how to get it out when we get to that point."

Bailey gave him a salute of understanding and dipped back down, closed the hatch, buckled-up, turned to Betty and said, "Hold on sweetheart, this might get a little bumpy."

Betty closed her eyes wondering what this lug-head was about to do. "Just do it already, before you run into something and mess up our new ride."

Bailey slipped the G1000 helmet back on, waited for the visual visor to pop back up before moving forward. He read the terrain pictured before him. Bailey slammed the little dozer into drive, flipped around and drove it up on the hydraulic lift. He put it in park, unbuckled himself, opened the hatch, and poked his head out.

"How's that Grandpa?" He rhetorically said. DR. EL still grinning with Ryan looking up at him.

"Just fine junior, hold on to your underpants, you don't want to lose them." He sarcastically said. DR. EL walked close to the end of the front wall after getting off the lift. He found a keypad for the roll-up door. He pushed a button that showed an up arrow as the door moved toward the ceiling. Bailey shot forward and almost got air-borne off the lift, squealing tires while burning rubber. Ryan closed his eyes, so did Betty who was buckled in screaming internally like she would kill him if they survived.

Bailey saw what looked like the truck by flashing images centered in his visual visor. He whipped around it in a perfect frenzied circumference. Betty opened her eyes when he stopped. "What's wrong sweetheart? You lost control and wet your pants?" She glared a punitive smirk and then bit her bottom lip.

"You're such a dork! Where'd you get your driver's license?"

Bailey ignored her, while considering the Q-Tank handled fine, "why the look of indignation princess?" Betty thought of punching him like Jackie did to Ryan but reconsidered. She narrowed her eyes and perched her lips.

"Don't make me hurt you." She said with that building urge to punch him again. Bailey tried to kiss her hand, but she flicked him on the nose with her finger. It actually hurt as his nose turned red. Bailey's eyes started to water. Betty put her hand to her mouth and held back a giggle. "Oh, I'm sorry. I didn't realize your nose was so close." A small touch of blood came out of Bailey's nose, and then it wasn't funny anymore. He reached up to stop the trickle. "Sorry. I wasn't thinking." She said.

Bailey was more embarrassed than hurt. He didn't say anything, but she saw the look of pain. He only unbuckled his belt and crawled out of the hatch. Betty felt terrible. She pulled her backpack up out of the hatch after getting free.

Ryan saw the spot of blood right away. Without thinking, Ryan said what he was thinking. "What happen she smack you?"

Bailey didn't say a word, but only looked at her with a fading acknowledgement. He lied to cover his embarrassment. "No. I was moving down when she was moving up. Her head bumped my nose. It was an accident." Betty didn't want to say what happened. She knew he was trying to make their situation easier. He figured it was his fault anyhow since he started this. Betty opened up the back of the truck to make a lunch of it. Then she reached in her backpack for the first-aid kit. Seen by DR. EL's expression he figured foul play but didn't respond. Bailey sat down against the back tire by the right side of the wheel-well. Not thinking of her little flicker of pain, but the tunnel left behind. He was thinking about that hole in the abyss where Betty's grandmother was caught in the tunnel with the left behind hearse. He noticed Betty had lowered the tailgate of the truck. This was her banqueting table for lunch. It was high off the ground, about three inches below her shoulder. From her backpack, she pulled out egg-salad-sandwiches, water, chocolate-chip cookies, and potato-chips, with six-oatmeal-granola-bars, three cold bottles of coke, left over peach-cobbler in Tupperware, napkins, paper-plates, plastic-forks, and the thermos of coffee. The coffee thermos made DR. EL smile. He knew she had thought of everything. She was well taught by a grandmother who always pushed her to be better. Betty had referred to her grandmother's prodding as Betty's boot camp for beguiles of her own personal blunders.

Dr. EL sat down next to Bailey as a father would, fatherly order making a statement. Bailey browsed up at him with a simpering stare. He was aged in his eyes in a physical stance, yet looked permanently damaged from what he could tell. He had the normal middle-aged spread, but not overly heavy, about 190 pounds, being six feet tall. Ryan took to the other side of Bailey. The small boy looked concerned about the couple of drops of blood that already started to dry on Bailey's top lip.

"Does it hurt?" Ryan said. Bailey only showed that pasty-white hesitation with a blank expression. Something in his eyes relayed a message for this to be a touchy subject. Ryan backed off, knowing closeness and friendships had their limits, secrets to keep at bay, and being composed for distances of respect. He was only seven, almost eight, yet a hard lesson to learn brought the memory of Jackie punching him for not using good judgment. He was criticized harshly, from a physical stance without knowing consequences of sharp words said, don't always go unpunished. He was learning the lesson of wisdom, *you know, that wise old man that shows up every once in a while, to point us in the right direction.* A lesson learned is a lesson earned—like badges of courage. Ryan leaned his head against Bailey's right shoulder as he took his first bite of sandwich.

From a quiet distance, Betty displayed a hurtful glare. Her face was flushed red. She was thinking of that love-hate relationship when mingled with that obdurate boy to always confuse her. She tried to keep her stare away from the three males, knowing their way of thinking was all too different than the average female. According to her, they were a team of consorters, and she viewed herself as the last man standing—or woman.

Dr. EL broke the ice. "So, how's the Q-Tank handle?"

"Good," Bailey returned. "I want to see how fast it goes, before we take it into the tunnel." This made the doctor's curiosity perk.

"Why so?"

Bailey looked at him. "I don't know. I feel a little strange about getting so far up the road without being close to the gates." Dr. EL wasn't sure what to think of Bailey's lack of confidence. He thought of the tunnel, but couldn't think of anything that would go wrong, not unless Bailey was holding something back.

The doctor left it for the boy to figure out. Betty, knowing Bailey's hesitation, and knowing she wasn't done reading the manual pulled it out of her backpack and started flipping through pages. Two curious men and a small boy looked up at her. She found what she was looking for and smiled.

"Maximum speed for the JR22 Q-Tank is 55miles per hour." Her eyes flickered from delight knowing she could offer Bailey a token of *I'm sorry for giving you a bloody nose.* He looked up and smiled. She sensed a jolt of competition flashed before his eyes. He would have to test this out. After lunch, they helped clean-up as Betty saw the boy of silent words head back to his task at hand, pushing the JR22 Q-Tank to its maximum speed. She sensed him not backing down. Ryan showed a flicker of hope.

"Bailey!" He yelled, "can I ride with you?" Betty thought this to be an enjoyable time to part ways and let Ryan have a chance of seeing the Q-Tank in action. Once buckled in they were off down the road.

Betty had a hurtful look on her face, and it showed when they took off in the distance. Dr. EL grimaced and sensed fatherly advice down the road might be fitting for the young couple. After ten minutes of surging forward and spinning in loops Bailey came back around and opened the hatch. He popped his head up out of the hole before letting Ryan out. After getting out, Ryan walked up to Betty and said.

"He wants you helping with navigation." Betty's eyes flickered toward the Q-Tank, knowing this was his way of saying he didn't hold anything against her. She slung her backpack over her shoulder and headed for the Q-Tank with a sparkle in her eyes. Ryan looked at Dr. EL like *what's got into her?* Bailey waited as she closed the hatch and Betty had just slipped into her seat. He reached over and tenderly kissed her stealing her breath away. Her heart started to pound. She pushed him away to catch her breath. A puzzling wonder crossed her mind as she looked at him. Who was this strange boy who stole her heart? Bailey turned his head back forward and buckled himself in. She did the same. He acted as if nothing at all had happened. Bailey played with the scoop shovel up and down, to get used to it. Betty covered her mouth to hold back a giggle. To her, he looked like a little boy playing with his favorite tractor. She could read his face like an open book. He pretended all his attention was absorbed by the job at hand. The Q-Tank was an electric all-terrain vehicle ready-as-Freddy to do some damage.

Two hours later, they decided to stop for the day. Bailey dropped Betty off at the warehouse opening, and then picked up Ryan before heading for the Zoo. He shot down the other side of a dirt road viewing the tunnels ahead. In the distance, the electric carts could be seen as blinking specks of red. Two little girls immersed in the darkness as George let them off the golf-cart to wait for their next ride. All Bailey could see from the visual visor was three moving images and the golf-cart engulfed in red. He pulled up short, unbuckled his belt, pried the hatch open and yelled. "Want a ride?"

Jackie surprised by the sudden outburst said, "Sure, where do we sit?" Bailey, from the very first time, noticing the Q-Tank from a distance, had two seats on the back with pull-out lap belts. He pointed to the back. Jackie moved her eyes in the direction he was looking. Bailey was suggesting they hop on.

"We sit on the back?" Jackie said. Mattie looked over.

Bailey only nodded, pulled free from the top to help the girls into their new seats. George waved good-bye at a distance. Ryan had the other helmet on noticed once the girls were buckled in, a small visual reminder popped up on the right outside corner of the screen, connected to some type of sensor. This was letting him know they had outside passengers aboard and needed to drive with caution, making sure the driver was aware, not to drive through a wall or go into water. Bailey reflected a quirky acknowledgement as he shot to the top of the Q-Tank, closed the hatch, and prepared for the bouncing jaunt back to the Atrium. He could hear the girls screaming as they bounced up and down in their sits as Bailey made the ride a bit off-roadish from the few curved contours as the Q-Tank caught air. Viewing the camera from the side, Ryan got a big smile on his face when Jackie's skirt lifted up over her face and showed her undies. He saw her fighting with the wind to make for adjustments, pulling at her skirt. He looked over at Bailey and said what he was thinking.

"She's wearing pink." Bailey held a flickering look at the boy for his unruly behavior. He winked as they pulled up next to Dr. EL and Betty, still flustered from his abrasive manners.

Bailey opened the hatch and got out. He released the two little girls from their bonds of brisk rides of bouncing about. Jackie's face was flushed, and Mattie's nose was flared from their fitful flight through the air. They were both breathing hard like they just got off a roller-coaster.

Jackie asked. "What is this thing?"

Betty showed a fading acceptance of comprehension, "It's called a Q-Tank. Bailey can tell you about it later, right now you two girls need to go up and take a shower. You both smell like poop." The girls both looked at each other and giggled.

"I'm pooped, and tired of scooping up poop." Jackie said. Both girls giggled. Ryan cringed at the thought. As the girls walked toward the elevators, Jackie continued her little recital of pleasures. "We're professional pooper scoopers, and I'm pooped." Mattie's eyes brightened, while holding her hand over a missing-toothed giggle. They were little girls in the bond of friendship. Betty looked at the two girls as the group headed to the fifth floor.

"Well, I'm glad you two enjoyed your day with the Zoo-Keeper." Betty stated.

"He was nice to us. Being a Zoo-Keeper is challenging work, but the animals are neat and fun to take care of." Jackie responded. "George has to monitor their health and fitness too. It can be detailed and tiring. I'm glad the day is over." Jackie looked up at Betty before continuing. "George said that normally it's not that hard, but because he got stuck in the monkey cage from the day before, he got behind on work duties." Then Jackie developed a little curved smile in her eyes. "I like the gorilla. His name is Tito. George said he was born in the jungles of Honduras. He has a mate named Mini." Jackie giggled from the thought. "But she's not so little. She's big and pregnant." Betty smiled at this added information. She knew Jackie was quickly getting attached to the animals.

Suddenly, the door opened, and the small band of misfits trudged toward the Penthouse door. Betty moved in close to the door, so it would catch her eye through the scanner. Two smelly little girls pushed through the front door leaving a trail behind. Ryan fanned at the air but kept quiet about smelly moments of scooping up animal dung. Betty turned around and stopped Bailey at the threshold.

"Can we stay in for the rest of tonight, and not have to fix dinner for everyone? I'm bushed." Betty showed a flicker of affection in her gaze. Bailey didn't really care one way or another. He was happy to stay with this dysfunctional group, as long as they weren't wallowing in muddy pig-poop he didn't care. Swatting at flies was his limit.

After baths and naps and little girls of pulling at hair, they sat around the coffee table in the living-room and played Monopole. The girls were giggly, and Ryan was giddy, while Betty smiled at a distance. She liked this place they had found dug deep in the mountains. A resting place, a place of comfort, a place to heal, but she liked it because she felt whole for the first time in her life. She felt love seeping through the cracks and walls of this warm and comforting apartment. She felt her heart about to explode like she found this was the place to be. This was her family now. This was a place she would always feel at home.

CHAPTER 17

The Cavern

The alarm sounded jolting him awake. Bailey laid there rubbing his eyes trying to draw focus. It was time to get up. He rolled out of bed and staggered toward the bathroom. He accidentally bumped into Ryan down the hall. "Are you okay?" The little chap inquired.

"I'm okay squirt, just trying to wake up. I think coffee will do the trick." Bailey walked into the bathroom to pee. He forgot to close the door as he began spilling splashes below. As undiluted pressure built up from behind, he farted, causing this unannounced incidence of potency to sound off a warning, like a ship at sea coming to port.

Betty walked by at the right moment and caught the whole scene in action. She scrunched her face in surprise. She couldn't help but say, "Nice, that's showing some class." She shook her head after passing him by. "I'm glad no one else saw you, my commander-in-chief doing your thing!"

Bailey, surprised by her quick sarcasm, comprehended he'd forgotten to close the door. This reminded Betty of a baboon from the bayou, pissing on a tree. Now he had something in common with Ryan. More than surprised by her quick-witted judgment Bailey responded.

"Sorry. I'm not myself this morning. I just woke up." Bailey hesitantly reached over from behind him to close the door. No light from above had left him in the dark. He sighed heavily, before reaching back behind him to turn the light switch on. When finished doing his little deed, he took a long hot shower to wake up. Then quickly got dressed and made his grand appearance. His condemnatory constituents were sitting quietly at the breakfast table. Still clouded by fog-like sleep, comatose conditions, unavailable intelligence. Bailey reached behind him to scratch his rear. Not thinking to be a picture worth a thousand words, he took a seat. Betty looked down and covered her eyes. *Oh my God.* She said to herself. *Forest Gump has a little brother.* They stared at him all wide eye catching his every move. Ryan wrinkled his forehead but smiled like all little boys had problems. Some were more visual than others. But then they were eating—weren't they?

Betty had a puzzled smirk doubting he could keep from doing anything more stupid than scratching his rear like one of those monkeys in 'George's Jungle.' She wondered if boy-wonder was off in la-la land trimming trees or hiding under some mental bush. Yet Bailey had no such intentions to mislead young hearts with impressionable egos. In innocence, his mind was a blur. *A couple of gulps of coffee would do the trick.* He thought. Ryan, with a peculiar devotion touched the awakened dead to get his attention. He shyly scratched his bottom lip. "Did you wash your hands or were you picking fruit?" Ryan got a tickle in his belly. The two little girls giggled. Bailey looked over at Betty like she had a new recruit helping her keep everybody in line. He causally rolled his eyes, shook his head, and said…"oh brother." Jackie and Mattie giggled.

Bailey reached up above Ryan's head and rubbed his fingers through his hair. Ryan pulled away, believing Bailey had unsanitary hands. Betty thought to keep her jaded heart of sarcasm crisp and well-tuned by infusing more attitudes across the table. "What's on the agenda commander-in-chief?"

Bailey looked up with an unsettling glare but ignored her; he comprehended her irritating smile to be over doing it. Then she looked at him with a little indignation. "Don't be so smug. I'm just playing with you. Is that not, okay?"

Bailey had enough of her verbal rough play. He wasn't awake yet and didn't appreciate her prodding. He finally pointed it out. "Okay, so I'm not the model of superior class. I'm just some country bumpkin that got lucky and found this hole underground with a mysterious road leading to here, but I didn't cause the end of the world, so lighten-up!"

Betty noticed his eyes were set afire. She knew further negation would start an all-out fight. Something she didn't want to do in front of the others. Betty backed off and rolled her eyes to the side and crossed her arms against her chest. To make up for her attitude she got up and set a warm plate of pancakes in front of him with his usual cup of coffee.

He looked up, offered a lop-sided grin, and said, "Thank you."

Ryan changed the subject. "Hey Bailey!" Ryan looked at Betty like taking his cue from her, "I mean, commander-in-chief. Can I ride with you today?" Ryan reflected an air of excitement mimicking someone a trifle bit older who drank all the coffee and was hyped-up on caffeine.

Bailey turned his glance in Betty's direction and knew she was still staring at him with a piercing glare. He felt her x-ray eyes were boring holes in the back of his head. Bailey got up quickly and slid his chair away from the table. He felt his face heating up.

"What!" he said, "I'm just sitting here!"

Betty moved her eyes away from him. Ryan sensed a fight brewing and decided to hold back any excitement. Everyone finished their breakfast and left the apartment to the elevator to attend their separate duties. The heat of the moment started to cool. He looked at her. She looked at him, and then turned away. The couple kept their distance for the time being. Betty reached down and kissed the little girls goodbye. She smiled while pushing hair back from Mattie's eyes. Then Bailey thought of an idea. "Want a ride to the tunnel?"

In the elevator, both little girls perked up. Jackie developed a smile. Mattie's eyes widened.

"You mean on the back of the Q-Tank?" Jackie asked.

He grinned at the two little girls with the impressionable minds. "Yes, if Betty doesn't mind." The girls looked up to see if her resentful mood had changed. A small crease of adherence in approval crossed her face. Jackie knew that meant yes. The two little girls looked at each other with smiling eyes. Within a few minutes, everyone was down in the storage area waiting for Dr. EL to roll up the door, like meals-on-wheels had hit the street; the children were rubbing their hands together in anticipation. Bailey unhooked the familiar JR-22 Q-Tank and looked past the door. He rolled the electrical cord up and put it away. The doctor would take Ryan with him in one of the dump-trucks. Betty would ride with Bailey in this newfound modified miniaturized bulldozer with no windows, and hopefully everything would be okay.

A sense of worry crossed the doctor's face. He glanced Bailey's way wondering if boy-wonder would have the stamina to endure through the day, within dark tunnels, eerie developments or sudden unplanned situations that might come up. He didn't know why he was worried, but the feeling of regret pressed him to be careful. Then Dr. EL broke the ice.

"Good morning young man, are you ready for a glorious day in the tunnel?"

Bailey returned. "I think so sir."

Dr. EL was trying to show an air of confidence, despite being in the mix of overconfident children without knowing what was to come. No government to give directions, no rule books to guide them by. They were on their own. No city lights exposing life from below. No sounds of excitement from people walking in the brightness of the sun warming their skin. There was no living hope or proof that anything would go back to normal. Only this small band of misfits was left in the wake. A wave of emotion flickered from Dr. EL's eyes. He looked at these innocent children like they were the crumbs of left-over cake surrounded by starvation, yet blind to any future results, expressions of trust in their eyes, fragile bodies, and minds. They were children, how would they cope? They were buried beneath tons of rock and earth with no one around to care. Dr. EL felt a continued stirring in the depths of him. Why none of this make sense? They were making a stand, but a stand to do what? They needed to prepare, yet the doctor sensed their efforts to be futile. Limited to people, limited on patience, what were they thinking? What kind of push for mankind could they make? They were too young to stand against the odds of survival. Who were they kidding?

Bailey looked over the top of the Q-Tank. "I'm ready. I'm dropping the girls off on the way. I promised them a ride to the tunnel." *Don't forget your promises made to children*, was his thought. *Earthquakes devastated cities; rouge-waves sweeping across skyscrapers, genocide and starvation killing thousands, no control left in the world, but just don't forget your promises. They held a purpose.*

Jackie and Mattie climbed on the back of the Q-Tank. Bailey made sure their safety belts were secure. He and Betty slid through the top of the hatch and buckled themselves in. Readied themselves for a jaunt through the darkness, an abyss of the unknown lay ahead. Bailey started her up. The Q-Tank responded as he began pushing and pulling on switches while Betty did an equipment check to make sure they were ready.

Dr. EL and Ryan pulled up next to them in a white shimmering brand-new dump-truck. It wasn't a vehicle considered as a bad ride, but it did have its own personal appeal as if to say, *I'm bad to the bone, and don't mess with me.* Dr. EL wasn't sure how he would do with shifting a six-speed transmission. He didn't have homed-to-trucker skills to awe the children with. He was a scientist of weather, not a lug-head scratching his hemorrhoids.

Dr. EL, being a smoker, had the dreadful vision of dropping a smoldering cigarette and burning himself. It caused him to smile as he pushed forward taking the lead.

Ryan placed a curious stare across the dash. "What's so funny?"

Dr. EL, still with the waning smirk responded, "Nothing…just thinking."

Ryan went back to staring out the window as the passing air hit his face. Bailey followed closely behind. From behind the Q-Tank, Jackie and Mattie had the wind whipping through their hair. The Q-Tank and dump-truck headed down the service road in the direction of the three tunnels in the distance, a three-quarter mile romp on dirt roads.

Bailey pulled up short in front of the middle tunnel, as George waited patiently on one of the golf-carts. He popped his head-up out of the Q-Tank and pulled himself free, releasing the two little girls from the back of the Q-Tank. He brushed back Mattie's curly hair, with a missing tooth and freckles, she was adorable. Jackie glanced at Bailey as a newly adopted brother. He walked over to George with a friendly gesture of kindness while holding a smile. He shook his hand in greeting.

"Hey George…we're off…so keep my girls safe will you…until we get back?"

George had a curious expression. "And when will that be?"

"I'm not sure, depends what we run into." Bailey replied.

George didn't like the sound of the unknown. He always liked a sure plan. Mattie and Jackie gave Bailey a hug, and they were off down the road into tunnel number two, as the sign of 'George's Jungle' on the back of the golf-cart faded in the dark. Bailey looked up at the monkey with the two hairy coconuts in his hands showing teeth and gums and shook his head. Something the government let happen, he smiled bearing in mind the government had really monkeyed up their chances of survival.

Once in the Q-Tank, Bailey had to try and readjust driving by the G1000's monitoring system. Clicking buttons, and flashing lights, he was totally surrounded. Betty was watching gadgets and time-to-time looked at the manual for future knowledge would help them when short on proper planning. She also noticed from snooping about; another compartment was placed behind their seats. The items she found showed effectiveness of purpose, items she could use in the near future. She found climbing gear in the back, which looked quite familiar. She found a flare-gun kit, and a long rope, with ascenders to help inch her way to who knows where. There was a small hand-pick for climbing rocks, several LED flashlights, specially made shoes, gloves that climbers used for inverted landscape. She acknowledged this gear was here for a reason, but all she could think of was why do we need these things?

Dr. EL took the far outside tunnel to the left as he was heavy on the gas pedal. Bailey had trouble trying to stay up with him. He was still trying to learn depth-perception without the aid of a front window. This was a bit difficult. He looked down and noticed the battery-pack showed a full charge. From the manual, Betty read the Q-tank was good for about eight hours of work before another charge was needed.

From ahead, Dr. EL glanced in his rear-view mirror seeing the couple lagging behind. This made him worry about the Q-tank in an emergency situation. The road was angled down and askew at first, but then rolling curves later like turns on a roller coaster. It was dark with diming light, yet Dr. EL internally felt chancy about what lay ahead. It was a half mile up over the next break in the road leading over another bridge, which featured a gorge below to the left. Bailey couldn't identify the bridge as seen by the doctor, and he couldn't see this gorge below either. His judgments were perceived as colors only from a three-dimensional perspective on the G1000. Judging distance and corners, it was all line-of-sight, and a stiffer-wrist for tighter corners. He knew if he turned to sharp, they would fall off the deep end of the road, plunging down into the gorge. The worst things thought of, would be sharp rocks, the bogeyman, and creatures of the black lagoon. Everything an imaginative boy could think of. Bailey gripped the steering wheel harder shuddering at the thought. It was time to keep his imagination in check. He had to blink several times to pull his attention back to the road. He followed Dr. EL over the first bridge, staying a steady speed of fifty miles-per-hour. Betty was consumed by the three-dimensional-screen, the colors, the lights, and watching the terrain up ahead, became so overwhelming.

Once over the bridge, there lay about three-hundred fifty feet before he could see distant lights flashing on a computer screen. Dr. EL got out of the dump-truck and walked over to a wall mounted keypad/scanner with the flashing green colors. He placed his right hand over the scanner and waited for the ten-inch-thick steel plated gate to open. Once open, Bailey whipped the Q-Tank around the big truck and went through the opening. Betty turned her eyes at him wondering why he took the lead, but then it dawned on her that he and she were the only ones familiar with the tunnel where her grandmother had died. Bailey stepped on the gas pedal until he cleared the massive bridge. Then he stopped short of the tunnel that they needed to go up and unbuckled his seatbelt. He reached up and opened the hatch of the Q-Tank as he anticipated for the good doctor to catch up. Dr. EL pulled up next to the Q-Tank and rolled his window down. Bailey could tell from the size of the dump-truck there was no way Dr. EL could flip the truck around inside the tunnel if they had to leave quickly for an apparent emergency situation. He was limited to backing the truck up, which was a good mile up the road.

So, Bailey came out and asked him. "You think you can back that truck up? You won't be able to turn around otherwise." Dr. EL looked up the darkened tunnel feeling an eerie presence might be waiting for them on the other end. He nodded quickly, then looked back at Bailey wondering what this boy was getting himself into. Once acknowledging his plan, Dr. EL flipped the truck around, as Bailey watched. Ryan glanced across the dash trying to figure out what was going on. Driving backwards didn't look like a good plan for them. Ryan raised an eyebrow with a curious stare. In front of him, Bailey shot forward into the unknown. The Q-Tank tore up the next tunnel. Within seconds, Bailey felt a cold chill go through him. Even though the cab of the Q-Tank was quite warm the chill was evident. Just the memory of the fire, the hearse exploding, Betty's grandmother dying—it all became surreal. Bailey had no visual aids to warn him of the roads end. Most of what he'd go by would be intuition. And maybe a few limited skills acquired from past experiences, yet he remained nervous. He wasn't an expert at video-gaming either. He was an amateur at best. He looked at Betty for moral support and sensed her somewhere else. Quickly, Bailey began to slow down when he noticed the colors on the screen turned black. They had only been driving for about five minutes when he felt like he was misreading the screen. This didn't make sense. What was he looking at? Bailey slipped the Q-Tank in park, unbuckled his belt, opened the hatch, and poked his head out of the top. They were sitting in complete darkness, and that tainted smell left behind had become a quick reminder of things gone wrong. It didn't feel right to be here. He recalled from four days earlier the lights blinking out behind when the hearse blew up. There was nothing left as a visual aid. He had to think. Then it came to him. He dropped below in the Q-Tank and looked at Betty.

"Can you turn on the head lamps?" She looked over to the left side of the panel looking for an indication of a round black button with a pictured white diagram of headlamps. She found it and pulled it on. Bailey saw the headlamps shoot forward into the darkness. The hearse that was there from before was gone. Only blackness lay before them and a short ledge on the left side jetting out from the tunnel's floor, about two feet wide of floor was all that was left. Everything else was gone. Forty feet of stretched out darkness dropped below, and a smoky stench rose above and hit Bailey's face. Its smell was so strong it gagged him, what he was breathing wasn't even considered breathable air. It was an intrusion on personal space, and Bailey wasn't buying it that everything was to be hunky-dory. What lay below was a well-hidden cavern hollowed out from underneath them. Something most alarming. Betty pulled free from the Q-Tank, and with an LED flashlight, lighting a pathway before her. Thinking of the climbing gear in the storage bin she had a plan. Being the good sport that she was she'd thought of everything. She'd brought her backpack with her, and the walkie-talkie attached to her belt. She was every man's dream where they had fallen short of being prepared. She was a Joan-of-Ark, a Princess Diana, and a First Lady in the second running. Bailey had a curious expression developing on his face. Two minutes later, Dr. EL had the dump truck backed up next to the Q-Tank. The small group of four got out of their vehicles and looked down into this blackened abyss that seemed bottomless. A weighing murkiness mirrored a smell of burnt metal and old fermented flesh. And what was that smell? A cold eerie dampness rose from below as the four peered into the dark wondering what was down there in this place for the dead. Betty had brought Grandpa's loaded gun and the knife hooked to her belt. She was a warrior, even though a soft spot had started to develop in her heart for that awkward boy who'd accompanied her. She looked at him for a brief moment—a flash of her shower break-down, the awkward kisses, the pounding of her heart.

Blinking, Betty came back to present day happenings. She went through her mental checklist of items. She had retrieved the climbing gear out of the Q-Tank in advance. She knew the hole below was waiting for discovery. Without conversation, she started hooking herself up for the drop by tying the rope around the Q-Tank's front frame and adhering loops and belts around her waist.

Bailey had a dumbfounded look on his face, "Where are you going?"

She acted like she was in charge and needed no approval from the boys surrounding her. Ryan leaned over the edge and almost lost his footing. Dr. EL pulled him back with the back of his jacket.

"Wow…" Ryan said, "It's dark down there."

"Watch-it little man. It's more than dark down there. It's a long fall." Bailey embellished. Betty double checked that she had all the materials she needed to make the descent. Flashlight, flare-gun, knife, climbing shoes, ascenders, rope, LED light, Grandpa's pistol, granola bars, water, oh yes, she thought, my abrasive attitude to scare away the bogeyman. She thought of Bailey, but then she knew he wasn't quite the type to scare her. This caused her to show a chaste flicker of emotion in her eyes. Everything would be okay in the end. But then she flinched, when Bailey put a hand on her shoulder and startled her. She had the jitters and didn't know why?

"So, you're just going to jump off this edge without knowing what's down there?" Bailey snapped.

Betty showed a dim sparkle in her eyes. "Lighten up dork. I'll be right back." Betty checked the tied rope to the front bumper with double grip slip knots and tested its durability by yanking on the rope. She checked her walkie-talkie by turning her switch on and off. She looked at Ryan who had the other walkie-talkie in hand. She smiled slightly when thinking little boys with toys sometimes came in handy. Nothing to read into, she'd been accused of having a sense of humor sometimes, as long as boys behaved themselves and kept their stupidity down to a minimum. "Keep it on squirt," she said, "just in case I develop a problem or two down there."

Bailey looked at her like she was weird. "Be careful going down there, it doesn't look like a stroll in the park." Betty took one last look with a flickering glare. Then she dropped off the edge. The two men slowly lowered her into the darkness. Bailey didn't like the fact that she was so bull-headed about doing things her own way, and she wasn't usually one to take advice. If anything went wrong, he would go down after her, was his thought. But then this was his first inclination of reasoning, and the fact that he was afraid of heights. Well, come to think of it, he was afraid of Betty too, and might have better luck with the bogeyman.

Ten minutes had gone by before Bailey saw a light turn on from below. He saw it flicker in a complete circle. Something wasn't right. The light had dipped high and low like in a panic. Bailey held up from lowering her farther. From what he could tell, she was close to the bottom, about ten or twenty feet away. She was already two-hundred and forty feet toward the bottom, and the air was worse than before, and that continued smell was so pungent. From the top side it looked pretty far. From Bailey's point of view, she looked as if in trouble. She was a lot braver than anyone else in their little group. Bailey began to take tabs on the remaining circle of rope piled behind him, two-thirds gone, and at the moment she had stopped her descent.

Below, Betty flashed her LED light and shined it in a complete circle. It slipped in her hands, as she nearly dropped it. She saw the remains of what used to be the hearse. All battered and burnt to a crisp, with a piece of bumper sticking up with shredded metal extending high. She could hear water running toward the bottom—empty space of darkness all-around. Light adaptation would begin to take over. Small flickers of light from above would start to make sense, revealing shadows and forms of whatever was down here.

Suddenly, this hole had begun to get really creepy. Something wasn't right about this place, a frozen chill of air swished by her back with a splash of water. There was something down here, but what? She was hesitant about continuing her descent and felt at the same time the rope tightened. She looked up and barely saw three shadows standing still. She didn't know if they were getting the same vibes she was getting, but she could tell by their stillness something was wrong. Betty grabbed for the rope unexpectedly while flaring her legs, when something else brushed by her from the front, startling her, making her lose her composure. She was about to scream out yet stopped herself. That could be a mistake if something were down here. She would become a sounding bullseye for anything of the dark. She had to use common sense. Betty closed her eyes and took a deep breath. She felt watched. Like she was stuck on sticky tape, similar to a fly for all to see, but her audience was hidden in the dark. She felt this was all consuming. Betty flicked her LED light back and forth, trying to make heads or tails of her situation. She swished the light behind her. Something was there, she could feel its presence, but she was so alarmed, she tensed. Betty felt a body of air move past her from the front and from behind at the same time, causing an elevated heartbeat and rising emotion to set her in a type of panic mode. She'd never felt fear like this ever before, this was too strange to feel normal. She felt alone, with no surefooted way to make amends for what she had done by coming down here in the dark. This was crazy. She didn't think wisely about coming down her at all. Now the fear filled her like a burning fire taking control of its surroundings, and she wasn't sure what she could do about it. She wanted to panic, but then she might lose her perspective of her surroundings and that wouldn't be good. By now, Betty sensed several unknown predators were captivated by her presence, like the hungry glare of hunting cats. She was on display like a tease toy. This feeling caused her to reach for the flare-gun. She loaded it and aimed the warning weapon at the ceiling angled away from the rope. The light from above projected the ground at an angle, with rocks along a riverbed bottom. Betty shot another flare, except in another direction. From this angle she saw four or five strange looking creatures clinging to the cavern's walls. Something she hadn't seen before. Something stranger looking than ever imagined from a frightened girl losing her way. The flare didn't last long enough to get a focused visual. These things were moving about so fast, they were like a blur. She began to panic and grabbed her walkie-talkie. While turning it on her hands began to shake. *How could I be so stupid climbing down in this hole without a clue?* She thought. Then the reality of the situation hit her right between the eyes. She was like a piece of beef-jerky hanging on a piece of string, waiting for these things to strip her off this rope. Betty kicked forward to try and get a better grip on the rope to climb back up; she felt an instant sting and blood started dripping from her calf. Something had just grazed her leg with a very sharp object, but what? Then she heard the squawk-box come on with a familiar little voice.

"Hello Betty, are you okay!" Ryan asked.

Betty noticed her walkie-talkie was at full volume. She reached to turn it down. She heard sounds coming at her from all around. She yelled into the microphone, "Pull me up!"

She didn't wait for the men to comprehend. She started to pull herself up, hand over hand. The pull on her back and neck caused her to tense.

Ryan didn't understand. "What'd you say?"

Betty had gotten only ten feet higher before barking orders. "I said pull me up! Now! There's something down here...hurry!"

Bailey looked over at Dr. EL and knew she was in trouble. He detached the other end while keeping it taunt, then hooked the rope to the wench on the dump-truck and started cranking the handle as fast as he could. Dr. EL went back to the truck and found a bigger LED light to shine down into the hole. Ryan could barely see Betty scurrying up the rope as fast as her arms could move. She had a muscular athletic body, fine-tuned, like a gymnast. The muscles in her neck bulged. She was red-faced, scared, and running out of time. She could feel more blood dripping off her leg. Whatever cut her went deep. A wave of nausea hit her throat. She held her breath in rapid gulps to keep from throwing up. She was in an unpleasant situation. She could feel a sense of death hovering over her.

Bailey kept cranking the wench until his arm ached. Dr. EL went over to help him to speed up the process. Ryan shined the light below. He could see Betty's face was pale and wet from perspiration. She had a look of panic in her eyes, but was still moving quickly toward the top, never stopping, never pausing to get her breath, a constant movement toward the light above. Ryan saw scurrying from below her. What was that, something big, something that could climb, because he saw it scurry up the wall?

"Hey Bailey, something's down here, and it doesn't look friendly!" Ryan screamed out.

Bailey ran over to the edge of the hole to help finish pulling Betty up by hand. She lunged for him. Bailey had grabbed her wrist. His shoulders tensed from feeling the weight of her. He started too slide forward and grabbed for the Q-Tanks bumper with his right hand. Being left-handed he had ninety percent of the small girl's frame. Ryan pulled on the back of Bailey's belt to keep him from slipping any further. Even the smallest of members could do their part. This was a rotten hole from forgotten days. Betty was spent beyond measure, breathing hard, she never lost her stride. She had a look of panic plastered on her face. Bailey saw the glare of panic in her eyes and wondered.

"We've got to go! I mean now!" She yelled. Betty unhooked the belts as the shovel fell from her backpack to the ground. She didn't wait to fill in the rest. She grabbed Ryan by the back of his jacket and air-lifted him up over the entrance of the open Q-Tank.

Ryan squealed out, "What's goin on! I'm not carry-on luggage!"

Bailey grabbed the shovel as it had popped open to its full extension. Suddenly, he saw something move toward the top of the gaping hole. It didn't look like anything he'd ever seen.

Betty grabbed her pistol and yelled at Bailey. "We've got to leave… now!"

He was so dumbfounded about the shovel he forgot to let go. Something belligerent behemoth bellowed a defiant cry as a creature leapt in his direction, with a flaring sound of rage while calling others, like a pack of wolves. He had hot smelly breath, jagged teeth dripping with a greenish drool, and blackened eyes bulging with fused fury—only inches in reach. This creature pressed Bailey hard against the Q-Tank. He was incredibly indomitable. Bailey didn't stand a chance going hand-to-hand with this monster. This creature had his own rules of survival, and it didn't include friendly handshakes or gestures of kindness. It meant to kill Bailey, as fast as it could. Bailey knew he was finished if he couldn't get past his fear. The shovel had trapped Bailey against the Q-Tank with the shovel end buried in the creature's belly and the handle end lodged up against Bailey's shoulder. He started to scream, but nothing came out. Only a squeak of air escaped him. Bailey felt like a deer cornered sensing eminent death as it crept from over this edge of defiant demise. Dr. EL had run to the dump-truck and locked himself in already shooting down the road. He didn't wait for the kids, and Bailey didn't blame him for taking off like a madman with his face lit on fire. Betty had reached up over the front of the Q-Tank and popped off two rounds from Grandpa's pistol toward the creatures head. The thing fell dead off to the side giving his victim only seconds. Bailey scrambled backwards and physically fell into the open hatch. He grabbed the hatch door and slammed it closed. He didn't wait to check and see if everyone was comfortable and strapped in. He started to hit buttons and switches then slung rocks and dirt as he tore a 180-degree angle back down the road toward home. Bailey barely got his helmet on and lit up the visual visor before bouncing off a side wall. Ryan was crying with a raging sound of terror squelched in the back of his throat. Bailey knew he needed both him and Betty to focus, because what had come out of that hole was in hot pursuit, and he wanted no part of it. He looked over at Betty's right leg and saw it was covered with blood. He turned his glance at the crying boy of over exposed senses. "Ryan," he said, "Listen to me, and listen well if you want to survive! I need your help!"

Ryan turned his head with blubbering lips and quivering hands. "What was that thing, Bailey?"

"I don't know Ryan, but I need your help," he repeated. He flicked his eyes quickly in Ryan's direction. "Betty needs your help too." He emphasized. "Two things little man. Do you hear me?" Bailey had raised his voice to make sure he had Ryan's attention, as he bounced the side of the Q-Tank off another sharp turn. The visual visor showed a mass of these creatures gaining ground about a half mile behind.

Ryan finally swallowed hard and choked down his tears, "What do you need?"

"Get your walkie-talkie and call Dr. EL and tell him…tell him I need to talk to him!" Bailey didn't want to mess with the walkie-talkie. He wanted to focus. Ryan didn't waste any more time. He turned on the walkie-talkie, waited for the static noise to come on to channel three, as they had discussed earlier. Ryan wiped tears away with the back of his hand—snot, sweat, tears, and urine, all the fluids of little boys in a heated panic. He had to draw the doctor's attention somehow. Ryan pushed the call button down.

"Calling Dr. EL over, calling Dr. EL over!" His small voice projected over the engine with emotion. Bailey kept the Q-Tank to maximum speed, with hundreds of these creatures filling up his visual-visor like an Ebola virus epidemic, preying on the weak. Red blinking lights of constant movement. The next corner, Bailey had the Q-Tank sliding sideways just missing the wall from the other side of the open cave separating two tunnels, as weighing darkness below them slid by. Betty flinched from being bumped about. Her leg was engulfed in blood, and the pain was almost unbearable. Her difficult climb up the rope and the cut to her leg had taken its toll.

The doctor's voice could be heard over the speaker. "Yes, I'm here. Those things are on our butt!" Dr. EL belted out.

Without a filter Bailey returned, "No shit Sherlock, tell me something I don't know!"

Dr. EL surprised figured the boy was coming into his own. Ryan controlled the walkie-talkie as Bailey spoke.

"We've got to beat them to the gate! Can you block them off?"

"Yeah…I think so!" Yelled the doctor, "I'll leave enough space for you to get through, so don't make any mistakes gringo your lives are at stake."

Bailey went back to being focused on what was up ahead. They were five-hundred feet from the large, massive bridge with steel arms and legs—a monstrosity stretched out across the gorge. Bailey turned the Q-tank sideways, twelve spinning tires digging in. Rubber met the road burning black smoke behind. They passed the bridge and headed up the next tunnel—screeching tires, smell of burnt rubber, they were homeward bound.

"Ryan!" He yelled, "Find something in the back to cover or wrap around Betty's leg!" Ryan was hanging over the console quickly flipped around and opened up the storage bin behind. At the bottom he found two white army towels. He grabbed one and handed it to Betty. She took the towel and started wrapping it around her leg to slow down the bleeding.

Bailey looked at Betty. He mimicked an expression of concern. She was pale and depleted and definitely overheated—just a young girl. "Are you okay?"

Sweat ran from her face with a clammy expression written in her eyes. "I'm okay, just a little shaken up from that smelly hole in the ground, it gave me the creeps."

"I'm sorry I let you go down there. What the hell were those things, Betty?"

"I don't know. I didn't stop to ask." Betty replied.

"That beast in front of me was extraordinarily strong. It didn't look human." Bailey reported with a flicker of fear showing in his face.

Betty looked at the speedometer. "Will this thing go any faster?" She asked.

"If it does, I don't know how." Bailey squeaked out.

Around the next corner, he saw on the screen the dump-truck up ahead, set up for some type of diversion. The doctor had turned the bad-to-the-bone truck sideways across the road. He had jogged past the entrance of the smaller gate and waited for Bailey to get past its borders. Bailey measured the distance mentally. He took the next curve drifting at the same speed toward his destination. The small area left between the wall and this diversion was a perfect fit. Bailey slid to a stop as Betty popped open the hatch and saw the good doctor standing in the distance, fifty feet from the dump-truck.

She yelled out, "What's up Doc?"

Dr. EL pointed to the road leading to the gas tank of the dump truck. "You think you can hit the tank from there?"

Betty smiled a snooty expression as her eyes lit up. She reached for the flare-gun, loaded it, aimed with two hands.

Bam!!! Fire, metal, and steel flew in all directions. Creatures were climbing up through flames blocked by the truck. The air was filled with screaming cries of rage. They were in a frenzied motion. Terror gripped the small band of dysfunctional members. Bailey screeched past the gate. Dr. EL hit the close button as the gate shut just before something slammed into its armored plated separation. Earthen dirt fell from above. DR. EL fell back on his butt, in shock as the creatures tried to gain entrance by slamming their bodies into the steel. The violence, the rage of the creatures left quite the impression. They were behind the gate of safety, overwhelmed, overrode emotions, listening to loud rumbles as the gate was swarmed. Dr. EL sucked in air as his heart felt like to explode. He said, "I'm too old for this chaos!" As he got up and headed for the Q-Tank. The rumbled noise of fury faded in the background. The sound of chaos was left behind the gate of safety. Bailey glanced at his visual-visor—no movement from behind. DR. EL pulled the weight of his body onto the Q-Tank and strapped himself in. He felt the adrenaline rush. The four surviving souls made their way back to the compound. Bailey saw the reminder that he had a rider from the top right-side corner of his screen. He lifted his view and took off up the next tunnel.

Betty looked over and saw his paling expression. "They don't make creatures like that." She said.

"Who are they?" Bailey asked.

"You know. The U.S. government, that's who, those government people that didn't make it." Betty continued her thought, "How could they make a creature so strong that could run like a cheetah?"

Bailey developed a confused stare. He continued to press the Q-Tank on the road to the compound, a place of safety, a place to regroup. There had to be an answer to what lay behind. He finally glanced over at Betty. "Why ask me?" Bailey resounded. "I'm just a stupid kid from California. I don't know anything about science. This was something created by some mastermind, not ordinaries like you and me."

Betty thought for a moment. "Those things weren't human. I don't know what they were, but we can't go back there. They're too dangerous for a hand full of kids to contend with." Betty's hands were shaking, and she began to feel the toll of shock and losing too much blood. Ryan reached down a pulled a bottle of water out for Betty to drink. She chugged it like she hadn't had water for several days. She grasped for air when done. Ryan looked at her with a concerned glare.

"Are you okay?"

Betty didn't answer him because she started to drift into another world of dizziness. She was done. She was spent to the point of no return as Ryan considered her ability to focus.

Bailey could tell by the look in her eyes she was close to passing out. He pulled the Q-Tank up next to the roll-up doors featuring the warehouse front. Dr. EL unbuckled himself and slid off the back of the Q-Tank. He had sweat, worry, and a defeated look on his face. He had a hint of despair in his eyes. The shock of survival from these creatures was a miracle to still be alive. Bailey helped Betty out of the Q-Tank and set her gently to the ground. Ryan got on the walkie-talkie to call George.

A few minutes later, George was rolling up the dirt road driving one of his modified golf carts. He saw Betty prostrated on the ground. Her right leg was a bloody mess. Bailey was set into an emergency mode.

"Where are the girls?" He asked.

George's face was masked with curiosity. "They're still cleaning cages and feeding some of the smaller animals. Don't worry. Jackie's caught on quite well."

Bailey reached down and picked up Betty and straddled her over one of the bench seats of the gulf-cart. George looked at the cut and knew it was deep. He could tell Betty was in a lot of pain.

"Let's get her into my medical lab. I'll fix her up there."

Betty's eyes were glazed over, then suddenly closed her eyes. Ryan stayed with Dr. EL. The couple took the short ride back to the zoo with George pushing the golf cart to her full speed. His had the pedal to the metal with a serious look in his eyes. He was focused on what he had to do. Bailey saw that Betty was out. Her eyes fluttered closed. He pushed back her hair from her face, wet, warm, a soft rhythm of breath coming from her chest. He was worried she wouldn't make it. A wave of emotion touched Bailey with a wistful expression in his stare. She remained quiet, clammy, still, lifeless. He choked back the sentiment as he touched her face. In all her misery she was still beautiful, petite, soft and surrendering, just a young girl. He felt the drawing of tenderness—a memory of soft and warm kisses and fast-moving glitches. She was a warm acceptance of his embrace. He rubbed his fingers across her arm, a slight prickling of hair. The breeze whipped around him, cooling his face and arms. Sweat ran down his back. A gentle emotion stirred in him. He didn't understand what he felt, but somehow, he knew he felt for her, even though she had a rough disposition. She was a part of this little arrangement of family and friends. This was their journey together—unsettling at times, but a worthy journey to take. Yet the journey wasn't based on how difficult this road could prove to be. It was a road that had to be taken. It was journey mapped out from long ago. It was a road that Bailey had to take. He would go back and make a stand. They were set on a course of a predestined way of life, in their loving innocence, in their unplanned bravery. It didn't matter, as long as they were together. Bailey set his jaw in a grimace of anger—thinking of those creatures invading their lives. He would think of a way and go back to kill them. He didn't know how. He didn't know when, but he would do it. He played back the last two hours of memory, flashing glitches of time, key sporadic flickers of chaos. What had happened to them? Bailey felt a sudden surge of naivety, like he'd been caught in a quagmire of misunderstanding, left in the dark. Something wasn't right about this place they had found. The government had caused its own personal genocide, but who was to blame? Who would take up the slack and make everything right? He sensed a decrepit feeling go through him. What did they get themselves into? The gulf-cart pulled up next to this small office building of a creamy grey color. This was the familiar makings of a veterinarian's hospital. This was George's sanctity for sick animals, from caring hands, a guiding light. 'Healthy animals were happy animals,' said the sign above the door. It made Bailey smile. Set back in a cozy corner of trees, a building for the fixing of broken bodies, or blundering bruises, medicine for mending. It was home for the hapless, for the weary wanderer from walloping wounds, survival of the fittest. This refurbished jungle styled home for those of the animal kingdom, put in the care of a man with a plan to heal, to comfort, through a touch of personal dedication and finesse.

Inside, Bailey laid Betty on a medical table that was padded gray leather like you would find in a dentist dental room. George started getting the tools of his trade out, scissors, antiseptic, small tweezers, and a syringe full of medicine to fight infection, gauze, with a clean white bandage to cover the wound. George washed his hands and then reached for a pair of thin-elastic gloves from a box placed neatly on the counter above him. He cut away some of Betty's pants from below the knee. He took a clean wet cloth and started debridement of the wound like a professional. Bailey seemed cheerful to have two doctors in the house, one for medical manipulation, and the other for the science side of sensibilities. George looked up at Bailey. "The wound's deep. I'll have to suture the cut, and then I'll wrap it nice and tight to keep germs out." George said, like he'd done this before.

After cleaning the cut really good he gave Betty a shot. She still lay unconscious. Bailey turned his head, not wanting to see the blood oozing out of the cut. He seemed a bit squeamish to George. George smiled, sensing Bailey to be somewhat of a lightweight when it came to seeing blood flow, *Bailey, a tough guy. ...Huh.* George thought. Then George pulled a trusty tool out of a drawer that looked like a staple gun.

Bailey winced. "Is that what I think it is?"

George smiled as Betty came to. She jerked awake with this sour look on her face. "What's happening to my leg?" Betty said, with a wince of pain.

"I've got to add a few staples my dear. It might hurt a little, but it's necessary so I can stop the bleeding."

Betty looked up, "oh well." She said. "Get on with it George. I've had a few scrapes before. Just tell me when."

"When," George said, and away he went.

"Ouch!" Betty yelled, "I said..." She began, and then was reminded he did say when.

Bailey closed one eye and hardened the other. "You okay princess?" He asked.

She had a dismal stare in her eyes. "Stop calling me that. I know that tone. You're making fun of me."

Bailey raised both eyebrows. "No, I'm not. I'm trying to be sweet."

Betty flinched from the next staple. "Well, don't do me any favors commander-in-chief."

A weighing smile grew on George's face. The he chuckled. "Sorry you two, it's just, you two sound like you're in love. Don't mind me."

Betty fluttered her eyes at the thought. "Huh?" she said, like she was hacking up a hairball. This made Bailey smile.

Then she said. "In love with him?" like there might be a crowd in the room of people.

George looked at her, thinking she was seeking further investigation of who was left in the room. George looked around then flushed a pinkish color not wanting to be the third wheel among the abrasive turning of the other two wheels in the room. A devious smile crossed Bailey's lips. He then let out a quiet high-pitched sound of a kitten. This made Betty smile, George too.

"I'm not being difficult," she said.

George inserted the last staples as Betty scrunched her face. Bailey shook his head, but only smiled at her brazened acknowledgment of pain. Sensing she was the pain and not so much the cut on her leg.

Bailey carried his new acquired, injured, sweetheart, to the elevator as she pushed number five. She saw the vein stick out in his neck and forehead. That caused her to feel heavy. She hoped he was straining. She weighed only 105 pounds. Not enough to jolt a big boy who would bend at her every disposal. The boy of bashful beginnings had an irritated look on his face, but he wouldn't drop her, not if he cared, was her thought, but then, would he? The elevator door opened on the ninth floor.

He could feel his heart weigh heavy about their situation, not thinking about her actual weight. A dreaded snowstorm, a buried place of refuge, a government's hidden secrets, creatures of the blackened night, injuries of pain, Betty not trusting, little girls on their own, too much to worry about. He needed help from something bigger than he was, bigger than his imagination, bigger than any confidence he could ever envision.

Bailey knew they weren't here by chance, but they needed a different angle, a sixth man in the game for a competitive edge. This life before them was fleeting. Options were almost obsolete. There had to be something left behind by the government, something unique, out of the ordinary that could give them a sense of hope.

CHAPTER 18

Military Crates

Bailey laid her down across the king-size bed. She seemed cold and clammy, soft, abrasive at times, but showing delicate features. He looked at the peacefulness of her face. George had given her two types of pills, one for pain, and the other for infection. Bailey's mind was focused on those creatures experienced. He was driven to find answers to those things left behind, answers for all of them. He leaned *in* and kissed her on the forehead. She had fallen asleep. He left her alone but would soon send Jackie back to be with her. He had to find a cure for those creatures left in the dark. What else was the military hiding in secret? What had they planned? He thought of the crates below and left for the warehouse with a competitive nature in his walk. This was what he was groomed for, giving his best, looking past adversity, past pain, past defeat.

A few minutes later, Bailey met Dr. EL in the warehouse below with all the crates holding secrets. The doctor handed Bailey a bottle of water. He chugged it without thinking. The drama of the day had taken its toll. Ryan showed a pasty white face of demure. Usually talking and moving about, he kept his words a bay. They walked to the center of the warehouse wondering what they could do. Dr. EL rolled a large toolbox from a primary mechanics garage, big, bulky, dark blue with a shimmery shiny metal top. Without saying a word, the doctor handed Bailey the largest hammer he had ever seen. This was his year for massive things and big moments, he felt ready. Dr. EL grabbed a crowbar. Ryan watched. On top of the toolbox lay another schematic. *What's up with the government and schematics?* Bailey thought, but then he smiled. They hide so much stuff they forget where they put it. So, schematics have their place in the mix of chaos. Bailey remembered getting mail from the government telling him to sign and return the forms sent back in the envelop they provide with the paperwork, but no envelope was provided, or asked to stand in the red line when there was only white and blue. He called that patriotic confusion. He remembered his uncle telling him once that most government people hired were hired by other government people with a position that didn't exist, for a position based on seniority, not how smart they were, but who was next of kin. Once, he remembered seeing a cartoon in the early morning edition, showing new hires for a governmental position, reading an eyechart while showing the answers in big letters on the left and right. When people off the street stepped in line for the same job, they were asked to wait in line 36, which was out the door in another building called The Last Line of Defense. Didn't take a genius to figure out something was wrong with their hiring procedures. This made him think. *They stole someone else's idea* Bailey thought. *They held someone at gun point or threatened to kill someone's family? Who knows?*

Dr. EL wheeled the toolbox where they could get to easily. Reading, as before, Dr. EL flipped through the schematic to find something of particular interest that forced his eyebrows to shoot up. This was it, the jackpot, the whole spill, the big Kaduna, the one that didn't get away. Dr. EL looked over the rim of his glasses. "Are you ready to search for answers?"

Bailey's forehead wrinkled. "Is there a choice?"

Dr. EL smiled in a form of comforting bliss. He pointed to the page he had his finger on.

Bailey looked back in surprise. "You're kidding me?" as if to not trust the government, black-suits and red ties, home of the brave and free—yes, as long as they knew your every step taken, who would you trust otherwise? Bailey said sarcastically, "I don't have to mail anything back, do I?"

Dr. EL smiled and shook his head. "It should be there." He said it like he would trust them for once, considering this might not even be their find—could be someone else with the brilliant mind with separate hands in the work, while as usual good old U.S. of A. taking credit. All kidding aside, Bailey read the schematic like it was scripture. It almost made him smile. He thought that this might be inspired like the word of God, adjusted to fit the occasion like the government adjusting the constitution to fit their situation. Then the scripture Romans 3:23 came to mind: *For all have sinned,* except the government who makes things work instead of—*and fall short of the glory of God...* The New King James Version. The other version inspired by government people that don't exist, and if it gets out of the room. I never said it. Then Bailey came back to the land of the living. The schematic was opened to page 265. The number by itself didn't stand out as anything significant, like a neon light hanging from the rafters but the picture in front of him did. It was a detailed description of a nine-foot tall, gold, and green Robot. A childhood fantasy, something seen in Hollywood, but not from the government, this had to be a joke. Sure enough, a picture, as the saying goes, was worth a thousand words, and not one word shy of that quota. Bailey was surprised. He responding as the man-child he was.

"It's a Robot?" This got Ryan's attention. He bobbed his head and looked up under sleepy eyes and the lack of information.

"Where...?" The boy of leisure said.

He got up off a wooden crate he was dosing on and looked in the doctor's direction. According to the schematic the robot was in crate 2743, row ninety-three, under space ninety. This was like a game for children. Ryan was in. Bailey looked at the numbers painted in red on the floor. Ryan ran over to the schematic to look at this said robot. He sucked in air.

"Dang!" He said with more emphasis than air. "Where is he?" Bailey ignored him because he was focused on finding this coherently illustrious imaginary form at any cost. He saw row after row of wooden crates, lost in the illusion of likeness. Bailey looked down at the number below him. He was in row eighty-six. He was close. This was strange, Robots, creatures from the black lagoon, what was next, robots with friends?

Bailey looked up. "This way," He said, as Ryan closed in on him, almost tripping his mentor of the last four days. "Dude…please…let me find him first, and then you can help." Ryan backed off with flickering eyes of coherence, thinking he'd stolen all of Grandma's cookies without being caught. Then Ryan developed an idea for buds arm-in-arm.

"Can we share him?" Bailey wrinkled his forehead. Dr. EL smiled. The search was on.

Bailey looked in front and saw an odd-looking crate of substantial size. This had to be it. It was bigger than life. He stood there staring at this strange looking box, one so peculiar was pulling his mind to its exact location. A wave of emotion chilled his back. The government was holding secrets in one of the many schematics of hidden treasures waiting for these boys of curious minds to find. Deep in this mountain, buried beneath cold and blinding snow, the answers to all their problems lay near. The number printed on the side was 2743. Bailey looked over his shoulder.

"What's that number again?"

Dr. EL leaned in the schematic's direction. He felt a wistful stare of wonder. "2743" he repeated. The crate was ten feet tall and six feet wide. Bailey took the hammer that Dr. EL had handed him and started banging on the sides. Splintering wood, echoing noise throughout the warehouse, Dr. EL came over to help, and so did Ryan. Ten minutes later, after banging, sweating, and digging deep for the prize, everyone stood back, shocked, dismayed, and fit-to-be-tied.

"Wow…" Bailey said, "It *is* a Robot!" Little Ryan speechless, he reached over and finished pulling out Styrofoam and packing tape, as the shimmering shine of metal reflected off golden light. He was so pretty, he was blinding.

Ryan turned back from this marvel of mayhem and asked the doctor. "Does he talk?"

"I don't know, but we need to learn how to power him up first." The good doctor responded. Dr. EL noticed a 'how to work' manual adhered to the side of the Robot's leg. This looked handy. He took the manual and opened it. Flipping through the index of operations the doctor read in silence. Two boys waited in anticipation. Dr. EL moved over and sat down on a smaller crate next to the open crate.

Ryan couldn't turn his eyes away from the shiny gold color. He had his mouth open with his tongue pushed to a corner, with wide-eyes and a blank stare. Turning back to look at the doctor he said, "What's his name?"

Dr. EL looked over the rim of his glasses with a slight grin, and then back at this odd little book of knowledge. He flipped to the front of the table of contents looking for a certain page. "Found on page three." The doctor said. "His name is T-DEXTER...made by a company called Trio Sonics Systems. He's from the TX3300 series of robotic programs."

"Cool!" Ryan shouted.

The doctor continued reading. "According to his specifications, he weighs nine hundred pounds. He can run up to forty miles per hour, and he has jets in the bottom of his feet."

Ryan got excited. "Dang...Dr. EL lets light him up!"

Dr. EL shook off the thought with smiling eyes. Then he continued quoting from the manual. "His body is made of heat-treated titanium steel that's able to withstand temperatures up to three thousand degrees. He's also waterproof."

Ryan had his mouth open sucking in drool. Bailey pulled back with flared nostrils, not wanting to get any little-boy-drool on his arms. Ryan ignored him.

The doctor read on. "He can sustain pressures up to sixty tons on his frame." The doctor stopped to look at the boys, who were both staring at this golden sparkle of light. They were held in some magic spell. Ryan grabbed at his wiener and adjusted his legs, little boys, and their lack of manners. Bailey looked at him with a raised eyes and growing wrinkled brow. They stared at the robot. T-DEXTER had emerald, green eyes, and fingers, and green in his chest's body armor, but nothing of significance looked out of place. He was like a brand-new penny just off the mint.

Ryan repeated, "Let's turn him on!"

Bailey put his hand on Ryan's chest to hold him back. He was acting like the ever-ready-bunny with new batteries, tap, tap, tapping' across the floor.

Dr. EL hinted a giddy expression and continued. "Hold on little man. There's a lot of information about the robot that we need to understand before we upload his system." Dr. EL looked down at the small boy with the pent-up anxiety then continued. "He has a voice activation system with multi-language choices. His vocal patterns are copies of famous people in history."

"Wow…" Ryan said, "Can I play with him when you guys figure him out?"

Dr. EL laughed and Bailey giggled. Ryan scrunched his nose in a show of confusion.

Dr. EL read on. "He has a pet dog according to the specifications in this manual." Dr. EL looked past the robot wondering if his sidekick would suddenly appear at his side.

Ryan yelled. "Pet dog? Where?"

"I'm not sure." The doctor got up and went back to the schematic. He flipped two pages ahead of page 265, "Bingo!" He said.

Ryan emphatically asked, "Where is he?"

Dr. EL looked back at the crate he was sitting on. "He's right here!" Pointing at the crate he was sitting on. "He's in crate 2744." The other crate was right next to T-DEXTER. If it would have been a snake he'd be bitten.

"Can we open the crate?" Ryan belted out. He sniffed while biting his lip.

"We can, but nothing gets turned on until we totally understand all about our newly acquired friends. Got it?" Dr. EL said.

Ryan shook his head like he was the most conforming child on the planet. Bailey wondered where all the energy had come from, when fifteen minutes ago he was falling asleep. "Okay," Ryan finally said back. "We'd get to know all about them first. I got it!" Ryan pulled up his pants and dragged the back of his hand across his nose, sucking something back in that should have been blown out. Bailey recoiled. Dr. EL pulled a handkerchief out of his back pocket and handed it to the small boy of nasty habits. Ryan blew really hard and wiped his nose really good, then tried to hand the discolored handkerchief back.

"No, you keep it." The doctor stated with a look of disgust.

The two boys and the science weather senior grabbed their hammers and turned to the next crate. Banging and splintering wood, sweating, and pulling at packing wrap, jiggling, and jarring loose pieces of Styrofoam and plastic, they had finally gotten it open. Wood and debris was everywhere. Ryan saw him first. He had pushed the rest of the Styrofoam and packing tape aside. A curious cringing glare flickered across the small boy's face.

"I wonder if the robot dog bites." Ryan said. "I don't like dogs that bite," He looked up at Bailey as his mentor of the last five days.

"I'm sure he won't bite us." Bailey said with an odd smile as he rubbed the top of Ryan's head. Ryan stared at the piece of work in front of him for a minute, considering the metal-mutts angle. He had deep blue eyes, black and silver colors throughout, pointy ears like a Scottish-Terrier. He wasn't that scary looking like a mini-Godzilla-fire-breathing-dragon, or pit-bull barking snarls of drippy fangs, while pushing persistence of dominance. He was a cold storage critter reflecting silvery stiffness. He was comparable to a mummified mannequin you'd see in a display window showing off the latest fashions of doggy-world collars or perfect wintery weather sweaters. Yes, he was stoically big for a seven-year-old to picture, but scary, no. He didn't look too much of a threat, the over imaginative boy thought. Ryan finally glanced up at Bailey with an inquisitive stare.

"Does he have a name?"

"Well, let's see what his manual says about him." Bailey said. He flipped back a few pages from where he was. "Oh yes, his name is SNARF." Bailey barked out. He had found the same type of manual adhered to the side of the metal mutt's side.

Ryan crinkled his forehead. "What kind of name is that? That's a dumb name." He doesn't sound like a tough dog." Ryan insisted.

"Yes, it's kind of dumb, but one you'll never forget." Bailey said.

Ryan had to think about it for a second. "Well, I guess you're right. I've never heard that name given to a dog before, and he's different. He's got his own special look. So, what's his name mean?"

Bailey read on. "Well squirt, it stands for **S**ystematic, **N**ucleus **A**ir **R**etrieving **F**ield-Unit."

179

Ryan raised an eyebrow. "What the heck does that mean?"

Bailey showed a growing annoyance, trying to accommodate the boy's many questions. "Well, it means nobody better mess with you, or you'll sick your robot dog on them." Both men laughed.

Ryan didn't see the humor. He continued with the questions. "What does T-DEXTER's name mean?"

Dr. EL flipped back a few pages to answer this one last question of quarry. The boy with rude habits was wearing them out. "Let's see..." The doctor said. "His name means...oh yes...**T**urbo **D**ensity **E**minent **E**xpunging **T**ransport **E**nhancement **R**obot."

"Wow! That's a mouthful," the overexcited lad said. "Can he fly?"

Bailey's face grimaced. "Hey little man, we've had enough with the questions. We need to read more about the two. Why don't you go upstairs and help the girls make dinner, since Betty has to stay off her feet. I'm sure they're tired from working all day. Everybody's got to do their part."

Ryan achieved a big frown. "Why me, I always have to help out with the chores."

Bailey was losing his patience. "Look, just do it. I'm not going to argue about it. We're short on people. Everyone needs to do their part, so lighten up. We're a team."

Ryan got a flicker of hope in his eyes. "Will he be my dog if we train him together?" Ryan asked.

"I think he's T-DEXTER's dog, but you can help take care of him. Just make sure you don't mess-up." Ryan finally turned around, and skipped toward the elevator, assuming he made out like a bandit at his favorite bank making a huge withdrawal.

Both men went back to digging through the manuals to learn everything they could about their two newest members. Bailey stopped to reminisce. Thinking aloud he said, "I've never had a robot as a friend." He insisted, as if finding it funny. "I guess there's a first time for everything sir." They looked at each other. The men of discovery continued their readings. The robots had so many talents and capabilities that the two men were intrigued for quite some time. They were entertained on an intellectual level. Their interest pushed time to move on. The night grew late without much notice. Yet they moved on not comprehending some hidden secret, something not said. Their findings were fresh territory of discovery, this would change their circumstance, give them a unique angle of hope. Their studies would give them a chance to have an altered experience. Robots with friends, who would have thought. According to his manual, SNARF weighed two hundred pounds. He had razor sharp teeth and could run up to ninety miles per hour. It was like watching old re-runs of the Keystone-Cops in super-fast mode—a blur, an enhanced vision, a pathway onto stardom. Bailey could imagine their bright colors of gold and green blue, black and silver. They were a pretty pictorial— close to being set in motion, close to becoming stars. This caused Bailey to think of the Star-Wars movie when it first hit the big screen. Chewbacca could play the part of one of George's gorillas, Princess Leia Organa, playing Betty, R2-D2 the quirky droid playing the metal-mutt, and C-3PO with his brassy logical silly personality that played as T-DEXTER, if he were willing. Except T-DEXTER, having many talents and fighting skills. The famous Jedi-Knight Obi-Wan Kenobi playing Dr. EL, Luke Skywalker taking Bailey's role. He didn't have a spot available for Han solo yet, but maybe in time—Bailey's imagination was running wild. They were set to clash intelligences and wit with Darth Vader and his evil Clone-fighters set in that hell-world below them, that malevolent abyss.

Coming back to reality, he read there was a voice box sound control implant in SNARF's sound modulator. This was buried in the metal-mutt's neck. This information would pop up on a video screen with three-dimensional graphic cards enhancement and task performance from hologram imaging when lit up—making green colors stand out like phosphorescent light. From reading on, he noticed through several screens later, the video hologram enhanced different schematics of representation. He had detailed diagrams of the robot's configurations. He was a complicated, emancipated, rejuvenated, piece of work. The metal-mutt was a video Drone without a home. He was a two-eye, four-legged, butt breathing dragon. He had highly sophisticated gadgetry. He was a chutzpah character enhanced with flare. There was a video camera seen through or envisioned by both robots. They had the vision of super-computers, superior eyesight greater than a hawk. They took readings of thermal-Nuclear devices. They also detected any signs of danger from intruders, or getting too close to danger zones, pitfalls, or changes in the environment. They had a visual visage of an unmannered clout. They stood up to anything that capered about. They could be raucously flamboyant in fits of approval, screaming ululations of intimidations, reacting and removal of all condemnations. They could even smell invading dangerous substances or changes in the air's chemical composition. They both would record everything around. A similar screen reflected where Bailey could change the robots personality. He didn't want to mess with perfection. Dr. EL read that T-Dexter had computer jack inserts placed in his back with a platelet covering from a hidden entrance. This was something he'd have to check out. Furthermore, behind the hidden plate was a keypad for typing in directions or installations for disk-drive software for modifications of memory—a gyro-sized type of insertion. According to the manual, T-DEXTER had pre-programmed computer chips installed into his hard-drive to modify memory for advanced personality adjustments. Dr. EL smiled, wondering if the robot might have the capabilities of PMS, Post Mandatory Stiffness from sitting too long in cold storage. T-DEXTER was programmed with his own personality, unique as in famous, quirky as in odd, but fun loving. General directions of control could be command-voice-activated by pre-programming voice description with audio-enhanced-voice-pads located in the back of his neck. T-DEXTER was a complicated and expensive piece of work. His main programmed function was to find and eliminate alien hostiles. *Something didn't sound right about that.* The doctor discerned.

He displayed an air of surprise, "This is something that's *never* come crossed my desk—alien hostiles?"

"Maybe the government already knew of our cadaverous creatures found by Betty." Bailey replied. "You think maybe the government kept this a secret for a good reason?"

Dr. EL rubbed the bottom of his chin in deep thought. "I think they kept this and other things in the warehouse a secret for many reasons, but the most important that of a foreign and domestic influence." Then the doctor read the next few paragraphs with raised curiosity.

"Young man, T-DEXTER is commanded and controlled by the first voice that he hears. His owner wanted a quick response in the making. There's more to him that meets the eye?" Dr. EL read on.

"Punching in the letters of his name into the keypad would light him up. T-DEXTER has a superpower mode only used when totally surrounded by enemy hostiles." Dr. EL looked up over the rim of his glasses with a lit cigarette. "The manual suggests not voicing a command when the robots are in this mode unless there's no alternative without depleting their total energy source. Both robots power-sources are a high-energy magnetic-arch of light held together in a diamond-faced-octagon, surrounded by a reflective interface of honed-magnetic-energy." They were like Buzz-Light-Year or Bolt animated from cartoons to real life. The doctor knew nothing of the robot's power sources. This was unfamiliar territory of understanding. He was left in the dark. He read on in silence. Two beams of light traveling in a circular motion, at a speed not comprehended, was what the diagram showed on page 279. The doctor thought, someone was up late most nights burning the midnight oil. They were complicated inventions. Their telepathic inclinations were ones that involved quantum-physics, magnetic-fusion, and a whole lot of an extraordinary imagination. They were new to a world turned upside down. They were slick talkers and fast walkers by the evidence seen, yet nothing compared to their robotic functions. Someone really smart had created these two robots, too smart to still be alive. He read the last paragraph and paraphrased its meaning. "Both robots have fusion reactors placed in the center of their chests." He whispered. Dr. EL well thought-out the information and so did Bailey. This was most alarming. "I would let little Ryan know that neither of these robots are toys to be played with. They are highly dangerous, sophisticated, expensive pieces of work, and who knows what they are capable of doing beyond the realms of this compound?"

Bailey wondered what was next on the rise. What epic beginnings could they be faced with around the next corner? His mind couldn't comprehend the caliber of what was to happen in the next few days. What past things would come to life as the days moved forward? He was still too young to understand all of the dynamics of this new world ahead of them. These new creatures that were in it were not of the norm. Everything in this strange place, built by the government, was still a mystery slowly unfolding before them, something extraordinary was beyond anything ever imagined.

It was way past midnight as both men began to grow weary. The dawn of a new day was shortly upon them. "We need to get some rest sir." Bailey said.

Dr. EL shook his head. "Not yet. First, we need to upload our newly acquired friends. I don't feel safe without having some type of backup in the compound." Bailey understood the doctor's way of thinking. "If those creatures get past our guard—we're done." Dr. EL stated. They both looked at each other knowing what they had to do. Dr. EL read the key loading plates on either Robot could be manipulated or opened by key-codes entered into their keypads. This was handy. A super-hero, a pre-Iron-Man robotics design, a concept not thought of by any previous masterminds. In this age of discovery, they were of a scientific invention with serious intentions. Bailey pushed the rest of the crate pieces away from the robots so they could move about both units freely. He retrieved a ladder from a side storage room just to the right of the office. Dr. EL slid the ladder behind T-DEXTER for better handling and reaching. After climbing the latter, he pressed the letters of T-DEXTER's name into the keypad. Quickly, Dr. EL got down off the ladder, and slid it to the side. He then moved to the front of the robot and waited. With T-DEXTER standing over nine feet tall, his wide shoulder's sparkled with golden light. The boys of discovery had to look up from a safe distance. The key-code plates automatically closed up behind. The robot had an effective way of construction. He was a big bad man with good intentions. Body armor with shielding titanium plates jetted across his body high and low. He was set for battle. He was intimidating in size and stance. He was to be reckoned with in a military fashion. Bailey jerked back in surprise. Dr. EL put his hand across Bailey's chest to help him step aside to give the robot room, like a guiding father would do. T-DEXTER lit-up like a pinball machine plugged into a high-voltage circuit breaker. He stood at attention. A voice came from his mouth that sounded all too familiar. Bailey recalled the voice of Steven-Tyler who sang as lead vocalist in the Aerosmith rock-band. Not that he was this man of fame but held a voice of repetitive likeness. This caught him off guard. Dr. EL saw T-DEXTER's eyes draw focus like two microscopes taking pictures of some distant planet. Infused life became a part of him. Movement and coherence forced the robot to comply. This reproduction of the famed voice said, "What's up man!" The precarious familiarity, "What can I do for you or what can you do for me?" A chuckle of laughter came next. The robot seemed to take on the personality of the famed person he would imitate. Dr. EL wondered about giving this outlandish looking robot direction—since he insisted.

"We have enemy hostiles outside this compound. Your duties," he said, while looking at the Robot dog, "with your trusty sidekick will be to protect those left inside." The doctor then explained what had happened to earth in detail to fill him in—the super-storm, and the government being left behind in the wake. What would they do next? T-DEXTER knew more than the doctor had figured from sitting in cold storage. Dr. EL didn't gather he would know more than they assumed as being pertinent information embedded in memory. Whoever had built him didn't make known everything about him. Some things were kept secret until now. Someone else had learned the government's old tricks of misrepresentation. T-DEXTER saluted the doctor in a mock military persuasion. He had a replicated voice of Steven Tyler down to a hilt. Dr. EL gave the robot detailed schematics of the compound, the tunnels, the hotel, and zoo. Then T-DEXTER responded to their situation.

"Man, oh man that's a doozey! We'll keep you in line big bro of the jungle juke box…I'm your man yea, yea!"

The doctor looked at T-DEXTER wondering if he was half crazy. He was confused about his programming. Something had gone wrong inside of the robots memories or his circuitry. He wondered what the boy-wonder thought of their new toys in a man's size type of way. He looked at Bailey and said. "He appears to take on the personality he reflects. We can change his character."

"Change him?" Bailey said, "I think it's bad-boy-funny. This takes away from his hard-core demeanor, adds to the bad-to-the-bone capabilities, and lightens him up a bit. Don't you think?"

"You have a point there. This does add a little flare to the personality."

"He's different than anything else we've seen yet, he's better than a kick in the pants." Bailey blurted out. T-DEXTER looked down at his sidekick. With exclamation point he said,

"Tewalawalabebanchew…" The robot dog, SNARF began to light up and move about. He wagged his tail while barking twice. Except that his bark sounded like a roaring lion.

"Holy Toledo…" Bailey embellished, "He scared me!"

Dr. EL flared his eyes at T-DEXTER. "How'd you do that?"

The robot showed an idiosyncratic air of acknowledgement. "I take the load off you man! My little sidekick is voice activated. He's in tune with my voice. He's a baaadddd dude. The dirt-digger has some moves that are just too cool." T-DEXTER raved. SNARF blew a flame out his backside. "Watch the back burner. It will heat up your drawers and singe your attitude." T-DEXTER embellished, like he found humor from his sidekick blowing flames out his backside. "Okay, big boss, where do we lay our tracks?"

Dr. EL expelled serious intent. "Guard and keep safe our little family within the compound. They are asleep for the night up in the hotel room. Don't disturb the animals down in tunnel two at the zoo. George, our zookeeper, and animals need to be left alone."

T-DEXTER laughed with a chuckle. "I'm not a space-case big boss. I know the difference between zoo animals and alien hostiles. I'm the big bad dude with a big bad gun, you tangle with me. I breaka your face."

"Okay T-DEXTER, I get the message." Dr. EL was well informed with a curious flicker set in his eyes.

T-DEXTER pushed a button on his wrist. "My sensors detect seven humans within the compound, and two hundred and three animals at the zoo. There's also over 2300 enemy hostiles left behind in the cave below us. Whewwwwee! Those are nasty smelling critters. I might have to wear nose plugs to vamoose their carcasses."

Bailey looked up at the strange looking robot and made introductions. "Hello tall and handsome fellow. My name is Bailey. It's nice to meet you." Bailey held out his hand as in a friendly gesture of camaraderie.

Like Steven Tyler in his true form to character. "Out of sight… It's nice to meet you too little brother." The big robot put his hand out for Bailey to slap in a high-five—a suggestion of sealing the deal of friendship. Bailey responded to accommodate by slapping the gold and green Robot's palm but had to do a jump slap to accommodate.

"Ouch!" Bailey yelled.

"Sorry about that little brother. Yes, I forgot you're a little soft around the edges." The two looked at each other astonished.

"Well, anyhow," Bailey said. "We're headed off to bed. Watch our backs. We'll see you in the morning." T-DEXTER did a little jig of groovin' with a skip and rhythmic dip causing the two men to feel a tad nervous about T-DEXTER's frame of mind or programed circuitry.

"Right on, right on little brother. I've got you covered." T-DEXTER raved,

"See you on the flip side, and we'll do another day." The big Robot held up a piece sign as if departed President Richard Nixon was in the house, submitting this goofy loyalty pasted on his face, like Bailey was truly his little brother and he would defend him and the others at all cost. T-DEXTER sighed transparently with a huff of imaginary air, as if breathing, and his stance of remembrance was both political and intriguing. He stood there stoically, like a refugee in memory, as in days gone by, another day done on this mounded millennium, or another cross to bear was tolled across some make-believe line. They had submitted to other battles of conformity that young Bailey had missed. Anything was possible. Nothing had been planned or set in stone. The metal-head warrior was lost from their point of view yet shaking his head in retreat the robot pressed on. He wanted to make sure there weren't any loose cannons or loose ends running about in the compound. This was a territory for the living not for those misinformed of who was in charge. He was a Politian in the making, a goofy soul of conformity, lacking rules and religion. Yet he was at his best. He was a clown of clarity, a mongrel of many missions, but he was himself—tall and glittery like a shiny brass new golden coin. He stood out prepared to do battle or sing a song with silly tunes all night long. His own unique character inlaid to a key, clarity of wisdom, he housed a mass of information in his hard-drive, confident as a Canary, and he was ready as Freddy. T-DEXTER took the stance corresponding that he was in charge now, if all else failed *now* he would take full responsibility and have a full report of duties first thing in the morning. Bailey looked at him with a hesitant salute. "Wow…a robot, with friends. Who would have thought?" Both men left the robots behind and headed up to bed. It was now past two in the morning. A long day of close calls, near misses, casual losses, a day this small band of misfits would never forget.

CHAPTER 19

First Fight

Betty woke early that morning. She was stiff and slow to move about. Her right leg felt engulfed with burning flames of fire. The pain had overwhelmed her. The cut's protruding appendage of wrap felt similar to a tight vice of pressing inflammation. Her face was a bed of wrinkles and worry. She reached to the side of the king-size bed for a crutch. She was unsteady at first. Slipping on her good leg then catching her fall. The bathroom was only twenty-five feet to the right. The flicker of not-so-distant memories flashed before her. Her hands were shaking, and she'd pondered her heavy weight of wonder and doubt. These were not normal memories for a young girl with an impressionable mind. They were memories that could tear her world apart if dwelt upon. She was alone, secluded and deluded in her way of thinking. And where'd everybody run off too? The suite appeared as an abnormal place for the blind and weary. She was left in the dark. She felt disoriented as she blinked and tried to draw focus, forgetting where she was.

From the other side of the large apartment, she could hear a slowly increasing vibration. Along with that, came a quiet thrumming of footsteps from a distance. She cautiously comprehended the quiet closing of a door. A hush of air blew past her. She knew it was him. Mentally, she viewed him as a rhetorical, plutonic awkward talker with a tacit stare. He wasn't a rebel rouser, a peeping-tom, or a bad-boy-do-gooder of shady deeds. He was just a boy with brave intentions through unannounced innocence. He expounded a presence no one else had. He was a tad-off in stride, when it came to saying the right thing, but he never ran away from a challenge. He was a gentle moving spirit, had calm clarity, his imagination was full of potential. His mind, his athleticism, and his youth, all played a part. He was the man of the hour, the super-boy of salvation. In the past he showed himself to be trustworthy. Betty wanted to grin, yet her pain stopped her. He had a certain rhythm to his every step. A shadowy silhouette had cast against the wall as he approached her. Her heart skipped a beat. She had made it into the bathroom, rinsed her mouth and ran her fingers through her hair. Dual points of delusion crossed her face. She felt and looked awful. She wasn't ready to see him. To her, he was a man of many secrets, a man of mystery. She didn't totally trust him yet. She didn't want his company at the moment either as most girls don't want to be seen by guys in that position, of uncooperative stares and insecurities. She wanted to be alone. She didn't know why she felt irritated, but she did. And he was the only one around to vent on. He was setting himself up for the fall. There was no one else to connect with at the moment, except that lanky boy headed toward her. Her problem was not to be with him in the near future, it was to be with him right now. Not with the way she felt, not like this. She wanted him to leave.

Bailey crossed the threshold of the door. She had just finished in the bathroom as she stood on one leg and reached with one crutch under her arm. The last five days of her life were unbelievable. Nothing had made any sense to her at the moment, too much mystery had happened. Strange feelings had taken over, creatures below trying to kill her, now injured, confused. She wasn't ready to change her whole life overnight, not today, not since her grandmother was gone. She began to modify her way of thinking in an assertive emergency mode that an awkward boy in front of her would never understand. And with changes come frictions. And then to top it off, she was stuck in this giant cave, with three degenerate children, and a drunkard has-been-scientist. Plus, this weird chubby little man named George stringing along a bunch of monkeys and guerrillas, trying to conform to this new world of undiscovered secrets. They were all just hanging on to the end of this long rope trying not to lose their grip, as she'd done from the day before. They were like small cats on a piece of string, ready to fall and be swallowed up by all their problems. She had no knowledge of the outside world just yet. What was happening out there? What would happen to them? Where else would they go to find safety or other people? And who would come and rescue them from their miseries of solitude? Of all people, Bailey stood before her like the old Forrest-Gump. She could imagine him giving advice to the children with that stupid slogan, 'stupid-is-as-stupid-does.' And then at that moment she looked up and saw that stupid grin. She wanted to cringe from his presence, but she couldn't because she could tell his face showed good intention. He was like a lost little boy with a backwards grin. She didn't even want to be here herself, yet she was. She had to face him, and their bleak situation. He wasn't going away by what she could tell. And Betty felt dirty and soiled and lacking a bath. She never had time to even change her clothes. She still had sweat and blood and something dripping from the corner of her mouth. What was that, drool? Her reflection even frightened her. She left the lights off so he couldn't clearly see her. When he reached for the light, she stopped him. "No, don't, I like the dark." She said, confusing him the more. This boy was delusional to even come here without some type of warning. He should've stayed where he was. Why couldn't he just understand and give her some personal space? She was in her worst of form, after going through so many bad situations that day. She had bad breath, bags under her eyes, bad intentions, and itchy underwear. She could imagine him getting a whiff of her tainted smells of misery—him regurgitating and running for cover, like a skunk crossing his path. This caused her to tense.

With no lights in the room, there appeared to be dark shadows crossing his face. He was silent but willing—young, naïve, and presented his stature as green around the collar. An expression her grandmother made. He was a dork in her book, awkward, senseless at times with a quirky sense of humor. Yet somehow, she knew she could count on him in all her dreadful hours. He had integrity. He didn't need much, just her company and those with their stubborn stares. That look was on his face again. He looked like a strange little boy who'd just got paid with a pocket full of nickels. She could imagine her Grandma giving advice on how to handle such a boy. She wanted to be pleasant but held back. He was lost according to her, and she didn't know what to say.

Watching his frame pass through the dim light, she suddenly broke the silence,

"My leg hurts pretty bad. I forgot to take the medications George gave me." She said it like she was filling in moments of too much silence. Bailey remembered seeing the pills left on the kitchen counter and turned to get them. He returned with a glass of water and two pills. She sat on the edge of the bed as he handed them over. She expressed a look of painful indignation. Bailey waited in silence knowing she was not up to giddy conversations, being in her condition. She looked irritated. He was sorry for something he had no control over, her piqued attitudes, and painful grimaces kept him from sharing. Then finally, he broke the icy conditions in his meek words of submission.

"I'm sorry that I let you down into that cavern." He tried to make eye contact with her, trying to fill in grim moments of perception. Betty turned her head to avoid his stare. She didn't want to face him in her circumstances, besides, her head hurt, her heart hurt, and her leg was beyond hurt. She was vulnerable, like a vixen of unsolvable solutions.

Left in the darkness of the room, Bailey continued. "I had no idea those things were down there." Betty didn't answer. She was glaring at the floor as if confused about something. She then looked up and gave an irritated answer.

"If I didn't go, you wouldn't be here right now. We'd be dead." She said,

"You don't have any climbing experience. You wouldn't have been able to pull yourself up as quickly as I was able to do. I'm lighter than you, besides," She said frustratingly, "Those things were fast." Betty rubbed the top of her left shoulder. She'd pulled a muscle without knowing how.

He watched her with curious eyes. "You, okay?" He asked.

She had just swallowed the pills while chugging the whole glass of water. She gasped when done. Then she narrowed her eyes as sweat beaded on her forehead.

"Do I look okay?" She said with flaring eyes. Bailey lowered his stare, comparable to a conforming puppy that'd been spanked for missing the paper.

"I didn't mean…" He started saying before looking up. "I know you're hurt. I mean are you *okay*, okay?"

She didn't answer again. He sensed something brewing. Betty knew he wouldn't understand her heart, because she didn't even understand herself, like a freight train going full speed set afire. She was comparable to a bright burning blaze of lights flaring at both ends, like candles leaving wax all over the floor, to scorch him with. He was just a crazy boy with a crush. He'd be over her soon, and off to better things. She knew she had an abusive behavior that would soon *get* to him, forcing him to make decisions that didn't include her or these degenerate kids missing parents. He would move on. He'd figure *way* beforehand that all of them were too much drama for a nineteen-year-old man-child to take under his wings. By her look, Bailey felt her flaming sarcasm rising steadily. She was in pain, and he was the scapegoat of her delusional nightmare. He looked at her like she was a loaded gun. If he didn't learn to duck and cover, he would be her victim of circumstance, and she was familiar with both barrels, smoking aces without a thought of consequences.

Bailey wasn't sure how to break the news about what was found below. Those metal mechanical wonders were viewed as back-up, was his train of thought, but how to express it without giving too much away was another deed he'd thought impossible. He noticed how battered and beat-up she appeared, but that wasn't his concern of the moment. His concern was her frame of mind. She didn't look like her normal self. She looked unwilling.

Betty's eyes crossed his glance. She'd looked as if wondering about this boy of melancholy moments, and less blissful beginnings. She was like a pissed-off pit-bull ready to fight. No rhythm or reason of calm clarity or thought-out cohesion. She was a venting vixen blocking his momentous abreaction of light. Their trains were on different tracks. At first, she had no intentions of ruining his day, but with each passing moment things got stranger.

"I need to sleep a little more before going downstairs." She briefly said, as she tried her unsettling hint of reason. They weren't on the same page of understanding. His mind was racing with answers of antidotes, and she was focused on her conditions. Somehow, they couldn't match up a successful way of thinking. Bailey answered with a disconnected thought of perception.

"The doctor and I were up pretty late last night. We all need to sleep a little more," not to feel concerned about her condition, yet not purposely. This caused her eyebrows to flare with untimely perceptions. Bailey continued his thought.

"We found something most peculiar. The government has left us some pretty strange artifacts left in cold storage. The most concerning of things held in secret. Well, I mean we'd wanted to share them with you, but I'm a little lost if you're up to it, or you're not." To her, he sounded like a rambling little boy about to be scolded for doing something bad, while hiding his intentions by telling a lie. Yet he didn't, even though she assumed he was hiding something of particular interest. And she was sure he wasn't quite ready to tell her. A vein was sticking out in Betty's forehead. A heated face, with wrong intentions started to show. Bailey knew.

"What are you mumbling about? Nothing what you just said makes any sense!" Betty continued, "Don't talk around in circles with me. If you're going to say something, spit it out!" She yelled. "Make some sort of sense with your words before you come barreling up here like you've got something important to say!"

Bailey was appalled. He dropped his words that he was about to say and lost his train of thought. He looked as if she'd slapped him. "Okay, I'm sorry, I know things have been difficult, yet we've all been through quite a lot." He said, including everyone as a unit. Betty took over. At the moment, she wasn't feeling the same vibes of wanting to do her part. She wanted to get up and hit him with her crutch.

"Well, since you seem to have all the answers, what's next hot shot?" Bailey stammered for words yet found none. He was stumbling and stultified by her daring submissions of understanding, even though she had none. She was acting on pure rage of the moment, without considering his heart.

"I'm trying to tell you." He said.

Betty used every word coming out of his mouth against him. "There you go, talking in circles again." She said, "Come to think of it, Ryan was saying something about having a robot dog you said he could play with. What nonsense were you feeding my nephew? Don't be giving him hope for something he can never have, he's too vulnerable right now."

Bailey's face flushed red. He didn't know what to do, so he said. "I hope you have fun getting through this without me—I'm done."

Betty was so surprised by the sudden proclamation she'd pulled back from saying anything else. He had stumped her with this vow of silence. Bailey stopped long enough to gather a few things and left the room. Betty heard the door in the front of the apartment close behind, leaving her in the silence of her own miseries.

He walked the hall with a blank look on his face as he entered the elevator to head for another floor. Quiet, unbecoming, he couldn't figure her out. And furthermore, he wasn't putting up with her unrealistic attitude anymore. Then he'd remembered she was hurt. He wondered if he did the right thing by leaving, yet at the moment, he was too heated-up to care. Bailey stopped the elevator on the seventh floor. This wasn't too much different than the ninth, except not as luxurious, and the doors were smaller from the outside of the rooms. And the paint and the decorations weren't so God-awful rich looking. There was dark green carpet with a light color of buttery paint with a light olive color of crown moldings all down the hall. Sconces hung in brassy thick golden fixtures on both sides of the wall. They were spread out about ten feet apart every other one, setting off a diffused mix of a mannerly glow. From a distance, Bailey noticed a door slightly open from the other end of the hallway. A vaguely graceful light sprung out drawing his attention. He left a backpack of clothes in front of room 704, and then made his way down to the open door with the catchy reflection of light. Once there, Bailey pushed the door all the way open. In front, hanging on glistening golden circled hooks were keys to each room. Something was strange about keys hanging on hooks, and no one around. Someone had left in the middle of doing their job. A bell or siren went off, he figured, and they couldn't stay to finish whatever they were doing. He grabbed the key to the room opposite his backpack. The number 704 stood out in the gleaming light. Turning his view back toward the closet, he noticed a wheelchair leaning against the wall. Not too big, folded inwardly not taking up too much space, silver in color, polished and clean. It was just what he needed, and excuse for going back to the penthouse. Bailey glared at this welcome discovery. A wheelchair could be a wonderful thing, when used in the right manner—a life saver, it could relieve one of a most particular predicament, a helpful instrument of handiness. Thinking of his unsettling situation with Betty, he knew directly that the heated mess he had left behind reminded him of Betty's condition. He frowned and felt the guilt of leaving her stranded and knew for the best of reasons he had to go back. There was no other choice. Bailey put the key in his pocket, grabbed for the handles of the wheelchair hesitantly and wheeled it to the front of room 704. He stopped. He reached down and picked up his backpack, unlocked the door, slid his backpack inside the door. Closed the door and left for the elevator wheeling the wheelchair weightlessly forward. His thought was he'd only stay long enough to drop off the wheelchair, and let her consider her words of harm, while he'd snooze off some of his problems as she tried to take care of herself without his assistance. This was payback. But then Bailey wasn't usually the type to take revenge on helpless little girls with attitudes. After calming down, he waited by the elevator for twenty minutes before entering. He wanted enough time to go by before confronting her again just in case she was still full of spiteful spasms of spontaneity, so easily ignited by a flickering flame. Face it. She was nitroglycerin concisely, a bomb of bombardment, a harassment of heresy. She was a pain in the butt. He didn't really know what to do, but he knew she needed the wheelchair, so he swallowed his pride and wallowed back-up to the ninth floor. When the elevator had opened, in the distance, he could see her struggling past the door. Betty was one crutching it through the open door, when she heard the noise of the elevator opening. It startled her. She dropped her crutch. She then lost her balance and fell to the floor, crossing the threshold of the door. Bailey saw her in the distance and the guilt hit him. He moved quickly down the hall and helped her into the wheelchair. He noticed she'd been crying. Small stains of liquefied bereavement marked her with two lines of trailing tendrils on a dirty face. She still looked a mess, but he wouldn't mention it.

She wiped at the tears while staring at the floor. Bailey felt stupid for getting mad, and he could tell it had really bothered her when he'd left. Betty was the first to speak.

"I'm sorry," she said.

Bailey smiled slightly from a quivering grin but was still confused. He said softly, as if teasing, "You're what?"

Betty heard the tone and knew he was trying to get her to repeat what she knew he heard.

She smiled with sad eyes and heavy heart. "I said I'm sorry. It's really not your fault."

Bailey looked into her big-brown eyes and said, "I didn't mean to make you cry. You just get so wound up you don't let me talk."

"I know." She said. Then she noticed he'd not returned with the backpack. She looked up, as he looked down. He made the connection and reached down and kissed her. Soft lips, warm bodies, her heart started to pound. He finally pulled back from her showing a hesitant stare. He wasn't sure if she'd try to kick him with her better leg. She suddenly realized he'd kissed her without considering her conditions. She covered her mouth and blew her own breath back toward her face. This made her cry. *Oh no*, she thought. *He kissed me and I smell like Godzilla rampaging in the hills of Tokyo.* She hid her embarrassment from his view as he'd wheeled her inside past the door.

Quickly, he turned around and said, "I'll be right back." He left her with the door open. Bailey was gone about ten minutes before he returned. He crossed the entrance of the door and finished pushing her in and closed the door from behind. While he was gone, she'd been staring in space, sitting there thinking about all the strange things that had happened to the lot of them. All the circumstances that had happened the last six days couldn't be just by pure luck of the draw. They were down here for a reason that they'd all soon find out—but what? She looked up at him with a hint of embarrassment.

"Can you come back later? I need to clean-up."

CHAPTER 20

T-DEXTER

Twelve o'clock...

"Hey, what's goin on?" Ryan was banging on the door of the primary-suite. He yelled through the door, trying to penetrate the impediment of silence.

"You need to come down and check-out T-DEXTER and his dog SNARF! They're way to cool!" He said it like he was an over-heated puppy. Ryan continued his barrage of brisk abetment of a little boy's playtime. "Hello...Houston...the captains calling and wants your help!" This caused Betty to open one eye. *What was Ryan talking about? They found others.* In her awkward condition, Betty slid out of bed, in dark red shorts that hugged her tightly and a pink Aero-Smith t-shirt she'd put on from the day before. She was tired of sleeping and wanted to see what the boys were up to. *Here,* at her door, was another eccentric boy trying to move *in* on her own personal space—those two ill-mannered boys and their flamboyant toys and their repartee attitudes. What was next? She might have to start carrying a big stick and start smoking cigarettes. With a bad-boy attitude like in a western movie—but a girl, of course, small in stature but big on making an impression. She opened the door with a wrinkled, sleepy, aplomb expression plastered on her face. Her hair was sticking out in all directions, sleepy-crumbs, swollen eyes, and Godzilla breath. Ryan pulled back with widened eyes.

"Dude…" He said, "What happened to you?" He finished with an overanxious attitude. Then the non-filtered boy finished, "You'd better clean up. You might scare are new friends." Betty slammed the door. Ryan yelled through the door. "Where's Bailey? I haven't seen him since yesterday!"

Betty yelled back at the door with a raspy voice. "He's staying in room 704, two floors down."

Ryan's face lit up. "Okay…I'll go wake him up. We've got things to do!" He said with a high-pitched squeak in his voice. She heard the pitter-patter of small feet running away. The two little girls were already gone to the zoo to help George. Betty thought of ringing Bailey's room, but she only stared at the phone on the nightstand. She knew Ryan would roll him out of bed eventually, besides, she'd done enough damage from the day before. She stood on one leg and reached for a crutch.

The elevator door opened, and Ryan ran down the hall. He couldn't wait to wake up Bailey. He saw the number 704 and tried the handle first. The door was unlocked. Like all little boys who enjoy searching and discovery with curious minds. He wondered why Bailey took refuge in his own personal suite. He had an expression of curiosity when he tiptoed across the room bent over the bed real quietly and blew into Bailey's ear. The sleepy-head Sasquatch took a swing at the air like trying to swat a fly. Ryan pulled back and held his breath. He covered his mouth from leaking giggles. This was fun. He liked this game of cantankerous teasing as most little boys like causing chaos and pulling bigger boys off balance. This was his chance. Ryan reached down and stuck a wet finger in Bailey's ear. This caused him to shoot straight up. Ryan started laughing, then said, "How'd you like that wet Willy?"

Bailey not being in a playful mood said, "How'd you like me to shave your head and make you walk backwards?" This statement confused Ryan. He didn't understand the older boy's motives. He considered it for about two seconds and then moved on.

"Whatever dude…We've got work to do. The robots are waiting."

Ryan paused for a minute allowing Bailey to focus. "Why are you sleeping down here anyway?" Not understanding the heart of courtship of little girls and abrasive attitudes. Bailey slid across grasping sheets in his boxershorts. He had to play two roles all at the same time, being a pretend big brother, and a mentor of mental-metal-marvels.

He finally answered him. "Betty and I thought it best. We're not an official item yet." The boy of unruly behavior didn't understand. He wanted to be Bailey's best friend of the hour, but this girl thing was strange. He grabbed for his hand to help him up. Little brother helping big brother, it was a game of trust. Bailey played along not to damage his delicate ego of not adhering to playful moments of misunderstanding hearts. Then from a distance, of only a few feet away, he watched Bailey's every move, like he was watching Saturday morning cartoons. The Road-Runner, Porky-Pig and that funny little bald man called Elmer Fudd. Not thinking of danger or the creatures left behind. He was in a playful mood with a curious mind. His only concern was being that little boy that he was. Bailey opened one eye and dragged his right hand through his unbalanced hair then yawned.

Ryan looked at him with a distorted view. "Looks like you and Betty crawled out from under the same rock." Bailey batted his eyes, knowing Ryan was aiming for negative attention, but he wasn't biting. He smiled knowing Ryan was only trying to bond with his uncooperative movements and misguided judging stares.

"So, what's goin on compadre? Where's the fire?"

Ryan confused about what a compadre meant, and he hadn't heard anything about a fire. "No fire," he said, "We're meeting downstairs is all. Want to see the robots?" Bailey knew Ryan was trying to be friendly past what an adult male wanted to endure but held back. He put his hand up as in a high-five. Ryan slapped his hand to accommodate.

"Okay, I'll let them know you're coming down." He said and darted out the door.

Speedily, Bailey remembered the forgotten girl in room 903. He began to worry about leaving Betty unattended. He hadn't checked up on her all night. Tired, disconnected, and so much energy was expended the last two days, needing to reboot from the lack of energy. After taking a shower and getting ready for a new day. He dialed her room, but no one answered. She wasn't close enough to pick up the phone. He let go of the thought and started to get dressed. A few minutes had gone by. Something was wrong. He could feel it. Something he felt internally made him think of her on a bigger scale of consideration. It wouldn't hurt to quickly visit on her, besides, she was hurt and couldn't get around to good on one leg. He was just being a good citizen and doing a good did, and anyhow, there was no one else around to care. So, it was settled, he'd take a brief look. *She* if she were still around, still breathin in air, still kickin, as long as she didn't kick him in the teeth, everything would be okay.

Once at the door, Bailey considered knocking but knew this to be more of an inconvenience. He could imagine her pushing herself across the floor in an unbalanced procession. Therefore, without further ado, he let himself in. The boy of bashful-beginnings crossed the room of both the kitchen and the dining-room. The master-suite lay ahead down the hall. It was on the right side a good forty feet with obfuscated shadows lining the walls. The door was hinged open three or four inches. A small amount of light crossed her face from a skylight. The ceiling was dormered to fit the acquired projected construction of the room. The Artificial bleeding of light angled from the top of the ceiling like it was inundated from one place of mystery. Only a circle of light came from the top as the rest of the room was opaque with shadows. Betty was still crashed-out on the king-size bed. Lying on her back, with her hurt leg uncovered. Her right arm draped across her stomach with her shoulders leaning towards the outside of the bed. Her left leg bent in and her right rested on one of the many pillows. Her hair was pushed back strung across the left side of her face leaning on one of many pillows. Pink pillows fluffed and trounced in dimming shadows all around the bed. Pillow heaven was his thought. A large hope-chest of dark engravings lay at the foot of the bed. The room was filled with intricate rhythms of Betty's breathing, up and down. He judged the room by its conditions of luxury for a few seconds. He looked at the angled shadows crossing the room, he looked at the dresser and the vanity mirror, then noticed the glass door closet of clothes which were bought and placed by someone else. They enjoyed the riches of others, after leaving everything else in their lives behind. Bailey sensed the emptiness of starting over. Quietly looking back at Betty, a deference of emotion welled up in him. She was peaceful, beautiful, soft delicate whispers of air moving in and out. Drawing focus, Bailey noticed the wrapped wound on her leg showed no signs of changes of extrication. Everything was in order. She was dressed, and cleaned up, a modern miracle of mad marvels. He thought. She got up earlier and then became conscious of her situation, comprehending not to be as strong as she first had thought, lying back down, to gain her strength to be placed in a better mood. She had fallen asleep. That was his best guess, yet something was divergent, not normal, a tad off. Still focused on details, noticing she had brushed her hair, and was wearing a clean pair of jeans that showed her figure, petite, gentle curves of feminine proportions of perfection. She had rolled up her right pant leg from where her calf was carefully wrapped up to the knee. She had on a tanned-collared-short-sleeve-shirt showing her fading tanned pigment of conditions. He noticed a delicate golden necklace around her neck of a small, reproduced Fairy *that,* wore dancing shoes with a flicker of pink in her wings. This made Bailey smile. Betty had freckles and hair showing the frizziest, and he could imagine in all his dizziness when she was close in his arms. He'd visualize a locked warm embrace, but then she wasn't conscious. Her face was peaceful, gently molded, she was dreaming about something. For the oddest of reasons, by which he did not know, exuded from him was this bazaar attraction. He kept staring, and by even a stranger adherence he knew they were a perfect match, even understanding together they were the opposite of the spectrum. They were comparable to Bonnie and Clyde, or Tom and Jerry, Lewis and Martin, the Mummy and Cinderella, except she looked like Cinderella but played the part of the Mummy. When he got closer to her his heart started pounding. This made him think about coffee, but he hadn't had any that morning. It was her. She was causing this strange stirring of fascination, but he didn't like it. It made him wonder if he was okay. He reached up and felt his own heart—tap, tap, tapping in rhythm of a bad dream. But was it? He saw the beaded sweat on her face and knew something was wrong. He leaned closer to see if she was breathing. He couldn't feel any breath but noticed her chest moving up and down in soft whispers. This made him smile in a bleak sort of way, but then he thought of her devious ability to be able to catch him so quickly off guard. He dropped his grin and pulled away. Not wanting to be considered misaligned in his way of thinking. He went back to concentrating on her medical conditions and not so much the force of her chest moving up and down. She would defiantly consider him an altered-ego-infidel if caught looking at her, so with that relinquished plan of entertainment, he drew focus on her physical conditions only. Bailey reached down to touch her forehead. She was burning up. He thought of getting her into a cold-water bath, but then no. Like the comical expression, 'yeah no you're right.' which is it, yes or no? He would really be considered an ill-mannered idiot by the lot of them if caught. What can I do? He thought. Then he ran from the room...

Bailey proceeded down the hall, back to the elevators, got in and pushed number five. This was taking *way* too much time, from his point of view. He had to hurry. Once the elevator had opened to the fifth floor, Bailey took off at a full sprint across the warehouse floor. This wasn't fun. The faster he ran the scarier he thought of Betty's condition. What if one of those creatures scratched her? Would she get sick? Would she die? Then he certainly started to panic as he made it out into the hallway overlooking the atrium floor. From above, looking down, he could see the robots doing some daredevil stunts. Seeing an over apprehensive little boy below and a doctor-dare-to-do-little lost in leisure entertainment. They were viewing the new metal marvels of a mechanically sophisticated world displaying non-emotional movements of quickly quirky antidotes of overanxious friends. The doctor was giving directions of cohesion for their two new additions to their little family. He was trying to keep both robots in tune for future endeavors. Dr. EL stared at the manual in his hand, looking for further inductions of intelligence. *He* experimented with what he considered tricks of the trade, similar to dogs of denial being led astray. He had SNARF spinning in circles and chasing a ball. Bailey looked down and grimaced. What the heck, he thought. They were military marvels, not a circus show. Bailey yelled with all his might. "T-DEXTER, come here quick!" Bailey wasn't sure if he'd been heard or not, so he yelled the more. "Hey...anybody...I need help!" Being a metal-mutt with well-tuned ears, SNARF looked up and barked. Well, not a bark, but similar to a lion roaring his loquacious benevolence towards the sky.

T-DEXTER turned his head upward. "Looks like Bailey's in quite a fix!" Bailey, looking down and noticed the unreserved robot. He was pointing to the fifth floor above. T-DEXTER saw movement of shadows at a distance and zoomed in. From a closer picture of focused intent, he saw the stretch of worry crossing Bailey's face. T-DEXTER looked down and pushed on his video screen placed on his wrist. He was taking thermal readings and looking to find anything that seemed a little odd for those in the compound of safety. T-DEXTER popped his head up quickly then said. "Hey cooled dudes…little brother needs some help." He looked back at his scanner sensing something else. "Oh no…" T-DEXTER exclaimed. "My bio-scanner detects a nasty infection in the little lady upstairs. "Eweeh, that's a nasty cut. I hope that's not the scratch of one of those creatures. She needs a stronger medication." T-DEXTER said. Dr. EL glanced at the gold and green robot with extended arms.

"George will know what to do. He's the one with medical mentality, with extraordinary flare." T-DEXTER didn't wait. He took off in the direction of the zoo. He shot across the atrium in a sudden zoom. He zoomed and jetted, zipped, and soared, a blue-burning streak of light. In a blaze of glory, in a push of persistence, he was determined to meet the demands of the boy. Bailey took the elevator to the ground floor, met by a sudden streak of light. T-DEXTER was already back. In the circle of friends, he floated two feet off the ground, blue flames shooting all around. The atrium was set in a blaze of light; persistent heating from T-DEXTER's cheating. SNARF wagged his tail in delight. George, in the grasp of T-DEXTER's hands, looked petrified. A miserably poor reason for the lack of treason, he had no recollection of flight. George almost left this world on short notice by the pounding of his heart. T-DEXTER had squeezed George so long. He let out a long undiluted surging hot trumpet of air. Ryan caught the end of it and fanned at his face. Then he giggled and the two men laughed, but George didn't see the humor in respiratory conditions and pounding of his heart. Ryan looked up at George curious about what just happened. "Dude…did you just mess yourself?" George was embarrassed, but stared at T-DEXTER like he was abducted by an alien.

Bailey tried to explain the intrusion of privacy. "Sorry George. It's an emergency. Betty's sick and T-DEXTER acted on instinct."

Ryan said without thinking. "Yeah…his end stinks alright."

Bailey ignored Ryan and explained to George. "We found him buried in the warehouse."

George insisted. "Well, put him back. He scared the…well simply scared me senseless…"

Ryan took it. "You can change over there. There's a bathroom in the corner."

George looked down at the boy, and said, "What?" The two men were still laughing.

T-DEXTER looked at George acting on Ryan's cue of misunderstanding. "You smell like broccoli and eggs gone bad."

Ryan looked up in discuss, crinkling his nose with a twitching awareness. "Dude please—go away!"

Then to make it worse T-DEXTER grabbed George again and raced him up to the third floor. He said without hesitation. "Go into the medical lab, third door down the hall. Betty needs an I.V. bag for fluids. She's dehydrated, and full of a nasty infection. We're not sure what it is yet."

George looked at the big, bold, gold, and green robot. "Don't do that again. I almost died from heart failure!"

T-DEXTER confused explained from his limited skills of understanding. "Well don't go just yet. We need your assistance if you wouldn't mind. The young lady needs your attention."

George looked at the robot wondering if he was missing a few cubes of clarity. "I got the message." George spouted out of necessity. "Now put me down and move aside!" George said with a flaring temperament, "I've got work to do!"

T-DEXTER left without a moment's notice returned back to the atriums floor.

Ryan still fanning at the air said, "Who eats broccoli and eggs on the same day?" He looked up at Dr. EL. "Isn't that like mixing chemicals?" Dr. EL smiled and left the smell of broccoli and eggs in the wind.

Bailey made his way up to the third floor by way of elevator. As the doors opened, George walked out of the medical lab with a handful of needed items for Betty's condition. Bailey wondered if George was still a little bit shaken from being swooped off his feet. Yet George looked more concerned for Betty. Knowing Bailey was serious about their situation quickly running south. He pushed out a raised acknowledgement from the corner of his mouth. For George this was an awkward moment.

Bailey was the first to speak. "Are you okay?"

"Yes," George said. "I'm fine. Let's get this done before I change my mind and leave this place." The men of a like minds walked enroute to their next adventure.

Once at the President's suite, not abated by confrontation, since they both assumed Betty would be unconscious. From memory, Bailey recognized the first of shadows would return lining the hallways. He reached for the light to the left of the primary suit. To his surprise Betty was up. He could see the king-size bed had left her impression. She was in the bathroom. George had gone to the kitchen to fetch more water and two more pills. Surprised to hear noise Betty stumbled her way back into the bedroom. Bailey reached to help her get back into bed. George behind them came into the room from the kitchen with needed pills. He had an I.V. bag, syringe, another bandage if needed, and elastic gloves in case he had to clean the wound.

"Hey little lady," He said, "You got to take it easy." He looked at Bailey who appeared concerned about her as George continued. "You lost a lot of blood the other day. You need to rest. Don't get up, and don't walk on that leg. It takes a while for your leg to seal that wound." George glanced back at Bailey taking on the aura of a busy doctor, and Betty was part of his rounds. Looking at Bailey he said, in the most conforming of ways. "Make sure she gets plenty of fluids. She needs to stay off her feet." He reintegrated with a wrinkled brow. Bailey only nodded and showed a salute. He was instantly signed up for his latest duty of his sergeant's orders. George got the I.V. bag ready whereas Bailey went to the closet to grab a metal hanger that George had asked for and bent his find into a hook shape. Betty laid back down without putting up a fight. She took the pills that George had brought. George removed the bandage to check the wound. He gently wiped the cut and returned a fresh bandage, as she grimaced from slight pressure. Within a few minutes after the procedure, she had fallen asleep. Bailey reached down and kissed her forehead. Then the two men quickly left the room.

Jackie came up as requested to keep an eye on her. She was instructed to give her soup and crackers, and something to drink when she woke up. All was well in the president's suite.

About an hour later, Bailey was seen back in the atrium to meet with the doctor, and the two robots had joined them. Ryan was at the doctors side. He was watching SNARF chasing a small ball. Dr. EL would throw the ball, and the metal-mutt would catch it before hitting the ground. He was faster than the average dog doing tricks. He was lightning fast according to Ryan. Dr. EL was reading that SNARF had the ability to crush anything with his jaws. He could dig under walls and create his own tunnels at inconceivable swiftness. This made Dr. EL think of the creatures left behind. How could they defeat them? And how long would it take for these creatures to figure out a way into the compound? Something was aloft, something not thought of before about all this mess. The good doctor glanced up at T-DEXTER fearing what was ahead of them. He knew the robot had information about what festered behind in this place of decrepit space. Something not seen lay between the road and the cavern, something they were not prepared for—a holding place…for those creatures. Imagining them slithering by in the night or crawling and craving human flesh. They were here to annihilate. In a brief period of time life had flown by as fast-moving glitches. The cavern wasn't a place they could survive to long without food or a water table—envisioned like a den for wolves. Yet these were wolves of a different kind, ferocious, carnivorous, strong, and carriers of an infectious virus that was ever able to sear through human frailties.

"T-DEXTER!" the doctor yelled, "What are those things below? I mean what are we facing ahead that we need to know about?"

T-DEXTER stopped giving his sidekick directions and looked down at Dr. EL. "Pull-up a chair boys, I'll explain our situation."

Ryan and Bailey took notice of the informal invitation and made their way to the back of the truck. *Being* that it was only a few feet away, Bailey lowered the tailgate, and they took a seat. T-DEXTER mentioned a paradox from a three-dimensional screen like an electronic chalk board in bright blue colors hanging in the air. Accept this chalk board showed schematics, and graphs, along with pictorials never seen before. Screens of history were on the first few schematics, experiments of another day gone by, treachery among the ranks, and a particular scientist held in secret. T-DEXTER was showing detailed descriptive information downloaded from his hard drive. They were all seeing the screens for the very first time.

"Well, those indomitable creatures that you've met are known as Pailoids." The robot looked around for a minute to wait for several screens to slide by on his three-dimensional hologram, before continuing. Pointing out as a teacher would do. "The pending snowstorms were meant to change the surface of the world. But after the Pailoids became the main event when first discovered. The government thought the storms weren't enough to cause sufficient damage. But *that* wasn't the only issue they had brewing. Something not mentioned from before was spilled into the mix of chemicals and contaminated compound they were working on. And then, one of the scientists had cut his finger. Well, to make a long story short, you can understand the results. The compound was introduced to human flesh for the first time. And the host began to change. The one infected began to feed on others. The bio-department couldn't stop the results of what had happened next. It spread too quickly. The creatures couldn't be controlled. In the rush of panic, the government did something unthinkable. Three years ago, a group of scientists who were working for the bio-department had spliced several compounds that created a weapon to be used for military intelligence. Something went wrong with the experiments they were testing. Something for which they weren't ready. The results were something never imagined before by anyone. Later, they labeled the compound HN-1. Their new creation was kept a secret. It was never meant for the outside world. The bio-department used the virus, first on several animals, and then later on inmates at the prison. The military thought this to be a breakthrough for the weapons department. Then, without warning, treachery slowly developed among the ranks of higher-ups. They tried to separate the infected from the healthy, but it was too late. A few of them had gotten out of the cave, and you know the rest." D-TEXTER waited for a few seconds to get a reaction.

Ryan interrupted T-DEXTER with a raised hand. "Yes, little man, you have something to say?"

Ryan's eyes lit up. "They really scared us. They were really fast and strong!" Bailey placed a hand on Ryan's shoulder. T-DEXTER cuffed like a big cat. He touched Ryan on the top of a dirty baseball cap.

"Sorry little man. I should have been there for you. As long as I'm around this won't happen again." T-DEXTER looked back at the others.

"They do have a weakness though. Their sensitive to light. Their eyes do work, but they only see shadows. They retain direction through what they can smell. It's something that the HN-1 compound does to their system. An animalistic instinct takes over." Then T-DEXTER gave his own personal view on what he had learned. "So, dudes, it's not to kosher to have the local boys of the club below for dinner. You'll be on the menu."

Bailey stood up and looked at T-DEXTER with a serious stare. "So, what do we do then?"

"Fortify our compound, maximize you firepower, and immortalize your physical conditions." T-DEXTER answered with his flamboyant mannerism and caught Bailey off guard. He personally had nothing against this voice of the famed vocalist. Actually, he loved the band. Yet he was a little concerned about T-DEXTER taking over, and asking for courage that couldn't be given. What was that all about? He was just a silly robot with a life programed by his maker, with his own unique personality. But something was missing from the equation. He was on his own, leaving Bailey without knowing what T-DEXTER really meant.

"What's the best way to get rid of them?" Bailey asked.

"Well, maybe draw them out with some type of bait, like catching fish." D-TEXTER replied.

"And how do we do that?"

"It's pretty easy. They're attracted to the human scent."

Bailey understood from the visual of first introductions, when pinned up against the Q-Tank. He didn't like the sound of being hunted down by Pailoids. This was serious stuff.

"I'll let my sidekick draw them out with a good piece of meat and then the not-so-sharp Pailoids will be drawn to one area—then bam, we'll hit them hard." T-DEXTER was already pulling up schematics of the underground cavern below. He knew what to do.

"Wow," T-DEXTER said. "There are plenty of pickings from this warehouse for explosions." He flipped through a couple of visual screens to show the doctor and the two boys. Then T-DEXTER noticed something most alarming.

"Oh no," T-DEXTER yelled out. "An explosion would cause the inner structure of this compound to give way. The support beams would collapse beneath us." T-DEXTER pointed out where they were vulnerable in several areas, by showing the structure beams below on one of his holographic images. It didn't look good from Bailey's perspective. They had to find another way to draw the creatures out. The robot measured the information he had. "Maybe my sidekick and I might have underestimated them."

"I don't think you two can survive without some help. There's too many of them. They'd overwhelm you." Bailey said while looking up. "There's got to be a better way, than a frontal attack inside that cavern. They boldly have an advantage from my perspective with their numbers."

"Well, little brother, your help is more than welcome. Whatever we plan needs to be quickly before they have a chance getting in here." T-DEXTER raised his wrist to get a better look from the image. "They prefer fresh meat from warm bodies…those that are still alive and kickin." The big robot exclaimed. "T-DEXTER shook his head cuffing like a big cat. "Man, oh man—what did you guys get yourselves into?"

Bailey looked a little pale. "Well, we really don't know."

"Don't worry about what hasn't been seen yet. I'll cover your back," The big robot cuffed loudly, while reciting a strange poetic song, "hang it in a shack, shack…just breath in relax and listen to the facts. We'll be groovin to a movin to the rhythm of the dance." The big robot went into a jig. He was getting into the mood of the groove.

Bailey wondered if there was a loose bolt in the robot's brain pan. "His personality throws me off a bit." Bailey looked at the good doctor. "He doesn't make any sense at all sometimes, yet on a logistical level he's prime when it comes to having courage, and fire power."

The doctor wondered with a raised eyebrow. "Hey, you wanted him to lighten-up a bit, remember? It was your call. And sense you'll be the one out there with the robots, they'll have your back."

Bailey's eyes flared when hearing this. "What do you mean?" Then Bailey quickly understood. "Oh…you meant I'll be out there fighting with them?"

The doctor nodded with a raised eyebrow. "Who else…" as he held his left elbow and ran his fingers through chin hair with the other.

"There's nobody else, except you and handful of kids. I don't see anyone else to come and rescue us, and besides, you can't do it without their help." Dr. EL tried to instill confidence in the young lad. He didn't want Bailey falling apart before the big show. Then Dr. EL considered something funny. "We could change his voice patterns to one of the presidents. This would make him have a feel of a politician more than a robot of war." The good doctor said.

Bailey considered the change for his new arrival. "No thanks. Leave him the way he is, I'd trust the famed voice of Steven Tyler more than one of the presidents, and at the same time he'd be fairer."

Dr. EL looked over the rim of his glasses. "Well, between you, Betty, and T-DEXTER, you're the only ones to care. You guys can draw up your own plans, since you'll be the ones going out there and not me. I'm sure the voice is not as important as his frame of mind."

Bailey didn't like the sound of heading into battle with a beast with which he was unfamiliar. This was unfamiliar territory. A week ago, he was a prized runner, now the end of the world, a leader, one that included battling creatures never seen before. This was nuts. What was next, putting on spacesuits and flying through the air?

The next day, Bailey went to visit Betty in the president's suite. She was in better shape. She had her strength back. The color in her face was stronger and ruddier. Jackie had persisted in getting a little more food down her. She was still using the wheelchair to get around. Yet the stitches had finally taken hold, and the cut was starting to heal. Bailey had run into Mattie as the elevator had opened up. She was coming up from the bottom floor, and it stopped on his floor before reaching the ninth. She smiled and knew where he was headed. She looked up into his eyes, just before the doors to the elevator shut.

"Do you miss Betty?" She asked.

"Kinda, but I don't think she misses me much. She was upset with me last time I'd seen her." Bailey remarked. The elevator opened while Mattie reached over and took Bailey's hand.

"I think she's over that. She's been asking for you, but Jackie told her she couldn't get up. So, she stayed put."

Bailey looked down at Mattie with a growing grin. "Well, for all our sake, I hope she's better." He said. Ahead, Jackie met them at the door. They stepped into the penthouse and closed the door behind them. Bailey had turned back around, because someone had knocked on the door just when he'd closed it. He reached back and grabbed the handle. Ryan stood there with an odd look on his face.

"I was getting hungry and was wondering what's for dinner." The small boy of unhealthy habits had said. Ryan had come up on the next elevator. He'd been about hundred feet behind them. Bailey walked into the kitchen and opened up the freezer. There, he found two generous size frozen pepperoni pizzas. It brought a smile to his face.

"How does pizza sound squirt?"

"Hey!" Ryan yelled. "Sounds like a treat."

"I'm starved." Mattie said. "How long does it take?"

"Not too long, it'll be ready in about thirty minutes." Bailey removed the pizzas and turned the oven on to pre-heat.

Later, all the children and he gathered around Betty on the king size bed. They talked about what they had been through the last few days. They talked about Grandma. They talked about things ahead, and they talked about good projects for them to do in the near future. They were bonding. They had become closer through their experiences together. They were a family, dysfunctional at best, and not yet obsolete, but still a family. They had learned to share these pangs of life together. This was a good start. Bailey sat down on the edge of the bed and accidentally leaned in on Betty's damaged leg.

Betty yipped out a high pitch squeal. "Ouch!" She yelled.

"Something's digging into my cut. Something sharp is poking me." She exclaimed further.

Bailey looked at her surprised. "What do you mean?"

"I don't know. It feels sore, and there's this strange pressure."

Bailey looked at her with a curious glare. "Mattie, get me that magnified glass and the tweezers in the bathroom. We're going to check Betty's cut. See if there's something in there, something left behind." Betty wasn't sure if she wanted Bailey digging into a cut that had already sealed and was healing without anyone touching it. But at the same time, she wanted to know what was pricking her calve, and digging into her skin. Mattie was back quickly with the items requested.

Bailey carefully took off the bandage on her wounded calf and made her turn to her side to get a better look what was underneath. Bailey washed his hands before touching her. Once he returned, he took a closer look starting at the top, and working his magnified glass all the way down to the bottom. Betty had prickling legs, causing him to smile, fading tanned skin, and particularly something else that seemed quite peculiar. Something was sticking up from the bottom of the cut. He saw a small fragment, something metal, something odd looking. He fingered the tweezers perfectly to get a better grip on the upper end of the tweezers because he didn't want to poke the cut or break off whatever it was sticking out of the cut. He looked up at her as all the children held their breath.

"There's a small sliver of something working its way up out of the cut. Hold still so I can pull it out." Betty showed him a malevolent stare. "This might hurt a little."

"Ouch, which hurts you nimrod!" She said. This made the children giggle. Bailey was focused on this little piece of, well, a piece of metal he thought. "If I could only get a hold…"

"Ouch!" Betty stated again. "You're hurting me with those moronic tweezers!"

He glanced up exasperated. "Come on. Hold still, so I can pull it out!"

Betty fluttered her eyelashes with a bit of snootiness. "Well hurry, before I change my mind."

Bailey rolled the tweezers once and took another stab at getting a grip on the small piece of metal. "Yeah, that's what it was." He professed. "It's a piece of metal. Look." Everyone looked at what was pinched between the tweezers. It was a quarter of an inch long.

"Hey, that feels much better." Betty showed equanimity, "What took you so long?"

This made Bailey smile. "You're endearing difficult attitude sweetheart." The girls and Ryan giggled but didn't say anything. Bailey required more information. "What else was down in the hole in the ground?" Bailey asked. Betty knew she'd forgotten about the hearse rear bumper. A flash of memory was a quick reminder.

"The bumper had metal sticking up from the end, but I was confused because of those creatures down there were shooting all around me. It threw me off." Bailey raised an eyebrow.

"Well sweetheart, you weren't scratched by one of those creatures. You were cut by the bumper of the hearse. You had us all scared. I'm glad you're okay." Bailey said. "Why didn't you tell us about the hearse bumper sticking up?"

"I don't remember why. I was scared, wouldn't you be?"

"You have a point. No harm done, as long as everything's okay." Bailey cleaned the cut as a small amount of water and blood ran from the cut from the lower end. He applied medicated ointment and put a new bandage on her calf. He made it snug then looked up at her. With a troublesome grin, he leaned in on her and kissed the top of her forehead.

"What was that for?" She said.

Bailey smiled with that elusive way he always expressed in his eyes. "No reason." He said, "Just glad you're okay. I mean you're really going to be okay."

Betty had a strange expression on her face. Suddenly, Bailey heard the timer go off on the oven. Betty stated. "Don't be such a dork. I'm not going anywhere. Get our dinner before it burns."

"Yes princess." He said mockingly.

She held a heated glare. "Don't make me get up and hurt you."

"I'd like to see you try." With a sparkle in Bailey's eyes, he got up and took the pizzas out of the oven. They had hot pepperoni pizza and coke for the end of a long enduring day.

CHAPTER 21

Government's Secret

The next morning, Bailey received a call from Dr. EL. He wanted to see the both of them immediately. They were to meet him in the office, where they had met before. Bailey was a little concerned about the sound of his voice after getting off the phone. Something was aloft, something that wavered in the doctor's tone made Bailey feel uneasy that morning. Discernment he couldn't quite read *in* to.

Ten o'clock that morning, eleven days after they first arrived in the cave, this place of safety, something odd began to take form hidden from the eyes and ears of the last few survivors. Only a bleak world left behind in snow and ice. Everything was changing. They were lucky so far on this strange journey to still be alive. They were wondering about the bizarre account of governmental secrets yet to be heard.

The office was brightened by florescent track lights ten feet above them. Spread four feet apart from four rows of corrugated beveled corners. Bailey acknowledged the room as a standard office setting, a black computer monitor with seventeen-inch screen, a grey metal desk with a black leather chair on roll wheels, several file cabinets four feet high with four slide drawers in each, a large aviation chart tacked against the wall with red, white, and blue colored plastic tacks, each pin-pointed to strategic locations situated on an aviation chart in front. A chalk board with three pieces of broken white chalk, a chalk board eraser covered in white dust, and a trash can to the side of the desk made of a grayish metal. Below was a shiny clean cemented floor. From across the room, they sat in two brown metal padded chairs toward the front side of the desk, a small globe on a circular spinning-rod with a brassy metal base, a metronomic art piece that click-clacked back and forth with small brass balls.

Betty reached over to stop the rhythmic click-clack. She turned with a slight flicker of coherence. Bailey saw a thirty-gallon aquarium on the other side of the room with four lonely Goldfish swimming in slowly circular movements through a bluish tinted background. A quiet thrumming could be heard from across the room from the water filter pumping whitish bubbles through the top of the tank.

Dr. EL had set up the LED screen of the computer for them to view. What he had to present was something alarming to the few.

Dr. EL looked at Bailey and Betty before slipping the CD into the disc-drive. He had an unusual stare that Bailey couldn't quite figure out. Betty reached over and took Bailey's hand. She was nervous and didn't know what to expect. This surprised him. He turned to view her with an acquiescent stare while squeezing her hand. They sat quietly and waited for the twenty-minute video to finish. Dr. EL reached up and turned off the computer with an unsettling look crossed his face.

"So, as you can tell," Dr. El said, "we're in a strange situation. The creatures below this compound were not by accident. The government had been using the prison inmates for the last few years. I'm guessing for a foreign and domestic concern." Said the doctor. "But something happened—something terrible. And now we're facing what's left behind."

"Dr. Alfred Geneses produced the HN-1 compound as he was told to do, like it was a regular drug you'd for a common cold. Then this secret society was to come in later and change the way the world lived down the road. A worldwide panic would be anticipated and handled. Of course, the two-fold freaky phenomena would put everything to rest. The government wouldn't take the fall. They'd blame everything on these bizarre circumstances of the weather." Dr. EL pointed in the direction of the gates behind them. "What was left out in those caverns wasn't meant for this world. It was supposed to be set up like some freakish accident, something not expected. By then, everyone not connected with this branch of government would be left in the dark about what was going on. This new world order would try and set things straight—in their deceptive way of gaining control. They'd cover their tracks, get rid of any evidence left behind. They would replace the old government by a decommissioning process slowly exterminating those do not worthy of their new world order. Thus, by using the HN-1 compound to implement their plans. They would start anew. Then, when nature had taken her due course, they'd use the robots to clean up the mess.

"But nature had her own plan that didn't include them or their new world order. With our natural resources depleting to an all-time low over the next ten years, they used this excuse to implement their control. No more social disorder in her ranks of government, yet unfortunately their plan backfired. They were lost in the numbers along with everyone else. Their timing was off by a few weeks. They had planned for their new world order to take over after most of the people were already dead. These Pailoids were smarter than what they first assumed. They began to hunt in packs, like wolves—except different. They still had memories of human instincts that made them smarter, focused, learning from errors previous." Dr. EL dropped the two-inch file in front of Bailey and Betty. "It's all written here, in this file." Bailey and Betty looked up bewildered.

Dr. EL paused for a minute to let the young couple soak up the information before continuing. "Consequently, we still have this alarming problem. They were set to release the creatures out into the cities after they were safe within the compounds walls. That didn't happen though. The problem we have now is we don't know if these are the only creatures. There might be others. We need to find out and find out fast. This could mean something altogether different."

Bailey didn't like the sound of the world being taken over by the Pailoids—a gestating creature with a hunger for flesh. This gave him a chill down his spine. They were in a tough situation, yet without more manpower they didn't see what angle of attack should be used against an enemy so violently reformed into something indefinable. Dr. EL concluded his findings. "Nature has her own natural way of cleaning up our mess, but we need to help get her back on her feet. If those creatures get into our little compound…"

Dr. EL didn't finish his statement. The couple got a vivid picture of what he meant and stayed silent for the moment. Thinking about all that was said. Betty's hands were clammy, and Bailey was too stunned to comment.

T-DEXTER was standing behind them through the open door listening and recording everything said and seen on the CD, and now explained in detail by Dr. EL. The couple heard T-DEXTER's sensor probes going off, which caused them to turn suddenly with surprise. They heard a quirky high pitch whistle, mimicking the droid from the famed Star-Wars movie. T-DEXTER alerted them to what he'd found. He was flaring his arms in a panic. "I found something for you to use little brother," addressing Bailey. The robot explained with his raspy voice what was to follow. Sounds of flipping through recorded music, like fragments of old LP albums running backwards on a stereo. T-DEXTER started reading information he found on his bio-scanner. "Listen-up compadres. I found something you might want to use against those smelly Pailoids below." T-DEXTER let out a chuckle of coherent laughs, tricking his limited audience. He rubbed his hands together as if to warm them. "Yow…yow…listen up!" T-DEXTER flipped his hand back and forth like a famous D.J. pushing an L.P. on a turntable. The three bewildered office individuals were wondering what this racket was all about. T-DEXTER stood and gave an account by popping up several screens of dire information—something out of the ordinary, something in their favor. "My scanner detects a suit that I ruminate as a scientific find. Something else also created by Dr. Alfred Geneses. This is a suit to boot beyond your wildest dreams. Oh man, lights out, it's tight and ready to fight, that's what I'm talkin about, a Dream-Team, an unplanned scheme…a roller-derby of military militia. Stand back, don't give me any flack. It'll light up your life and set you on fire." T-DEXTER was Wiggin. The three curious minds wondered what was up with this rambling robot, he had a screw loose or maybe he was one chip shy of a complete mega-byte. "Furthermore," T-DEXTER said. "A project that involves quantum-genetic-fusion. I believe it's the invention of the century, a modern marvel of right on, right on. This is the substance of Matter interfaced into a metamorphosis base with unstable composites of magnetic energy. Well, only stable within the molecular structure of this suit. The equitable fusion of matter has interrelated parts that are controlled and re-circulated into a compressed compound of energy. This compressed energy is magnified by making interrelated connections with protons, neutrons, and electrons moving at incredible speeds, speed of light, no less, a curved bending of light honed and controlled between the body of the user, and this suit of composites, thus, creating a super physical state of being. This energy is then conducted by using the electrical signals that the human body produces to enhance the physical and mental performance of the user. The super physical energy of the suit controls and magnifies the user's abilities. The suit produces what has been termed as Crepto Energy. It stands for the following: **C**ontrolled, **Re**-circulated, **E**nhanced, **P**erformance, **T**ransport, **O**perative. This enhanced energy was not experimented with before now. This is new. Whoever wears this Crepto Suit will have superhuman strength, epic vision, and mental capacity, and will be able to fly or travel at extremely high speeds. They will have sight that penetrates the thickest of walls. All their senses would be heightened, and their bodies mass would be impenetrable to armor piercing rounds or shrapnel due to high explosive devices. Pressures outside the suit will not be able to crush the user inside. He or she would be totally protected from the outside world that might come against them per say in battle or dual to the death. It is by far a perfect blend of enhanced body armor that has ever been created. It's a suit of superficial finesse, a dual imbued influence on both inside and out. Dr. Alfred Geneses was forced to release his invention into this new world order's control. The Crepto Suit is located in the sub-basement warehouse in crate 2750, aisle ninety, and row ninety-three." The numbers sounded familiar. Bailey turned to look at the doctor.

"Sir, I guess we should find this crate and check it out. T-DEXTER is on to something, something quite spectacular, beyond anything found so far in this warehouse." Dr. EL turned toward the robot.

"Thanks D-TEXTER for sharing this information. We'll take this under advisement and consider its viable content." The doctor stated.

"Just doing another day doc. Stay real. You're the man." The big robot showed a thumps up. This was his gesture of understanding.

Dr. EL looked back at Bailey with a smile. "Young man, you are the only person that can actually wear this so called Crepto Suit, there's no one else qualified to do so. I'm too old and worn out, plus I need to stay here and monitor our weather. George will continue to take care of the animals. Betty's here for the children. That leaves you." Bailey glanced up at the doctor with a startled expression.

"But I'm just a boy. I don't have any outstanding skills to enhance this suit with, except in running. How can I be a success without having any scientific knowledge or know-how?" Dr. EL smiled with a deep impeding glare that comes with aged wisdom.

"Well, I see you as the perfect candidate—unless you see anybody else around gearing up to fight those creatures below." Bailey couldn't imagine facing up to the Pailoids. Last time he was even remotely close to one of them, it scared him to scurry away without a second thought of wanting to fight back. A shuddering chill went down his spine.

"But sir, I don't even know what I'm doing here. It was an accident. We're not even meant to be here."

"Well, we're here, and we're staying." The doctor said. "So, get ready to rumble because I don't see anyone else standing in to take the job." Bailey wasn't too keen on fighting. He had no previous fighting skills except for a couple crummy karate lessons at the Y. What was the doctor thinking? Is he nuts?

He turned toward Betty and said, "How are you feeling sweetheart?" *She* feeling Bailey meant it in a mock way, considered an unhealthy dose of attitude fitting for a return remark. The robot gave the impression of being caught in the middle. Betty finally answered.

"I'm fine dork. Why'd you ask?"

"Just wanted to make sure you're okay before we go traipsing out into the tunnels again." Bailey barked back. Not minding his own business, the robot wanted to feel like he was bonding with the compounds local socialites. The robot asked the most precarious of questions.

"What's a dork, young lady? I don't seem to have that expressive word in memory?" Betty smiled trying to accommodate the big guy.

"Well, Tin-Man." Betty said, "For the record, so you have everything in memory—it's a clumsy, awkward, skinny, useless, dumb-founded piece of work. Did you get all that?"

T-DEXTER looked at the smaller than normal girl with the attitude and sharp expressions of coherence and began to laugh. "You've got jokes," T-DEXTER said.

Chuckle…chuckle…"oh man, oh man…your cruel to the bone, she's out to burn you at the stake little brother." The big robot continued to laugh at Betty's gestures of love.

"Don't I know it?" Bailey said while shaking his head.

"You two are a pair made in heaven. So, what do you think?" T-DEXTER said, still continued the dig that Betty started. Bailey looked up at T-DEXTER with a smirk.

"She loves me. I don't take to heart her little gestures of pain. She's only playing around. It's her way of getting attention."

T-DEXTER put his hand up for Bailey to slap. Betty rolled her eyes and said, "Oh brother," She whispered. "Things are heating up." Bailey ignored her and slapped palms with T-DEXTER. The boy of bad beginnings looked at Betty but angled his view toward the big robot.

"I'm glad she's okay. You know," He started, "she saved my hide at the cavern five days earlier. She's a fairly good shot with that gun. She shot that smelly Pailoid and caught him right between the eyes. I don't think the creature knew what hit him." This made Bailey smile from his own memories of survival. "She takes no prisoners." Betty ignored the comment.

T-DEXTER piped in, "Right on, right on little brother. I feel ya. You're speaking my language. You're in ship-shape, you two young turkeys are in a turkey trot, and you're a bashful boy with boots on. Don't you frown? Keep your feet on the ground. She had your back. Shift your gears into the shack tracks—move low I'm your brow. Hang tight you're out of sight." Bailey wasn't quite sure how to take the robots words of encouragement. He seemed a tad off.

From the center of the room, the giant hydraulic lift came to the bottom sub-basement floor. They were all just standing and looking. Dr. EL, of course, had another set of schematics in his hands. He was trying to match up rows with figures and numbers, and varied sizes of crates.

So much looked the same. T-DEXTER turned on his bio-scanner and began helping to search for this mysterious crate that had been held in secret for the last three years. "It's right close to where you found me and my sidekick, in Crate 2750. It's not too big. It should be lying flat." T-DEXTER said.

They walked over to where the other open crate material was still scattered all over the place and began reading numbers on the floor. T-DEXTER found it right away and pried the top cover off with his strong steel hands. It was a cinch, an easy fix. Everyone looked down into the crate with a look of surprise; even T-DEXTER couldn't believe what he saw.

The suit put off a warm, transparent glow. It was a shiny coppery color that looked quite becoming. Coppery colors made from materials of a distinct soft flexible, synthetic metal mesh. Something none of them had seen before. Since he'd be the one wearing it, he stared at it like something would float out of this box and slap him across the face. This could be an enlightenment of a physical nature. He wanted it to slap him out of this delusional dream and give him a sense of reality. But nothing happened. It was similar to metal-mesh used to make a knight's armor—a shimmery shine, a golden sparkle of light glittered off the top of the suit's wavy appearance. The suit had curvilinear extensions wrapped into circles with spaces of about four inches apart from each other. It also had an inseam stitching between the divisions of circled material. This gave it a rounded muscular riveting glow, similar to shiny new brass pots and pans. Bailey showed an inquisitive stare. He was mesmerized by the shiny colors of light. It sparkled like T-DEXTER did.

There were no holes in the suit except for the back that had an opening to slide into. It included a head piece or mask as one unit connected to the rest of the suit. Bailey would have to slide in first, and then pop his head underneath the covering of head gear. A twofold operation of adherence. It didn't really weigh too much either, fifteen pounds. The suit was about the same height as Bailey. Betty knew it would fit him. She shook her head when she saw him bending over to pick it up. She knew he'd be the right person for the job too. Bailey was afraid to pick up the suit. He turned to look at Betty to ask her approval. "Don't look at me," she said. "It's your funeral. At least we won't have to buy another suit. We can use that one." Betty pointed at the suit like Bailey was funeral bound. Remembering them being chased by those Pailoids in the dark. He showed a twisting glare.

"Whatever," he said. T-DEXTER began to expound on his previous findings.

"You need to trust the suit." The big robot said. "It will enlighten you to its energy source. The longer you wear it, the more you become familiar with its capabilities. Once you've worn the Crepto Suit, no one else can put it on. The Crepto suit becomes automated to your body chemistry. It won't change to fit anyone else after the suit has accepted your chemistry. If anyone else puts on the Crepto Suit after you've worn it. Well, it just might kill them. Make sure, when you are not wearing this to store the suit in a safe place where children can't get to it." Bailey nodded in understanding T-DEXTER'S directions.

"Yeah…okay…I'll find a safe place to hide it. So, what's next?" Bailey looked over his shoulder.

T-DEXTER wobbled his head side to side and then said. "You've got to trust what you feel in the Crepto Suit. It will enlighten you to what to do next."

Betty interrupted the two in conversation. "I'll wear the suit," she said mockingly. "So, I can kick everyone's butt."

T-DEXTER jumped the gun with an awkward expression, "Holy moly little lady—you're pissing vinegar!"

Betty showed an eccentric stare. "It's full of piss and vinegar Tin-Man. Learn the lingo so people don't think you're a dipstick."

Bailey turned his stare acknowledging Betty was coming into her own. He then looked back at T-DEXTER. "Hey, big brother, do we have any big guns in this warehouse?"

"What's your pleasure, Crepto Man?"

Bailey gazed a pertinent stare. "What did you call me?"

"I called you Crepto Man. That's who you'll be after you put on that suit. There's no turning back after you and that suit become acquainted with each other. It's the bond man…it's out of sight. It's better than smokin aces. You and the suit to boot will light up the skies. Hey man, it's the invention of the century! My hat's off to Dr. Geneses. He broke the mold on this one." T-DEXTER raved.

Bailey showed confusion. "Are your side bolts off a little Tinman?" The big robot laughed with a cuffing whiskey sound, like a cartoon character.

"No, not really, just having fun man. I'm feeling good, I'm flying high today little brother."

Bailey's look of misperception. "Let's open up some Christmas presents Tin-Man. I'm feeling lucky." He was riding his expressions on the robots demeanor.

"Crate 2227," T-DEXTER said, with his gamboling playfulness. "Let me introduce you to all my little friends." He said with an indomitable personality.

"There's Crappy, and Lug-nut, and Mini and Boo, Short-Stack and Roundhouse, and Winnie-the-Pooh? Who's that—how'd he get in there?" T-DEXTER acted resembling to tossing out an old CD—flipping and juggling imaginary two-sided-vinyl. Then the robot went into a little jig and made up another chorus line of phraseologies to fit a second verse. Betty wondered with raised eyebrow if she was watching a really bad movie.

She finally said. "Can I at least get some popcorn, while Tinman tries out for cartoon aerobics?"

Bailey glanced up at the space-case of robot aerobics. "Dude... really, come on...get serious."

T-DEXTER shook off his little pleasures of fun. "Well," The robot cleared his imaginary throat. "Let's see...oh yeah...back to crate 2227." He said. "Stop your grinin and drop your linen.' This is laser cannon!" The robot raved on. "You have the right to remain dead, after I shoot you in the head! You have the right to be escorted off the planet. Anything and everything will be used against you, my big gun, my big deltoid reflex, and my big attitude."

SNARF tried to squelch out a howl, yet it came out like a tiger growling loudly. "Papa do run—run!" T-DEXTER belted out. Out in left field, Bailey had thought, as T-DEXTER looked down at his scanner. "Hey...I found something for the little lady!" He turned his stare toward Betty. Bailey had wheeled her to the center of the room. The wheelchair was turned at an angle between the other two men. The warehouse was all lit up like a Christmas tree, flashing lights, sparkly presents, and an attending audience. T-DEXTER walked over to the side of where everyone was standing. Stooped over and grabbed a small crate to his left. He sat it in front of Betty. "Hey, girlfriend…you can get your groove on with these."

"What's in the box, sugar-pops and crackerjacks?" Betty displayed an eccentric sneer.

T-DEXTER reached up and scratched his metal chin, like he'd want to scratch if he was itchy, but being a robot, it was highly unlikely. "I don't think so, but let's take a look." T-DEXTER pried the top wooden slates off. Underneath was an impressive set of two barreled six-shooters. All shiny and silvery, long barreled, ready to blast any bad guys out of their boots. T-DEXTER handed them over. Betty looked down the barrel of the first gun like a professional. Eyes focused, checking out the smooth in lined surface, the flashy color, the spinning cylinder, the handgrip, the hammer-cock, its cold mesmerizing steel. The robot reached down and picked up a box of ammo at the bottom of the crate.

"Here you go!" He said.

Betty loaded the gun knowing she'd done this before. Click spin, click spin, click spin cock. She was ready. T-DEXTER reached in the box again and dug a little deeper. There was a leather belt with two holsters for the left and right. This caused Betty to grin—a disheartening grin, from Bailey's point of view. "It's what I've always wanted." She said. Some girls get dolls of Barbie's boyfriend Ken, but Betty gets six-shooters from overanxious friends. Her hands were small, but she'd developed a perfect grip. T-DEXTER walked over to the next crate on his bio-scanner he'd detected something strange. Something round, something brassy, big, and bulky. Something that Bailey would need. Another crate, another gift, Christmas was definitely here. They resembled mock teenage soldiers of fortune. Their fortunes to come would come from their individual efforts, their creative thinking. Yes, misfits they were—survivors from a time that could not be reversed. Yet together they would unite and find the answers needed to achieve success.

Inside the next crate was a sword and shield proportioned to fit the Crepto Suit perfectly. The shiny green and gold robot pulled the shield out first and handed it to Bailey like handing him a toothbrush. The bulky brass cylinder clanged to the steel worthy floor. This embarrassed the boy with bashful behavior. He didn't know what to do. He lifted, prodded, poked, and strained, and finally got the shield up to his chest. It had to weigh over eighty pounds. Betty saw his face turn three different shades of red. He was dead if he turned any more shades of red.

And Betty, who was ready as Freddy looked at the boy who was almost dead from being red and said. "That looks heavy." She saw his cheeks shake and his bottom lip quiver. This gave her a chill. How would this boy whose face was turning red, keep from being dead, with a girl who was ready as Freddy?

Furthermore, T-DEXTER held the sword that matched the shield that matched the suit that matched the boy who was almost dead from being red, staring at the girl with the guns ready as Freddy.

The nine-foot robot took the sword and waved it through the air. Coppery glow of a shimmering light reflected off the blade. This quick slashing of sword cut through the cold chill of open space, it was light for a robot, clean looking, and sparkly, flickering vivacities of light across the room. The sword and shield were meant to be together, they were a pair, like the girl in the wheelchair and the boy with a difficult beginning was meant to be. Though young and vulnerable, they would be pulled together by the silent moments between them. They were destined to share jointing space, like hammer to nail, carpet to floor, bee to pollen, bereavement for the dying, they all had their place—life with the living, a time for even giving like Christmas in this warehouse, rhyme and reason, time for each season. This was theirs. They were a team.

After dropping the shield Bailey showed a transparent awareness.

"I meant to do that," he said. "No rest for the weary." He proclaimed as if in some glorious contest of resistances, an actor, a façade, a mirage of understanding. T-DEXTER wasn't buying the act. From the robot's perspective of gradation, Bailey was at his beginning of growth. He saw him as only a man-child learning his limits, his ways of seeing life would change. All that was happening was relevant to a cause beyond his understanding. Bailey would learn of his true purpose in life, one step at a time. T-DEXTER reached down and helped the individual boy pick up the shield, to take the strain off of his shoulders. T-DEXTER was Bailey's strong arm of support, a friend when needed, a component of camaraderie. The robot handed the sword to Bailey. It wasn't as heavy as the shield, but in his present condition Bailey would not be able to lift them together. He needed the power of the suit. After setting the sword and shield by the roll up door he walked back where Betty was present.

He wheeled her near the roll up door. Dr. EL hit the button. The roll up door began to lift. The courtyard lay ahead in open space that jetted to the top of this cave. A good place to start for target practice, and besides, Bailey needed to try on this suit that he had thrown over his shoulder.

"I can't shoot the laser cannon in the courtyard," T-DEXTER said. "It will do too much damage, but we can practice with the other weapons on hand." T-DEXTER flew out past the center area with a large crate about a hundred feet or so, far, but not too far. Betty was setting the grips on the handled pistols. She looked down the long barrels again, her last few visual adjustments to the sights. The distance to her appeared to be far for shooting pistols. What was T-DEXTER thinking? She thought. Six soda cans and two coffee cans were spread-out across the top of the wooden crate. T-DEXTER was back before she knew it. Betty took aim for the first can to the far left. The first can rocked a little before she continued a bombardment of three shots from both pistols, every other shot from each one. She made connection with all bullets except the last shot because the right gun slipped in her hand. T-DEXTER went to check out Betty's progress. He understood she was consistent. She did well. She saw his nodding glance of approval. Looking over her shoulder at Bailey, seeing he was still holding onto that crazy suit.

"It appears you are a little skeptical about putting the suit on." She said. She didn't know about this strange boy, who appeared to hold back; too shy, too intimidated by the unknown. She'd remembered how skittish he was when she first met him. *He,* being afraid of heights, afraid of moving forward in the dark, she knew he needed her. She was strong where he was weak, and vice versa. His face was red from forcing the heavy shield up to his chest. He couldn't really lift it high enough and hold the sword at the same time.

Betty raised an eyebrow. "Quit playing with that sword and shield and put the suit on!"

Bailey gave her a dour expression. "Maybe you'd like to try it." He said. She ignored him. He knew she was right but didn't like being pushed into something that made him feel uncomfortable. Sensing the suit was inscrutable. He just had to try it to know for sure. That was the only way. This was a game of change. A bridge in the gap of events not yet known, a swirling tide of circumstances, a disconsolate bend in the road, and a quagmire in the making. Putting all that aside.

"Come on!" Betty shouted. "Don't be so concerned about what's going to happen. Just let go." She insisted. "You'll be okay." She glanced at D-TEXTER who'd been really good about not getting in the middle. Bailey had picked up the suit again by now, and was considering the best way to slide in. Impending butterflies began to kick up in his stomach. He wasn't sure about this side-stepping robot's point of view or Betty's. This strange girl appeared to go out on a limb at times, not considering consequence from a logical perspective, leaving behind most individuals precariously blowing in the wind. She tried to take up the slack where he lacked. This was the only reason Bailey had even hesitated. T-DEXTER finally stepped up to give Bailey a little reassurance that the suit was on the same side.

"Hey dude," He said. "Calm down. The suit is your friend. It won't swallow you up."

Bailey's face twitched from nerves, most likely. He turned one last time in the direction of the others and said.

"Well, here goes nothing," and sidled into the suit. Slowly and willingly the Crepto suit began to change his environment. At first, Bailey wanted to panic, but knew doing so would only make this more difficult.

"Hey little brother, flow with it. It will take a few minutes to adjust. Give it time." T-DEXTER said. Bailey felt the Crepto Suit made a direct connection with his mind. Heat and adrenaline flowed through his veins. His senses heightened. His energy level began to elevate. His eyes began to see what he normally could not see without the suit. His peripheral vision was enhanced all around him. The suit added a chaste feeling to his aura. He became calm, connected—his environment gave him confidence that would otherwise not be there. The Crepto Suit expelled a sinuous presence to Bailey's mind and body. They were like one. He could smell, see, understand, envision, and think more clearly. He could move faster, felt stronger, he had a better strategy toward making decisions.

Bailey tried to relax and let the Crepto Suit do its thing—whatever that was to be. He felt his mind making connections to every cell, every atom, every electrometric pulse that touched his nervous system. A susurration of sounds in the distance became efficacy in ones ears. He heard the gibbering of birds in the distance. He could hear George singing in the galley. This caused him to smile. His breathing came easier, his sight was more in-depth. He felt a surfeit of power course through him. He was infused by an incessant circumstance out of his control, like roots of a tree growing and touching the very nerves that give life.

"So how does it feel?" Betty asked.

"I don't know yet. It's getting to know me." Bailey said. This statement caused Betty to be apprehensive. There was an incongruous sensation that had passed through Bailey. He turned and saw more than he had bargained for. He turned his view away from Betty. Not wanting to see her in an embarrassing manner, since he could see through clothing, it didn't seem appropriate to stare back at her. He'd blush a brighter color of pink if he continued. This suit was extraordinary. It caused Bailey to feel ubiquitous to his surroundings.

Glancing past the gates ahead. Nothing on the other side except the bridge. Skid marks left by the trucks tires. No Pailoids could be seen, no round up of the dead. It was silent like the reins of chaos before showing a pedantic ending to life. Bailey felt at that moment, some synesthesia in this bizarre connection of coherence. The suit was him. It was the roots of something beyond his understanding of existence. He had a personified strength of awareness. The Crepto Suit was power under control, pushed by the persistence of a sharp mind, which was created by the intelligence of Dr. Alfred Geneses. He was a mastermind of science. He had a grand plan for a hero. Unfortunately, a plan short circuited by a corrupted government. Now, on the edge of despair, this small band of misfits was destined. They were destined to become the heroes of the end of the ages. Bailey was no longer some young runner from a city by the sea. He had become a man with purpose to survive, a well-rooted *will* transformed into a hero, a hero to be remembered till the end of time...

CHAPTER 22

Crepto Energy at Work

"So, what's the secret in working this suit?" Crepto said. He turned to look at T-DEXTER. T-DEXTER had the key answer to the why's and how's of the suit. Crepto felt a surge of equanimity engulf his character. It was something that set him up on top of the world. Feeling and seeing everything, similar to a fly with a thousand sets of eyes, and keen ears tuned to the softened sounds and brilliant sights of everything around. Feeling an explosion of knowledge, flashes of changes glitch by before his very eyes.

Then T-DEXTER answered the long-awaited question. "Express what you want the suit to do. You are one. You are the same."

Crepto held a wrinkled expression. "What?" He said. "You mean we're inseparable now?"

"Well, kind of," said the robot. "It will respond to your heart, your head, and your desires of dominance."

"Dominance? I'm not trying to dominate anyone. It's just a suit. I'm still me."

"No! You're more than you. You're everything. All powerful, all consuming, all knowing. Well...it will take a while before you understand the suit in that way."

"So basically, I communicate with the suit with my thoughts?"

"Yes, I believe this to be something closer to that, than anything else little brother." Crepto raised an eyebrow. What was this strange robot actually saying? He was confused.

"I've never had the pleasure of wearing the suit so I can't be exact. I'm going by what Dr. Alfred Geneses has put into my memory, and what logic has been placed in my data center. I take the logical equations and find the best route. A choice made by intuition."

He wasn't sure about this oddity of the robot and his data opinions. Bailey made some really bad choices from earlier times. His intuition wasn't erasing any of his past. It was best to see all angles, was Bailey's form of thought.

"You and the Crepto Energy are bonded for life. You're as one. You're the same, like your fingers are a part of your hand, so the suit is a part of you. The suit is molecularly constructed, combining scientific research and the delicate infrastructure of the human body. Both capacities united, bonded into one source of energy—Crepto Energy. Your emotions will have the greatest effect on performance. Your drive, your ability to withstand pain, your ability to go beyond the boundaries set by the human heart. As you were pushed by your human desires for success as a runner, the same will happen between you and this suit. Together you will combine both knowledge and power, learning to understand each other's motivations. What drives the Crepto Energy, and you together will fetter this bond to become stronger. Trust the Crepto Energy."

Bailey wondered if being a future superhero would then connect him with the suit permanently. He was concerned about the attachment. Would this peculiar suit someday take over? Would he become like the Hulks mysterious second personality? Would he revert back to the dark side? This wasn't a dream from a Hollywood stunt. Would he be become like Xavier from the secret institution for gifted mutants? Or a boy with special powers. This was crazy superpowers from a suit. Being able to fly into the air, super-human strengths, like superman. Yet to him, all this special power talk appeared a little unsettling. Bailey knew he had to test the Crepto Energy. A scientific invention researched and taught from the mind of genius. There was something right about this energy that couldn't be explained with words—as blue skies can't be explained to its balancing colors, or the universe drifting apart to further its dimensions, inexplicable on a universal plain. And as this Crepto Energy would learn its purpose of being, they would become complete. Bailey's mind raced with metaphors of disturbing images…

Bailey, now Crepto, reached down and picked up the sword and shield. No weight was even noticed. He spun the shield as three-inch razor-sharp spikes jetted from around the edges. The blades held a relentless gyrating motion while picking up speed. Dr. EL moved Betty to the side to avoid the energy being seen in surfeiting effect of efficiency—a brightening of light shot forth from the shield, intertwined with heat. This caused everyone else to cover their eyes. T-DEXTER used his body as a safeguard for Dr. EL and Betty. The exposure of the Crepto Energy was a pervading growth of light. Crepto was in a zone. A superfluity of power made the suit glow to a point to cause impaired vision. Ryan turned his view away from the glow of brilliant light.

"Dude…" he yelled. "That's burning my skin!" T-DEXTER pulled Ryan under his protective armor with the others. As Crepto's shield spun he sensed the energy building with each passing second. The suit has an infinite ability to diminish its drawing. This was all pushed by the boy's emotions in the suit. He had to learn its limits and not to overplay his role.

Crepto swung the sword in line with the constant spinning of the shield, building momentum, finding a rhythm. He could see, feel, and sense, all through the suit. A sense of dominance was seen through the eyes of the boy in the suit. Crepto through the sword in the direction of the crate a hundred feet in front. The sword, not usually used in a manner such as this shot like a bullet from a gun. The stentorian sound echoed throughout the compound as heated synchronicity of motion was quicker than a blink of an eye. Time slowed to a coalesce moment, a fraction of a nanosecond, a permutation of reversed order. A division of time was separated before acknowledgement. Betty covered her ears. Ryan dove to the ground. T-DEXTER did a jig, and Dr. EL grappled for air. The force was so great that it pulled the air from the atmosphere.

The crate splintered to pieces as the sword continued to travel past its mark and bury itself into an oak tree. The power was beyond human comprehension.

"Now, now little brother, don't go overboard! We have to live in this facility! We don't need any extensive damage done to our new home!"

Crepto turned to acknowledge T-DEXTER, yet every slight movement caused Betty to scream, because he'd turned the blades of the shield in her direction. He needed to refract the heat and light.

"Turn that thing off!" Betty yelled.

Crepto had been so focused on powering the sword that he forgot the shield was still spinning. It caused coruscated blindness to overtake their senses. Once the temperature and light diminished, Ryan got up off the ground and brushed himself off.

"Dude…" he yelled. "That was awesome!" Ryan turned to look back at the crate. It was gone. Betty's face showed the visage of a woman with a querulous glare. The facial expression alone told Crepto he'd gone too far.

"Sorry guys. I didn't know it would be so strong. I guess taking it down a few notches would be good." Betty fluttered her eyes and expelled a deep wrinkle in her expression.

"You don't have a clue what you're doing—do you?" Betty insisted. Ignoring her, Crepto noticed T-DEXTER was still doing a silly jig, acting as a boy receiving his first puppy. SNARF, this dumber-than-normal-named-dog cranked back his head and let out an ululation of celebration. Everyone stared at this new, secretly discovered, strange-looking, overwhelming piece of work. Crepto had game. He wasn't a rocket scientist, yet in the suit he was a boy turned into an upgraded cohesion of conflict—an inclusive spike on the rector-scale, a pipedream, a missile of reclamation, a bionic aberration, a sick psyche-out of eccentricity.

"I feel strange with the suit on. It'll take a while to get used to sharing space with its energy." He said. Betty covered her eyes with her right hand to block partial light still emanating from the glowing glitter of illumination.

"So, now you move from dork status to one with solemnity." Betty professed with eyes unblinking. She took in the countenance of this odd boy turned into what—a superhero. "Don't wear that dreadful thing if you don't have too. I'm afraid you might hurt someone."

In the distance of the second floor, Crepto could feel George calling to them from the galley—a sense of urgency played on his mind. Dinner was ready. What was this, telekinesis on a different plain? So, he suggested.

"Hey guys. It's time for dinner. George made fish and chips. It actually smells quite tempting."

Betty whipped her head around. "Don't tell me, you can smell dinner from here."

Crepto nodded. "Yes, I can."

What Bailey, from the inside of the suit wanted to say, was he could feel George's intentions of calling them to dinner, but decided this was to be too much to share.

"How can you smell dinner from here?" Betty asked.

"I don't know, but the metal-mutt can smell it too." Trying to take some of the attention away from himself while leaning in the direction of the metal-mutt. *But then how would he know the metal-mutt could smell dinner too?* Betty thought. SNARF growled with a disapproving glare, Crepto past the torch to T-DEXTER'S sidekick. Betty wondered what else could be manufactured from the abnormality of the Crepto Energy?

"Don't wear that suit to dinner." Betty said. "And don't have it anywhere near the children. I don't want anyone to get hurt."

"What? I don't like wearing it *now*, what makes you think that I'll wear this blasted suit all the time?"

Betty snubbed her nose. "That's the scary thing. "She said. "You shouldn't wear it at all. The dreadful suit will be the end of you."

"Now, now little lady—what's the big deal with wearing the suit?" T-DEXTER said.

"Don't get in the middle of our conversation Tin-Man. I wasn't talking to you!"

"My bad little lady—didn't mean to step on your toes." The robot said.

Bailey tried to warn T-DEXTER before saying anymore. "Never get between two cats Tin-Man. It might ruin a good coat of paint."

"Nice to know little brother, I'll go guard something. I'm out of here." T-DEXTER left the immediate area so not to be in the direct line of fire. SNARF ran after him in a fit of retrieval.

"Look," Crepto said. "The suit is new to me. It might take me a little time to adjust to all the changes." Betty looked up at him.

"Well, you better have a talk with that suit. Or I'll be putting it in the garbage can"

Crepto was tired of dealing with her attitudes. "I should let you wear the suit." He suggested.

"Why's, that?" Betty asked.

"Because you're full of piss and vinegar like the robot said. Besides you're more the warrior than I. I'd try to make peace with everyone, and you'd want to blow everyone away." He said. "The problem would be the suit might suggest killing everyone else and you'd think it was okay."

Betty didn't appreciate his answer—he'd gone too far. He had taken a lot of flak from her previously though and this had put a barrier between them.

He turned the wheelchair around to face her. "Why don't you just kill something and get it out of your system?" He said.

Betty picked up both pistols and shot Crepto right in the chest. He was blown off his feet and fell backwards hitting the ground hard. The wind was knocked out of him for a brief moment, but no permanent damage. He struggled to move as Betty screamed.

"Oh my God… What did I just do?" She tried to get out of the wheelchair as she noticed Crepto still sprawled out on the ground. She stood on one good leg and fell on top of the uninjured idiot.

"I'm so sorry! Are you okay?" Betty overwhelming said.

"Do I look okay? You just shot me!" He tried to push Betty off without being too aggressive, since he was in the suit and didn't appear to understand the full involvement of its powers.

"Well, I didn't think it would hurt you—did it?" Betty professed.

"Those weren't Beebe's. Yes, it hurt! What'd you think would happen, the bullets would tickle! I'm not the man of steel. I'm just a kid in a stupid suit." He reinforced. "You need to be medicated."

This made Betty smile. "Medicated—why medicated?"

"So, you don't hurt people. I'm going to put a collar on you and take you to obedient school for wayward young girls of inferior minds."

Betty lost the grin. "I'm not inferior. I just like things done in a particular way."

Crepto raised an eyebrow after standing slowly and dusting off the suit. "Yeah…the hard way…" Betty showed a fading sparkle in her eyes.

"I don't expect you to love me you big dork?"

"Yes…like I love alligators, but that doesn't mean I'd tussle with them." Crepto held back a grin. "I'd be crazy to get affectionate with one so scaly."

Betty showed a hurtful stare. "Why are you comparing me to an alligator?"

"Well, for starters you both bite. And you both have a dangerous snap. Your skin is scaly from this cold climate like those unfriendly critters at the zoo, and your temper scares people. Do you always leave clutter everywhere you go? A sweater here, shoes in the middle of the floor. I'm always tripping over your stuff, and you're so bossy with everyone—need I go on?" A scathing chuckle came from the boy in the suit. She didn't like this new man in the suit. He was obnoxious. She reached up and smacked him in the chest.

"Stop picking on me or I'll shoot you again!" Betty said this with a chagrin expression.

"You do and I'll file charges." Crepto reported.

"You wouldn't and couldn't besides…there's no one to report a crime to and…I didn't hurt you anyhow—you big baby." Betty said this with an exasperated appeal.

"But you did. I'm filing assault charges first thing in the morning—assault with a deadly weapon." She looked at him as he held a straight face. She couldn't figure him out to be serious or not.

"I didn't assault you." Betty retorted. The boy in the suit shot out a smidge of a smile. He couldn't hold it anymore.

"Well, you emotionally damaged me then." He said.

"Someone's gotta keep you in line, if not me, who then?" This was Betty's unabated attempt to defend her honor. Crepto continued his prodding.

"How about Dr. EL, he's the senior adult here. He's the one with all the experience. Or you would prefer getting spanked like a little girl."

"You wish," Betty narrowed her eyes. "Watch it wise guy you're pushin' it."

"Okay, so you're not into spankings, but you need one. I could get that metal-mutt to lick you to death."

"Now you're dreaming. Just be quiet and take that dreadful suit off." Betty said.

Crepto reached down to kiss her, and she poked him in the eye… "Ouch!" He exclaimed.

"What'd you do that for?" He yelled out. She was lethal.

"So, do you abuse all your close friends like this?"

Betty smiled as she pulled her fingers back. "No, not really…" She said as if she got the best of him. Crepto broke out another stupid smile.

"Now…about that spanking…" He said. "It's still on my, to-do-list."

Betty rolled her eyes. "You're not some type of pervert, are you?"

"Okay I'll stop…" He said. Betty tightened her eyes while cross examining him by his last statement.

"You better stop, or I'm leaving."

"Hey…sorry, didn't mean to be a killjoy. I meant it as a joke. I wouldn't really spank you, besides that would look weird to the others."

Betty glanced up at him with wondering eyes. "So, are you going to be nice to me now or am I going to have to hurt you again?"

"It depends on you."

Betty tapered her eyes. "You need to be flogged." Betty said it like she'd be the willing soul to do it.

"I was flogged by a Molly once, she was hot." Saying it with the same temperament. "She could flog me anytime she wants."

"Oh, you're such a big dork. I know you're talking about that rock group called Flogging Molly. No pretty girl is going to let you have your way with her. You're flogging days are over." Betty put a hand over her mouth and held back a giggle. Crepto grabbed her wheelchair and spun her about. He then crawled out of the Crepto suit and pushed out a slow breath of air. It was hot in there. He threw the suit over his left shoulder. His body was wet from the heat of the suit and his shorts were riding up where the sun doesn't shine. She noticed his awkward moment when he walked in front of her to push the elevator button. He moved his legs to try and remove the shorts without physically touching his tethered crease. This caused her to smile. *He was a big dork.* She thought.

Once in the galley, everyone turned to look at the suit, but nothing was said. They were still in a bit of shock over the Crepto suits eminent power. Bailey knew his emotions were flared a bit too much from first introductions with the Crepto Energy. He needed to take it easy next time or there might not be a compound to come back to.

Bailey looked at his small crew of members, then back at the suit wondering why everybody was silent. He looked up and suddenly said, "What? It's just a crazy suit! There's no ghost that lives in there. I'm just new at this, okay!"

Betty wondered about his excuses and spoke in a soliloquy way. She acted as if the only one in the room. Everyone turned to look at her. Mattie and Jackie giggled. Betty didn't like the boy being a pain in the butt.

"So, now you're going to be in charge?" Bailey could feel his face flush.

"I'm not in charge. Nobody's in charge." Bailey was getting frustrated. He turned to get moral support from the doctor.

Dr. EL looked precociously at Bailey. "You know this is going to take a while before everybody begins to except this suit as a normal thing. Right now, it's a bit odd and scary at the same time. To see you do incredible feats with such power. It's hard to explain." Dr. EL noticed everyone staring. "We're a little concerned how far you'll take this."

Bailey couldn't believe what he was hearing. "I can't believe you guys are already turning against me. I've worn the suit one time. I just need practice—that's all. Enough about the suit, okay?"

The rest of the room remained quiet while George served up this heavenly fish 'n chips dinner. *It smelled awesome.* Ryan thought. The boy felt his stomach touching his backbone. He was starved.

George poured wine as he told a few jokes. The little girls and Ryan drank tea and so did Bailey and Betty. When all was said and done the girls and boys helped clean up. Yet the real issue at hand was still ahead of them, the battle to come.

What the young hero thought and what others had thought were two diverse ways of thinking. Bailey figured not to plan at all, but to only take a lot of firepower and hit them hard and without mercy. After dinner, he stood to address everyone at the table. He waited until he had everyone's attention. The dining room grew quiet, then Bailey stood. Betty was wondering what this boy had to say. Now, he'd been a little different after spending a few hours with that involved invention.

"First I want to say," Bailey professed, "is that I'm glad we have survived up to this point. We've been through a lot together, so your trust is warranted. All we've got left is each other, along with T-DEXTER and his metal friend. We're a team." Bailey paused for a few seconds to get his thoughts together. Suddenly wondering where his confidence had gone, after getting out of the suit, he was just Bailey. The mental connection had been severed.

"Tonight, we'll try to find the best way to form an attack. Their numbers can be overwhelming if not properly prepared."

"Well, if we're going to make a frontal attack, we need more guns." Betty said.

Dr. EL turned in the direction of the bewildering girl. "The armory below should accommodate those wishes." He said. "We need to look a little harder."

Bailey finished the short speech. They knew they had a lot to do. He and the others started making their way to the subbasement floor to get lots and lots of guns...

CHAPTER 23

Hangar's Stockpile

Bailey pushed Betty in the wheelchair toward the elevator. Dr. EL followed behind them out of courtesy. The three slipped in the double doors as soon as they opened and headed for the bottom floor. The hangar still presented a lot of areas of searching they hadn't yet uncovered. They had a few hours to make plans and finish everything that needed to get done. Time was of the essence. From the center of the warehouse, lay a chilly crisp feeling that hung in the air. A balmy fifty-five degrees kept them quite cool as their efforts would take much needed energy for later. Betty was staring at the thin dorky lad that had given her such attitude. She liked him, but she didn't like his sarcastic demeanor. She wondered about that name given to him. *Wow, Crepto Man, how can you top that?* She sat in the wheelchair wondering about those creatures left behind the walls of safety. They were a memorable impression she'd never forget. From those fleeting memories of that first day of horror, she'd begun to feel a growing presence hidden behind these walls of secrets. How could they have been so stupid not to notice the danger signs along the way? A cave hidden in secret that no one else knew about. Who were they kidding? They were just a bunch of kid's unprepared for their future. They'd gotten a crazy idea to go off into the wild white wonder of the storm to save themselves, and now they were facing the end of the world, challenged at every corner of concern. Something one day would come to try and take this place of safety away from them, but when and how she did not know. Yet Betty also sensed that this journey couldn't have been by accident because too much had happened already, and for the apparent reasoning they were still here, still trying to fit all the pieces of this giant puzzle together no matter how difficult. Furthermore, the hours had advanced so quickly, and nothing could be left tussling in the wind without first bearing in mind the future to come. They were in the last stages of finding some type of success. Some of the pieces were slowly beginning to surface. Betty knew with the help of the guns, the robots, and Bailey's new suit they might have a chance. But they had to see every angle of the fight before facing it. Still needing to safeguard the children before leaving this place.

Being in the warehouse already twenty minutes, Dr. EL turned to look at Bailey with an expression of deep concern. "Hey, where's the suit?"

Bailey turned and noticed his first rule had already been broken by leaving the Crepto suit behind. He looked up with a timorous stare. "Sorry, I left it in the banquet room by accident." As Bailey finished his sentence, he noticed Ryan right behind him dragging the fifteen-pound suit over his left shoulder like a good little soldier was meant to do. Bailey was curious. "Hey squirt, how'd you get to the bottom of the sub-basement floor?"

Ryan pointed in the direction of the office. "There's stairs inside to the right of the office over in the corner." He looked around wondering why the questioning. "I found the stairs yesterday when I got bored. There's a secret compartment too. It leads into that cavern below."

Bailey's eyes perked. "What cavern?"

"There's another way out of here, but I think it's barricaded by several doors, looks too spooky if you ask me. It's not a place for children to play for sure."

The men looked at each other. "We'll have to check-out what Ryan is referring too." Bailey said. "We can't leave any stone unturned."

"You're right. I'll have T-DEXTER check it out later." The doctor responded.

"Alright sir. That would be great." Even Dr. EL didn't know about the stairs, but now they all did. Ryan insisted Bailey take a look. He was all hyped up from dragging the suit down three flights of stair and across the hanger floor. Bailey assumed the casual aberration of the boy was something to learn from. Curious minds of curious young hearts were always looking for secrets, and Ryan happened to run into one of the biggest secrets unrevealed until now. Tired of looking, tired of dragging himself around, from one event to another, Bailey stood at his feet. He felt lackluster to move any further.

Ryan noticed his condition too. "Hey, let me wear the suit. I'll take better care of it than you will, and besides, you look beat."

"Sorry squirt, it's my responsibility. I'm tired, but thanks for retrieving the suit. I owe you one."

Ryan's eyes lit up when he'd sensed Bailey was showing him an appreciation for helping. "So, what's in the crates for me Dr. EL? I mean if we have to fight and all, do us kids get to fight?" Ryan blurted out.

"Well, not exactly. You get to learn about some of the weapons, but you won't be in the middle of the battle, besides those creatures are a lot stronger than you think?" Dr. EL explained. "We all need to figure out what we're doing before starting to make plans of where everybody needs to go."

Betty interrupted. "Little man you're small to be facing those creatures out there, remember last time, how scared you were? They're fast."

Ryan's eyes moved quickly back in the doctor's direction. "Well yeah, I guess your right about that. It was scary, but what do us kids get to do?" Bailey looked down at Ryan while the doctor was looking out in the warehouse. Then Dr. EL walked over to Bailey with a line of curiosity written in his eyes. Bailey ignored Ryan when the doctor walked between them.

Ryan waved his hands in front of the doctor. "Hello? Dr. EL…hey I'm talking…" Ryan turned to look at Bailey, frustrated, and upset about being ignored. "Does Dr. EL have a hearing-aid problem?"

Bailey smiling while looking sheepishly at the doctor. "I think he's trying to get your attention."

"Oh, pardon me young man. I didn't see you there."

"Yeah, I kind of figured that, but, if you're listening to me now, what's our part in all this?"

The doctor looked down at the irritating boy and considered his words. He put his arm around the little man's shoulders. "Well young man, we'll just have to see what T-DEXTER can find, and when he does find that perfect gift. We'll let you know. How's that young fellow?"

Ryan wasn't sure about being brushed off like his name was Rex. He displayed a hand-dog look. "Okay..." while lacking enthusiasm, swinging his shoulders, and rolling his eyes from side to side. "I'll wait and see what T-DEXTER finds."

Then the good doctor went on to more critical issues, involving their future to come. Glancing at Bailey he said. "You need to be in the suit, so you can sense where to locate such items—you know. Feel one with the suit, like T-DEXTER suggested."

"Yeah, I guess you're right." Bailey returned with a slight twitch in his eye of comprehension.

Ryan, begrudgingly, went over and handed the suit back to the appointed super-hero as he hung his head expressing a disconsolate attitude. "I know. You guys think I'm too little too fight." He got close enough to where Bailey could sense his energy. Freckles and curls stuffed under a baseball cap. Light brown hair in a disarray of messiness. Big brown eyes of a natural size that matched Betty's. He was a pint-size prince and a pain all mixed into one, with a little boy's thinking of playful mishaps while speaking his mind. A little round tummy stuck out to give his tightly fitted blue shirt form, one tooth missing in front from a perfectly formed row. He was a worthy addition to this party of members. And definitely worth protecting. Bailey measured the boy, with all his questions and childlike attitudes. Serve up one bottle to go of his innocence. He couldn't imagine such a child being torn apart by one of those creatures. This made Bailey's stomach churn to even consider such an event. Somehow, someway, they had to find a solution.

Looking at Ryan he said, "Please don't worry about fighting. You know how dangerous and scary we found the cavern. Let us make it safe, for all of us. Help us to do that, okay?"

Ryan only nodded. They were facing a future of which they were not sure. Then the thoughts came to Bailey. The place hidden below, was a place no one would ever want to go without a lot of back up fire power, and a big-bad-dude standing to the side, shooting ammunition from big guns or missiles over ones shoulder to protect what was considered precious. Because the big bad dudes found in this basement weren't going to be push-over's. They were here to fight, and fight to the death they would. Life didn't always require a moment-by-moment reproduction; it usually required first a willingness, a desire for achievement, and a courageous beginning. To have the will to look beyond failure and see a different light, something not seen but felt in the innermost part of a soldier's heart. As young boys would become men, and young girls would find courage, they were destined to be heroes, to grow, to learn to be leaders of a new and changing world. Yes, this alluded place where those of integrity didn't take to loss without a fight—a fight to the end, and with the support of other big-bad-dudes along the way. Then casually, Bailey reached for the Crepto Suit and sidled into it, as it quickly closed up from behind. He stood for a few minutes while the suit began to conform to his body again. His momentum seemed to leave off right where he was last time.

Crepto drew his focus back to the enormous crate laying toward the back of the warehouse, hidden on the floor beneath them. The writing on the side of the crate with the words, *do not remove,* highlighted with bold red paint. The same type of stamp Bailey and Ryan had seen on their very first day. Crepto detected a hole beneath the floor. It was hidden for a reason, away from the eyes of others. Another minute went by, before he walked over and thought it was a clever idea to remove the crate to the side. *Let's find out what our government was up to with their old tricks.* Crepto thought. Yet for some particular reason something was held back by them that had wanted a promising ending to an unpleasant situation. The suit held him in an eternal trance of memories flashing by. First the storm, then the death of Betty's grandmother, being chased by those irritating creatures, and them just trying to survive. This wasn't a pathway *to* another life going in another direction. It was a pathway leading to danger. Something intangible lay between a good life and that twisting fate of terror below. They were separated by only inches of safety. This was not anything for children or family members wanted to experience. A few minutes later, Crepto turned to look at the others.

"This is the other opening to the cavern below." He said. "This is the same cavern Betty climbed down into, except this is the other end of it, maybe a few miles away from here. It's where they have survived. This is where we'll make the drop. "

T-DEXTER walked over to lend a hand and help his acquired little brother move the crate out of the way. Once the heavy crate was removed, both heroes of the moment stared at the hydraulic door left undercover. They were stalled for a few seconds, to find answers. As if this door to another world would show them something of mystery. They wanted to know what to do next. Crepto turned to look at Betty, who had just pulled up along the side of them. She always had some smart comment to make or idea that might even be of some help. Of all the times to have a dumb look on her face, this was not the right time, because time didn't appear to be on their side. Crepto wanted her help.

Betty looked down at the hydraulic door. She noticed when first arrived, a timer was set to go off three hours from now. But who had set this timer? What was planned so efficiently that didn't include them?

T-DEXTER moved on to other things. He lost interest in the door and went back to opening new crates. Off to the right, he noticed a medium size crate about six feet long and three feet high, and three feet wide, and lying flat on the cemented floor. On the side, was stamped a caution sticker that said high explosives. The robot opened this crate gently not to disturb anything that might have an explosive attitude. He didn't feel like tethering robot parts back together. And didn't want anyone else in his party getting injured either. Suddenly, T-DEXTER drew their interest away from the door by yelling.

"Hey little lady! Look what I found!"

Betty wheeled herself over where the big robot was staring. Then looking down she saw what he was looking at. She smiled and looked up. "Toys for the boys." She said. "You'd better let me have that, so no one gets hurt."

Crepto glanced over from hearing added information. "Sure… take them. Just don't roll them under your bed. They might change your attitude." Betty wrinkled her nose knowing he'd spoken out of turn.

"Never mind what I do with them, you just concern yourself with those creatures below. We can't allow them to get in here." Crepto was sorry for mentioning personalized comments about grenades changing attitudes. He was still staring at this mystery door.

Back where Betty was seated, T-DEXTER brought out one package of C-4 neatly stacked in the bottom of the same crate covered by bubble-wrap. Also, lying at the bottom was a metal briefcase with spongy gray foam. Betty could only imagine was that was. T-DEXTER gave the girl some room. He noticed she was totally engulfed in their recent noise of opening so many crates, without the doctor's approval. There was packing tape and Styrofoam everywhere. What a mess.

"Maybe the grenades would come in handy on the open road." Crepto said.

"You might me right…" T-DEXTER replied.

"We'll load the Q-Tank up with them. The Pailoids will get a blast out of them. To keep them from hanging onto the sides of the vehicles."

Crepto noticed the sword and shield in the distance. Someone had left them about forty feet away. They were leaning up against a crate behind him. He wondered if T-DEXTER was the one that brought them back to the warehouse from yesterday.

Looking back at the sword Crepto thought if they were damaged in any way. "Did anything happen to the sword?" He asked T-DEXTER when walking up.

"There's a few scratches," The robot said, "but hey little brother, take it easy next time, this was just practice. You can save the gusto for later."

"Sorry big brother. I didn't know what the suit is capable of doing. I'm new to this. It's still all a little confusing." Then his memories of the Star-Wars episodes came to mind. *Luke, let the force be with you.* He could imagine being like the famed Jedi-knight Obi-Wan Kenobi, being led by the force to some mystery planet to be trained by Yoda the Grand Jedi Master. Yet maybe his imagination did run wild at times giving him some type of creative force to help push him to make better decisions. Who knows, there was a little Star Wars in all of them when pushed to be their best. Then this weird aura of enlightenment circled in around him. Crepto thought of the dangers facing them soon if they weren't more pressed to finish in a timely manner. He looked up suddenly to see a divine revelation. Concentrating on what Ryan had said to all of them earlier. There was something for the children to use for protection. And then it hit him. He couldn't chance one of the children being scratched or bitten by one of those creatures below. There had to be something in this warehouse that the children could wear to protect them. The suit pulled him to a different area where a smaller crate lay close the back wall away from the sight of others. The crate looked like any other, but for an apparent reason he knew something in it would be a good find for the children. He walked straight to the crate and dismantled the top. Ryan was curious why a sudden change of direction too, so he followed Crepto to the wall.

Inside the crate were three small, suited vests made out of a synthetic metal mesh like you would find on a knight's armor. Crepto pulled the three suited vests from the crate. When doing so, he noticed something else strangely placed in the bottom of the same crate. There were three, three-foot black sticks, similar seen from policemen of the 1930's would use on a normal beat of duty. On closer examination, He also understood they were different from any night stick he had ever seen. There was an on and off switch on the side giving it some type of purpose of which he hadn't thought. Holding the odd stick out in front of him, he pushed the switch on. A blue blaze of light shot from the end of this most magnificent find. A blue arc of light gave off a bolt of electricity. This was cool. Betty would be pleased, was his next thought. Speaking of Betty, she'd just rolled up next to him. She imagined him being a lost little boy with his over exuberant imagination getting the best of him.

"What's in the box?" She asked while looking up at him with her usual untrusting glare.

Crepto raised an eyebrow and looked down. They held a mutual bond of skepticism. "Something for the children to wear, I mean, if it's okay with you."

Noticing the suited vests too and the over-exemplified night-sticks, she was sensing a bit of caution crossing her mind. "Well, if you insist, but they need to be careful with them." She said while a suspicious glance flashed across her eyes. "Make sure they know how to use them in the proper way. You know how Ryan looks at everything being like a toy."

Crepto reflected a flicker of comprehension with a nod. He wasn't sure he was buying *in* to her doubtful acknowledgment. "Yeah, I know. Ryan's got quite the imagination." Then turning his head Crepto called out to Ryan. "Hey squirt! Put on one of these—let's see how it fits."

Ryan didn't know if he liked this latest attire. Moving his eyes side to side he looked a bit skittish. Grabbing for one of the night-sticks first swinging it around like he was Zorro. Maybe marking the backsides of his latest victims would please him quite efficiently, like a game of tag. Taking aim at the seat of someone's pants. Having his victims running for their lives. *This might be fun,* Ryan thought. This brought a smile to the boy's face.

Abruptly, Crepto grabbed what Ryan accepted as Tinker Bells wand of wonder made him drop the silly grin. "Hey! Give me that back!" Ryan yelled.

"Now hold on!" Crepto yelled back. "This is not a play toy! Be careful!"

Ryan had a devilish sparkle glazed in his eyes. "I'm not going to touch anyone with it. I just wanted to see what kind of juice it has. Just give it a test run." Crepto kept him from getting the wand back.

T-DEXTER took a step behind Crepto. The devilish look in Ryan's eyes would be something to be afraid of. Who knows what the child was capable of. "Hey squirt, which could mess up my circuit boards." The big robot said. "You'd better watch where you're pointing that thing."

Ryan was leaking giggles. Betty fed up with boy's and there silliness came over. "Stop it Ryan or I'll send you to your room!" Ryan looked back at Betty and knew she were serious, so he held back from reaching for the black stick. Crepto put it back into the crate. Ryan stared at the metal-mesh-suited vest. "So, what does this thing actually do?" Ryan turned his eyes to his mentor of the last 11 days.

"It will keep you from being bitten by one of those creatures."

Ryan raised both eyebrows. "Oh, well, I guess I'll be wearing one of these vests then." Without making it a contest, Ryan tried to figure out how to crawl into the funny looking metal vest. But once he was in it, Betty's smile widened when seeing how cute he looked. Then she covered her mouth to hold back a giggle. Ryan glanced up at her with this dumbfounded expression. "Why are you looking at me like that?"

"Nothing really, you look cute, like a little night from King Arthur's court."

Ryan wondered if they were all smiling for the same reason. "Maybe T-DEXTER can be my jester and I can play funny tricks on him." Then everyone was smiling, except T-DEXTER looked confused.

T-DEXTER ignored the boy with the vivid imagination as he opened another crate. This next crate was full of walkie-talkies and gadgets with a bunch of batteries in the bottom. Ryan saw the walkie-talkies and walked over. T-DEXTER, still a little leery about the small boy prodding his back side, or searching for a lost watch, he didn't know. Only showing a little doubt about Ryan's true intentions. T-DEXTER handed the misguided youth a walkie-talkie. Ryan played with the buttons for a few seconds, and then looked up at the funny looking robot.

"It doesn't work." Ryan shook the walkie-talkie. He figured that by shaking the gray communication box it would start to squawk.

T-DEXTER mouthed, "Hey squirt, it needs batteries—here." He handed Ryan a hand full of batteries.

Ryan rolled his eyes. "No duh! I'm not stupid you big dork." Then Ryan had recalled on several occasions Betty calling Bailey that famed name of worthy-hood. He grinned and looked up at Crepto who'd already sensed the young boy's personification.

"Don't look at me like that. That's not what she meant." Crepto said.

"Yeah, it is. She thinks you're the dork."

Crepto smiled but said. "How would you like me to put a grenade in your jump-suit squirt?" Ryan got an imaginative smile as another giggle leaked from his mouth.

"Those can't be any worse than my farts." More giggles leaked out as he tried to cover his mouth. Crepto ran over and carefully picked him up with one leg while tickling him. Ryan had to catch his breath from being flipped upside down. He giggled while releasing one of his deadly bombs right in the direction of Crepto's face. Everyone smiled when this happened. Crepto, outgunned by Ryan's backside sat him gently back to the ground. Ryan, still giggling, turned red.

"Okay…that's enough boys. We've got work to do." Dr. EL said.

T-DEXTER jerked back and smacked Ryan lightly on the butt while going into a spastic jig and song routine. "When you're hot you're hot…when you're not you're not! That's the way…aha, aha…I like it. Aha, aha…" This was a song by KC and the Sunshine Band. T-DEXTER moved in the groove of the music. "Do-do-do-…do-do-do…do-do-do… that's the way [uh-huh, uh-huh] I like it [uh-huh uh-huh] that's the way." He was moving his robot hips left then right while dipping his arms down in a circular motion, flexing his head in the same manner. Ryan looked up at him all bug-eyed.

Betty was surprised by the sudden spastic bit of humor. She said. "You okay, big fellow?" Betty expressed a sarcastic manner. "Want to borrow my wheelchair?"

T-DEXTER chuckled as if he was flying high on his own sense of belonging. "You guys need to lighten up a bit, learn to love, live and boogey!" The big robot was still chuckling at his own personal performance.

Ryan glanced up at him and said. "Are you low on oil or something?" Everyone laughed. Even Betty squeezed out a few chuckles about the misalignment of his spastic humor. He was fun to be with. The robot, although a bit odd, added some flare to this little family. Even Dr. EL sensed they were bonding. Their focus was off, but the camaraderie and mixing of emotions for the moment gave them reason to be hear, however that was meant to be. They were a dysfunctional group at best, but they were a team.

In the distance, Betty was pulled mentally to a long and tall, strange looking crate over ten feet high and eighteen feet long. It was so big no one had even considered the crate as being a part of the rest of what they'd seen here, below in this warehouse. Something out of the ordinary had to be behind its covering—something that might change their odds. She signaled for T-DEXTER to come over and give her a hand. He looked down sensing her abrupt curiosity strange. It was sitting on its own, detached from everything else. The crate was just waiting to be discovered. T-DEXTER and Crepto came over to help dismantle it. Once the crate was taken apart from the front view everyone stood in awe. Betty had her mouth open. This was another vulgar display of wealth by their government. Standing before them was an over-sized black Hummer just sitting there on wide tires, pretty and shiny and built like a modified tank with two Gait 30M machine guns attached to the top. No one said anything for the moment, because it was never meant for the plebeian person walking the streets. It was meant for someone with a chutzpah character and lots of money to throw around. It was a vehicle of the future and not of the past. *It would run over anything and keep going,* Betty thought. And unexpectedly, she reached up with one of her pistols and squeezed off a round. The bullet rebounded off the window and went buzzing in Dr. EL's left ear.

Dr. EL shouted. "Hey, hey, little lady those are real bullets! Don't be shooting them off in the hangar! You might hit one of us!"

"My bad Dr. EL. I just wanted to see if the Hummer was bullet proof. I got my answer." Betty sat staring at this modern marvel. It had all the latest gadgets for the over imaginative mind. It was slick, stylish, overbearing, Jacked-up, bad-ass, black as night, out of sight, exactly right—according to Betty. She felt like a kid scoring her first bicycle. She'd made up her mind. "This toy's mine," she said, as she looked at Crepto. "Since I can't walk, I'll drive this baby. They'll never know what hit them. I'll show those creatures what a one legged, two pistol gripping, long range shooting, four-wheel-driven, five-foot three step-in tomboy with a deranged attitude is all about."

This got Dr. EL to smile while Crepto looked back peculiarly and shook his head.

He walked over to the Hummer and heaved it up off the ground. He sat it on his shoulder like a bag of dog food pulled off the shelf at the local supermarket.

"That looks heavy." Betty said.

"Not really," Crepto returned, "feels a little awkward that's all." He sat the over emphasized Hummer gently back to the ground.

"Be careful with that." Betty barked. "I wouldn't want you to put any dents in my new ride." Everyone turned to look at her. Betty got up on one crutch as Crepto opened the driver side door as a personal invitation. The Gait 30M machine guns at the top were controlled from the steering wheel by easily maneuverable joystick placed in the middle. Betty turned back and smiled. "Screw the Barbie-dolls," she said, "look at this." The ammo for the guns was connected by two large metal boxes sitting in the back area where usually a bench seat would be, but it had been taken out and modified for military missions, not for comfort. The front console was a dream in itself. It had relay buttons for self-loading cartridges that would auto-feed new ammo slides with a sequence override switch after automatic ejection of used shells. This modified war machine was self-reliant. A hydraulic lift on a computer monitored screen released a scud cannon that sprung from the roof for Missile discharge. "Wow..." Betty exclaimed. "That might leave a few holes in this mountain."

Crepto absorbing everything in front of the console then said. "Well, you'll just have to be careful what you aim that at."

Betty smiled while looking at the young super-hero. "All I need now is my Tank-girl T-shirt and I'm ready to go!"

A smile broke out on Crepto's face. "You can lead with the Hummer, and I'll follow behind and clean up whatever you miss. The problem is..." Crepto said slowly, "I'm not sure about leaving this compound unprotected is the way to go. We need a little more fire power." He assisted when glancing back at Dr. EL.

"Sir...you can draw up the schematics on this facility before we go off on a whim. I want to make sure every corner is covered."

Dr. EL's ears perked to the message and nodded with an understanding glance.

Crepto opened up the conversation again. "I feel that Betty and I can draw them out with something that will force them from their hiding place. I think the robots would only scare them farther back into that cavern. We need to hit them with something strong enough to make them leave their place of safety." Crepto leaned over and whispered in Betty's ear. "So, what you think?"

Betty surprised by Crepto's quick insertion. "Well, my personal opinion, I think you're nuts, but what the heck, I'm in. Try to stay close to me. I wouldn't want you to drift too far back and leave me on my own. I'm not sure how much abuse this Hummer will take." Betty said in one long breath.

"We won't know until we get there." Crepto responded back. "Dr. EL will get us through the first gate on the other end of the compound. He's the only one who has a hand and eye signature fitted for the electronic gates." Crepto said. "Right now, that's our only way out of this compound, unless we blast our way out, which I don't see as being a good idea, since it's colder than the last ice-age out there." He looked into

Betty's eyes to make sure she was listening. "It would leave this facility unguarded. So, blasting our way out is not an option."

"Maybe we'll find something else before we leave?" Betty wondered if there could be something else of significance yet to be discovered.

"Like what?" Crepto said.

"Maybe we'll find another toy like our friend over there." Betty responded, as she looked at T-DEXTER. "Besides we haven't seen all that's down here yet—you never know."

"Point taken, but we're running out of time. Those creatures below sense us to be their next meal. They're not going to sit tight for too much longer." Crepto said. "I wouldn't doubt their hunger will push them to come this way—you get my drift?"

Then Betty thought of the perfect diversion. "Dr. EL…those creatures below don't they breathe air just like we do?"

"Yes, so what's your point young lady?"

"We can gas them out. Wouldn't that work? I mean any toxic chemical breathed through the air will be toxic to them too. Wouldn't that be a correct assumption?"

"Yes. You've got a good point there young lady, so what do you have in mind?"

"What about a chloride-based compound mixed with ammonia, doesn't that make a type of lethal gas?" Betty asked.

Dr. EL reached down and kissed her on the top of the head. "And of course, the smartest one in the building would have to think of the perfect way to draw them out. Good goin girl—I had a feeling you'd produced something." Crepto rolled his eyes seeing that her head was already getting too big.

Betty expelled a slight hesitation. "So, my idea is workable?"

"It's more than workable—we can do this. It will only take a little planning." Dr. EL said. He turned suddenly and started walking toward the office a good two hundred feet to his left and up a flight of stairs. When getting there, Dr. EL picked up the phone to call George and gave him the news. A few minutes later Dr. EL was back with a smile, and new sense of direction.

"What's the smile about?" Betty asked.

"George has a fifty-gallon barrel of ammonia and a considerable amount of bleach. He said he'll have them up here in about an hour. In the meantime, we have more crates to open."

Betty stared barking orders like she was in charge. "Ryan, go help George get all the bottles of bleach and ammonia up to this warehouse with the girls, Crepto, T-DEXTER, we need for you two to keep opening crates. Dr. EL get the schematics for this compound, we've got to cover all the weak points in this structure, leave nothing overlooked."

Without responding, Crepto was drawn to the far-left corner of the warehouse. He walked a good two hundred and fifty feet from where the others were standing. He sensed something strange, some type of support that they couldn't live without, but at the same time something redeeming from what had normally been found in this secretive warehouse. Crepto reached down and pried the lid off the top of a crate that looked a little bit thicker than a casket. Surprised by what he had found, yet there it was, a life size man or what appeared to be a man in military attire. Crept reached down and picked up this soldier of fortune, this G I Joe of a military persuasion and sat him straight up, on his feet. He was motionless, surreal, a strong looking masculine type. The soldier looked about six foot three, a good 250 pounds, if he'd been of the human species. But Crepto figured him more like four hundred and fifty pounds, considering he wasn't made from flesh and bone. He looked right through him and knew he was different in a way that no ordinary soldier could ever be. He was a force to be reckoned with for sure. A soldier of an altered state of being, even though he had skin, and even put off the scent of the human male. He wasn't human. Crepto took in this optical impression and noticed through closer examination that this soldier was a complicated piece of work, with computer graphics throughout his system. Intelligent and sophisticated piece of equipment. He was a one-man dream-team. He was a terminator of a military influence. Crepto had no idea how to wake this Cyborg up. And he didn't know if he would be of a cooperative nature even if that was possible. Within a few minutes, everyone was drawn toward this piece of work pulled from the crate. Betty and T-DEXTER were spell-bound by what they saw. Ryan had left for the zoo already and was gone. DR. EL would soon return with the schematics they needed. Betty had circled around this pretty piece of equipment and wondered. She smiled and looked at Crepto and T-DEXTER.

"He's not bad looking from my point of view. A little too muscle bound as for what it's worth." She is smiling a hint of jealousy from Crepto would suit her fine. Crepto shook his head and passed her playful stares off as immature.

Dr. EL was back and noticed the Cyborg right away. He walked over to the crate he'd come in and began looking for a manual for the Cyborg, but all he could find was a gun too heavy to pick up in the bottom of the crate.

"So how do we turn him on?" Betty said.

"Well not by batting your eyelashes at him." Crepto remarked.

Betty ignored the remark and got up out of her wheelchair on one crutch. "I think he has a keypad like T-DEXTER." Betty said. Right away, she noticed the number 731 tattooed on the back of his neck. Betty without thinking, not wanting to offend anyone, lifted the soldier's grey T-shirt from behind and saw a hidden flip-plate in the middle of his back. She pushed on the flip-plate with her index finger. It rotated around and a keypad popped open with lettering and a numbers system displayed on a small monitoring screen of a bluish tint. Betty pushed in the numbers 731 and hit enter. She backed up while the screen automatically closed up from behind and pulled his shirt back down. Right away the Cyborg began to move and opened his eyes. Startled, unsure where he was at, didn't hesitate to reach for the gun left behind in the crate. T-DEXTER reached over to stop the Cyborg while Betty flipped around in her wheelchair and got out of the way. Crepto reached over and grabbed the startled Cyborg from behind to keep him from grabbing the heavy gun. The Cyborg matching T-DEXTER's strength. He pushed T-DEXTER a good thirty feet away to clear a path for the gun. Crepto kept him from advancing though.

"Let me go!" The Cyborg yelled.

"Hold on man! We're not here to hurt you! We're on the same side! Give us a minute to explain!" Crepto said. "Who are you?"

The Cyborg still struggling. "I said let go of me!"

"Not until you calm down. We don't want to hurt you. This is a military installation, but we're not in any immediate danger. We need your help." These words caused the Cyborg to stop struggling, and he noticed the girl in the wheelchair wasn't looking too much of a threat, and no one else had any guns. He blinked his eyes a couple of times as Crepto let go. In a lower voice Crepto began to tell the Cyborg the account of the last eleven days of solitude, and the creatures below. After about ten minutes, the Cyborg loosened up. He sensed nothing remained a threat by what he could tell. Then, he began to share his bizarre account of the last three years.

"My creator was a scientist named Dr. Alfred Geneses." *Not surprised in the least Crepto thought.* "He had programmed me for the end—the end of all mankind, chosen for destruction. I was set to help in the destruction of those creatures you've mentioned."

T-DEXTER put out his hand as a friendly gesture of approachability.

"Well, big fella, put it right there. We're on the same team." The Cyborg looked down at the hand and didn't know what the robot meant by his over friendliness. The Cyborg gave in and grabbed T-DEXTER's hand in introductions. After a few minutes, this eccentric Cyborg with the square cut jaw, blue eyes, and dark military haircut, shared of what he knew.

"My name is Bristol. I'm a sergeant by rank. I'm a Cybernetic unit created from the 731 series of the Cryobines Intellect systems. My system is fully charged with an Intel Nitro pack placed in my hard drive frame. The Nitro pack is good for about 150 years. My command module was pre-set by Dr. Geneses three years ago from today. The government tried to modify my unit to fit their needs, but Dr. Geneses put an override chip within my circuitry board, which superseded all other commands. My mission was and is to save the humans from their own destruction. Dr. Alfred Geneses saw the end coming. He died by protecting me. I owe him my gratitude. The government could only control me by disconnecting my power module." Crepto and Betty were surprised that this odd-looking Cyborg named Bristol would hold an emotional connection to his creator. They looked at each other not knowing what to think. Crepto held out his hand.

"Well, for second introductions Sergeant Bristol my name is Bailey outside this suit, but they call me Crepto, when I'm wearing it."

Bristol looked confused by Bailey's introduction.

"And this is Betty." He pointed to T-DEXTER's sidekick SNARF and Dr. EL and made their introductions also.

"It's a pleasure to meet you. This military facility you're in is something we found by accident—well except Dr. EL and George, who have their place here, besides that, we're all on our own. Nobody else made it past the gates." Crepto paused for a second letting Sergeant Bristol make his way around to each individual, while he noted there was only a hand full of them. "Dr. EL will explain in a minute what we're up against." Within a few minutes, the doctor took over the conversation and began to explain about the homemade gas bomb they'd intended to roll into the cavern below, and their desired effect of drawing those creatures out. When done, the sergeant glared at his newly acquired friends. This was quite the predicament they were in, and he didn't really know what to say in return, except for the bare essentials of moving forward with their plans.

Then Crepto informed him. "We need your help in facing what's ahead. Are you familiar with the JR-22 Q-Tank?"

"I'm familiar with all the military equipment within this compound." Bristol stated. Without being noticed by the others, he had mentally scanned the whole inside warehouse taking in all the military vehicles and made detailed registration of them in his memory.

Crepto stated further. "This is the only facility within hundreds of miles that we can make a stand and have a chance of survival. The weather outside is at its peak maturity. Nothing human or animal not acclimated to freezing weather climate, outside these mountains could last exceedingly long in the weather. This is the only place of safety."

Bristol showed a nod of understanding. "So, when do we get started?" The sergeant asked.

"Shortly, probably within the hour if all goes well." Crepto looked around the warehouse briefly, reconnoitering the present conditions of their equipment before heading into the unknown. From a distance, Crepto saw George driving a miniaturized electric truck with the drums of needed liquid materials in the back of the bed. He was up on the second level, so Crepto made hast in that direction. Together, with T-DEXTER's help, they moved to the first level to retrieve the materials needed. Once back to the bottom level, they lifted the cleaning liquids from the truck bed and sat them to the side of the front unopened hydraulic steel door. The timer was only a few hours from expiring. And they weren't quite ready to open it. They had a limited window of opportunity ahead of them. Their timing had to be perfect. No margin of error would be allowed.

Betty, with Ryan's help, had loaded all the equipment she'd need for the drive down the tunnels. Ryan kept the medal vest on. The little girls were made to put the synthetic metal mesh vests on too. Each was shown the proper way to use the modified night sticks with the electrical charge. They were almost ready to leave. Bristol road in a Q-Tank modified with the Gait 30M machine guns mounted on top. It was just what he needed—to give him a little more fire power.

Looking back at Betty, Crepto was concerned about Betty's leg and driving the Hummer. She insisted everything was fine—so they were ready.

Ryan saw them looking at each other. He stared at Bristol wondering how they got so lucky. So, they were on their way. Time had flown by. They were spiked by the rules of engagement. Ryan walked over and opened the other side of the Hummer and crawled up over on the seat and closed the door. His eyes surveying this over exemplified vehicle with gadgets and switches had him all bug-eyed. *Wow,* he thought. *We're going to kick butt.*

CHAPTER 24

Preparation

The hangar had half the crates emptied by now. All the crate pieces strung out all over the sub-basement floor. T-DEXTER, Sergeant Bristol, and Crepto pushed the empty crates out of the way and neatly stacked the broken wood and swept the floor clean. Starting from nothing, they took the gathered household chemicals from the zookeeper and created a two-fold siphon system from two containers to one, bringing both chemicals together into a large glass beaker type of system. The liquid appeared to cloud as the two began to join as one. Only a few minutes remained on the timer connected to the hydraulic door. It would be ready to open any minute, just a turn of a handle would break the barrier of two worlds. George had brought several gas masks that T-DEXTER had found in the storage warehouse above. Betty, George, Dr. EL, and Ryan had put on the masks, just in case some of the chemicals were aired within the compound. The robots, Crepto, and Sergeant Bristol waited for the timer to expire. But Crepto and the sergeant wouldn't be here when the door was finally opened. It was 8:30 P.M. and Betty was tired with her bout with the cut and having been stuck in the wheelchair for a good many hours without circulation. Her once sallow color reminded Crepto of the turmoil she'd faced a few days back. They were spent from the last eleven days of mayhem, but without doing anything further, things would worse as the night progressed. Bailey in the suit was worried about Betty's ability to perform among the ranks of the Pailoids and doubted her stamina to endure. Yet he knew she was too stubborn to be left out of this little skirmish. He remembered that she hadn't had a Tetanus shot from the metal that had caused that nasty cut. Suddenly, knowing the importance of being safe, he darted away from their presence and flew up the stairs to level three where the med-lab was. He retained certain items needed to procure desired serum and syringe to administer a shot to Betty before they would be led off down a tunneled dirt road towards a mission thought almost impossible. Crepto knew nothing would be better, thinking a healthy dose of serum before giving your life up to some mystified creature not understood. Besides, better to be in tip-top shape, one shot left before the silent gibbering of deaths toll. Death could be what was considered by the few, the grim reaper peering through nefarious eyes fading in the vestiges of fleeting heartbeats. As viewed, those creatures mimicked a time not recorded in anyone's history. They were a new species waiting in the darkened crevices of this Earth, ready to pounce upon its wanted victims in the abattoir of a final soon end. Each species leaves their epoch marks weighing in the portended reflections of their fading existence—to wreak havoc of those of the human species. Crepto's imagination peeked by the seething metaphors flashing before his eyes. There were no limits where his imagination would take him with the connection of the suit. Those duped images of torment that he had experienced, were mindful of the creatures which expelled no pellucid adherence of gender. They were as one mind of confusion giving only purpose to hunger, to destruction, to the end of all life, separate from the frozen world up above. They were left behind, forgotten, making a way for a new species to take the lead.

Once returned to the sub-basement floor, Crepto rolled up Betty's sleeve and administered the needed injection.

Betty yelled. "Ouch, which hurt you big dork! I'm not your punching bag! Go a little easy on the needles!" This caused Bailey in the suit to smile. She was back to her usual self. This pleased him as he knew she'd need this recent spunk to get her through the next couple of hours. Looking beyond the borders of the compound, Crepto sensed the fight ahead would help her blow off some personal steam that had been building up from the last few days. She was due to placate the mounting tension of being held back. And noted her sitting a lot the last few days had taken its toll.

"Can you drive with the bad wheel? I mean your leg?"

Betty's eyes flashed a sign of equanimity, like her veins were infused with a soothing drug of self-reliance. Her nerves were on edge, but her mind was clear, and her pose held to their mission ahead. "I'm fine." She said without elaborating.

Crepto sensed her insight to be as a vivid picture of fearlessness. A rebel in the worst of forms, an injured bear searching for her lost cub, or a vampire smelling the last remains of blood left on Earth. She was like an unlit pack of dynamite raucous to the terms of waiting. She was the alpha of their soon to be omega. She was termed as a terminator covered in silk and lace to confuse the enemy with her true intentions. She was ready like Freddy, and she exposed her objectives in a sullen way.

"Why don't you ride with me?" Betty insisted, as she looked at the surprised Bailey hiding behind the suit. "Besides, Sergeant Bristol knows what he's doing. I'm the injured one—remember? We should stay together."

"Yes, I guess you're right."

"And" she said. "You don't stand a chance without me."

Crepto looked up at T-DEXTER, after ignoring Betty's last comment. "You and your sidekick will stay here and make the drop. Don't let anything pass this door, and if they do get passed the door you have to kill them all. Leaving nothing to roam this place. You get me?"

T-DEXTER gave a salute from the head. "Got your back little brother, we'll keep them out." Bristol finished equipping the modified JR-22 Q-Tank and double checked all the systems. He was ready and steady with nerves of steel.

The children were made to put on the synthetic suits for protection. Ryan walked up to Crepto with a curious expression on his face. Wondering what the pint size boy was about to say jumped the gun when saying. "Let's lock the children in one of the Q-Tanks and lower it into the lagoon. The creatures won't be able to trace their scent. We'll draw the Pailoids away, if they get beyond the gate's borders, you'll know what to do." Crepto finished saying.

Ryan interrupted him. "Can I go with you guys?" Betty sensed the boy was feeling a little insecure about being left behind. Crepto looked at Betty as she noticed his unblinking stare.

"So, what ya think? Should we take Ryan with us?"

Ryan's eyes flared with excitement. "Well, I don't know? We might not come back." Crepto said.

Ryan expelled personal exasperation by the huffing of discontented air. He'd quickly folded his pint-size arms across his chest with his bottom lip hanging out. He was quite the actor and selling his image on a very committed act.

"You guys might need me as back-up. I can hand you things and make calls to the others if your hands are full, and besides there's only enough room in the Q-Tank for two. The girls will be fine without me in the middle of everything, and I think I'd be of some use coming along, and besides," He over emphasized. "I'm the youngest."

Crepto eyed Betty for an answer, but she'd left it up to Crepto to make the right call. Somehow, there was no way a small boy could have his part in the violence that was to come, but also, Crepto knew that taking Ryan would be a learning lesson that would stick with him the rest of his life. Yet, he still remained hesitant about putting Ryan in the forefront of what was to come. Crepto nodded as Ryan showed a cheerful glare. He ran to get his gear. Betty wondered if they were doing the right thing, yet somehow deep inside her, she knew this would cause Ryan to quickly grow-up, omitting any obfuscation of previous. Somehow, they would protect him from what was to come. He would be tethered between them in the heat of battle. The little girls would be left alone, with Cuddles, buried in twenty-five feet of water. While T-DEXTER would be on the other side of the compound—far enough away not to offer a protecting hand. If those creatures passed T-DEXTER's guard, would they even be safe? No one was safe anywhere, from Crepto's point of view. They were all taking risks, yet running could never be an option. Fighting for their rights to live was their only option.

George and Dr. EL would take the lead in the four-by-four red truck, only procuring them through the first gate, and then taking them to safety behind its thick protected layers of steel. Later, they would be there to let everyone of their party back through the opening, and then close the gate leaving what was left of those creatures behind. George was a little nervous. *Why do I have to go?* He thought. And Dr. EL was no spring chicken either. They were two old men taking the lead for a bunch of kids to go into battle, with a futuristic breed of Cyborg with no sense of humor. *Who were they kidding? A bunch of crazy kids not* knowing *what they were doing. God help us all.* George thought.

Dr. EL leaned out the window feeling the cool air hit his face. They were really doing this. Where was my say-so, I'd never agreed to this insane cause after thinking about it. The doctor thought. What if they all get killed? Who'd run this place then?

The air beat against Crepto's face in an awkward procession, like memories of his life passing through his hair. He wasn't Superman or that big green guy with the extra muscles, and even if they had the guidance of the Crepto Suit and that strange looking Cyborg, what were their odds of having success?

Crepto had loaded his shield and sword, along with Ryan in the back behind the large shadowy grey metal boxes of ammo. There was a small space for Ryan back behind the passenger seat, but this would place him just in front of the firing shells expelling heat. From the front seat view, Ryan looked a tad nervous. They were all anxious, showing nervous tension. This was a mistake in bringing him. He was just a boy. This was the first time he'd been seen with a taciturn nature, usually Ryan was the first to speak, and last to follow critical directions. Crepto turned back to view him for a second, dubious of bringing him along, of course, feigning emotion so Ryan would take this seriously. Betty reached to flip the high beams on as the road up ahead was blacker than night, eerie shadows loom of noncommittal in form. It gave Betty a creepy feeling rising on the back of her neck. *What's going on?* she thought. They were behind Dr. EL who was driving the red four-by-four truck. Dr. EL was showing nervous tension within every nerve-racking turn and shift of change. Betty almost honked to give him a wake-up call, then had second thoughts, knowing any extra noise right now might be a bad call.

The girls were already in their own Q-Tank. Crepto had settled it to the bottom of the lagoon. Only the robots were left behind. This made him worry.

Suddenly, Betty heard the squawk box make a high pitch squeak. "Q-3 this is Q-5 over!" A young girl's voice came over the speaker. Betty grabbed the connection to the walkie-talkie. "Q-5 I hear you. What's your twenty?"

Three seconds went by before Jackie's voice came back over the speaker. "I just wanted to say be careful. I mean don't be heroes." Betty turned to look at Crepto from the passenger seat. Then she said.

"Jackie don't worry. We'll be okay. You girls stay quiet until we get back." A long pause before Betty heard a returned answer.

"We'll be okay Q-3—I mean Betty." Jackie said.

"How's Cuddles holding up?"

"She's fine. She's nervous just like the rest of us, but she'll be alright."

"You girls be good. We'll be back in a couple of hours."

"Ten-four, love you…over and out."

Betty's eyes got watery from that last response as she hung up the receiver. Crepto saw the look from across the dash and knew Jackie had hit a soft spot. He turned to look back at Ryan, who held a pasty white glare in his eyes. He could tell Ryan wasn't sure about what they were getting into. He had sweat already beading on his face, so Crepto tried to calm him. "Are you ready little man?"

Ryan only nodded.

Crepto understood the curious glare of fear crossing the small boy's face. He looked back at him again. "If you get scared, I want you to crawl up underneath this seat and cover your head and say a little prayer if you can't think of anything to do. Don't look at the blood."

Those five words made Ryan's heart sink. *Blood, why would there be blood? And whose blood was he talking about? Wait a minute.* He thought. *I should go back.* Yet it was too late, they were already on their way and close to their destination.

The Q-Tank was about a hundred yards behind the Hummer. Crepto could see through the body of the Q-Tank, so he looked into the side behind them, nothing but emptiness of a cold dark tunnel lay behind, and what lay ahead was still held in mystery of the road ahead. He was worried. He wondered if this slower vehicle would be fast enough to flee the defiant enemy that was soon to greet them. What were they doing? And why all of a sudden did he feel his stomach drop below him like a heavy weight? Is this something they really had to do? Then the burned-up hearse pervaded his memory. And that strange hideous creature that blew hot pungent breath in his face caused him to shudder. Betty looked over and caught the gesture. He felt the chill of death hovering over him, like the lucidity of the moment was forthcoming, and there was nothing he could do about it except face the fire coming up ahead. Crepto felt a florid rush of heat run through his veins. They had to be smart about everything they did that night in perfect order as their phalanxes should be, every angle of attack had to be measured, every decision concise without making any mistakes, because anything short of perfection could mean the end of life as they knew it. And Crepto wasn't buying anyone not doing their job to the line of the letter. He didn't want to underestimate this enemy. And he was sure they wouldn't underestimate them. They were a driving force.

Just ahead, Crepto saw the first barrier separating them from the other side of their long-lost awaited destiny. It was the first gate…

CHAPTER 25

The First Battle

Dr. EL got out of the red four by four truck and hurriedly walked toward the utility pole with the green glowing phosphorescent light. The light blinked portended signs of things to come. The gate before him was a stoic reminder of the massive gates outside the compound. And it was a reminder of also where Bailey and Betty had first found out their fate. Their future destiny as seen in the signs was to be experienced in the not-too-distant future. They were pictured behind the walls of fortitude in this quickly fading world of yesterday. Crepto got out of the Hummer for a minute to make sure they were on the same page of understanding. Dr. EL would stay behind with George to make sure they had a way back in. The dark recesses of this pervading world that lay ahead was hermetically sealed from the world outside…a separate life was facing them. Yet if those creatures got into their compound everything would change for the worst. Their first decadent beginnings with those below left a sense of trepidation in Crepto's bones. He was bent on changing their situation, even at the expense of self-sacrifice. He had to draw focus, and not let his feelings get the best of him. Yet knowing what to do and when to do it was not written in any language he'd ever understand. He had to go off instinct and what the Crepto Energy propelled him to do. Nothing was by chance or accidental consistency. It was destiny that had marked him, and through the time to come he had to face something not human head-to-head.

Dr. EL turned to look at Crepto with a disconsolate glare that usually comes with fright. The doctor's vivid memories of the creatures experienced, from a few days ago, appeared to be mirrored in his eyes. He didn't want to open the gate. Yet he knew this boy who'd taken on a role fit for a hero would not give in, he would fight no matter what the doctor said, or did. Their time was now. And the paling lights of the night flickered in the distance as their emotions began to rise for the occasion of the night was at their very door. They were headed down a road leading to a justifiable end.

Betty looked out toward the two men who spoke in the silence of unheard words. She wasn't the same girl that sat on the edge of the bridge eleven days ago. She was in complaisance about their journey even though numbness had left a dour expression on her face. She'd moved on from a little girl onto becoming a vixen of visage, a warrior waging a war with the support of those seen as hero's, pulling them along with her on this dismal night. She was polluted by the rage they were soon to face. Soldier's fitted for a course that an ordinary man or woman would not walk, who would soon return with the scars and memories of what was left. As her grandmother had taught her so well, to be strong; it was embedded in her character.

Ryan sat quietly in the back trying to draw up the courage for what was to come. In all his innocence he'd placed himself in an enigma—no turning back, no going home. The thrill of what walked and crawled and scurried in the night left a chill reaching to his bones.

Bristol grabbed the com-line when he pulled up next to the Hummer. "Q-5 this is Q-7, what's your status?"

Betty reached over and grabbed the com-line. "Q-7 we can't make the call until we're next to the hole we left behind eleven days ago."

"Roger Q-5, I'll wait for the call…over and out."

Bristol was anticipating the call to T-Dexter to open the hatch and make the drop. Their liquidity of misery was about to unfold. They wouldn't get there for at least another twenty minutes. This would cause a flurry of rage from those odious creatures below. The Pailoids would break free from the top and flood the cavern with the hundreds. Betty felt a chill go through her. Her hands were sweaty, and sweat was already running from the back of her neck. She had a flush of humidified nerves.

Crepto walked back to the Hummer and got in. Betty revved the engine and peeled out. They shot through the first gate of safety. Getting airborne over the first little mogul on a road going nowhere. Bristol closed in behind with the Q-Tank. Dr. EL was more than happy to shut the steel gate to safety. He let out an ambiguous nervous huff once the gate was closed.

The visual visor on the sergeant's video screen was a perfect adaptation for the Cyborg to follow. He knew every bend and curve of the road ahead to perfection. He was a mean machine cut strong and lean. He was a highly tuned taskmaster, a demolisher of redundant demeanor. He was a good reason to leave the scene. He was a venturing vicious military man of vituperations. Bristol drifted into the first sharp curve and got airborne over the first uphill turn. From Betty's rearview mirror she made the connection. She smiled knowing this Cyborg was cut from the same type of rock as her, hard and steady determination and ready to rock and roll. She flashed her lights to get his attention. The Cyborg ignored her and kept moving toward the dark. Pulling his high beams on, focused into every turn, every change of coming circumstances or bump and curve. Betty felt her veins pumped with adrenaline. This was something for which she'd been geared. She was ready as Freddy and kept the Hummer steady. She knew the sergeant was a good addition to their team and wouldn't disappoint. He was the man of the hour, a soldier with superpower, a mental message of monstrosity. He was motivated to manipulate his way with a gun.

Betty started to slow down because she wasn't quite sure where the drop was, considering she didn't want to be added to the numbers who'd fallen in such a hole. But even at a distance she started to smell what was up ahead. It turned her stomach, and Ryan's.

Ryan covered his nose. "What's that smell Betty? That's gross!"

Betty pulled a Wet-One out of a plastic lobed canister and handed it to Ryan. "Here, breathe into this. It won't seem as bad." Ryan took her advice and breathed into the lemon scented wipe.

Crepto reached over and turned on several spotlights to get a better view of what was ahead. "There it is!" He said. He turned to look at Betty as she pulled up twenty feet shy of the hole. Ryan poked his head up to get a better view.

"What," Ryan said, "It's just a hole?"

Betty had pulled to the far left to make room for Sergeant Bristol's Q-Tank. The windows rolled up, everything quiet, nothing stirred, nothing out of place, like the calm before the storm.

"Are you ready?" He asked. She reached over and took his hand.

"I'm ready, if you are." Crepto saw the determination in her eyes, but a slight quiver of apprehension stood between them. Betty reached for the com-line as Sergeant Bristol pulled up next to her. In the distance of the hole, straight ahead the trail continued toward the bunker in the darkness. The strangest thing suddenly hit Betty.

"Crepto," she said. "If those creatures run the other way they'll head for the bunker."

"Yes, your right. We can't let them have a way out of this place." Crepto remarked.

Betty made the call. "Q-7, do you read over," Betty waited for Bristol to answer.

"Q-5 I read you over…"

"We need to seal off the other end, so they don't have an escape route in front."

"Roger that Q-5 I'll seal this area, so they have nowhere to run."

Betty wasn't sure if she liked the sound of facing this enemy to run only in their direction. They could get run over in the midst of all the chaos to come, like a stampede of raucous cattle. Bristol pushed a button that elevated a rocket launcher that pointed toward the ceiling forty feet past the hole below. A rocket shot toward the ceiling as debris, rocks, dirt, and boulders rumbled in their direction but stopped shortly after the hole. It looked like a good shot from Betty's point of view. They felt the whole mountain shake. "Q-7, get ready to rumble, making the call to home base." Betty barked out. Her eyes were set aflame.

"Roger that Q-5 waiting for the call."

Betty took over. "This is Q-5 calling home base. Home base this is Q-5 do you read, over?"

T-DEXTER, having a radio frequency imposed in his line of communication responded. "Hey little lady what's up. Home base ready and steady, you just say when. I'm good to go little lady!"

The Cyborg listening in appeared to show a little confusion by T-DEXTER's wacky acknowledgement. Betty hesitated for a brief second as she let in a deep breath of air before letting it out in a slow shudder. She was anticipating the drop like the others. Ryan thought he'd see what would happen next. Sensing this, Crepto looked back at Ryan.

"Don't think so little man. You won't like what you see." Ryan crawled back under the seat. The three heard the robot's voice blast forth from the walkie-talkie, and yelling and firing on the other end—then it was cut off…

"Tinman, are you okay?" Betty asked, yet it was already too late.

T-DEXTER, without answering, opened the metal hatch connected to the floor.

Betty knew they only had but moments. She looked over at Crepto. "They got in from the other side. I hope the girls will be alright?"

Crepto had a determined expression written in his eyes. "They'll be fine, just be ready. This won't take that long before…" Crepto didn't have time to finish because all of a sudden, hordes of Pailoids shot up out of the apocalyptic hole. The hole from both ends had been breached. Betty started firing the Gait 30M machine guns right away. Bristol took her queue of vengeance and lit up his gun like a rampart of redemption. Ryan covered his ears, yet the noise was unbearable. Betty and Sergeant Bristol cut through them with a sinuous movement of effort.

The air was filled with impetuous sounds of the dead. A cumbersome wave of trepidation flowed while crushing flesh and bone marked the tunnel as it splattered remains. It was a slaughterhouse for the dying. It was a battle of fading bliss. Betty put her windshield wiper blades on. The Gait 30M's echoed out killing five, ten and then fifteen more. The day of the dying seethed through the air. This cavern below was like an open tome bringing forth the mockups of the dying as rolling thunder. The lithe movements of these warriors piled the mangled, piled the malevolent, which gave back of the dead, as life was taken away this day in the life of dread. This was a production of chaotic reflections left behind catastrophic effects—a rhythmic movement pointing them to their doom like the pied-piper in melodramatic fashion. The Pailoids frothed forward in the rage of feral emotions and succumbed to the reason of dread, raze became the forbearance of the things to come, which led down a road of the dying, no longer was the living geared for a better way of life as it was not in them to hand out the gift of life for the lonely or down hearted, only those marked by a higher calling were honored to carry on life for the lost. Those left behind in the spillage of blood, the breaking of bones, fragmenting those of rage to set a course not justifiable of those marked for their end. They spilled forward into the giving of flesh and blood. They were a churned dynasty of senselessness. They moved forward in a congregated effort of togetherness. This enemy had been duped, overwrought, and become chancy in believing their finality was good reasoning to a sure end.

Sergeant Bristol stood up on top of this miniaturized Q-Tank and fired his gun in a circular motion, lining the walls with bones and blood. Their insidious cries defied all manner of existence. They plunged forward venomously with their cause. The rumble of feet and bodies building momentum lost their reason for existence.

Ryan yelled into Crepto's ear. "I can't breathe! The air's to hot!"

Crepto reached down and turned the air-conditioner on. Ryan had a look of terror in his eyes. He wanted out of this chaos. "What should I do?" Ryan yelled out with pasty white skin and quivering lips.

Crepto turned and said, "Get behind the seat and cover your ears and head!" Crepto looked back behind the ammo boxes and grabbed his shield and sword. Betty was overcome with the violence in front. Bodies stacked like a wall of a malevolent mass, which kept pushing forward into the unwanted ranks of the dead, as soldiers, marching on to the flowing into the fury of nonexistence. A thousand rounds for a thousand sets of eyes lay on this particular road of dread, in the embittered realm of the dying. They were marked in blood and left in vivid memories as extricated souls lost in their cause, as they left behind their brothers in a flow of blood who had met this road leading away from life to an end, for an ending was the cause. Betty's hands were shaking but continued to fire. Sergeant Bristol was out of rounds and started using a flame thrower to slow them down. Betty was almost finished with the two large boxes of ammo in the back of the Hummer. Smoke and ash detached the air from the tunnel as they coughed and huffed to find clean air to breath. They had to find another minute of life as their time to eradicate these creatures from memory was running out of time. They stood out like no friend or foe could ever manipulate their way with a gun towards a better way of life. They cut down this foe that recognized no light in the world they had become accustomed too. This was their end. This was their way to a better life, only painted in the mind of the dying as the distance of light shot forward into the night showing a different path to take—one that eluded their way of thinking. They were tricked. They were fooled to take this road to their end.

Betty glared at Crepto, "I'm out of ammo, but they're still coming!"

Crepto knew he had to take the fight to the Pailoids. Their numbers were overwhelming as they hit the front of the two vehicles like they weren't even there. This pit was comparable to a hive for man-size bees disturbed from the nest. Crepto glared in Betty's direction.

"Betty...just listen...open the roof hatch when I tell you to!"

Betty flipped her head in his direction. "Do what?"

"I said open the roof-hatch when I tell you to!" All of a sudden, there was a break in ranks. Their numbers were depleting. "Now!" Crepto yelled.

Betty reached over and pushed the roof-hatch button as it began to open. He took sword and shield and flew through the top while spinning shield and waving his sword. Spikes on the end of the shield jetted out. The brightness of light and heat was a gyrating rotund of terror, cutting and slicing, dicing, and removing, leaving the enemy in shambles. The bodies of the dead piled up even more. Crepto noticed that Bristol was becoming overwhelmed by those creatures surrounding him. He turned his rage toward the sergeant and swung sword and shield to free him. An opaque smoke flailed through the air leaving a tainted embodiment of putrid smells and sinewy flesh lay in heaps of emptiness. The piles of the dead, their visage left as a reminder of war. The dead could tell no tales, yet the living understood the words not said—a delirium of acts from the living to surprise those unaware of their fate, their demise, that road that leads to destruction. A pathway not visualized by the dammed, they were adherent victims of circumstance. They were on a road to a better life but lost their way and were sidetracked. This was their end.

This was their outcome. They were malicious creations from a sadistic mind. They were created in an image used for a discordant end. Betty and Ryan could smell the pungent drifting of the dead through the air-conditioner. Ryan swallowed a lump of vomit. Only a few creatures made it past Crepto's blades. Hundreds and hundreds of them came to meet their maker. No mercy was shown by the sword and shield as they spun in unison to hand out the dead their endings. The light of the Crepto Energy burned their skin. Betty's face was covered with the soot of blackened mortars projected by the extractions of shells. Ryan was in a befuddled arrangement of shock. Shaking hands sweat and soot from the remains of mortar shells left behind in the wake of the dying.

Betty had enough of this flaring smell left in their pathway. They needed to recover. She was out of ammo, and Ryan was almost comatose from the visual of the violence. The sergeant signaled Betty to flee the immediate area.

She could see him waving her off the front of the kill zone. "Go back!" He yelled. "Your job here is done!"

Betty didn't want to leave Crepto behind, but she knew Ryan and her couldn't face too much more of this decrepit violence raging in the air. Betty slammed the Hummer in reverse as Sergeant Bristol used his laser cannon to keep as many as he could from following after. She whipped the Hummer into a 180-degree turn, squealing tires and burning rubber down the road. The Hummer was a welcome sight. Beat-up, banged-up, no longer the pretty shiny black color as before. It was marked by war. It was one vehicle wreaked from recognition. One fight short of disaster. Four wheels of burning flames of burnt bodies, burnt nostrils, and fleeting courage. Betty choked down her vomit as she headed down the road. Ryan had tears running from his face, not so much from fear, but from the smoke and ash of burnt cinders. She tore down the road and left the visage of war behind. It was an encumbrance to the living to stay in this battle. It was a place only for the dead to recognize as they had found this road to a better way of living in finding death to be their friend, as their fear of the enemy enlightened them, which held them to this road of disaster. There was no turning back from this road that had led them to their end.

Crepto raged on into the oneness of fury. He flew high, and then low into the mouth of the cavern. The streams of the dead slowed down to a trickle, but they were still amongst the ranks of the dead—their bodies thrown into this hole, as if a pit of roiling confusion.

Betty yelled across the dash. "Ryan!" He looked petrified. "I need you to call Dr. EL. He's in the Red Truck, channel three! His call sign is T-4!" She yelled again, "Ryan, you better snap out of it and get your little butt up here!"

Ryan shook his head. Wiped a tear from his eye and crawled over the front seat.

"What? I'm here." He said back while wiping snot on his sleeve.

"I said call Dr. EL, channel three! We need the gates open before those things catch up to us—okay!" Betty took a quick glance at her little nephew, who started to pull it together once leaving that scene of death and mayhem behind.

Ryan reached for the radio control handle and practiced pushing the button a couple of times. He brought the mike up to his mouth as he pushed down on the call button. "T-4 this is Q-5 do you read over." Ryan let go of the button and waited for a response, but none was given, so he repeated the call. "T-4 this is Q-5 do you read over."

Then Betty and Ryan heard the radio squawk. "Q-5, I read your transmission, go ahead."

This made Ryan smile as he looked over at Betty. "T-4, we are headed for the gate." Ryan paused to look at the clock. "Our ETA is maybe two minutes, over." Betty was proud that little Ryan sounded like a professional.

"Roger that Q-5, ETA is two minutes, have your back, and on track."

Exactly two minutes later, Betty and Ryan went flying by the opening of the first gate. Betty slid the Hummer past the opening and turned the big vehicle sideways as it slid by thirty more feet. Both older men looked up in surprise. She yelled out her window when she saw George and Dr. EL standing in awe that she'd even made it back alive. "Is there ammo in those guns?" She asked.

Dr. EL nodded. "Yes, why do you ask?"

"Because those things were on our butts, and they can't be too far behind."

Dr. EL ran to the computer mounted pole and hit the close button. The ten inch slide gate slammed shut. Something slammed against the gate as soon as it closed, knocking Dr. EL back on his butt. Dirt fell from the ceiling above him. Dr. EL crawled backwards to push distance between him and the gate. He looked up in astonishment.

"What was that?" He said.

Betty widened her eyes. "What do you think it was? Those creatures weren't far behind me. They pulled all the oxygen out of the air. They won't stop until every last one of us is dead. You got that?"

Dr. EL didn't appreciate her sarcasm, but he wasn't about to get judgmental at this point, since she still was jacked up from the fight. "Where's Bailey…I mean Crepto and Sergeant Bristol?" Dr. EL asked.

Betty ignored the question while she bent over to throw up. Ryan mimicked her twelve feet away. The doctor turned his head and covered his mouth. He could smell the burnt remains of those creatures permeating off the body of the Hummer, and seeing chunks of what Betty had left in her stomach gave a vivid picture worth a thousand words. The machine gun in George's hand began to shake. Ryan reached up and steadied his hand.

"Are you okay?" Ryan barked out while looking up at the Zookeeper. Dr. EL got up and brushed himself off.

"Yeah, I'm okay, I'm…"

The doctor didn't finish because more waves of slamming against the door caused him to stop, like a sounding herd of cattle crashing against the gate, trying to flee from the rage of fire and flame. The doctors were left behind in the shelters of zoological predicaments by cleaning up after hairy little monkeys and pushing computer buttons on greenish backdrops of a seventeen-inch screen. They were left in a frivolers world of yes and no, not gasping for air while in the shivery of their shorts. They were left behind the walls of comfort, not the insanity she'd faced marked by smoke and a trail of blood, and broken bones and urine.

At the moment, Ryan felt tougher than his mentors of the moment. He sided with Betty like she was the Queen of the day, and he was one of her concubines. They were royalty marked by the incessant trail of experience and were soon to be marked for leadership down this road leading to a better way of life. They were shortly to be exposed on someone else's reflected screen of importance as they were recognized on a new trail of supervision—and if any further happenings made itself known while they traveled this dangerous road, quickly to be exposed, they would add this to their accomplishments, which was not meant for the weak and weary to be caught by surprise as the quickly fading thunder behind them was pushed off to the side. They were on their own road leading to redemption. As a ship is to the sea-tides-journey of her waves, or as a lighthouse burns bright on the darkest of nights, so those of experience guard the hearts of the innocent.

Sergeant Bristol was overwhelmed with the swarming of the enemy. They tore through his chest and poked out an eye. His right hand was missing. His clothes were completely torn from his body. His neck leaked a greenish fluid as his lubrication left him. He didn't have the pretty boy face from before. He was a mess. His movements had slowed to a crawl.

Crepto swung his sword mightily cutting through the ranks of the dammed. Quickly noticing he was losing his second in command. Crepto flew up over the top of the sergeant's frame and quickly cleared the area of the infestation. The light and the heat had overtaken them. They fled back into the other direction of safety, drawing the fight away from the fast-depleting Cyborg. This new Gambit had become one with his sword, in a zone not too far from home. He was hotly heated, tired, and depleted, but he now stood alone. He was the cause of this immolation of a tough situation, a home wrecker, a rebel rouser, a two-punch knock-out in the tenth round. He was the man of the hour, a super-power, a done deal with the super-meal, except minus the toy.

He was Crepto Energy in the worst of ways as this battle of refutation was done.

Crepto grabbed the Cyborg and gently slid him into the top of the Q-Tank. After pushing the mass of the dead back into that apocalyptic hole. He joined the sergeant in the Q-Tank and headed for home.

The frenzied motions of the Pailoids disappeared in the distance. Crepto lit up the Q-Tank and flipped her around, pealing tires and spinning wheels. It had been a long inscrutable night. No one would believe them if he tried to explain the unexplainable. It was a justifiable day to remember, one marked by the offsetting of scales, releasing the anatomy of the epitome of the not so lucky into the hands of the dead. One more game chalked up on the wall of humanities accomplishments— one more day to stay alive, one more day to take that long drive home, a day to thrive and survive on what was left.

Crepto grabbed the com-line to call Dr. EL. His motions were fine-tuned, hitting a mark. He sat in his deluged aftermath of exhaustion.

"T-4 this is Q-7 we are homeward bound." Everyone on the other side of the gates yelled with hands and arms lifted toward the caves ceiling.

Dr. EL smiled as a tear of joy ran down his face. "Roger that Q-7, this is T-4 we hear your transmission and are at the gate. Check the area for stragglers and let me know when it's clear."

"Got you covered home-base. I'll see you at the gate." A few seconds past before Crepto came back on-line. "I don't see any stragglers on my radar." Dr. EL reached over and hit the button on the gate after letting the eye and hand scanner complete their cycle.

The Q-tank shot past the gate. Dr. EL closed the gate behind. Crepto looked over at the Cyborg. "Are you going to be, okay?"

Sergeant Bristol let out a leaking green smile. "I'm fine," he said. "Might need a slight tune-up, but I'll live to fight another day."

Crepto glanced over to his right showing a fading smile, "A tune-up huh? You might need a few fluids too." Both heroes' laughed.

Betty came back over the com-line. "Are you two, okay?"

Crepto smiled as he drove toward the compound. "Well, I'm fine," while letting go of the com-line. He looked back at the Cyborg and shook his head,

"But our friend here might need patching up." Sergeant Bristol coughed a flow of green leaky fluid out from his neck.

Ten minutes later, they're all back in the safety of the compound. Betty jumped out of the Hummer with a machine-gun braced against her shoulder. Ryan slowly got out of the other side. Crepto shot from the top of the Q-tank, but at the same time he heard gun fire. And not too distant in front he saw what looked like one of those smelly Pailoids jetting across his pathway. He flew above them. He shot straight past Betty. He quickly gained ground on two Pailoids heading for the zoo. He was quick on the path of the two little girls soon to be discovered underwater, hidden in secret. One of the creatures dove for the water of the lagoon hoping to elude his captor. Crepto grabbed the creature and hauled him backward out of the water from below. He reached and snapped his neck in an obdurate demonstration of emotion. Betty took aim at the other and cut it down with her machine gun.

T-DEXTER came out to greet them as he heard Betty zipping bullets across the landscape ahead. She turned her aim in the direction of the robot. He raised his hands in obvious surrender, "Hold-up little lady, I'm on your side." Betty's eyes darted his way.

"Have you seen any more of those pesky Pailoids hanging about?"

"Well, I don't rightly know. One of them broke my scanner—so maybe two or three of them left." T-DEXTER glanced in the direction of the zoo.

"Where'd Crepto head off too?"

"I think he went in the direction of the zoo, but I don't see him, so I'm not sure…" Betty glanced up at T-DEXTER.

"How many of the blood suckers got in?" T-DEXTER shook his head.

"A dozen or so before I got the hydraulic door shut. They're pretty fast."

"Yeah, tell me about it. They almost took out the Hummer!" T-DEXTER glanced over at what was left of Betty's prize and temporary possession.

"Wow, they did that?"

"And then some." Betty overstated.

From the other side of the compound Crepto dove into the lagoon below, and before pulling the Q-Tank beneath the protection of lost scents. Crepto hadn't realized his suit was burning up. The water cooled him quickly as he stayed at the bottom for a few minutes and let it cool. He felt everything around him becoming clearer. For some reason, the suit had heated up to a point that caused him to lose sight of his full powers—something not known from before. This Crepto Energy had this one weakness or flaw to account for. It had to be cooled every so often.

Hanging from the rafters above the lagoon at the water's edge, one of those insidious creatures hung in waiting. Ryan had left Betty's side wondering where Crepto had gone to. Grabbed up his purposeful night sticks and took on a run in the direction of the lagoon. Presently, he was seen as a target by one of these creatures hanging quietly from above. Crepto, being focused on the safety of the girls, had not known of Ryan taking off on his own, without making sure the compound was safe. Two minutes had gone by before Betty noticed that Ryan had eluded her position and had taken off without letting her know. She looked up at T-DEXTER and began to panic.

With this friendly fire stick of an electrical current, Ryan felt like the head of his own destiny. Not thinking of harm or being cornered unnaturally by one of those nasty Pailoids. Finally, he found his way through the garden, through trees that passed by the area he'd remembered burying his grandmother. This drew his attention for a brief moment, not noticing what was above. After his short visit to his grandmother's grave, he stood and walked in the direction of the lagoon. Ryan could see a few hundred yards in front that Crepto was pulling the Q-Tank from the water. Without paying much attention, Ryan tripped over a loose root while passing a tree. Not being able to place his footing in the right manner, he fell, losing his grip on the black night stick as it sprawled out of his hand and rolled to the left. Suddenly, the creature hanging from the rafters took more interest in the small boy who'd shown himself vulnerable in the eyes of the swift and cunning. Ryan rolled toward the sky and saw this abrupt shadow making haste in his direction. He lunged and grabbed at that awkward stick at just the right moment, yet nowhere to run. He had to face the creature. Then suddenly, realizing there was nowhere to go. Thrown to the side, Ryan held on to the black stick filled him with courage. He had surprising clarity. The creature walked back and forth in a cunning way, sizing up this smaller than usual victim. Ryan's eyes drew focus. He was having none of what this creature had in store. Even as being as small and vulnerable as he might be. He clicked his magic wand in the direction of this awful beast. The Pailoid roared to set his presence known. Ryan held strong to the stick. Even though scared, and even though intimidated by this creature of the pit, he secured his boundaries of safety sliding between the aftermath of two large stumps, rolled out on the ground, hollowed out for the perfect size of fitting dimensions. Fingering his trusted wand between him and this beast. Suddenly, hot breath leaking from the Pailoids mouth stood and eyed him, making judgments of which way his victim might run. Claws and teeth and adrenaline running rampage of a bad dream. The Pailoid sunk claws into the flesh of the hollowed-out logs just inches from Ryan's small face when falling back between the logs. A pungent smell drifted in the air—*stinky breath* was Ryan thought. Wanting to wince in disgust yet holding back, he stayed focused. Abating when to strike, when to hold up, when to force his opinion by lighting him up. Ryan, suddenly saw the right moment to move with the stick. Moving at the same time this creature did, pushing the black stick right down it's throat. This was the perfect position of prodding. A blue flame shot out at the other end of the pole. The creature lit up like a candle of burning wax. Ryan became persistent about his position to fight back, to hold his ground, giving his left hand to secure his right to live. This creature was driven by rage rather than by intellect. Ryan lit the creature up like the Empire State Building with a fanfare of blue Christmas lights. He kept his fingers steady and true as this most adherent buzz of blue light exploded through the top of the Pailoids head. Crepto flew by at just the right moment to see the creature surprised, as Ryan's magic stick finished off the Pailoid. Crepto swooped down and pushed the Pailoid a good twenty feet away while snapping his neck. A lifeless burning, flickering, turn of events. Ryan had killed one of the beasts.

Quickly, there was a crowd around watching Ryan get up and brush himself off. Still a little shaky, he was a paler color of white, but he'd won a victory not only for himself, but for all that had given this day of all days of the grateful dead.

Crepto sat the Q-Tank safely to shore. He sensed the air was different than what was its usual form. There remained the tainted smells of battle, not wanting this, not wanting any part of this abnormal situation, as he couldn't forget remembering the dead. He didn't like the feeling, but without war, without drawing this imaginary line of acceptance, there'd be no life for the living, but life only for the dammed, so frequently made known of their situation. What was left would keep pushing him to be on alert, looking for clues, looking for distractions from others of that other world. Never be satisfied with the sanctity of the compound, keeping a look-out for change, for red-flags drifting in the wind. Living in a impossible world of the dying, a world of dismemberment, Now setting history could be the only way to live inside the compound.

Crepto standing next to Ryan placed an arm around his shoulder. Still wearing his dirty baseball cap looked up.

Betty came from behind on one of George's miniaturized golf-carts. She glanced at Ryan with a mournful stare. Ryan turned at the right moment and got an eyeful. "Where'd you go squirt?"

Ryan lowered his eyes, but then raised them again. "I wanted to find where Crepto was, and I brought my weapon with me, but I didn't see the creature above me. I somehow got lucky, I guess…He had no idea what I could do with the wand…"

Ryan trailed off…Betty engulfed his tiny frame close to hers. She was glad that he had made it. Crepto reached the top of the Q-Tank. The girls were fast asleep like slumbering sleepyheads. Cuddles from below, growled at this strange coppery man in the shiny suit. This startled the two little girls awake—a yawn, a stretching arm, and several blinks of curious eyes of little girls looking up.

"Is that you Bailey?" Mattie asked while Cuddles growled then barked in his general direction knowing he was one of them. Cuddles was shaking while tucking a tail under her legs.

"Yes, it's me. Are you girls alright?"

"Yeah, were fine, it's a little hot in here, that's all, but how'd everything turn out?" Mattie said while rubbing her eyes.

Crepto looked at Betty, and then saw T-DEXTER shooting across the sky to meet up with them. "Fine Mattie dear, everything is fine and dandy young lady." T-DEXTER flew in at the right moment. Dr. EL left behind in his office up on the sixth floor—drinking again was Crepto's thought. This had all been too much stress for him.

Bailey pulled himself free from the suit—tired and sweaty, drained from the long day. It was already past midnight. It was time to take a long shower and go to bed. Dr. EL would sleep his miseries off in the closet most likely. As most people in the world have their vices that at times are kept in secret. But Bailey understood this man who had their back could only be strong in character at certain times, sometimes his heart and mind were not strong enough to endure those things that overwhelmed him on certain days of the year—like Christmas or New-Years or battle days from the pits of that pungent hell.

What lay below was another world from days gone by, turned upside down, in another tunnel, on a different road leading nowhere, to the end of life as those creatures of a different kind had found out on the worst of days, as far as they could tell, their ending of a crossroad relieved them of their miseries of another day.

T-DEXTER reached over and touched the suit before everyone got up and headed off to bed. "Wow," He proclaimed. The Crepto suit is hot!" The robot started another one of his goofy sayings. "When you're hot, you're hot…when you're not, you're not. Push it in pull it out hot, hot…push it in…pull it out…not, not!" He was doing a little jig again offending Betty, showed by her two raised eyebrows.

"You better scrap the robot. He's at it again. Check his circuit breakers in the morning." Her voice faded in the distance as she walked toward the elevators. T-DEXTER said his goodnights after showing his spastic routine trying not to offend the children. Betty waved him off like she was swatting at a fly. This was a long day done lost in the many to come.

The children went off to bed. Betty leaned against the doorframe with the dim light from down the hall silhouetting across her face. The boy of bashful beginnings brushed his lips gently with hers. He didn't smell his best, but neither did she. He waved goodbye as he faded in the distance of the hallway. Betty closed the door as Bailey made his way to the seventh floor. This was a place of sanctuary. This being a place he could unwind and rest without the judgment of others breathing down his neck. A new day would soon be upon them. Bailey got into the shower and washed the filth of the night as it drained off his body. When done, he placed the Crepto suit into a tub of chilly water to wash the blood and sweat and smell of the dead off, so to meet another day head on without reproach or due process of personal litigations, bound by the epitomizing eyes and noses of non-acceptance. When slipping between sheets of comfort, Bailey began to dream away another night, to live through another fight, to breathe fresh air from day to night. This was a day branded in memory…

CHAPTER 26

The Secret Entrance

It was twelve o'clock before anyone from the small band of misfits stirred awake to face a new day. Life of another time was one of close calls and gut-wrenching memories, and sleepless churning. Bailey was awakened by the phone ringing in his ear. He stirred enough to feel the stiffness in his legs and shoulders. A totally diverse set of muscles had been pushed past their limits of pain. He rolled to his side trying to find reason to get up. After stretching and yawning, he stood in his boxer shorts as a chill of cool air hit his body. What was to come next? When would the struggle end? Would they ever find people again that they loved? He wondered if they'd find success—he was full of worry, and full of doubt. All he wanted was a normal life but knowing that his old life was gone caused fleeting hope to cross his mind. Nothing would ever be the same again. They would all live by a separate set of rules, a set of values that weren't their own. Feeling the synchronicity of living in two dissimilar worlds— one of before and one of present. The past and present were irrelevant to what was to come, and what was to come was still hanging in the short distance of only a few weeks, a few days, or hours.

Bailey speed-dialed the number back that he'd seen flashing on the screen. An older gentleman picked up the phone from the other end. Suggesting they get together for a late breakfast and coffee. As soon as Bailey hung up the phone, he heard a light knock on his door. He slipped on his pants and made it to the front door. A translucent light reflected off Bailey's face. Ryan was standing there with this chaste expression in his eyes. Bailey comprehended the solemnity in Ryan's demeanor. The small boy crossed the threshold without saying a word. Bailey comprehended the boy had a tough go at yesterday's violent reform. He pulled a chair out for Ryan to sit down. Hesitating, Ryan's eyes wandered back and forth as if a mounting anxiety was at a peak turning point of emotion.

So, Bailey asked, "What's bothering you squirt?"

"I'm not sure what to think about yesterday. I mean, I don't feel right about everything that happened." Ryan stated. His hands showed nervous tension. His face was drawn with big circles under his eyes, and he had a sallow pastiness to his color. Ryan put his head in his lap and covered his face with his hands. A susurration of emotion crossed his mind. Bailey's implicit reaction to the young boy's demeanor was one of complex circumstances. He knelt down and put his hand on Ryan's shoulder in a measure of gentle awareness. There was a bonding of two boys. They were a forced cohesion by the dour incongruous memories. Ryan was involuntarily pushed to his limits by an enemy stronger, by an enemy with a burning incessant rage. The boy felt a sickness take over from the visions of the eviscerated dead, along with an air of cumbersome defeat. His youth was tempered in the thrashing of wills, in the changing of circumstance. The days of his youth had become banished in the inability to hold on to pain, hold on to the horrors left behind from the rage.

"I'm sorry about yesterday. We should have left you behind with the girls." Bailey said.

Ryan looked up beneath tears of remorse. "Why didn't you Bailey? I shouldn't have been there. It wasn't a place for children."

Bailey knew they'd made a mistake by taking the small boy with them. Death had its own way of leaving a trail of memory from the transmuting images of the dead.

"I didn't know. I mean we're all new at this." Bailey stopped because he really didn't know how to word his thoughts. He was put into a position to mentor this small boy, but *he* is being a boy himself didn't quite have the words to say to a seven-year-old. And he knew Ryan wouldn't understand his way of thinking. His perspective was too innocent. Ryan looked up at him with curious eyes, wondering if this older boy had any understanding of wisdom to impart. Bailey was trying to understand Ryan's heart. But he sensed this a job for someone with a lot more experience.

"Sometimes," Ryan said, "when I would ask Grandma if I could do certain things, she would say no. She'd say no because she knew what was good for me or what was not good for me." Ryan looked at Bailey to make sure he was getting his message. "She was an adult. She knew better than to put me in a tough situation. She knew what I could handle." A tear rolled down Ryan's cheek.

Bailey was getting the jest of Ryan's guilt-trip. "I'm sorry Ryan. You're right. I should have known better, but I didn't. Do you know why I didn't?"

Ryan looked back up through tearful eyes. "No. Why?"

"Because I'm just a kid myself, and I'm learning as I go. I will make some mistakes along the way. Do you understand?"

"But why didn't you just yell at me and tell me I needed to stay with the girls?"

Bailey shook his head, and then looked back into Ryan's eyes. "I didn't really think that far ahead, and in all the confusion, and other things to deal with, I was scared myself. I didn't know how bad it would get until it happened."

"But your older and should know better because you're an adult." Ryan concluded.

Bailey stared at the boy for a few more seconds. "I know, you're right to a point, but remember this conversation when the subject comes up again, because you'll know we had this talk—okay? What you did yesterday in the garden was awfully brave of you. You know?"

Ryan's eyes twinkled in the confidence Bailey was feeding him. Ryan knew he used his age as a form of manipulation, but he also sensed this time it had backfired and caused him considerable mental stress. He thought about that creature for a minute. The memory of him was still fresh in his mind, so penetrating, so final.

"I was lucky more than brave. It had me." Ryan said. "I felt his anger, but it didn't make any sense to me. I could see the pain in his eyes before he weakened. They don't know they are bad. And if I didn't kill him, he would have killed me."

Bailey could tell that Ryan saw the senselessness in the dying. That's what stole his sleep away. He had this carrion image replaying in his head. He was vulnerable. He was weak in the placing of his own personal vices, without realizing it could have cost him his life. Those vivid nightmares from his experiences left him wanting—wanting a clearer picture, a better explanation of the end, and the reasons for dying held no purpose. This was something he'd never want to experience in his youth again, yet it was a reminder to Bailey that all boys and girls of many shapes and sizes feel pain and hurt and know when one's dying has a permanent effect on those that it incurs. Death wasn't an easy thing to face. It showed painful remissions of an end, which pulled confidence and strength from the very soul of what makes us human. It left its scars on the inside of his unprotected heart. It was a replication of an incessant reminder whirling and twirling in a finite existence—never stopping, always impeding relief for the soul. Bailey stood up and Ryan threw his arms around him. He shouldered the small boy with a hug similar to what a father would give to a son. As love goes, and the mysterious ways of its effect as a boy and his mentor would share. Bailey held his breath in a moment of silence as he felt Ryan's heart turbaned to his emotions. It exhibited an eternal flicker of love that was worth all the battles and setbacks that life presented, it was worth the lesson of pain, but more so, it gave him reason to live. Yes, this would take Ryan a few weeks to get over. Yet Bailey knew Ryan would be the better boy for it in the end.

Minutes later, both young men were headed for the elevator. Bailey had the Crepto Suit thrown over his shoulder, and Ryan caught up to him to take his hand.

When the elevator opened, Betty was standing with a cane knuckled under a bent wrist and two little girls at her side.

Startled to see them, Bailey said, "Good morning, ladies. It's nice to see you. How'd you sleep?"

Jackie was the first to speak. "I slept okay." She said. "But Betty woke up several times during the night." Not sure if she should say anymore,

Jackie looked over at Betty as if to win her approval. The boys only stared in silence as the elevator moved in the direction of the second floor. Betty returned the look but didn't comment on her ability to sleep or not. She reached over and took Bailey's other hand. Ryan looked up and smiled. The two little girls glanced at each other knowing Betty was learning to accept things as they *were* even in the dangers of the ever-changing world—a world that she thought lacked hope of a better future. The two little girls got out of the elevator first, and Ryan tagged behind. Bailey could feel Betty was hesitant about going into the galley. She pushed the close button on the elevator door, which surprised Bailey. As the door closed, Betty dropped her cane and threw her arms around Bailey. They stood in the closed elevator in each other's arms. Bailey could feel her trembling. He felt a drawn breath of emotion come from her. He felt the warmth and comfort of her small frame. And at that very moment she needed this. As the others in their group had felt at times, she was susceptible, she was weak and lost in the anguish of her nights revisions, and the only thing she needed right now was for someone else to understand her pain. Betty wanted to know by this emotional grasp that everything would be okay. They, as a couple, and their dysfunctional system would somehow make things work. And this unit of misunderstood misfits would be for the better. Bailey held her, yet he was unsure of her condition—her frame of mind, her stability of heart, and if she was able to go on. And he figured she'd finally acknowledged that this was the first of many battles to come, or it scared her to death—far worse than she would've first thought. From his point of view, he didn't understand why she was being so affectionate. Yet with a gentle smile he held back, taking it in with a gentle heart, knowing harmful effects are sometimes followed by good situations. He knew she was trying to draw strength from him by this physical connection.

Unexpectedly, in front of them, the door opened back up and Betty let go of Bailey as two little girls and a curious boy stood with curious eyes.

Dr. EL was standing over the galley stove cooking breakfast. This surprised the couple. Without too much hesitation Bailey said.

"What are you cooking this morning doc?"

The doctor turned with a placated expression. He forced out an impermanent grin. The galley was filled with the redolent of delightful home cooked food. Eggs and hash browns, and freshly brewed coffee got their attention. Dr. EL detected the couple and their little sidekick Ryan had endured an incredible amount of stress from the night before. Bailey picked up the Crepto Suit and walked into the galley and through it over a chair while Betty hung on his arm.

"Oh, good morning young man, you guys, okay?" As if the obvious was still burning fresh in their minds—fit, but stuck somewhere in the middle, they had crossed some imaginary lines, given up all the gusto, or had been burning their candles at both ends, and directly leaving anything behind. All the formalities that had gone unnoticed from before were evident by their timorous stares.

"We're okay," Bailey said, wondering about the doctor's frame of mind.

"How about some breakfast, are you hungry?" The doctor asked, knowing they had all taken quite the toll from the night's transitions, ready for someone to be understanding of their present conditions.

"Sure," Bailey responded. "We can all use a break. Besides last night, I think we're all lucky to be alive." All the children looked at Bailey wondering what he'd say next.

"We've got work to do ahead of us." He said. Dr. EL only glanced at the boy with unsaid digressions of the previous night's affairs.

"Sit, sit," the doctor insisted. All the children took a seat while Betty went over with her cane nudged under her right wrist for physical support and poured two cups of coffee from a pot sitting on the stove. Jackie got up and headed for the large double door refrigerator and pulled a carton of orange juice off the shelf and returned to her seat. Five glasses of orange juice she poured. This was a smaller than normal table fixed in the corner of the galley with five family members tightly fitted around. They were cozy and warm snuggled together from the heat of the galley. From the inside of this giant cave, they were where the kettle was warm and the comfort sweet, as time was running out, they took a moment to share breakfast. Bailey's eyes displayed a disconcerting stare. "We need to check this entire compound for weak spots that may have been overlooked—you know, just in case we missed something not seen before."

Dr. EL looked at the children knowing the eyes and ears of the young were like flies on a wall. They took in everything they saw and heard and waited for the doctor's reasoning. A perspective Dr. EL tried to pass on to the boy of the impatient heart. "In time dear boy, let's eat." Five disconsolate souls comforted by the warmth of a kitchen and the comforts of an old man of science shed a dim light of hope on their hopeless world situation. They were bonded by the reality of circumstances, merged by the uniqueness of timing, and the circumscribed adventurous placement of their hearts. They had united their wills in testament given by the force of violence, the force of the world's unnatural reform, and left with only scraps of a race almost extinct. Their courage had become depleted by their lack of energy and wisdom. Their faces were flexed in the mysteries that still lay ahead.

Bailey began to think of the robots and looked up at Dr. EL as he indicated concern.

"Have you seen T-DEXTER this morning?"

"Yes, he's already fixed his bio-scanner and is ready for his next assignment."

Ryan perked up. Thinking to never leave the robot's side they'd been through. In the company of laser blasts and flying friends would be where he wanted to be. No more electric cattle prods to be pushed in the faces of Pailoids. He was done being a hero. He looked up toward the wavering weather man. "Where's T-DEXTER sir?"

Dr. EL glared across the table to notice the boy's unwavering curiosity.

"He's downstairs. I'm sure you'll all see him within a few minutes." Dr. EL waved his hand at the boy while shaking his head. "Now do us all a favor," the doctor said, "and eat your breakfast, and don't worry about what the robots are doing. They have their assigned duties."

Ryan knowing, *he* had crossed a few lines of misunderstanding with him in the last few days. And the doctor had his fill of the troublesome youth. He understood the boy had manipulated his way into many situations of the past. Dr. EL continued with a roll of his eyes and glared at Bailey as if communicating with his obstinate movements from Ryan's limitless irritations. He wanted peace and quiet and not to respond with short tempers and lack of limitations. He fancied Ryan wouldn't take to lamenting over rights of who had done what. He was more concerned about the youngster not pushing his buttons. Bailey understood by a raised eyebrow.

Comfortingly, they'd finished their breakfast and talked about the day's events to come. Betty planned to spend part of her day with the children. They needed time away from their current conditions, and now or in the near future it had to be something light-hearted and fun. Betty exhibited a chastened stare toward the boy of bashful beginnings.

"Can we take the kids swimming today?"

Bailey, concerned about safety looked over. "I'm not sure. Around three or four o'clock we can fit in a swim if everything we need to get done goes okay." Bailey wasn't sure that Betty would have the same convictions as he felt, knowing, and sensing they still had dangers looming over their heads. So, he left that conversation for another time, knowing she had the children's best interest at heart, and not her own. He noticed her walking better from the day before. A slight limp in her stance, but to everyone else she was getting along better with the cane. Then Betty reflected an air of concern, she'd just remembered Sergeant Bristol was up one level in the Cryogenic chamber recuperating from his injuries.

"Oh…the sergeant…how's he doing so far?" Betty asked.

Dr. EL looked at Betty. "I had T-DEXTER lift the Cyborg last night and place him in one of the healing chambers, up in med-lab on dock eight, level three. The lasers do quite well at rebuilding his Cybernetic system to perfection. After three days, and several quarts of replaced fluids, he should be good-to-go."

"I'm glad he'll make it." Betty said. "He's a good addition to our little family."

Bailey showed a growing smile of acknowledging the same. "Yeah, he's a badass mother…" Betty put her hand over Bailey's mouth to stop him from saying any harsh words in front of the children.

Ryan knew the word and replaced it with his own word. "You mean mother humpier, right Bailey?"

Bailey took that as a clue that he'd said enough and let the statement's unwarranted replacement go, instead of saying another crass comment.

Everyone got up and headed in different directions. The little girls headed for the zoo as the rest walked toward the bottom floor. T-DEXTER was standing by the roll up door with his trusty sidekick. The robots had been busy that night cleaning up the mess left behind. Bailey, with his Crepto Suit draped over his shoulder stopped to acknowledge the robot.

"Hey T-DEXTER, how are you this morning?" Bailey trying to be cheerful.

The robot responded with high regards. "Not bad, little brother." T-DEXTER turned and pointed in the direction of the northeast side of the office door.

"A heads-up on what we've been doing little brother. My trusty sidekick reinforced the wall in the office leading down to a secret door. Ryan was the one to point out the compartment left undiscovered. We filled several areas with concrete and steel to keep out the pesky Pailoids from below."

Bailey responded with a skyward push of his right thumb, a visual for T-DEXTER's unwavering vision. "Nice goin' Tin-Man. It's good to know you have our backs."

The robot let out a chuckle. "Sure, thing little brother, no problemo, piece of cake, one for the Gipper, you my main man, smooth sailing, we're ship-shape, out of sight, give me some skin my friend." T-DEXTER held up his hand in a high-five. Bailey was confused with T-DEXTER's overanxious behavior but did a softer than usual tap on the robots palm.

He noticed that the lower compartments of the warehouse were ship-shape also, like the robot suggested and looked like nothing had been disturbed. Knowing the robots didn't have to sleep was a big plus. And having T-DEXTER and his sidekick around to do a lot of the dirty-work was an inspiration for those of a lesser number.

Then Betty stepped into the conversation. "That's a good thing about having them a round." Betty explained. "You don't have to feed them, and they don't leave a trail behind."

Bailey crinkled his nose. "You mean like horses do?"

"Yeah, something like that, they're low maintenance."

Bailey pushed out a smile from the corners of his mouth. "You got a point. They don't break things or get all emotional or throw their clothes on the floor."

Betty glared at Bailey with a sheepish twitch. "I hope you're talking about your clothes and your emotions and not mine?"

Bailey's nostrils flared with the continued jesting. "Yeah, of course, what… you think I was insinuating someone else?"

She raised an eyebrow. "I wouldn't put it past you—being the dork you are."

Bailey lost the smile. "Whatever man, I was only playing with you. Don't take everything so personally. I wasn't trying to get you riled up. I'm trying to change the mood of this whole place. It's drab with all the events that have been taking place."

Betty rolled her eyes. "Well, don't do me any favors hot shot." Betty folded her arms across her mid-section and turned her view in another direction. Bailey felt bad for even opening his mouth. The big robot stalled for more time to go by to see where this little skirmish was headed too. Then SNARF bellowed so loud Betty lost her balance and dropped her cane. She spun around on one leg and yelled at T-DEXTER. "Can't you change his voice box? The metal mutt needs to sound normal—not like a stupid lion!"

T-DEXTER reached up behind him and scratched the back of his head.

"Well, he'd suit a better selection of verbiage from a canine's clairvoyance. Well, let's see." T-DEXTER spun back when facing his second in command.

"Cewcewcachew…walawalabingbang," He belted out.

SNARF took a stab at his new voice pattern and barked several times.

Betty scrunched her nose and covered her head, like expecting phlegm to fly out of his mouth. "Well, I guess that's a little better than roaring like he's the king of the jungle." Betty squinted while covering her face. "Why's he always so friendly, like an over-heated puppy wagging his tail? Is he just trying to get attention, like our friendly super-dork over here?" She pointed to the suit wearer and giggled. "How's that for a mood changer Dork-Man." Betty covered her mouth in a mounting surge of giggles. She crossed her legs and put her hand in front of her, needing to use the bathroom.

Ryan couldn't believe these two were even friends. "Hey!" he said, "try a tree, it worked for me." This made Bailey raise an eyebrow.

Betty reached up and smacked Ryan in the back of the head. "Hey... nimrod...what'd I do?"

Betty put on a scowl. "You two boy's get on my nerves." Then Betty slightly giggled when noticing both boys frowning. "You two can sleep with the gorillas."

Bailey cut her off, "Hey you're the one with the unpredictability. I wasn't picking on you. I was just messing around."

Betty swung around with a heated glare. "I wasn't talking to you anyhow. Don't you have something better to do, besides bother me? Go clean the bathrooms or some doorknobs, since I never see you two washing your hands."

Bailey took that as a hint to lay-off the interminable judgments and leave well enough alone. He reached down and slipped the suit on. He thought, *super-dork.—huh...* He wanted something more inspiring to keep his mind occupied. He ignored Betty as he readjusted to the suit. Bailey, now Crepto, could feel a renewed energy starting to build, stronger than the day before. He ignored her while thinking. *I'm not a Super-Dork like she thinks.*

As the big robot walked away, he mumbled under his breath. "That Ms. Betty is a tough one to please..."

All was calm for the time being—too calm. In fact, no birds were flying through the air. There was a serene quietness throughout the compound, and above the Atrium level not a breath of air stirred.

Crepto flew to the compound's upper levels, crossing the Atrium a good fifty feet high toward the center of the cave. So, he could get a birds-eye-view of the recognized quietness. He waited for the Crepto Energy to reach a descent level before attempting to use his heightening senses. There was something not right out there in this place they called home. Crepto jumped to an implicit position to tune out everything else around him. The eyes and ears of those things he could not see or hear had once eluded him. But now, events of a different nature appeared to change. He looked back and forth from above to below. The trees off in the distance were too calm, too silent, no stirring of air, no sounds from above. He knew this calm was somehow a warning. Then it hit him. No sight of any birds or squirrels or the usual roaming of rabbits. This made him nervous.

Nimbly, Betty followed him out in the open and looked up at him.

"What's going on? Why are you looking so suspicious of the compound?" Crepto dropped down to Betty's side.

"Make sure everyone has weapons close by. I don't want any surprises from those creatures coming in here. Something's not right. I can feel it."

"So, what do we do?"

"Be prepared. Be paranoid, anything but normal. These fights are not over by a long shot. It's too quiet in here."

Betty didn't like the fact that he was nervous, even after putting on the suit. She looked high and low, trying to find reason for Crepto's sudden paranoid frame of mind.

Then T-DEXTER and SNARF came out in the open too, "What's going on out here—why you are hanging around out here and stalling?" Then T-DEXTER raised his wrist, popped on his bio-scanner, and waited for the readings to appear. He was expostulating about Crepto's nervous tension.

Precipitously, Crepto turned in the big robots direction. "Did you ever find a flame thrower we'd talked about yesterday?" Crepto moved his eyes toward the metal-mutt. "I mean besides SNARF, something with a little more gusto."

The all too jovial robot returned his stare. "I'll be right back." Bounding rapidly back where he'd had come from. The robot and his sidekick were off in a flash. T-DEXTER returned in about five minutes holding a nozzle of some sort with a tank hooked to his back. He had landed so hard that he'd startled his friends. Betty fell backwards landing on her butt. Crepto reached to help her up.

"Sorry little lady." The big robot embellished. "I'll try to be more careful."

In another direction, T-DEXTER shot a flame out away from the group. The air off the flamethrower blew back Betty's hair. She narrowed her eyes and looked at Crepto. "Make sure he doesn't set this whole compound up in smoke. I'm not so sure about using a flamethrower in here."

Crepto looked at Betty without responding. He stepped up close to the flamethrower to get a better view. A ribbed tank with a complicated nozzle wrapped up under T-DEXTER's arm. The tank was a shiny silvery color with a four-foot extending pipe connected with a cock-handle you'd find on a water sprayer for watering a lawn. A simple setup but deadly. Crepto walked back inside the bottom warehouse to retrieve his sword and shield from the Q-Tank he'd used from the day before. It still reeked with the smell of the creatures left behind. T-DEXTER hadn't had time to clean the pair.

When he returned, Betty covered her nose. "You mind getting that awful thing out of here? It stinks!"

Crepto rolled his eyes as he shot up in the air a good fifty feet above them. T-DEXTER, wanting to know what the young Gambit was doing followed closely behind. From a distance, he could see two Pailoids running towards a tunnel. *How'd they get in here?* Crepto thought. But then knowing they hadn't attempted to check out the last tunnel, not all places were examined as of yet. This caused a certain mystery to transpire. T-DEXTER saw the creatures too. Crepto didn't wait. He headed out of the compound like a rocket to the moon.

T-DEXTER stayed behind but hovered in the air. Not knowing if any Pailoids would get past his guard, and more concerned about Betty and the children. He then settled to the ground when she came over. "Sorry little lady. You're best protected behind the wheel of your Hummer." He stated. So, T-DEXTER scooped her up and flew her just outside the door. All beat up, and dents on every part, it was a disgrace.

"Now you're talkin." She said. Then Dr. EL walked over.

"What's going on?" The doctor asked. Betty swung around as she climbed into the Hummer. It was cleaned up on the inside. T-DEXTER had readied the Hummer for a new day. All the dents and damage on the outside were still there, yet it was ready like Freddy for another bout with the Pailoids.

"We've got company. Get in." She insisted. Dr. EL got in on the passenger side as Betty revved the engine and peeled a 180 turn, facing in the same direction as the tunnels ahead. Screaming tires and burning rubber shocked the doctor.

From the other side of the compound, Crepto cut through two bodies and laid them to waste where they fell. The air swished through trees when coming back around in front of the middle tunnel. He noticed right away George had rounded up the girls. Then suddenly landing in front of them.

"We've got company." Crepto stated. "And not much time. They found a way in."

Mattie and Jackie showed extemporaneous efforts to hurry along.

Crepto viewed one of George's gulf-carts close by and said, "Get in. I have an idea." Everyone, including George got aboard the small utility vehicle and held on. "Buckled up and get ready to go!" He stated. Crepto picked the gulf-cart up and flew in the direction of the compound, without wasting any time. The wind kicked up the girls hair and pushed them hard against the seats. This was no pleasure cruise, from George's frame of mind. This was serious business. Two little girls sensing a ride of their life held on tight. Jackie turned a paler white and Mattie gripped Jackie's arm leaving fingerprints that would stay. Both girls were closing their eyes. This flight kept them white, as pale as a polar bear in yellow snow. Jackie knew her heart was about to explode, and George in front didn't look any better.

Then George yelled as they came to the other side of the compound. "Hey stop!" George insisted. Crepto slowed suddenly like a jackhammer hitting steel, tearing flesh off bone was George's frame of mind. Two little girl's torsos leaned into the cross-chest seatbelts and pushed the air out of their lungs. George almost messed himself from the unannounced rocket to the moon. He wondered why no warning. Crepto, sitting the gulf-cart down, compared to a culinary turkey sandwich being placed with a gentle sweep of the hands. The girls had been holding their breath just before landing. Their faces were flushed, and hearts were pounding.

George unbuckled his seatbelt and lunged toward the compounds monitoring system keypad and slid his hand through the scanner. "I'm closing the gates. I don't want those things getting in the zoo." He said. "The animals, they're not safe..." George over emphasized his concerns.

Crepto walked over to the keypad as he looked around making sure none of those creatures were hanging around from behind. The doors closed suddenly, leaving the animals safe for now. George put a key into the lock to shut down the system. Generator lights kicked on as backup.

"Where's Cuddles?" Jackie whispered.

"We left her at the zoo." Mattie remarked. Both girls looked at each other. The girls were forced back into the Q-Tank for protection.

Within seconds, the compound filled with a stampeding hoard of hundreds of Pailoids moving quickly toward the Hummer and the robots. They were guessing they came from another tunnel. Crepto saw Ryan standing behind SNARF wondering which way to run. Ryan looked up when Crepto scooped him up off his feet...

The battle was on. Betty was in the Hummer with Dr. EL, T-DEXTER to her left and SNARF to the right, taking a military stance like birds flying in a V pattern.

Dr. EL shot a stare across the dash. "What do you want me to do?" He asked.

With a fermenting response. "Sit back, buckle-up, and close your eyes! This might leave a few stains on the hubcaps." The doctor held his breath and turned white. Betty had this quelling expression set in her eyes. She was unhinged, her autocratic mind flashing anomalies of this mounting situation. She was a badass Barbie doll set for butchery. Her mind raced with antecedent order. She was a war machine, fast and mean, locked, and loaded. T-DEXTER looked past her window and saw the crazed look in her eyes.

"Oh Ms. Betty looks pissed." The large robot responded. T-DEXTER warmed up his flame thrower with the first wave of fury.

Betty pulled her high beams on, blinding the Pailoids just in front. She double clicked her cartridges and unloaded. Wailing and screeching of the dammed filled the air. Dr. EL covered his head. Betty lit up the compound with 30M retribution in Gatling-gun style. SNARF tore through their ranks in doggy-done-did-it demonology. The air filled with a putrid stench of the dying. The running rage of this massive force pushed the two Gait 30M's to full volume.

Suddenly, a beam of light shot in front of them—Crepto was back as the Crepto Energy reflected an indubitable power. The suit shot heat and light in all directions. The burn, the power, the awesomeness of light—it was a metaphor of things to come—the burning of the bones, a rectifying of revenge, a day for disaster. It was a quest for the dying, a hindrance of havoc, a dripping of blood and the massing of flesh—embodied, broken, annihilated. The blood, the bones, the rage, decrepitude of madness chased them to the last heartbeat, to the end of the line, to this zone of reckoning, zealots of the dead. A suppurating seepage of urine, water, and blood trailed toward the centered gutters of the compound. A wasting of will and reasoning dripped into the gutters of denial. A black pile of muck lay burning in the middle killing field of stained constituency. This was to be as Armageddon, an abyss, a gulf of ephemeral existence—piled in the throes of forgetfulness. Smoke and dust, muddied in the piles of flesh and blood was a feast unrelenting.

T-DEXTER finished off the few that remained. Crepto had a yearning to find George. He left the scene to find his friend. The redundant burning of light pushed the suit to sweltering exhaustion. He headed for the med-lab on the third floor.

Bursting through the door, Crepto slid to a standstill position as Sergeant Bristol finished off a Pailoid. George was tucked between the cushions of a Cryogenic chamber with this bemused expression. "What took you so long?" A florid complaint was noted. The sergeant assisted George out of the chamber before getting back in his own. Bailey, inside the suit, peeled it off and dropped it to the floor. The burning of light flickered from its glow.

This day of battle had ended.

CHAPTER 27

The Gorge

The robots, along with their newly acquired friends, cleaned up the dead. The smell lingered through the air for quite some time. Dr. EL adjusted the ventilation units to clear the putrid smell, as George retained a fifty-gallon barrel of disinfectant for the exposed areas of battle.

The mystery of tunnel three was burning on Bailey's mind since their last battle. T-DEXTER had taken the Crepto Suit and submerged it in a tub of ice-water with a gentle cleansing solution.

Going back, Bailey had remembered the hoard of creatures that had come from this uncharted tunnel. There had to be a clue that lay beyond its borders, something missing. Something they hadn't seen yet. Without trying to alarm the others, *he* and Ryan had taken one of the Q-Tanks down tunnel one. Like all Q-Tanks left by the government, they were smartly fashioned, and built to take a beating, for times like these impediments of a darker world. Every Q-tank had a stealth mode with infrared cameras constructed in the computer's animated visual-visors. And for furtive reasons unknown, he felt safer behind the steel covering of the tank. And the fact that his suit had been left behind for cleaning and cooling purposes—they'd need the tank to fall back on as added physical protection.

So, without further consternation, the boys were left on their own. Ryan had tagged along to help with buttons and switches monitoring distance and temperatures or changes in road conditions—and also for conversation to keep Bailey company. They couldn't afford drifting too far from one side of the road or the other. Knowing Ryan was the only company for the moment, Bailey hoped not to see the small boy as a cumbersome pain in the butt. Furthermore, all the switches and gadgets lit up on the console in fine-tuned timing, accompanied by quirky sounds and three-dimensional screens. It was the perfect diversion for Ryan's playful mind of imagined missions and visual explosions of taking out his enemy. The view from the visual visor had become Ryan's clandestine delight. He had quite the imagination as he'd get lost in his make-believe world of crusaders and masked villains. Of course, he plays the part of one of the Avengers most likely. The mighty Thor or his all-time favorite superhero Iron-Man in his shiny red and gold armor. Bailey could hear sound effects of drifting splashes and explosions of military missions as seen from the contortions and movements of Ryan's whispering lips. He looked over and smiled. His face was lit up like a candle in the dark. A face of innocence as much as a child could expound. Freckles and frizziest with dirty hands and cheesiness that little boys string along, along with the imaginative expectations of his connecting bond—it's all part of growing-up from little boys to bigger boys with all their exotic toys. He was perfect in his form. One tooth missing and dirtied baseball cap. Left in the luxuries of what little boys could imagine in a world fallen apart. Bailey looked over and gave the befuddled boy a few assignments of duty.

"Ryan buckle-up and monitor the switches to your right. I've got the left." Ryan smiled.

"Got it chief, no problemo…" Ryan barked out as they shot down the road toward the mysteries of the dark…

Betty just remembered leaving the girls in a Q-Tank, on the sub-basement floor, hidden from the watchful eyes of their enemies. She looked up at T-DEXTER. "Tinman, I need your help. We forgot about the girls."

"You're right Ms. Betty. We better get them out of the Q-Tank." Betty, with her cane in hand, was swept off her feet. George and Dr. EL stood standing back in the distance—shocked by the robots sudden upheaval. T-DEXTER lacked the proper propriety of human traits, forgetting that bolting above with rocket like speed was most unbecoming. She closed her eyes and wished for smoother sailing transportation. She was livid with surprise.

Put me down!" Betty barked out, as T-DEXTER settled back to the ground.

"Sorry Ms. Betty, I thought hitching a ride would suit you better, considering the little girls were left unattended."

Betty looked up while brushing herself off. "Which Q-Tank are they in?" She insisted.

"Oh, the one on the end…" T-DEXTER embellished.

"I hope they're alright!" Betty said, while shooting a snooty glare toward this robot's impolite renditions. "Well, are you going to let them out or you wait for me to limp over and struggle with that heavy lid?"

Looking down at her wounded condition T-DEXTER got the visual. "Right on Ms. Betty, I've got them covered." The rambling robot reached up and opened the top of the Q-Tank. Two little girl's set in dreamy-eyes of fairy-princesses, soft cuddles of warmth and slumbering sleep-heads. Betty looked in on them and sighed with relief. Tender curls of little girls and soft shiny pink cheeks. Betty's shoulders began to relax.

Jackie slowly stirred awake. Blinking from the light breaking its way through the top brought her back to reality. Jackie reached over and nudged Mattie. "Hey…wakeup…we've got company."

Mattie squinted, then yawned erstwhile pushing her arms in the air, with bent wrist and over flexed elbow. "Where's Bailey?" Mattie asked, as if *he* is the only true Gambit among them.

Betty wrinkled her face. She whispered, "Whatever. The dork done did him-self in. He's riding on his ego down tunnel one."

"What?" Jackie said, not understanding. Betty rolled her eyes. "He's checking out another tunnel. We missed something." Jackie looked up still confused.

"Where's Ryan at?" This statement caused Betty's eyes to widen.

"Oh no, I forgot the knucklehead took my nephew." This lit a fire under Betty. "We've got to go!" Mattie showed a quizzical expression with sleepy interpretations of a few minutes before. Then T-DEXTER remembered Bailey had left the suit at his disposal, remembering submersing its contents in a tub of ice water.

Ryan reached up and twisted a knob that made the screen bigger on his visual visor. The darkness before them loomed like creepy shadowed arms elongated out toward this pervading mystery. They were viewing the tunnel ahead from a complicated headset. Most of it didn't make sense. This first tunnel was mysterious in an eerie type of way, a forbidden zone of confusion, a place dug out from the right side of this mountain with the wrong intentions of entering a place for the dead.

Bailey's eyes blinked from being tired. He wanted to pull over, but something pushed him to keep going. Something of mystery pulled him toward this obscurity ahead. He was traveling pretty fast, making pace with no reason in particular. Driven by this insane concept of finding hope for their futures but hope for them wouldn't be found on a road going nowhere. It would be found within each members own existence, their own manifestation of the living—not on this trail exploiting the ambiguities of something dead or dying. He really didn't know why he was pushed to find answers. What laid in wait in this tunnel to come? What had eluded them?

Bailey reached over and turned on his infrared cameras, and for the moment he had doused the headlamps. He was trying to brighten the area past the dark without giving away his position. This was a road that loomed in creepy shadows with unknown conditions. The tunnel was blacker than the blackest of nights, causing an impediment of sight, a mystery, a paroxysm on a different level. This was a place of nocturnal submissions untouched by the world from above—a world of bats and rats, and things that scurry in the night, from this cave leaving a chill in the air. Ryan looked across the dash wondering if they should continue.

"Those creatures came from this direction—right?"

Bailey glanced quickly across the dash. "Yes, they came from this way, but I think that was the last we've seen of them." Bailey said. "We'll be okay." was his thinking. Yet somehow a sensed deeper meaning were in words not said. Then knowing he had already climbed out of the suit, which would leave him unprotected if meeting these creatures again, but highly unlikely, was his train of thought. But his Gambit suit left an impression once understanding its use when looking at his situation from his human perspective. But that was exactly the perspective he'd taken—feeling something from the suit remained. There was a cohesive reminder on an extemporaneous logical level of what was to come buried in the back of his mind. Something lasting, something growing that would become stronger after each new use. The suit was slowly becoming a part of Bailey's physical body. An existence of both worlds began making a connection without the suit.

Coming out on the other side of the tunnel, Bailey could see through the darkness in this stealth mode. Lurking shadows advanced and moved toward them as they progressed forward. This gave Ryan a creepy feeling. "What is this place, Bailey?"

"I don't know squirt. We'll soon find out." In front of them lay seven towers, seven stories high mounting above them as Bailey reconnoitered their surroundings. He took in everything that he could feel through an intuitive sense. Something was wrong with this place, and something raised the hair on the back of Ryan's neck. He was afraid, but he held back. Ryan remembered this feeling once when he was a little younger, after watching a scary movie with his sister when grandmother was away. It scared him so badly he crawled under his bed and wanted to cry. He remembered eventually crawling in bed with his sister—this was different, this was surreal to the point of miscomprehension. They were inside someone else's world that didn't hold any logic. No color could be perceived in this impeding darkness. Their adaptation of almost no light produced a demarcation of how far they could go, how much they could see. Limited by obscure shadows and deep pockets procured. Behind them, to the left, in the distance, fitted between several buildings was the construction of a fifteen by twenty-foot utility shed sitting on a plinth. Connected above this diminutive building were several thick wires linked to the towers that jetted above. The blocked structure was surrounded by an eight-foot fence with razor sharp circulating barbwire strung out above. It reflected a prison atmosphere. A portended internal sense pulled at Bailey. He had remembered climbing a fence like this with his cousin back when he was sixteen. Now, for obvious reasons this was to keep out curious minds of a smaller stature—high voltage. Keep out--was the warning sign. This was an obvious roadblock, an appendage to impede personal resolve. It was to keep children and unlucky do-gooders of cantankerous deeds away. Then it made sense. This was the electrical unit for the entire cave. Bailey pulled to an unmarked parking area in front. Turning the headlamps on, in the same direction of this medium sized utility shed. He had predetermined what he wanted and needed, even though from a human perspective he hadn't a clue why he was even here, and with a small curious boy sitting at his side. Somehow, he knew the suit's impressions were still having an effect. To the left of the utility shed, all he saw was the darkness and the same to the right. Ryan reached into the glovebox and found a flashlight. He crossed the light past Bailey's gaze. Bailey looked over and knew it was something that would help him find what he was looking for, of course, that would be the main breaker-box to light up this cave. He wouldn't give in to not finding the answers needed before heading back to the compound. This was a point of no return. His pride wouldn't let him go back empty handed. An illumination of everything would give them a better view of what they were facing—what was hidden in the cold dark holes that surrounded them. He was the first to escape the top of the Q-Tank. Ryan was next, as he relentlessly scuffed his heels in the direction of his mentor. Ryan turned the flashlight across the path of Bailey's eyes. Bailey, more than surprised, pulled his hand up to block the light.

"Would you mind not shining that in my eyes?"

Ryan grinned and lined the trail of the light at Bailey's feet. "Sorry chief. It slipped out of my hands." Bailey playfully rubbed the top of Ryan's head above matted hair under a dirty baseball cap. He turned his head and looked in the direction of the medium-sized utility shed. Something told him that the shed was the immediate answer to any future questions that might cross their minds. Ryan held the flashlight steady as Bailey climbed the fence. Avoiding sharp curling wires and quick cutting abrasions was his first concern, and getting to the other side unscathed was the second. Bailey pulled off his jacket and threw it over his shoulder as he climbed in youthful fashion. He was nervous at first, but once past the top he strung his jacket over razor sharp wiring and catapulted himself over the fence. Ryan was all bug-eyed at Bailey's finesse. He stood up undisturbed. He whispered through the fence.

"Hey…little dude…toss me the light." Ryan did what he was told and threw the flashlight over the fence. It bounced from hand to hand several times before Bailey caught it and kept it from hitting the ground. Once procured, Bailey turned and headed for the crypt-like building, leaving Ryan behind in the dark. The headlights had automatically clicked off on the Q-Tank leaving the area totally dark. Ryan huffed out a large breath of air and looked around, not seeing anything he felt a chill go up his spine. And eerie feeling crept into the pint-size man-child when an undulating loud screeching noise caused him to freeze…

Betty helped the girls off the top of the Q-Tank as T-DEXTER secured the tank and closed the top. Betty was more concerned about two little girls than she would be about anything else at the moment. Even Ryan wasn't on her mind at present because he was in the safe loving care of Bailey's hands, and Bailey, she thought, had left his suit behind to cool down. She then turned suddenly to look up at T-DEXTER.

"Why, of all things, would that big dork leave his suit behind when he doesn't know if that tunnel is secured?" T-DEXTER showed a face of puzzlement. Without being told SNARF leapt over a chair and headed for the tub on the third level to retrieve the suit.

"What was he thinking?" Betty said, still limping. She started to walk across the warehouse floor. In the distance, she saw the Hummer beat-up and dented, yet it somehow was still able to roll. She turned to T-DEXTER. "I need your help. Since Sergeant Bristol isn't available, we're on our own."

Betty pulled herself across the seat of the Hummer. "You girls go to the penthouse and lock yourselves in. And set the alarm. I'll call you when we're back."

Jackie and Mattie looked like each other in a world of mystification. "But what do we do if something happens?" Jackie said.

"Call George, he'll keep you company." Betty retorted, sounding like her grandmother. She looked behind the back seat of the Hummer and had forgotten she had fired most of the ammo from their last confrontation with those malodorous creatures. Wish wrinkling face she reached over to push a button on the computer. The computer displayed a count of two-hundred rounds left. The ammo boxes when full held over a hundred thousand rounds. Betty knew this wouldn't even come close to being enough to face another attack.

"T-DEXTER, go get two more boxes of ammo." She insisted. "What's left won't do. And get that crate of C-4 and switches you found yesterday. I have a feeling we might need it."

"Right on Ms. Betty, I've got you covered." T-DEXTER did a couple of quick leaps over several crates and came back slowly with two more boxes of ammo—full, heavy, and ready to rock and roll. Betty had already opened the back left side passenger door, awaiting the robots return. T-DEXTER reached in and took out the two black powder burned boxes that were already in the custom-made area and replaced them with the new ones. Betty turned the ignition on. Rough revving of power roared to life as before. She pushed several buttons on the Hummer's computer. This would release the cartridge on the auto reload for the two Gait 30m's. It would also help T-DEXTER to reline the new rounds so they'd line-up through the auto feed to connect the two ammo boxes sitting in the back. The robot had to stop and clean both Gait 30m's before he could reload. Twenty minutes later, Betty's Gait 30m's were locked and loaded. T-DEXTER got up off his knees and went to retrieve the box of grenades and C-4 with the relay switches. Something he'd learned from enhanced programming in memory—setting up explosives. T-DEXTER slid the box of explosives in the back of the Hummer and closed the back door.

Betty yelled over the noise of the engine. "You two follow me! We don't have much time." Betty spun the wheels and burned rubber as the two robots chased after her.

Dr. EL, from the distance of the office, got up and ran toward the door—only catching a glimpse of the Hummer and two robots flaring off in the distance. He waved at the air in disgust. "Those stupid kids don't have a clue what their getting themselves into."

Betty took off in a trail of dust…

Bailey turned when this loud screeching cry belied through the darkness. He yelled through the fence to get Ryan's attention as mounting terror ripped through his gut.

"Get in the Q-Tank and wait for me!" Ryan couldn't believe Bailey would leave him on his own but didn't argue about what was right or wrong. He headed for the Q-tank and rapidly shot down the top with a loud clank. Ryan slid down into the seat, but then realized he'd forgotten to latch the top. He stood on the seat to reach for the top just before he heard this repeated ever loud screeching of ululation. Ryan was petrified but kept his composure enough to then lock the hatch. He slowly slipped back into the right-side seat. An impending bead of sweat was pasted on his brow. Ryan removed his Angel's baseball cap and wiped his sweaty face with a dirty sleeve. He still had the marks of impending war left from the compound—memories to vivid not worth repeating. Ryan got the little bit of composure he had left and began pushing buttons and switches while leaving the Q-Tank in stealth-mode. He had to monitor the movement just outside the Q-tank. Ryan slipped the visual visor on to look for anything that moved in the dark. Something big and shadowy from the right side of his screen blinked ominous movement.

Whatever it was, he thought. *It sounded pissed.* Then it just dawn on the boy he didn't have any way to communicate with Bailey. He was alone. This was the last place he'd ever want to be—caught in a darkened tunnel with some unknown predator headed his way. And by the sounds of it, he didn't sound small.

Bailey got to the door of the utility shed and hadn't realized that the door to this obscure building would be locked-up tighter than a drum. Leaving his jacket behind strung over the fence he'd remembered putting his pocketknife in one of the zipped-up pockets that hung low on the jacket. This was no ordinary pocketknife. It had special little gadgets attached to help those elude certain personal predicaments. He turned around and headed for where his jacket was when the screeching sound of ululation returned. It was comparably much louder this time, which caused him to freeze. What was that thing? And what had they'd missed that had become most alarming from previous? Scared that he'd been seen Bailey doused his light. Now he was really in for it. He couldn't see, he couldn't communicate with Ryan, and this feral creature was quickly catching up to him. He felt like Helen Keller reaching for the stars. But what stars could he reach for *if* he didn't even have the suit on? He felt vulnerable and at his weakest point. He felt naked. *He* was being a simple human trying to get past this adversity climbing an obfuscating fence without any hope, and something much stronger than *he* in its simplest of forms of massive size or whatever this thing stood to be, was stocking him and the boy by closely sniffing its way toward its next meal. Bailey became overwhelmed with emotion. A bleak hope shuddered through him. He sensed this was a predator of the worst kind that reflected a stentorian manifestation, but then there were the memories of the suit. His heart was pumping so hard he could feel the beat of his blood thumping around his neck and head. This was different, he was under-prepared, with an unmannered fear taking over. A new plan had to be invented for what seemed to be coming sounded quite different. To him it was like payback for all the dreadful things men of earth ever did to their people and their planet—retribution coming full circle, a sensation of compensation, and an unannounced proclamation opposite an explanation causing trepidation.

In the distance, Bailey heard rocks being extricated or torn from their current positions and falling down in the obscurity of echoing sounds. Was there another part of the gorge that lay close by? Was there another way out? Then more movement was heard yet closer. Whatever it was, it was headed in his general direction at an imbuing rate, faster than Bailey could handle. And Ryan might have been in its direct path too, from what he could tell. Bailey leapt in the direction of his jacket and heard it rip. He didn't have the heart to climb the fence at the present moment, knowing that what loomed in front would hear him stirring, giving the thing a clearer target of recompense. Bailey was stifled to stillness and didn't know what to do…

Ryan started looking in every compartment, cubby hole, and nook, under the seats to find anything that resembled a weapon. He needed a clearer path for a get-away—a distraction, a flamboyant bamboozlement to draw this monstrosity away.

Ryan accidentally leaned forward on the center console as a dim illumination of bluish light popped on. He reached for the center console and flipped a clipped handled door to reveal something hidden below. To his surprise, the deep pocketed console housed five odd-looking military grenades. Ryan reached for them but was careful not to accidentally push or pull anything to make them go boom. He cradled the five grenades and stuffed them carefully in his jacket pockets. Knowing he was armed with deadly weapons he proceeded to sidle back out of the top of the Q-Tank. His imagination of blowing up something big gave him confidence. And there was no way he was going to wait and be crushed by something bigger than his imagination would allow. Another squelch of reverberating terror vibrated within a short distance of a hundred and fifty feet. This was too close for personal comfort. Ryan pulled himself free of the Q-Tank. He could feel and smell the presence of this predator. Without light, without knowing his direction, Ryan began to run…

Bailey jumped a little higher this time and made a connection. The pocketknife fell from the ripped open jacket and landed in his hand. He couldn't see it, but for some mysterious reason he'd known it would be there—perfectly timed, of perfect dimensions, landing in his hand. He knew even through separation the suit made a connection within memory. Comprehended limber and acrobatic maneuvers he'd made the fence, without any difficulty, without much consideration finding success. Known from past experience, when wearing the suit—there was a link, something transferred and left in his cells, something of confidence, something real in an intangible way. He turned around and went back to the shed—quietly in solemnity moved forward in the obscurity of the dark. He took his pocketknife and felt his way back to the utility shed door, three steps up on a landing after straight ahead, about twenty-five feet then up to his left. The air developed a pungent smell that reminded Bailey of those creatures killed in the tunnel. He stopped long enough to flip open the pocketknife and turned the flashlight toward the inside of his shirt, away from the angle of where the noise was coming from earlier. A red beam of light flashed across the door handle, cuffed under his hand. He began to use his limited craft and worked at trying to pry open the door. The shuffling of large rocks could be heard extracted from behind. Heavy breathing and the smell of rot filled the air. Within seconds, Bailey had this utility shed open. He walked in, closed the door, and flipped on the flashlight. To his right, lay several electrical grey metal boxes connected to the wall. Bailey opened all three and started to match up breaker switches with what was written to the right of them. He read through the whole list before him. First, there was the town hall, the music room; kitchen galley, auditorium, banquet room, and then he went to the next breaker box, and finally found two breaker switches that read outside town lights and generator. Bailey reached for them and flipped both switches on. The lights outside lit up. Bailey heard a loud cry of warbling and ululation that sounded like metal plates scraping together. He felt a chill go down his back. This sound was different. Then he heard the scream…

Ryan had run in a direction opposite of where he should have gone. He stopped abruptly when he couldn't quite make out what was ahead. A gentle glow of lights was cast in the distance showing an unsure pathway just ahead. Without noticing, the boy had started crossing over a bridge that was a walkway, a driveway over to the other side of what he did not know. It led to an oblong shaped lawn about two hundred fifty feet long with several headstones at one end. And then a building that looked like a mortuary made of limestone with dormered windows. Standing over at the other end of the bridge was something hidden in shadows. Ryan stood on the higher end closer to the mortuary. This place gave him a hermetical feeling like he was inside an opaque bubble, claustrophobic, roiling together into a demarcated zone—a place to die, marked by the scent of sweat, and rage, and a fetid foul smell of death itself. Ryan learned a good measure of what deaths face looked like from the day before. He knew this thing was targeting him, whatever it was. The bridge was a good two-hundred and fifty feet long with a unique guard-rail about six feet high made of a brass color with points shooting across the top within a circled area turning inward to keep people from climbing the rail—not sharp but impeding as if to block ones progress. The askew road made of cobblestone of a tanned adobe. Ryan briefly noticed, beyond the rail, off to the right side showed blackness below. This caused Ryan's blood to rush to his legs with a sense of vertigo. It made his head feel light as he grabbed the railing and took a deep breath. Furthermore, off in the distance, past this bridge, next to this mortuary, on the right side was a Porte-Cochere where Ryan figured cars could drive around the back side of the mortuary to drop off the dead. A morbid feeling of seeing dead people caused a chill to raise the hairs on his arms and caused his bottom lip to quiver with a touch of emotion. Ryan thought of turning around and going back, yet sensed it was too late. Curiosity and a sixth sense pushed him to go farther. To the left, after the bridge, was this lawn he'd noticed when first making it to the other side. With a thick green golf-course type of grass with five headstones that had drawn Ryan's attention. This was angled between soft beads of coruscated sparkles of light. What had Ryan's attention *now* was coming from behind. It was the most disconcerting sound the small boy had ever heard. Heavy footsteps came to a stop. A cry of rage warbled from the back of this creature's throat. That's when Ryan turned to look. At that point, he was sorry for looking, because what he saw wasn't anything a small boy could even imagine. That's when he screamed…

Ryan turned and started running again in the direction of the lime-stone mortuary. He booked it as fast as his little legs would carry him. The creature behind him had just pulled itself up from the bottom of this enormous hole that lay below. The smell and feeling Ryan experienced from looking down made his heart sink. Several large boulders had tumbled toward the black left beneath as this creature clawed his way to the top. Ryan wanted to cry, but nothing came out because his mouth was dry, and because the fear that remained held him in check. And he'd also sensed that any susurration at this time would give this creature an edge. Ryan stopped and stood still like a desert lizard—not batting an eye, not moving a flinch. This thing on the other side stood on the end of the bridge, breathing deeply with a beastly stare—unchanging, unblinking, unmoving. The only thing moving was the movement of his chest sucking in air and something was independently moving on the surface of his skin. Ryan was staring into the face of death. He saw the look that shot through him as he let go of his urine. It flowed down is leg and out of his sock. Ryan didn't care. He was merely a boy with nowhere to hide, trying to keep this creature at bay. The bridge was slightly slanted going down showing a clear pathway, straight forth, toward this large production of terror. Ryan turned to look over his shoulder while viewing the mortuary. It was half the distance he was from the creature. He would make it, he wouldn't. This beast understood where Ryan wanted to go. There was something in his eyes that showed intelligence, a plan, a purpose in being here. When standing on all fours this Pailoid was over fifteen feet tall. This indomitable force was only separated by the distance of this bridge. And Ryan began to understand his form, his stance, his permutation of astute purpose. The giant Pailoids feet were fettered with long black-lined claws that were loped in two different directions. The boy sensed something had to be done and done quickly because the creature was on to his scent as seen by him sniffing at the air. A portended shock went through him when this monstrous figure's skin started to move in circular patterns. Ryan had to think, to do something. He had to get past the fright that had frozen him in his tracks. He didn't want to be overtaken by this prodigious beast.

All the color had drained from the small boys face. That's when Ryan remembered he'd had stuffed those five grenades in his jacket pocket. The creature that stood in the distance couldn't see Ryan, only shadows of obfuscated light, but persistently sniffed at the air. Even a small boy of seven knew what that meant. He was its next meal.

The creature of reddish muscling tissue looked festered and bulging with sores and rheumy fluid discharging from its face, yet something was a bit different than what he'd seen from the other creatures. This one looked like he'd been turned inside out. His flesh was a mess of reddish inflammation and movement on its porous skin, something imperceptible. From Ryan's point of view this was unacceptable. To even look at it caused Ryan to shudder. The creature's teeth were elongated and jagged dripping with long stringy greenish like phlegm or drool. He had blackened eyes, blacker than the hole below him. A sound of trepidation resounded back to the small boy. This creature was changing, he was transmuting at a metabolic rate. He was growing and expanding. A stentorian trilling sound shot forth from this creature's mouth. The changes were causing a substantial amount of pain and Ryan saw that as an opportunity to move forward and do something he'd never thought a small boy like himself would or should ever do.

Ryan took one of the grenades out of his pocket and pulled out the pin. He then released the grenade like a fast-moving bowling-ball rolling downhill. An arduous feat in the making, but Ryan found his angle of flight for the grenade had carried its momentum forward. Since he was on an uphill slant, the grenade bounced and rolled for quite some

time. It had rolled ten feet from this malignant beast before going off…
boom. The creature got pieces of shrapnel hailing toward him. Chunks
of flesh were splashed with blood, but nothing permanent seemed to
do much damage. It appealed to Ryan's better nature of a do-gooder
of quality deeds such as this that it could become all-consuming, like
taking shots with a Beebe-gun at a large Grizzly bear. There wasn't much
point to it. This creature wasn't going down easily. To be honest, it only
pissed the thing off. It started rumbling toward him in an unnatural way,
rapidly, like a Kangaroo, except bigger and broader in its jumps. Ryan
was still at a good distance, but this creature defied all laws of gravity as
it lumbered in leaps and bounds, not thought possible. Ryan turned and
started running toward the mortuary, hanging another hundred and fifty
feet away, which no more time to be given to think about the distance,
so that being said, it was an estimate of how far it was to the front door.
Ryan didn't know how he did it, but he'd gotten to the front door, yet
after trying the door to the mortuary several times he'd let it be known
that it was locked, and the fetid smell trailing behind him was quickly
discerned that this creature was close behind—he'd run out of time.
Suddenly turning, Ryan saw the creature clearing the bridge in a single
bound, landed fifty feet away as it slid to its left, cutting up lawn and grass
while knocking over two gravestones. Ryan took this as another good
sign and ran in the opposite direction, shooting around the side of the
mortuary headed for the back of the building. Ryan tore around several
corners, and at the same time pulled another grenade from the opposite
pocket. This time laced his left index finger through the pin. Ryan's heart
couldn't take much more of this, but another surge of moving forward
was a forewarning of a further chase to come, yet he'd still run in any
direction to try and hide or try to make distance between him and this
creature. Now, Ryan tried the back door, but soon found out that this
was locked too. And this nefarious beast came sliding across the back
court, and then screeched to a halt. Set on his trail to try and defy all laws
pertaining to the civilized world. The beast was only thinking about the
small boy drawing his interest.

Ryan didn't see any other direction to run, but at the last moment
saw three small windows glistening below in a sparkle of light. They were
below ground level about five feet apart, half sticking up on the same side

of the building as the door. Each window remained covered within each alcove, like a planter box. Ryan knew what he had to do. He pulled the pin, threw the grenade, and dove toward the first window…

Bailey heard the grenade in the distance. It didn't appear to sound too far, and being able to see now, he ran toward the fence. Bailey grabbed the fence with both hands as he laced his fingers through like a wench perfectly timed to catapult his body over the fence, clearing the top like a skilled gymnast. He had to think on the run, but then it dawned on him that the Q-Tank was locked and loaded and ready as Freddy. He moved toward the tank and made it to the top. He slid down the top and closed the hatch, with limited time, and a sense of urgency, started pushing buttons and switches while lighting the Q-Tank up. He ran up the road set out after Ryan, minus a Crepto Suit and two robots.

Bailey had the Q-Tank moving within seconds. And in less than a minute the image of a bridge came into his sights. From infrared imprints left behind he saw that the creature left a trail of blood and ooze and something else—plus its footprints. This was an easy mark to follow. Where was Ryan headed to? But then he saw it as Ryan had pictured, the same mortuary standing in the distance made of limestone, the railing to the right, and the lawn exuding a dark feeling to the left—except he saw the view in infrared.

Bailey didn't wait for his adjustments and focus to make tracks. He shot toward the mortuary and knew Ryan had run for cover, but also sensing the small boy was the one who had set off the grenade. He was armed. Then Bailey knew going in a guns a blazing wasn't such a clever idea. So, surreptitiously he put the Q-Tank in stealth-mode and crawled quietly over the bridge…

Betty had just cleared the tunnel when she saw the seven towers before her. They were a stoic reminder of our government's absurd waste of anatomical goods. The towers were beautiful. Condo units she thought. They were lined perfectly in red adobe-colored stones. Glass sliding doors on each one connected a small, covered quad or patio for a view for the end of the world, covered in dusty, reddish, muddy stones, with stalactites pointing down from above. It towered above everything, almost reaching to the top of this cave. At each breach of the tower's roof had what looked like satellites placed at the top? Then Betty blinked when the two robots startled her by flying.

T-DEXTER and SNARF shot past the Hummer as she left the fight for the robots and Bailey, for she had other matters that had drawn her attention. This hole before her stopped her cold. Since the robots had inside information on where the fight would be, she contended with making something of the relay switches and C-4. She wanted to close this hole before anything else got in. The robots were headed for the back of the mortuary. This creature they chased after crossed an imaginary line of retribution, a fast ride to a slow demise, a heads up to raze. Detritus fluids continued to drip behind the creature leaving a path easy to follow.

Betty slid the Hummer to a full stop knowing this hole in front had released something of an enormous contention—why else would the robots be so alarmed? Furthermore, this gorge, this gap, this hole abroad was left unattended and had been this creature's way in. Could there be more? Could there also be others below or already on their way?

She shuttled her way to the back of the Hummer, one crutching it in the distance on one good leg, with a scowl on her face and a sense of apprehension in the back of her mind. She was game even though she was worried. Betty was ready to set the C-4 to make the drop, but not so steady on one leg. She reached for the box of C-4 and relay switches. She was ten feet behind the Hummer with her driver side door swung open. Then she heard the noise.

It was bigger than she'd imagined, and her nephew was confronting something that would take him a part. A wave of emotion shot up through her, she wanted to run in the direction of the other side of this bridge, but this unconfident feeling enclosed around her. And being limited by her inability to fight, Betty stayed behind. She had to stay focused in case something came back her way. *Where were Bailey and Ryan, and were they safe?* She thought. They had missed something so significant and much bigger than she wanted to comprehend...

Ryan crashed through the top part of the first basement window. Shielded by his jacket he didn't get cut. But he did have to fall a good eight feet before hitting the floor. He rolled as he hit to break his fall. Then the grenade went off causing a stir of glass and flames and all-consuming heat, then that beast behind let out another roar. Ryan continued his momentum past the first wall. Then he heard the Q-Tank. *It's about time* He thought. Ryan let out a huff of air. He knew Bailey had followed him in that small sized Q-Tank. What kind of damage would it really do?

What effect would this tank have in this maelstrom event?

The giant Pailoid turned away after the blast had shot more shrapnel toward its face, and more chunks of flesh spattered in blood. Yet he was still standing. He was enraged. He was pissed like Ryan had mentally understood from the grizzly bear effect. Bailey got off a respectable number of rounds before this creature swung around and slammed the Q-Tank against another wall. It was caught in the air and slammed hard against a retaining wall connected to the next building, across the courtyard. Flying bricks and mortar tore into the retaining wall next door. Bailey was buckled in. Things started blinking on and off inside the Q-Tank into an emergency mode. Bailey was stuck. The Q-Tanks top had been smashed and bent in to seal him in from above.

T-DEXTER shot around the corner and unleashed the flame thrower into the Pailoids face. SNARF headed for the Q-Tank. While T-DEXTER contended with the beast, the metal-mutt tore the Q-Tank's top hatch off—with titanium treated teeth, was Ryan's thought, as he looked up through the small window from the other side of the courtyard. Bailey shaken up, but not damaged, crawled out of the top. SNARF wagged his tail and dropped the suit. Bailey didn't wait for explanations he quickly edged in the suit and warmed it up.

Within a few seconds, Crepto flew above the creature and pound him in the head with a punch so hard that the beast had forgotten about his main purpose of being here. Crepto quelled the giant Pailoid without too much effort. The creature roared and looked up. Clawing at the air, swatting at Crepto like a grizzly bear finding a hive of honey, but Crepto was too fast. He moved stealth like, zigzagging back and forth. The light and heat became overwhelming to the beast. Scorching her skin, scorching her eyes, she couldn't see this enemy. Crepto tried his best to avoid contact from returning blows. Racing high above to gain momentum Crepto flew in at an angle slamming against the creature's chest—a sound of cracking bone and tearing of flesh. The visage of the Pailoids face began to change. The rage was depleting, fading, draining of life. It collapsed to the ground, milled into submission. Crepto had cut deep into its flesh and tore out the beast's heart. Ryan looked up through the window and saw it beating while dripping of blood deluded his way of thinking. He then yelled out while turning his eyes away from the scene.

"Hey...I'm down here..." He said. T-DEXTER went over and pulled Ryan up out of the broken window. The beast lay in a slowing rhythm of his end.

Once dead, Crepto air lifted the beast high and dropped her into the gorge that lay past the bridge's railing. Her lifeless form dropped spinning and turning to her bleak termination too soon to be entombment of that pit below.

T-DEXTER helped Crepto turn the Q-Tank back right-side up. It had a few dents, yet it would survive. It was a worthy vehicle to ride in. Ryan looked over his shoulder at Crepto.

"Where were you? That thing had me." Crepto turned and saw the disappointment on the young boy's face.

"I asked you to stay in the Q-Tank, how'd you end-up this far?"

"I couldn't see anything. And besides, I had these." Ryan pulled one of the three leftover grenades out of his jacket pocket.

"They stalled that smelly thing long enough for me to get away." Crepto shook his head.

"I'm glad you made it."

Ryan glanced up. "I'm glad I made it too, but my heart's still pounding."

"Mine too." Crepto inflected.

And then he asked. "You think you can drive that Q-Tank across the bridge?"

Ryan's eyes lit up. "No problemo chief...I mean Crepto Man." Ryan responded, with a little more emphasis on the man part. He ran to the Q-Tank delighted to accommodate the hero.

T-DEXTER, Crepto and Betty put four sets of explosives together for this hole left unsealed. Crepto flew up and then down into this hole that reeked with the foul smell of the dead and placed each set of explosives strategically thirty feet apart. T-DEXTER had the relay switches ready. After a few minutes of pounding and burying the explosive packages in the mouth of the hole, Crepto returned to the top.

Then getting back a ways T-DEXTER pulled the switch that set off all four packs of C-4, all at once. The hole below began to cave in creating a forty-foot-deep rock ceiling blocking the passageway back up. After twenty minutes of the dust clearing, Betty went over to the edge and turned her LED light pointed down. The hole was sealed. Their job for the night was done.

CHAPTER 28

The Dream

Bailey had a dream that night. He tossed and turned in his sleep. There was this image of death that lurked in the city where he walked. No birds in the air, no playing in the frozen wasteland left in this rubble of the forgotten. Silence visited him in his dream. The only heartbeat that could be heard was his. The ache he felt shot through the core of him as if life had ceased to exist. His hands trembled at the sight of deceasing life. His courage had faded with the flurries of snow, blinded by the white mirage of passing. His feet were black from frostbite. His mind lost its focus. He was tormented by his companion, who held the cold scythe of the grim reaper. Love was burned out of his heart by the taciturnity of this frozen land that had passed the cries of humanity. All hope turned its back.

Hope died with the people buried in this wasteland of the dead.

Where would comfort come from to lay her warm blanket? Whose coals of fire would warm the bones of the perished ones? Who would care? Who would give back what was missing?

Bailey's dream felt real—a palpable vision of humanity's suffering.

He woke with sweat permeating down his back. He shivered in eradicated movements twisting and turning his body in morosely captivating shivers—a metaphoric fascination of the dead. Tightness rose up in his throat as if to smother. His eyes were swollen from the sight of remorseful alluring spirits of those unburied graves left behind in this frozen land of the dead. His heart could take no more visions of this forgotten place that soon would be erased. A precocious plan was not seen from his angle of sight. Bailey couldn't see what was to come, yet his passions would set a predetermined journey set to motion. He lay on the floor curled up into a ball, emotionally metamorphosed by the dream.

His tears were real, his plan uncertain. His heart was broken from his visions of the dead. His life was given to the dream for a predestined way of life, a harvest of prolific portions left of the living to be marked, to be set apart, a preplanned portion of the living was chosen to survive, on this bleak morning in remembrance of the dead—as seen through the eyes of this young Gambit. He was to become a leader not yet seen by his own rites of having a future. He was chosen from the many to represent the few left behind in a world turned inside out.

Bailey was becoming a man, without knowing his future, for his future would be carved out of what was left, controlled by the passions of the few willing for this journey to take place. He was to travel down a road not thought possible, a journey with no sure-footed footsteps taken. Away from home, hoping the of light day would take him through each day. Even as misfits to a world now gone but tethered together making a family of love and commitment, a bond of unity that would last through the ages, found on a dark and discontented road, a road that would lead to a future to save humanity or what was left of it. This journey, this place of redemption, was fit only for those who'd endured this test of time, through each stage of life, dug in these tunnels, deep in the heart of this mountain, down on Bailey's Road.

Betty was a young woman that fueled his strength and courage. She had become a light to him and the others down this darkened passageway, a spark of hope—she was. A woman with a plan to make sure, they as a group would endured, through intelligent planning, from settling goals from intelligent planning, as this apotheosis to come was a part of the journey, all willing to do their part. They would travel this road together in the silence of the humbling experiences. Her grandmother's place was now gone, she played her role as a good mother and grandmother for those youthful, through her 83 years of service, her octogenarian position, she did her part.

Her time had been for the children, now gone, it was up to Betty to take what she'd learned and apply the principles of what a grandmother's love could teach. Burning these lessons learned in memory of her last 18 years. Revealing what a strong character of a good life could represent, full of wisdom, turbaned with love. She would be the perfect example of reflecting a grandmother's elderly instructions to the letter for those who had been self-sacrificing for the many. To keep in her heart for a future use, while reflecting those good things learned. She was ready. By leading with love, and courage and energy by a new Gambit of the future, a hero geared for the end of time, a man for the people—Crepto Man, in his blazing light of glory was here to stay. Clearing the way of those dilapidated creatures left behind in the world of blinding snow. Now, at this new beginning, he would stand out on the edge of this apocalyptic end and find reason to go on.

Betty woke up with a small figure standing over her trying to wake her. It was Ryan with a testing weight of worry set in his eyes. He'd been stirred awake by Bailey, who'd been dreaming back in his own suite in room 704. Ryan had stayed the night with Bailey needing the comfort of his mentor. Yet he was stressed about Bailey being caught between worlds—the one they lived in and one of his dreams. Ryan looked back and forth with a worried expression. Betty's eyes snapped open after Ryan shook her awake.

"It's Bailey…he doesn't look right…there's something wrong with him." He paused as a small tear trickled down his face. "I think he's dreaming, but not a normal dream." He looked into Betty's eyes. "He needs you." The little man said. "I'm afraid of what he's dreaming about." A slight pause before continuing. "I'm afraid of that thing that chased us in the night. It wasn't afraid to die like we are." Betty, hearing the words, knew that her small nephew was still having trouble accepting their fate as a tangible way of life, with no sure confidence, no sure way of seeing the events for what they were. She put her hand around Ryan's neck and pulled him close, like a mother would do. He grabbed her around the waist and buried his head against her chest. He began to release what had built up from the last two days. He cried. Death had left its mark on the small boy, who'd intrinsically woven each particle played out into his mind by those decrepit visions. He had been chased by the visions running ramped in his head. Becoming overwhelmed, full of grief when the dying began.

Betty entered the room seeing Bailey still asleep in a heat of exhaustion. His body, his mind, his spirit was depleted from something overwhelming. She had felt for him, she knew his heart was trussed to the memories seen of the other night. Betty reached down after sitting on the edge of the bed and placed her hand gently against his face with a cool wet cloth for comfort. This caused Bailey's eyes to jet back and forth across closed eyelids. Slowly coming back out of this mesmerizing dream he abruptly sat up. A burst of air broke through his mouth as heavy breathing caused him to spray spit across the bed. Ryan moved with a flinch. Betty wiped his body to calm him down. Bailey's eyes blinked open. He saw his company sitting on the bed waiting. A gentle look was seen in Betty's eyes. A muscle in his cheek trembled. Ryan came closer. Looking perceptively at his mentor. "Are you okay chief?"

Bailey's eyes rolled in Ryan's direction. A crinkle of acknowledgement flared from his eyes. "I'm okay squirt, just a bad dream…that's all." Betty dipped her cloth into more water from a basin sitting on the nightstand. She rung the water out and placed it back on Bailey's forehead. Ryan reached over and took his hand.

"What was your dream about?" The small boy inquired. Hesitating while looking up, communicating with his eyes that the subject wouldn't be for a small boy who'd does not understand the dream.

"My dream…the dream," He rephrased, "was about a world we're soon to face shortly. I mean outside of this compound. It's a warning." Bailey said this as he turned his attention back to the dream itself.

"A warning for what…" Ryan asked.

"A warning to be careful and smart in everything we do, but the most important thing, of all things," Bailey over emphasized, "is to find others out there that might be close to dying."

"Do you think there is others out there Bailey?"

"Yes, I do, but we need to believe we'll find them—eventually. We have to at least try."

Ryan shook his head. "I think you're right. We have to try."

Betty reached down and kissed Bailey on the forehead. She seemed worried, but left words unsaid about that subject. It was already morning and the three heard a knock at the door. Ryan looked at Bailey.

"Don't worry. I'll get it. It's one of the girls." Ryan ran to the door. Wondering if it was two little girls, worried Ryan had figured. It was time to get this day started. Ryan opened the door and showed a discouraging hesitation.

"What do you guys want?" Ryan barked out. Jackie wrinkled her face and pushed through passing Ryan.

"Don't be annoying squirt. You're not the only one in the building and we have to leave soon to do our job. We're here because no one picks up the phone around here." The two young adults heard the commotion and turned their heads toward the front door.

Jackie turned to look at the phone on the table, noticing right away someone had unplugged it. She shot a heated stare across at Ryan.

"Who unplugged the phone?" Ryan showed a grimace but understood respect went a lot further than returning blows of nonconformance down a familiar road he'd already experienced.

"Sorry Jackie," he said, "I was thinking of Bailey when we went to bed last night. I unplugged it. Put the cuffs on me and haul me off to baby jail." Jackie had a scowl on her face, but she sensed Ryan was trying to be a good sport about it, so she dropped the subject and walked past Ryan to get a closer view of the two adults.

"We're leaving." She said. "We have animals to take care of. George is waiting for us. I wanted to make sure you guys were okay." Betty gave her a half hug and Mattie. Bailey looked up without commenting about chores to be done.

"Have a nice day with George and try not to step in anything that will get on the carpet later." This caused Mattie to giggle.

"We won't." Mattie replied, as two little girls headed back for the door. Ryan followed behind and closed the door like good riddance. He brushed his hands together like he'd just got rid of a giant rat and tossed it out the front door. Betty gave him a presaged frown catching the lucidity in Ryan's actions.

"Don't be so harsh with the girls Ryan. They're a part of our family. You should be thankful we have them. Or you would be…" Betty stopped herself from saying the words because she knew this little boy sometimes would take your words and use them against you in a heated discussion. "What I meant to say," Betty said, "was that they love you despite your abrasive attitudes. They would protect you if they could from one of those things—those Pailoids." Betty corrected.

Bailey backed up her message. "She's right squirt. They have your best interest at heart. Quit trying to bump heads with Jackie. You know she has no known family left. And she had a little brother about your age. He's gone now. She needs another little brother that can take his place." Bailey saw his lip quiver with a touch of emotion.

"I didn't know she had a brother my age." Ryan showed a touch of remorse in his eyes, and then his eyes began to water. He still was emotionally tied to all the bad that had happened in the last few days.

"I'm sorry she lost her brother. How old was he?"

Bailey shook his head. "He was…" Bailey finalized. "He was exactly your age."

A small tear dotted Ryan's eye. "It must be hard for her to think about him."

Bailey looked at Ryan as he tried not to lose his composure. "She's human just like the rest of us. She means no harm. We need to be there for each other, don't you think?"

Ryan hung his head as his bottom lip moved with a bit of emotion.

"I understand. I'll do better." He said, in a quiet whisper. "I'll do my best." Betty reached for him and pulled him into a hug.

"Okay sport, take your things and go back to the penthouse and get cleaned up. You still smell like yesterday's sweat." Betty smiled before smacking Ryan on the butt. The small boy reached over and high-fived Bailey before leaving the room. Once the door was closed, Betty reached down and kissed Bailey lightly across the lips. A twinge of a smile crossed her lips, before turning around and heading for the door like Ryan.

"See you at breakfast." as she turned around to view him one last time.

Bailey came out of the elevator on the second floor. The doors opened to the galley. Everyone was already seated, ready for this day to begin. He looked up and walked toward the group. George and Dr. EL were there. They were a peculiar bunch, Bailey acknowledged by the quick awareness he'd seen in the other's eyes. The little girls and George were getting ready to leave for the zoo. Dr. EL had sat a cup of coffee down for Bailey already, took a seat. Ryan looked at him with a curious stare.

"So, what's going on today?" Ryan asked. He switched his eyes back and forth from Betty to Bailey like either adult had every moment of his life planned out on some great schematic, in the order of what was next to do for little boy's to learn from.

Bailey answered. "I'm not sure squirt. It depends on what the doctor is up to, and if there are any more clean-up chores to do. The doctor had something in mind for Sergeant Bristol and me." Then Bailey stopped himself knowing that sometimes shedding to much information to the small boy wasn't in his best interest. "The doctor will find something for you to do—don't worry."

Ryan understood the misleading glare. "But I want to go with you to help rescue people. I'm one of the guys—right, we're a team?"

Bailey knew these words would come back full circle one day, and today was here.

"Sergeant Bristol and I might be in a lot of danger where we're going—it's not a place for children, its cold. A cold you've never experienced before, so cold it makes your bones hurt. And it's not even a place for me."

"I know. I wanted to help. That's all." Then Ryan got this huge smile on his face. "You should have seen that Pailoids face yesterday when that grenade went off. It was a shocker. I scared him for a second, but he kept coming." Betty glanced at Ryan knowing his memories would haunt the boy for quite some time. Each fragment of time would play out in his head repeatedly.

"I hope you find some people." Ryan professed. This made Dr. EL look up.

"Did I miss something?" He said.

Bailey closed his eyes. "We can't wait any longer. We have to look now, before it's too late." Bailey insisted. Dr. EL looked at Ryan sensing what he had to say wasn't for small boys with curious minds either. "Ryan," the doctor said.

"I've got several things I need you to do." Ryan came closer as the doctor whispered in his ear. Ryan got up with a big smile while taking off toward the elevator.

"Where's he going?" Betty asked.

"He's going down to the basement floor to help assist T-DEXTER and SNARF."

Betty wrinkled her face. "But won't he get in the way?"

"No. He'll be fine." The doctor stated, "It'll give him something to do, and keep him out of trouble for now." Then Betty understood that the good doctor was only trying to clear the room. She stayed silent as she waited for Dr. EL to begin a new line of thought.

"So, what's this mission you seem to be caught up in, of course, without my approval?"

Bailey noted the bit of sarcasm within the doctor's words. He didn't know where to begin. And Betty was curious about where this was going too.

"Let's go down to the subbasement—we can talk there." Bailey insisted. He didn't want to get the doctor all heated up before he had a chance to talk to Sergeant Bristol and T-DEXTER. Bailey wanted a clearer picture of some trip he hadn't quite figured out yet. Something to do with the dream leaving an impression. Dr. EL kept his words a bay as the three got into the elevator and made their way to the subbasement floor. Sergeant Bristol was standing and working on some equipment. *Getting ready for another bout with the Pailoids*, Bailey thought.

The sergeant looked up surprised to see the super-hero out of the suit. He was just a boy in his way of thinking, thin looking, with pale complexion, and working on a new mission. The sergeant put his hand out sensing a quailing in Bailey's demeanor. He looked unsure of himself. Bristol kept this feeling of apprehension immured. He was waiting for instructions, but also understood that this strange boy connected to the suit was a power to be reckoned with in the heat of battle. He'd won his respect; even though his outward appearances left him thinking things were chancy.

The handshake caused Bailey to comprehend this was no ordinary warrior or military person of remedial design. He was a terminable terminator ready for another mission with death.

"How are you doing sir?" Bailey greeted the Cyborg to confirm the handshake.

"I'm doing great." Bristol stated, as to show no emotional battle scars as the boy had shown by the previous day's renderings. Bristol was a fine running machine, cut thick and mean, determined in his character, fit to fight, not affected by the terrors mentally set in motion. He was ready for another day at the office. *Except his was on the battlefield.*

SNARF had submitted to his fetch duties and retrieved the suit. Its shiny coppery color sparkled in the light from above. It was a pretty piece of equipment when all polished up. Bailey slipped the suit on quickly, not waiting for any more misleading words.

Something was different about the suit this morning, something new, something enlightening. It was personified, electrified, emancipated, rejuvenated, corrugated, to face what was to come. And besides being ready the suit was steady as Freddy for a fight to fit the day to unload on, those creatures that hide in the shadows. The Crepto Energy began to give the suit wearer confidence that he didn't have as just an ordinary boy. The Crepto Energy was creating a new hope inside this young man's heart—a new way in facing the world, a new plan to understand, and a will to fulfill, as he walked toward Uncle Ron's red Ford truck. He had a mission on his mind that was relayed by this dream, a dream with quite the introductions. It was a scream, a bad-boys dream, a walk through a vision with a cold-hearted tug. Yes, it was a mean dream with unlikely schemes, but it was this screaming dream that caused him to move forward. Crepto was relegated to a different frame of mind, he was high stepping it with a strut and pep in it. He was a man with a plan, suppressing his emotions for another time. He was one to contend with in manner and clout. He's from a higher power, and even though he doesn't tower above all others, he eludes a peremptory authority from the energy released from this suit, to refute would be lethal.

His mind began to race to plan a rescue. He didn't know how to get out there, but he was determined to do anything, better than sitting around only thinking of his own accords. The suit had reminded Bailey internally: Let not the human spirit be overlooked or thought of lightly, for its ability to be able to rise above adversity gave man's first impression of will and courage in the fight. To push the body and mind beyond the boundaries of any traditional world's way of thinking as reflected from one's journey, so, there can be hope, there can be love, and there can be a worthy way of life. There would be pain through perseverance; knowledge learned from seeking, moments that take your breath away. For what are those things that bring out the best of what the soul imparts, are but truth to the heart. For what is hope, but the will to go on, to move forward, to get up, brush off the adversities experienced and smile at the outcome? The title of the victor is never measured by the finish, but measured by the focus one has on the journey itself over the span of time in one's life. Find those ingredients that burn like coals of fire within the very soul. Crepto thought, this road, though it be dark at times can fulfill moments that pull at the very core of the heart—as each moment of life is stretched out across the gulf of time, each day measured, and each journey different. The challenge of each journey takes its own road, for finding one's own redemption in the race is the cause of finding the mark. The reason for being, to somehow find a way through those secret places that lead to a new beginning, a new chance to let your light shine. A place that sheds a flicker or flame where there is no light, gives courage when there's none to be found, and supports when strength has failed. For what is life, but a road to be traveled on, never look for the end of the journey as the final outcome, but only to hope that the journey be one that reveals the reasons to go on. To find those answers that lead to an end, answers that show a way back, to bring hope to an effective way of thinking. To hope is to live, to live is to move forward, and to move forward creates momentum for the end, and for the anticipation of the end can leave imprints of the journey behind—for whatever your lot in life, shown through faithfulness in your journey, keep steady, stay on course for the fight to come is almost finished.

Bailey, now Crepto, was ready to face what this dream had imparted on his memory. He was ready to conquer the giants of this world, submerging himself in his work, his plan, and this newly conforming journey outside of this compound. To rescue those that could be found out in the frozen wasteland of the forgotten.

Crepto could sense that Dr. EL had been up most of the night studying the weather anomalies. He could sense his regret of any hope that there might be life beyond their borders. The radio station within the compound made no connection with the outside world anymore.

"Sir...we need to find survivors. I can't explain in a way that you'd understand, but with a little faith in me, and this dream I had, you'll find a way to accept Sergeant Bristol and I going out in the weather has its point."

Dr. EL looked up with an expression of puzzlement. "Dear boy, what are you talking about?"

Crepto was confused about the doctor's frame of mind. "You need to trust me with the foresight that this Crepto Energy has given to me. The dream I experienced last night left quite an impression on my mind."

"What dream?" Dr. EL asked.

He turned to look at Betty as if she might have an answer. For this insane man wearing the suit was crazy. The doctor suggested, "An epiphany or a beam of light from heaven—why are you thinking crazy?"

"I won't get into it. This won't make any sense to a man of your calling. You base most of your findings of nature by factual information that's learned from your own personal discoveries." Crepto said.

The doctor looked at Crepto like he was speaking Greek. "Well, wouldn't you consider that a good way to find facts, instead of the hearsay of emotional matters that bear no logic of order?" It looked as if Dr. EL's face was set in stone. Wondering why this boy with this delusional way of thinking was set on going out in the flurries of snow and death on a whim of servitude and personal guilt.

"The suit will protect me, and the sergeant can go with me. The robots will stay here to protect this compound. The weather won't have a lasting effect on Sergeant Bristol. The robots can stay behind in case there's any trouble." Bailey said.

"And what trouble would that be?" Dr. EL not only had a look of concern he was livid that this boy in front of him was thinking crazy. Crepto had started to get annoyed by Dr. EL's exacerbated appeal of leaving the compound without his blessing.

"For safety precautions, that's all." Crepto stated.

The doctor shook his head. "Why can't you offer me an intelligent response to my question? I'm not a moron who doesn't know his way around here. I'm a scientist, and a scholar." Dr. EL said brusquely.

The boy in the suit kept walking back and forth, trying to reason with the doctor on the subject—yet nothing made sense to the doctor from Crepto's perspective.

"I had a spiritual enlightenment from this dream. It was elating, mesmerizing, the most dramatic dream I've ever encountered. It drained my strength because of its vision. Its message touched the very core of my heart. I don't know how else to explain the veritable message seen so vividly. The premonition of its contents was so real. It has to be because I felt like I was inside the dream itself. It pulled me into a world so revealing."

Dr. EL stood with a blank expression pasted across his face, wondering about this young man's dream and the volatility of its message. He crossed his arms and put his right hand to his chin.

"So, you are going to be moved by a dream emotionally? Thinking your own personal impiety revealed some ghost like entity that scared the crap out of you?" Dr. EL couldn't believe he was hearing this and wouldn't believe it for a thousand years. Yet he thought Bailey was being self-deluded in reasoning, encountering this suit on another plan not meant for a normal human mind to endure. Furthermore, what was he left with eventually—a bedeviled boy strung out emotionally from his own personal demons, causing an inward rebellion about facing a fast and changing world?

"Get this straight." The doctor imposed. "If you've got to expose yourself to the cold out there, be my guest, just don't come back to me empty handed when I've already told you the facts. No one would or could survive out there in this weather. It's too extreme. It's not meant for the everyday man now set on foot. It's a different world altogether out there."

Crepto ended his conversation with Dr. EL and began to take things into his own hands, regardless what the doctor thought. He was a little disoriented by the doctor's point of view. He didn't want to leave on a bad note. But he also knew he wanted to make headway on the day ahead of him. He and Sergeant Bristol had a slim window of opportunity. The warmest part of the day was right now. If anything was going to be done that day, they had to leave soon, so he began to prepare.

After prepping the big red Ford truck, Bristol and Crepto loaded their gear and weapons into the back. Crepto put his sword and shield behind the seat. They were ready to take a chance on this crazy journey ahead of them. Betty and Ryan said their goodbye's for now. Betty had set her walkie-talkie on the same frequency as the truck's radio and his hand held. They had a box full of explosives with the relay switches and several machine guns as backup. Crepto grabbed two hundred and fifty feet of rope with the ascenders as needed in case the Cyborg had to do any climbing. They got into the truck and waved goodbye. Betty leaned through the open window and kissed Bailey through the suit. Sergeant Bristol's eye scan and handprint were placed inside the computer system so they could get past the essential gates. They were off.

They traveled down the first tunnel toward the far-left side of the compound. This was the same place where they first encountered the Pailoids. It was dark and the air was chilly outside the window, but neither Crepto nor the Bristol had felt any ill-affects while traveling this road. The tunnel had a musty smell of death left hanging in the air. The memories of that place of battle weren't too easy to erase. This was a place that the young boy in the suit would like to forget, yet knowing the memories were a part of his journey that would never happen. Bailey in the suit knew this would be something burned in memory to last a lifetime—to take with him wherever he might go. He explained to the sergeant about the internal structure of the tunnel and cavern just up ahead. He pulled to the side of the road just short of the drop. A pungent smell rose from below that flashed the memory of blood and flesh left behind of the dead. Looking back in the back seat Crepto hadn't realized that Betty had packed a cooler full of food and supplies. She was thinking ahead. She was showing a seed of faith that Bailey would find others along his journey to bring back to safety. This was the specific reason she had packed food and drinks to feed those they might find. It made him smile when thinking of her. *Always thinking ahead,* he thought. She shed a small light on his world to come.

CHAPTER 29

The Journey

The tunnel had that dark eerie feeling to it as they both looked down the undulating road ahead. A light smoky vapor rose from the ground as small patches of moisture seeped through the mountain.

"What do you think?" Crepto asked. Bristol kept silent except for the fact that he'd noticed two feet of edge that graced the left side of a hole in the ceiling of the cave below, which was their floor. Bristol pointed to the area he had noticed. Crepto got the view that Bristol was pointing at and understood. Using his highly skilled training, Sergeant Bristol set up a pack of C-4 to a relay switch and after surveying this edge to make sure it would hold him. There were wires hanging out of the explosives with a small antenna connected to a wireless remote. Once set, the sergeant walked carefully along the two-foot edge and strategically placed the neat little package buried in earthen soil and rock from above. He then turned around and came back. Then the sergeant looked back at a Crepto.

"Move the truck back about fifty feet. I don't think you want any dents in your new ride." Crepto did as he was told and moved the truck back fifty feet. Sergeant Bristol pushed the relay switch and ***boom***...

while watching a towering amount of rock and dirt tumble below. Swirls of intensifying smoke and dust pushed in their direction. A good amount of dust flurried in the air blocking their vision. Once the dust cleared, Sergeant Bristol looked back at Crepto.

"Okay, now it's your turn to do some damage."

Crepto was confused about what the sergeant was insinuating. "What," he said, 'it's still blocked?" The sergeant raised an eyebrow.

"Well, yes, it is, but you have the Crepto energy to clear what's left."

"What, you think I can punch my way through to the other side?"

The sergeant expelled a hesitating nod. "So that's your way of thinking too?" Crepto didn't know what to think of the nod—he could punch his way through or not.

Suddenly, something began to enlighten the young man in the suit; something was different from before, stronger, revealing, encouraging, moving, hidden, and holding a deeper meaning. He could feel an internal draw about what this suit could actually do was beyond the thinking of a boy in a suit with stronger powers. He stared back at Bristol for a minute, wondering about his assumption of current facts. It suddenly dawned on him that the Crepto suit had sources of energy with which he still wasn't quite familiar. Bearing in mind, he focused all his will on the Crepto Energy as it slowly began to build through internal instincts and through the walls of the suit, making a mental connection with every pore, every electronic impulse surging through him. What Crepto hadn't grasped until now, was that this first explosion had taken most of the forty feet of blockage away. It had dropped to the bottom of the cavern. It had built a perpetual rock ceiling below their feet. They now had a surfaced road under them, except for a few feet directly in front that remained blocked. After sizing up this thinner wall of rock through his stellar vision, he knew what he had to do. The thickness of the blockage in front was only about four feet thick, left behind from the explosion. Crepto studied everything about the blockage ahead. How much vertical ground would give way if he broke through, how would it impact the stability of this remaining tunnel, and what was the best angle to hit the blockage from this side of the road? Everything had to be calculated before jumping to conclusions. He didn't want to bring the mountain down on their heads.

After a few more seconds had gone by, with focused strength, Crepto flew back to the truck holding his body suspended in the air for a few more seconds to get his bearing's on the blockage ahead. He would seal the deal by flying ahead, a percussion of air striking earthen soil, to push the Crepto Energy passed any borders of comprehension. This was something new, something not of an ordinary man ever imagined. He would have to draw energy from a place held in deep crevices of his soul. Without further contemplation, flying at lightning speed, in the direction of the blockage, faster than a speeding bullet, faster than the speed of light. Even Bristol couldn't detect the amount of energy and speed from the suit. Crepto slammed against rock and dirt forcing his body through a slight opening, as a rush of air caused the Cyborg to slip back and fall on the ground. He got up quickly surprised by the loud cracking sound from earthen soil. It echoed off the tunnels internal structure, affecting this whole mountain with intense vibration. Crepto moved like a rocket that had been propelled to the moon, a missile of mayhem, a projectile of flickering light glowing in the dark. He was a battering ram of catastrophe, a burning bludgeoning of delight. His was an aristocratic mind in the body of an electrostatic climax of a different kind. He was a slick-do-gooder of non-shady deeds, a hero unhinged, and a super-fly in a zip of heat. He was the man of the hour with super-sonic power, and though he did not tower over most of those he'd encounter, he gave off a gleaming glow set to make history.

Crepto flew back and forth until he'd cleared the tunnel enough to pull the truck through. He brushed off the dirt and grime from the exposure of solid Earth he'd encountered and stood with a better plan in hand. He was ready as Freddy and geared to get it on. Sergeant Bristol poured a gallon of water over the young super-hero's suit, cooling the suit a bit before moving on. Once done, they headed toward the bunker about five or six miles up the road. The sergeant drove as Crepto read the map.

"There are only a couple of turns before we're there." Crepto said.

Sergeant Bristol looked across the dash quickly then back. Bailey in the suit had remembered running in life had taught him much to bring balance back full circle. He wanted that old life back. Yet he knew it was gone. They were faced with the changing formalities of a secretive government's twisted agenda. Knowing what lay outside in the cold was the only sure reality left. And he knew without doing something surreal, anyone else left outside would soon be dead. Their future started with today's journey.

"Stop here!" Crepto said. The sergeant saw the fuel tank to the right of the bend in the road and knew. They needed fuel. Crepto got out of the truck and opened the side gas tank door and the other end of the nozzle to insert gas. After filling it, Crepto replaced the cap on the tank and closed the hinged door, and then replaced the tank's nozzle on a hitch hook connected to the trailer, got back into the truck while Sergeant Bristol moved the truck the short distance remaining, close to Uncle Ron's bunker just up ahead.

"Now what are we to do?" Sergeant Bristol asked.

Without saying a word Crepto got out of the truck and glared at the bunker blocking the way. "Well, one of two things we can do." Crepto said. "We can either push the whole bunker out of this hole or we can pry the steel back like it's a can of sardines." He turned to look at Bristol. "You think we can do it?"

The sergeant showing a blank expression.

"I thought you would want to push the bunker all the way out in the snow, but the hole left behind would leave the compound vulnerable to those creatures."

Crepto understood what to do. "I see your point, so making a wider exit is our only choice?" Bristol looked back at Crepto then nodded.

"Yes, unless you have better idea that would be easier?"

"Well, let's give it a whirl and see what happens." The sergeant gave a salute to the forehead. Crepto, compelled to find success pushed while leaning *in* the doorway of the bunker. Pushing, moving, bending the metal with the help of Sergeant Bristol. Crepto pulled the back door off its hinges and set it to the side. Then both hero's began leaning further into the metal. The heat, the light, and the power of the Crepto energy started changing the metal of the frame, melting it, forcing the steel to bend like heated glass. Within a few seconds, the steel rolled to the side like paper from a paper mill. Moving to the other side, they did the same. The sergeant looked back at their work and saw the metal still had a reddish glow before it dimmed to its normal color.

Crepto started tossing everything below to the lower floor, except for a few things that wouldn't fit in the lower level, but then he noticed blood against the walls. Those creatures had already been here, and who ever had gotten here before them tore this place to bits, leaving no food below, ransacked to the last crumb. The front rollup door wasn't damaged, so after clearing the bunker with the truck Crepto rolled the truck past the entrance and re-locked the roll-up door. Then he grabbed the walkie-talkie and called Betty as Bristol was mentally surveying the area. The walky-talky's power button came on.

"Home base this is T-4 do you read, over?" Crepto repeated the call several times before getting a return answer. Finally, he heard Betty's voice.

"T-4 this is home base, read you loud and clear, what's your status?"

"We have cleared the bunker and are headed on our way out, over."

"Roger T-4 how's the weather?"

"It's clear at the moment. The sun is directly overhead with no wind. No problems so far."

"Roger that, take care and watch your backs."

Then Crepto had remembered. "Those creatures were here. They got in and killed whoever was here." A chill went down Betty's spine. She knew her uncle and auntie had been there, who else could have made it in the bunker without knowing the combination numbers and having a key. The door was almost impenetrable, was her way of thinking. Crepto realized that Betty was stunned after sharing this added information.

"I'm sorry." He said. "I just assumed by the blood, and there's no bodies, all the food was ransacked, nothing below that's worth salvaging. Everything has been torn to shreds." Crepto waited a few seconds before Betty came back on the open speaker.

"I'm sorry too." Betty said. There was a quivering emotion heard on the walkie-talkie. Crepto waited patiently.

"Okay…" Betty finally said. "I'll let the others know."

"I think there might be more creatures out here." Crepto mentioned. "There are footprints leading away from the bunker that don't look like anything I'd ever seen."

"Be safe." Betty said back. "And don't do anything crazy. You come back, okay?" Crepto could hear the emotion in her voice, knowing she was a little distraught thinking the others of the family didn't make it.

"Don't worry. We'll be fine, just don't let any more of those creatures inside our little compound, you got that?"

"Yes, I know. Talk to you soon." Crepto didn't give a solid answer about returning. He already knew the answer that they both might not return. It was the formality of saying the words not spoken. He didn't want to jinx their chances. Crepto signed off and got back into the truck.

Bristol looked over before slipping the truck into gear and drove up over the top of the first hill. No evidence of houses could be seen in this valley. No life stirred beneath frozen hills of snowy graves. There was no evidence of any type of life as of yet. The tops of a few trees could be seen, a few telephone poles sticking up out of snow by a few feet. A few tall buildings downtown were revealed in congregated blotches and patches. They both sat in the truck next to the church with the stained-glass windows—a vivid memory of some past escaped them. It was buried in snow and ice up past the top of the front doors. The windows had been broken out of the church, and a remedial attempt was made to board up the windows, but Crepto could tell where they'd been ripped free. Those creatures were too strong and determined to get past their guards—no borders of safety. All of the people left behind didn't stand a chance. *Dr. EL was right,* Crepto thought for a moment. This was all just a waste of time. He didn't know what to do. Should he move forward or turn back? Visualizing the lucidity of the aftermath. Pulling out his map to make heads or tails of the city covered by the waves of mounted snow and ice, a frozen wasteland of white leaving no trail or surefooted way back to reality. It didn't really do any good to think of a life of before that wasn't here anymore. Only to consider their present-day situation. Uncertainty crossed Crepto's mind when seeing this transformed world. There was no natural landmarks left, and if there was, exceedingly rare to find remained behind in the city. Most of it was buried beneath the memories of yesterday. It was almost blinding. If it hadn't been for the suit, it would be a hard picture to imagine such humanity.

The memories of the night's before dream weighed heavy on his heart. Something from the dream exposed a more tender part of Bailey's soul.

Finally, Bristol looked across the dash wondering why they hadn't moved yet.

"Where should we go?" Bristol asked.

Unsettling as the dream was, he looked back at the sergeant, still a bit lost, but then they had to do something, or lose any hope and go back.

"Give me a minute. I need to think." Crepto said. Waiting patiently, Sergeant Bristol was unaffected by the freezing weather or the conditions of a boy's heart, experiencing some confusing dream, as it seems. They needed to move on. Wanting only to complete their mission, to improve their circumstances. Bristol waited for the boy in the suit to find direction. Then suddenly, deciding to trust the suit, and move toward the East.

"Let's head East." Bailey in the suit said.

The suit knew what direction to go to find answers that weighed heavy on all of their minds. Suddenly, Crepto knew the mountains lying southwest of where the compound was located west of the city. Below the mountain's base heading west was a water basin beneath the mountains. How he knew this he didn't know. But Something revealing was soon to be exposed what they would end up doing. And knowing those creatures couldn't survive without a food and water source. This would be a good place to go if there were any survivors. Crepto noted, the truck had oversized tires to deal with the terrain. And the truck had a snorkel exhaust system in case they had to go through large unannounced dips or pot-holes full of water. The sergeant kept moving forward, going about 30 to 40 miles per hour, not too fast, not to miss anything seen while going in their current direction. Yet suddenly, Crepto saw something off in the distance that drew his interest.

"Go a little bit to your left. See that bridge over there?"

"Yes, about a mile out. I see it." Bristol said.

"Go to the top of that overpass. We'll have a better view from there."

Bristol only nodded and started turning the truck to the severed bridge, turning slightly left towards the top of this overpass that had drawn their attention. The bridge was grey in color like all mountains of cement when first constructed. It was broken at one end with ice and snow smothering it in white, except the bottom of its legs extended out as gray matter. It was a good fifty-feet below from top to bottom—*a sure death would be imminent,* was his thought. And at the highest end of the bend in the bridge everything from the top could be seen beyond the city that used to be. What had drawn Crepto's interest was the view at the top would give him a clearer picture of something to come. The bridge, of course, was completely covered in ice and snow, revealing everything past the city was the same. But something lay different, not to far up ahead. Something of perspective was set at an angle drawing his interest. Crepto got out of the truck and walked to the end of the edge of snow and ice and felt a chill of change had come. Fifty feet above the rest of the world. Looking down he saw this current world different than the one before, but it wasn't because he was standing at the edge of this said bridge, it was because he was standing at the edge of a new beginning. Not just for him, but for an entire world that had lost its way, one stormy dark night, when all was about to change. This was a new season for anyone left. His heart, his thoughts, his direction, was setting the stage for a new way of life. Pulling cold clean air into his lungs, he felt the warming surge of power flow through his veins from the suit. Bristle came out to meet him and stood at his side with a Gait 30M gun slung over his right shoulder. They surveyed the area like they were the last two souls of earth looking for any signal that there was still a flicker of hope in this daunting life left in the aftermath of a broken world. But there didn't appear to be anything that stood out that would lead them to a better way of life, because only what they could muster within themselves would then give direction. All life had ceased to exist, even up on top of the world looking down. There seemed to be nothing left. Crepto was taking in the burning cold, which swept across this barren land leaving behind death as a reminder of the time now come. It had taken only days to change the surface of the world. A lump of emotion pushed up into his throat. He held it at bay. He didn't want to seem vulnerable in front of this man of war that stood by his side. He had to set an example for those few that were left to support him. And knowing Bristol, wouldn't understand the conditions of a boy's heart from a human perspective. He was a man without a plan, but this strange suit knew of the boy's tender moments wouldn't be tied to the constrains of difficult moments, it would be tied to the instincts of survival when making choices. A translucent view lay ahead of them.

The sergeant looked over and knew the boy was thinking of something in his past and said. "This is a different world now. What used to be is now gone." The sergeant said. "You and your small band of survivors will have a different life now. You will set new standards for others to follow."

"I know." Crepto responded. "Let's do this. We're running out of time."

They got back inside the truck and the sergeant backed it down off the overpass and headed slightly southeast before turning east. After ten more minutes, something came to Crepto's mind. Reaching for the walkie-talkie, he turned it on and yelled words into the speaker. "Home base this is T-4 do you read, over?" Crepto waited because he sensed that Betty would be close by knowing they were outside, and knowing they might have put themselves into the pathway of danger, she'd be ready for their call. Just then, it hit him, he remembered Dr. EL talking about the men from the prison had been used by the government to try and find a cure with the RN-1 compound. The government had experimented with the drug. There was another way inside the compound that they didn't know anything about. Then Betty's voice came over the speaker.

"T-4, go ahead, this is home base, I hear your transmission, over."

"Betty, listen…find out the coordinates of the prison. I mean there's a prison out here somewhere, right?"

Betty blinked while looking at Dr. EL. "Yes, just a minute. I'll have T-DEXTER look it up." T-DEXTER was already turning on his bio-scanner floating through screens on different maps. A few seconds later the robot looked up at Betty and showed her what he'd found. The screen flashed before her a corroborating answer.

"I've located the prison. Give me a minute." Betty said. "It's at coordinates N38-68.22 and W103-47.12. Did you get that?"

"Yes. We got it."

"See you on the other side…" She was cut off. Betty didn't know what to think of that last transmission as she looked at T-DEXTER. Crepto broke off his transmission and looked over at the sergeant. Bristol set the coordinates and veered the vehicle in that direction.

"Heading is 92 degrees east for about five miles, by then we should be right over the top of it." Bristol said. Then understanding that Bristol meant that most of the buildings would be buried beneath ice and snow.

Bristol slipped the truck into four-wheel drive and headed east on those coordinates. Fifteen minutes later, he pulled up next to a grayish building showing only three stories above ground. The other three were below, and several layers below that. Crepto then realized that there had to be some type of subbasement tunnels underneath the prison. Crepto got out of the truck and started walking toward the west side of the building. After getting mid-point he looked at the Rocky Mountains pointed west and tried to line up an imaginary road on atop the ice— with his more than stellar vision he looked straight down into the ice and couldn't believe what he saw. Suddenly, seeing movement in a darker place below fifty feet. He knew what he had to do. He looked at the sergeant on his right. "I see movement, but I can't tell if it's human or something else."

The sergeant turned his view in Crepto's direction. "Their body temperature burns much hotter than the human body. Their thermal readings will be off the charts." Crepto said. Crepto looked back toward the bottom. "I believe it's the Pailoids for sure." Crepto remarked.

He went back to the truck for the C-4 and several relay switches.

When the sergeant saw what he was doing he spoke up. "And what's that for?"

Crepto raised an eyebrow. "I've got to make a hole."

"Not that way. Unless you want to kill humans along with those creatures, plus they'll know you're coming. Use that Crepto Energy like you did through the rock, it should work the same."

Think so?"

"Yes, why wouldn't it?"

"Alright...I'll give it a shot." Crepto pointed toward the mountains. "By what I can tell, it looks like this tunnel heads due west." He paused for a minute, rethinking his strategy. "If any humans survived, they'd use the same tunnels to stay out of the extreme weather. Once we're fifty feet below the ice, the temperature remains constant 50 degrees, and I'm sure not much colder than that."

Sergeant Bristol strapped on several guns and loaded his belt with ammunition. The sun was starting to make its way west as it sat halfway down from the top of the horizon. They didn't have much time left in their favor before the temperature dropped to twenty below. Crepto looked back at the sergeant. "See up passed that marker, about half a mile from here?"

"Yes. I see it." The Cyborg said.

"I need to drill there. It will get me a few minutes head start before they catch on. Meet me there with the truck. I have an idea that might work."

Sergeant Bristol got in the truck and turned it back on, he revved the engine a couple of times before following the icy road just beyond the prison tower. It looked rocky from the uphill angle. Taking his shield and sword with him, Crepto flew high and fast as the Crepto energy took him to new heights. Within seconds he was where he needed to be. Looking down through ice and snow, he didn't see any movement from this angle of sight, so he flew higher to build his momentum, slamming straight down against the ice with such force it cracked the ground echoing off the mountains laying five miles to the west. His building speed pulled the air from the atmosphere that lay close by. Crepto's flight was waged against the laws of gravity. He felt like one of those divers who dive off the sheer cliffs to awe-inspire their audience. Yet this was a little different from his perspective. He had to drill through over a hundred and fifty feet of ice within a few seconds. The Earth below trembled with vibration. Crepto flared a hollow point of five feet wide in the tunnels opening. He got to the bottom without much effort, forcing a gap between the tunnel and five feet of space above in the light of day. The sky above brought light in at an angle along with the freezing air. Below, Crepto felt a wave of fetid Pailoids rumbling toward him. There was almost no time to react. He couldn't see them, but he could feel the ground below moving with a building vibration. He spun his shield and whipped his sword in warrior like fashion and shot forward in the direction of his enemy with a stentorian sound wafting from behind. The pungent smell of the Pailoids drifted quickly towards him. Unaffected by the smell the suit took over. The Crepto energy was at its best when facing darkness of the dread. Speedy agility slammed the Crepto energy against body and bone of the living dead. These malevolent creatures shed flesh off bone that tore at the heart of the living. The damned gave away life as payment to ease the rage of hungered beasts. A new Gambit filleted through them like a skilled sushi chief in a culinary kitchen. Internalizing everything, the sounds in the tunnel, the chill in the air, and the rage moving in the stream of chaos. It was sensed in his skin, felt in his bones, and lived through the movement of the Crepto energy. It had lead straight to them.

Crepto tarried to use the light and heat of the suit to push back these creatures from moving any closer than they were. Hundreds of the Pailoids slammed against the rage of sword and shield in the burning of light in a day hence not seen from sight but only of vision. Blood splattered and flowed on a downhill slick of an icy chill in a forgotten manner of comfort, as the ending of bliss left no comfort for the dying as they dropped by the wayside of this day of the dead. This was a day turned night into the rage of chaos. This was madness. This was World War Z, pushed by fury, pushed by the hunger for survival. This was a ballroom blitz at the end of the line. They would not deny his blades this nonsensical end of life, as life was taken from them as payment.

The hole from above was a way in now, *there might be others.* Crepto thought. He could feel the temperature from above dropping down into the tunnel leaving an icy chill, a movement of correction on a downhill slide. They didn't have much time. It would soon be night, and those things of the night would take control to take away life. When the night came, a river of blood would flow freely. The Crepto Suit was heating up. Crepto needed the Cyborg's help, but what could one Cyborg really do except give him only a minute or two of relief? This was an insane idea dropping into this hole faced by the rage of the dammed—a sure end to a quick death, a suicide mission, a place where the dead rise from the grave and greet you without your approval. He was outnumbered in a numberless game of taking chances, faced with the fury of death at his door. Crepto couldn't stay too much longer. His hands and body were tiring, losing momentum, losing his will and strength to go on.

Suddenly, from above, Crepto saw a shadow cross over his vision like a giant bird casting its lot. When coming closer he understood Sergeant Bristol was coming down to assist him. He was strapped in, locked, and loaded. He also had packs of C-4 strapped to his hip. He was geared to get it on with those creatures coming towards him. He was ecstatic, automatic, brought his mean face, wore his long Johns, was ready and steady, and had determined to bring his best. He was dirty and mean and not so clean, and ready to rock and roll. This was his time. He knew this day would come. This is the life for which he was made. He placed C-4 just beyond the hole, up above Crepto, but for some reason he knew his season would be to finish in this cold hellhole dug deep in the darkness of another life. He set the charges and looked at the young super-hero. *Super-duper,* He thought. This caused a smile to grace his lips.

Crepto took a quick glance. "What are you doing?"

"I'm giving you a chance to get away! Take it while I'm offering. I won't ask twice!" The roar of bodies and bones were driven before the cries of their end began to settle in. Crepto knew he was done. He had to rest. He had to cool the suit off. He had to run to fight another day, to live through another night. Sergeant Bristol handed him a small box. Inside was a replica chip of his power unit, his memories, all inside a little chip.

Crepto saw him slip it into his suit pocket. "What's that for?" He asked with a quivering emotion building in the back of mind.

"It's a replica of my units memories. When you get a chance put it in another 731 series. I'll be back to fight again." A twinkling smile crossed the Cyborg's face. Crepto just looked back at him.

"Sounds like that's been said before…will you really come back?"

The sergeant past a final nod while dropping a belt behind him.

"Take that with you. Plant it inside the tunnel further down. It will cause the tunnel to collapse through this whole section. They won't be able to get through." The Cyborg cocked both his guns and leaned in with Crepto and said. "Go! You don't have much time!"

Crepto grabbed the belt and looked over his shoulder for the last time. "Nice working with you sergeant, I'll see ya soon." And Crepto was gone in the chill of an ending day.

He flew high above, then drove through three feet of snow piled high on both sides of the road above, quickly cooling the outside of the suit. Crepto had to hurry. He felt relief right away. But his job wasn't done. Passing three more markers Crepto dove straight down with sword and shield digger deeper, moving faster, contacting the same tunnel below, except further down into unfamiliar territory. He placed the C-4 in the ceiling like he was told by Bristol, fifty feet into the mouth to send the fire and heat vent up. Within seconds, Crepto heard the first explosion from where Sergeant Bristol had taken his place. He was gone. A flicker of emotion shot through him, knowing his short-lived friend had given his life to save the others. Crepto flew opposite the C-4 and set off the second explosion. Ice, snow, rock and earth fell and covered the tunnel behind. Crepto flew back up out of the hole in the direction of the truck. He was there within seconds. He grabbed the large cooler and several jackets from the back seat. Closed the truck back up and headed for the sky. He found the hole again from further down the line and shot down the opening. Once at the bottom, he flew in the direction of what he thought to be where their new home was at the compound. The suit was hot and dirty with the sludge of blood and mud and crud mixed together forming confusion. He was ready for a break—yet had no time left. He had to find survivors. This was a path where the dammed had walked and left their scent behind. Would he find others? Would he be in time? In the distance of elongated creepy shadows, he imagined seeing a flickering of light, something drawing, something interesting. Leaving the dark contours of esoteric conditions behind. The boundaries beyond the precursors of nonsensical logic felt but a dream. This was the end of the line.

Suddenly, Crepto comprehended something was there, something redeeming, something good. A reason for coming out in this mess. He could hear gunfire mounting in his direction. They were firing at him.

Crepto yelled. "Stop, I'm not the enemy! I'm here to help you!" A booming voice echoed in their direction.

Someone appearing to be their leader yelled back, "Hold your fire!"

The machine guns stopped abruptly and more than half a dozen dirty faces appeared out of the dark with children marked by war with a few unfriendly looking soldiers breathing hard in the dampness of lacking air. They were powder-burned, pale, chilled, and overwhelmed, faces of the slowly dying with children attached to them. Another wave of emotion pushed up in Crepto's throat. He almost lost his grip on the cooler. He sat the cooler down and handed out three jackets that he'd taken from the truck. A little girl limped forward and took the smallest one. Crepto looked at her while showing an emotional flicker in his eyes. He opened up the cooler as everyone came closer. A sparkle of light from a flashlight flashed across two dozen dirty faces. One woman started crying and covered her mouth.

"I'm here to help get you to a safe place, a place of warmth and plenty of supplies and food. We have places for you to live, for now, not outside." Crepto saw that Betty had filled this cooler with sandwiches and drinks, soda, water, orange juice. Then he knew the girl he left behind was more than he'd ever deserve. She had thought ahead to bring relief to the disconnected few. She had faith that Crepto would find them. He swallowed the lump of emotion that got stuck midway in his throat. The little girl who took the first jacket walked over and took his hand. She was trusting even though she lived not in a trustworthy world. She was petite with dirty clothes and bandaged knee. Crepto looked down at her and asked. "What's your name?"

"I'm Renee, and that's my dad and brother." Two worn out, and to dirty, with torn clothing; a powder-burned boy's face, sixteen, and his father stepped into the sparkle of light with shaky hands and pale faces.

"Hi, my names Rin and this is my son Jake. I lost my wife." Rin said, but he said it like the memory was still fresh on his mind, still lost from being in shock. He felt the many years they had been together. In memory, she still walked in the chaos close to his side. Crepto knew they were at the very end of hope, the very end of life.

Crepto reached over and touched Rin's shoulder. "We have to go. We don't have much time." Crepto said, as he pointed to the lower end of the tunnel. "You're going the right way, just three more miles." He informed them, but not knowing how he knew there was only three more miles to go, yet he did understand the suit had taken over.

As they walked in the direction of the mountains, Crepto told them about the facility they had found, about the food, about shelter, and about the government leaving everything behind. A mile later, the small girl that had been so trusting fell to the ground in a heap of exhaustion. Crepto reached down and picked her up and put her on his shoulders. She giggled and held on.

"Wow…" she said. "It's really warm up here."

Crepto smiled and said. "Yeah, it's the suit. It does that."

"Why does it get so hot?" Renee asked.

"Because it has Crepto energy working quite efficiently, in turn, causing the suit to get hot. I use the suit to much."

"You're okay, aren't you?"

"Yes, I'm fine, just a little tired from fighting those creatures back there. I don't like them." Crepto said.

"I don't like them either." The little girl said. "They smell awful."

"Yes, they do, and I'll be glad when we get home."

"Me too, I'll be glad when we get home too." That caused a tear to leak out of Rin's left eye.

"Are there beds for us to sleep in?"

"Yes, probably, a bed that we'll fit you perfectly, you can stay with Mattie and Jackie if you want. They'd be glad to have you." Crepto said.

"And what's your name again?" Renee asked.

"My name is Crepto, but you can call me Bailey when I'm not wearing the suit."

"I like that name Bailey better. It suits you." A sparkle of light glinted in Renee's eyes.

"You think so? I'm glad because I was hoping to keep it."

The little girl giggled and put her hand to her mouth. She was already getting attached. Rin looked over and smiled.

"Don't mind her. She's the talker in the family."

Crepto was glad he found this disconnected group of very few survivors. He looked over at Rin. "How many…?"

Rin looked back with a curious stare. "There were a hundred and fifty-seven of us when we first started. But after they picked us off one by one, there are only forty of us after twelve days." Crepto didn't know what to say to that answer, yet his heart was glad for the few that had made it this far. Several children ahead began to complain about being tired. Crepto looked back into the blackened tunnel and left behind nothing, no stirring, no signs of Pailoids. *What an awful name,* Crepto thought, *Pailoids, it sounds like something from a nightmare.*

A small voice could be heard from the front. "Can we stop and rest?"

"No. Keep going!" Rin yelled to make sure his voice carried to the front.

"Let's stop here." Crepto said. "I'll guard the back. Besides, I have this belt for C-4 and switches if we need to blow something up. I can light them up."

Rin didn't know if he'd like the idea of setting off C-4 in a tunnel so deep already. "We don't need to be burying ourselves alive now. Don't need anybody going pyro on us. You just keep those explosives to yourself."

"Yeah, sure thing," Crepto said. "No pyromaniacs—got it." Crepto looked in front then yelled. "Let's take a break! The young ones need a rest."

"Sure, you want to do that?"

"Yeah, I'm sure, unless you want some of them dying on you. Look at them. They're in sad shape."

Rin looked a little bit annoyed. "They're in better shape than the dead, so who's running this show?"

Crepto smiled and said. "I am. You want safety and food and a place to lay your head, you bet, I'm in charge, and when it comes to everyone's safety, I'm in charge of that too. Are you okay with that?"

Rin didn't say anything further, but you could tell by the look on his face, and knowing this boy in the suit had powers beyond anyone's control he'd leave it for what it was, for the moment nothing was said. *All things in suitable time,* was his thought. Everyone sat and took a break. Crepto reached for the cooler and opened it up. Small hands and big hands alike reached for something cool to drink.

Crepto was standing in a group of young men that had endured two weeks without hardly any supplies. Most of them looked a sight— powder-burned, and a paler color of the dead, and marked from being half frozen, black fingers and guessing toes.

Their leader walked over and introduced his good friend Jimmy, "This is Jimbo." He said. Crepto saw a big man come out of the shadows that took up enough room for two people. He was six foot nine with wide shoulders. Crepto had figured his tall frame had come in handy.

"We should be going." Rin said.

Crepto looked up and said. "Give them a few minutes. They will be better for the rest, and besides, I need to make a call." Rin nodded out of respect. Crepto reached for his pocket, but where he'd put his walkie-talkie? It was gone. It had fallen out during his flight. He shook his head and looked at Rin.

"Does anyone from your little group have a walkie-talkie?" Rin turned and looked at Jimbo, his best friend of the last eighteen years.

"Jimbo, hand me that walkie-talkie you found. Does it still work?"

Jimbo showed a big smile. "Yeah, it works. I just put batteries in it a few minutes ago. It's a military unit. It has a twenty-mile radius."

"That'll be good." Crepto responded. He took the walkie-talkie, turned it on, and turned the unit to channel three. He looked up at Rin before making the call to home base.

"Home base this is T-4 do you read, over?" Crepto waited for ten seconds before repeating the call. On the third call Betty cut in.

"T-4 this is home base, read you loud and clear, what's your status?"

"Betty, we found survivors. They're forty survivors." He heard yelling on the other end—as in a cheer. "Rin and his two kids are with them. No one else we know made it." Crepto said. It was a few more seconds before Betty responded.

"I'm glad you found them." She said, "Where are you guys?"

"We're somewhere east of the mountain. I'm guessing the tunnel where it comes up under our mountain, somewhere. Have T-DEXTER look for a secret entrance. It's got to be somewhere out by the main gates."

"Okay, I'll tell him, and we'll look. How far are you from the mountain?" Crepto called to his internal senses to get more of a fine-tuned answer on distance.

"We're about two miles before this tunnel ends. See if this tunnel leads to another gate. We don't have much more than a couple of hours before this freezing weather begin to set in and take their energy away."

"Alright," She said, "Bailey be safe, I'll call you back when we find something."

Crepto knew her message was meant more personal by addressing him as she did.

"Okay Betty, see you in a couple of hours."

"We should go." Rin said as everyone slowly got up and continued their journey to the lower end of where they did not know would end up. Rin stayed on Crepto's shoulder as they took to the rear of this human caravan.

"Do I know you?" Rin asked.

"Yes, you do. I'm Bailey, your cousin."

Rin was a little hesitant about believing Bailey was beneath the suit. "Betty is at home base with Ryan and Mattie. They're behind the safety of the compound. You'll see them in a couple of hours. I mean if we find a way through."

Rin showed a puzzling expression. "And you don't think we can get through?"

"I didn't say that. Those creatures are everywhere like you said. We don't know when they'll show up again." Crepto looked inside the cooler but hadn't realized that it was empty. He sat it back down and left the cooler behind. Jimbo cocked a shotgun. He had come closer to Rin's side. He was walking next to Crepto at the back of this human caravan.

"Sir shouldn't our new friend here do some scouting ahead," in a deep impetuous voice. "I mean to make sure we don't have any guests at the other end waiting for us?"

Crepto looked up to consider Jumbo's way of thinking. "I can, but you guys will be left on your own, and besides there's nothing ahead, all the trouble is behind us." Rin looked at the worn-out bunch of warriors and realized they could barely walk.

"Jimbo, if something happens to them, they won't have enough strength or fire power to take another onslaught from those creatures." Rin said.

"Yeah, I guess I wasn't thinking." Jimbo said.

He considered going on ahead, but with so many children being a part of this group he reconsidered and stayed. Yet all three, Crepto, Jimbo, and Rin took turns carrying several of the smaller children as they slowly traveled the remaining distance.

Jake looked back at Crepto. "Sir, if you're Bailey, aren't you, my uncle?"

Crepto turned to view the curious boy. "Yes, I guess I am…but I'm not much older than you are."

Jake looked up and smiled. "Well, that's not any…of my fault. There must be a cradle robber in the family tree somewhere."

Crepto took in the information wondering of family traditions.

Jake raised an eyebrow, sensing a subject to touchy to bring up. "Let's get there already. This bunch can't take much more." He said.

Crepto viewed the front of the line. He could see they had just a mile to go.

"Yes, I know. There's only a little bit to go." He reconfirmed their position.

Then this strange idea came to mind. "Listen up!" Crepto expelled with a loud voice. "I've got a plan." Crepto grabbed fifty feet of left over rope he had tied to his side. "I'm asking everyone to tie on to this rope by your waists. I'm going to pull you all to the end of the tunnel." He didn't wait. Tying one ended looped around his waist. Jake was second as each person tied themselves to the rope. Rin and Jimbo stayed to the rear to help the children from falling off the trail. Finally, everyone was linked together. When everyone was tied on, Crepto looked back. "The floor below us is slick with ice, just hold on, I'll do the work." Rin looked a little leery about being pulled down this icy path.

"You sure this'll work?" Rin asked.

"I won't go that fast. Trust me." Rin nodded, holding his daughter in front of him. Slow at first, Crepto leaned as the rope tightened. Within just a few seconds, he had them sliding in a steady rhythm. They were ice skating on worn out shoes at a good 10 to 15 miles per hour. The children were actually smiling when taken by surprise like this was a game.

Renee looked up at her father. "Daddy, this is fun. I'm glad we won't have to walk anymore." Her father said nothing in return. He was more concerned about the rumble from behind. Crepto could feel the vibration too. A quailing went through the group when turning to look back. They could see nothing, but the floor became unstable as Crepto got airborne and pulled them faster. He could see the end near. Once at the end, he heard the walkie-talkie blare. Crepto removed the walkie-talkie and waited.

"T-4 this is home base, do you read over?"

"Yes, I read you. We've got those creatures on our trail again!"

Rin came over. Crepto looked at Rin. "Talk to Betty, she'll help you get through the door. I have to make a stand. Take the children and the others through the other side." Rin nodded as he held the receiver button down.

"Betty this is Rin. Crepto has some work to do. I'll help them get across to safety."

"Roger that Rin. I've got you covered. What's your position?"

"We're at a gate, but I couldn't tell you where it's at."

Crepto turned. "It's under the massive bridge! Tell her to have T-DEXTER look for a hidden panel below." Rin turned and repeated the message back to Betty. Betty, from other side of the walkie-talkie turned to view T-DEXTER standing over her shoulder.

"I'm on it Ms. Betty…" T-DEXTER was already at the top of the bridge and had only to fly below to find this hidden panel. Within two minutes the robot found what Crepto had pointed out.

Crepto removed one of the packs of C-4 and looked back at Jimbo. "Sir, would there be one amongst you who uses a crossbow?" Jimbo turned to find a young girl towards the front named Natalie.

"Young lady, can you lend a hand with your cross bow. Our leader here needs your assistance." Crepto turned to take a glance at the young lady he was referring to. She had pretty blue eyes, with long blonde hair pulled back in a ponytail tucked underneath a baseball cap, yet it was hard to tell if she was male or female because she was dressed as a boy with over-sized clothes full of dirt and mud, and a face masked over with filth of the last two weeks. Crepto saw she had depth in her personality, one of character, one who'd seen death a few times already in her young life. He saw a warrior in the smallest of form before him. Who would have known she'd only be a child of seventeen? She showed a fading smile as she stepped into the limelight with her crossbow. She took a sure-footed step in front of noise coming their way.

"Sir, what do you require of me?" She said with a softly gentle voice. Crepto turned to look again. She had a placid manner about her and showed pretty hands even under dirt and blackened fingernails. He felt confident about this girl. Bravery eluded from her aura, unblinking, unflinching of the desire to kill. She knew the Pailoids were bound by a higher calling than the one she served, but it wouldn't make a difference. Her spirit was willing and her skill right on. Knowing her place was on the front line. A place where only warriors would make a stand against such enemies. A dissimilar set of circumstances gave her courage. Building certainty was glazed in her eyes. She had a warrior spirit pressed in her mind, exuded from her pores like blood flowing to give back life as payment.

She saw Crepto putting together some type of explosive. She'd seen this before. Her father served as a military man and had shown her its purpose. He took one of her arrows and laced it gently with this C-4 as he wrapped it around both ends. The rumble ahead increased with volume. But Crepto waited then looked at her.

"When you fire, we'll only have seconds to clear this area, when that happens…do not be alarmed when I carry you to escape the fury of what's to come." Natalie glanced over without a wavering eye or doubt of Crepto's purpose. Within a few seconds, she shot the arrow forward on a slight uphill turn that got lost in the dark only moments after. Within five seconds, the sound of a loud boom echoed back, resounding off walls and ceiling. The ground shook beneath them. The arrow, shot straight ahead, prevailed, won over a short victory of surprise, into the heart of what was to come—a journey recompense of desire, a place where dead men tell no tales of a ballroom blitz. A journey not for the faint of heart to set on foot, only enduring souls drained of emotion would know what to do. Crepto reached down and swept Natalie off her feet, turning suddenly to look away from fury and flames rushing towards them.

T-DEXTER was just getting the panel door open to this gate impeding their safety. They were running out of time. They stood between life and death. They were at the end of this lugubrious situation. A flurry of creatures tumbled through the darkness that could not be stopped. Crepto yelled into the walkie-talkie, with raised sword and shield while taking a stance against this enemy.

"Open the door!!" He embellished with this astute heart that beat in his chest. A fury unmatched by fire and flame overtook him. He was enveloped all around as the rage set the stage.

Suddenly, the door slid up as the mound of human bodies poured through it's opening with building anxiety. Pressing toward a day behind to find safety amongst the living. Crepto pushed Natalie through door, "Go, your safety is at hand. Don't delay!" Crepto turned to face the coming retribution, only seconds to spare separated him by just inches. Yet the rumble of bodies and the blood were not demurred from its purpose. They were as one, a unit pressing against the strain of survival of the fittest. The ones that have changed the faces of this universe were at hand. Crepto spun his shield and flashed his sword as he shot forward into the misery of the fight. The rage of the death met him in the middle. Crepto slammed against body, bone, and blood in the bludgeoning of fury chased to the grave—moving sword and shield weighing heavy on his mind. Heat and light were the same as friend and foe—life was taken from the many by shield pushed by the Crepto energy.

"Where's Bailey?" Betty asked. No one had an answer, and no one responded to go back except the young lady he had forced through the open gate. Natalie started to go back but was stopped by Rin.

"Don't, what's out there is not for you—it was meant for him. Let him be."

What they didn't know was that T-DEXTER was trying to rewire this gate because it wouldn't close and the rage that lay behind was still headed their way. T-DEXTER finally got the right wires connecting the gate, yet he wasn't just yet ready to close it behind, because an important part of their group was left in the burning of the tunnel.

T-DEXTER left his post and flew down into the secret place hidden passed the gate, below the massive bridge. Crepto was face-to-face with these creatures, and he was all alone. T-DEXTER shot through the opening and met the rage with little brother, as brother's always take the burden of the many to filter the pain of the burden which becomes too heavy, for the burden of the many is the cause that unfurls the strength of one or two, and two becomes the many, as the rage of the dying furls the strength of the two gain the strength of the many, and the strength of the many are consumed. For the dying of the many which the cause of the two leaves behind the strength of the many all consumed.

T-DEXTER pulled little brother from the fight and the two who were many left the scene not consumed. Once they shot through the open gate, T-DEXTER cleared the panel and closed the rage from behind. They were safe behind the gates as the rage of the many was consumed and the fury of the smoke of the two left behind floated high off the bodies of the many.

CHAPTER 30

The Arrival

The survivors were pretty beat-up. T-DEXTER opened the back of this large trailer that Dr. EL had pulled to the main-gate so the survivors could be taken to the compound and dealt with according to injuries or frame of mind, or needing normal human items of survival, such as food and water, or a shower and a warm bed to lay their head. T-DEXTER, even though a robot, acknowledged the downhearted distrainment of trying to herd them like cattle to another area. But at the same time, they had no other way to move them as a group through the tunnels. The ingress of the back of the trailer made it seem like they were victims similar to the holocaust. Dr. EL remembered the stories told of such in his youth. Crepto was quick to help the group inside the trailer in the back of the truck. He wanted to help them in as little time as possible to meet their needs.

When Betty saw the sad shape, they were in, the back of her eyes filled with tears. She saw the relentless rage of the dying in each set of eyes, as they humbly crossed a line of finding a new home—as each set of eyes expressed a deep inhibiting stare, almost lifeless. As she could tell, they had lost hope, for hope was just being rescued. They'd been running on adrenaline. Now strength depleted, barely surviving the aftermath of an end.

Betty came around the back side of the trailer to help others down off the lift. Two little girls were in bad shape when seeing them. One had to be hospitalized up on the third floor. George would help supervise any patients that needed constant care. Jackie had learned enough, with little Mattie, to be able to run the Zoo on her own with minimal help with heavier chores like, baling hay, or moving yard equipment to clean cages. Jake would help the girls for the next few days, so George could offer his services medically.

None of the injured were bitten by the Pailoids. Some had frost bite. Powder-burned, half-starved, cold, and afraid. Their whole lives had been taken by violent force.

George, Betty, and Ryan helped walk several of the injured up to the third floor to get medical treatment. George and Betty prepared a feast of sandwiches and drinks, potato salad, fruit, crackers with small bowls of soup, and water. Betty and Dr. EL were acumen of the needs presented. Several first-aid kits for scraps and cuts, along with blankets to hold in body heat had been handed out. George unlocked the downstairs bathrooms to help accommodate the many for personal hygiene. T-DEXTER had hauled a long table to the bottom warehouse floor to set up food and drinks to be dispersed. Everyone gathered round and took part in the meal presented. And clothing was handed out like jackets or a good pair of shoes to cover their feet. Even Dr. EL felt a wave of emotion, when seeing the sad shape, they were in—tears sparkled in the back of his eyes. They had never seen such great need from half-starved victims. It was a picture set in time that Dr. EL had remembered from school. Now, a reflective reminder pierced at the hearts of a small group of people. Even Ryan helped one little girl get her portion when she struggled to walk to the table. One of the mother's emotions had suddenly unraveled as she sat on the floor and broke out into tears. Another survivor helped her by getting her a plate of food and water and helped clean off one of the girl's faces covered in dirt.

Bailey crawled out of the Crepto suit. SNARF, taking that as a clue, came by to take it to be cleaned and cooled. Bailey walked up to Betty and gave her a hug. Dr. EL's face shows a bit of tension. Knowing he owed Bailey an apology for not having enough faith to find survivors. The doctor was prepared to say something to Bailey, but the boy held up his hand denying him the effort.

"It's not necessary sir. We were lucky to find them."

"Where's Sergeant Bristol?" The doctor asked.

"He didn't make it sir. He died in one of the explosions to save me so I could save them." Bailey pointed to the ones gathered around the table. Dr. EL wondered of the horror they went through by how they looked. Bailey reached to put a hand on his shoulder.

"What's the weather looking like out there?" The good doctor asked.

"It was almost unbearable out there sir. The tunnels were in the forties and fifties. They saved them from freezing to death. Being underground kept them from dying."

A surge of emotion raised up in Bailey. Knowing the survivors needed to know where they were going to sleep. So, clearing his throat to get their attention. Raising his voice to say. "We're happy to have found you before it was too late. I know some of you have injuries that need attention. One of us can show you where you can get medical treatment on the third floor in our med-lab. George will be there for the next few hours to help you with your individual physical ailments. Please feel free to seek any medical attention needed now or the next couple of hours. Don't wait until tomorrow. No one will be in the med-lab on the third floor tomorrow. What I'd like to point out would be that we do have an overabundance of supplies and resources to last a while, but please use things sparingly for we do not know how long we will be staying in this facility. Using a bit of intelligence, and common sense with our supplies might save our lives in the future by thinking conservatively. Except for that, I'd like to welcome all of you to this facility for our time here is short of divine, thanks to our government. Betty and I will give you keys to different rooms up in the hotel here for now, where everyone will have a chance to be close to food and water supplies. After that, if you would like a bit more privacy for families and friends, we do have condominiums down one of the other tunnels. There's a town in tunnel three that most of you will enjoy. We set some charges yesterday, and the air needs to clear there another day or so, before we let people down there. We hope all of you can find everything you need for the night. If you have any questions, please ask. Thank you." Bailey finished and started to help a few others to where they needed to go.

Betty started taking groups of families up to the seventh and eighth floor for room assignments. Bailey helped with his own groups as they all began to get situated for the night.

Later that night, Dr. EL, Bailey, and Betty, with Rin and met for a private dinner to catch up on family issues and events of an immediate nature. George came up later to get directions from the others of leadership. Dr. EL and Bailey took to the kitchen for the dinner's menu. Jake laid his sister down earlier for the evening. Meeting his father in the doorway of the dining-room across from the galley. "Dad, can I be in here?"

Rin looked up. "I don't see why not? Come in." Rin said.

Coffee was served while George brought out a fresh hot peach pie from the oven. Betty got the ice-cream scooped out for each bowl. She looked across the table, noticing that Bailey looked worn from that day's efforts. He had a glassy stare in his eyes. He looked sad, maybe because he'd left behind his friend. Sergeant Bristol will be missed. They just started to bond. Then Bailey pulled the tiny box out of a pocket and sat it on the table. She wondered what it was. Bailey looked across the table at Rin. Dark circles rounded the bottom of his eyes. His face was pale, looking tired, worn out. No words could be expressed of what they'd been through. Rin told them of about the last twelve days of fighting. After peach pie alamode, Jake and Rin left to their own suite to rest.

Later that night, Dr. EL sat on the ninth-floor patio of the penthouse, Bailey and Betty invited him to spend a few more moments together. A strange look of concern about the days to come was written in his eyes. Even though Bailey went out of his territory to find others, he knew the doctor would be incredibly careful in the future about decisions made. They were in a tough time of growing, a new era to making a living, worked out in a violent reform of survival. A new world facing them head on. Formed from the aftermath of what was left of a handful of victims. This was an apocalyptic time of survival. It was time to move on, to rebuild, start over, and create a new vision. Betty noticed the three children were in a hurry to get up and meet with the other children, for the next day. Betty went in and tucked the girls in snug in their beds for the night. Ryan got down on his knees and said a prayer. Betty never saw him do this before. It touched her.

Bailey sat with the doctor as he talked about events, they were soon facing in the weeks to come. There were several airplane kits and helicopters at the lower end. There was a pilot among the new group. Betty settled down for the night. She was filled with hope after the rescue. Happy to have the baseball park in Tunnel Three, the auditorium, the banquet-hall, and a bowling alley under the town hall.

Victims, survivors, an awkward bunch at best, now a part of a new race of people, having a chance for a new way of life. Seen as misfits before, but now considered plebeian. An oddity to the aftermath of what was left. No complete family had survived this apocalyptic end. Typically, all families, when viewing their situation, molded into one.

This was a new beginning, living underground in a world set apart, as companions, survivors, and leaders of their world. They'd survived insurmountable odds and remained intact of the living. For now, all were safe and at rest, and peace and tranquility became a haven of fortitude for the forty-seven souls that had remained. They were to become the foundation of a new society. Carrying on the legacy for all mankind. The road, though difficult, was a journey that had to be traveled. This small band of misfits, with their new friends, had found the key to survival down on Bailey's Road.

B G Simpson

AFTERWORD

Bailey's Road was a project I started back in 2011. I had several life experiences as a base before deciding to sit down and create a novel that reflected pieces of the type of stories told that I had always liked villains and heroes of an unnatural setting with a twist of fate. Unsettling circumstances and end-of-the-world scenarios appear to be the going thing right now as stories go. Stories about love and courage are ingredients we all tend to bend our ears to. A relevant story with heart-warming love and friction as told between the characters like Bailey and Betty tend to interest people also, considering no relationship in the real world is perfect. We all struggle with our imperfections. This story, as you can figure, started in San Diego where I grew up, and running in my youth was a big part of my life.

Stories like this about families and trying conditions seem to interest us all, with the climax of what to do or where to go when no one's around to care—the more imagination and detail we use with the right flare, the better. Colorado Springs, Colorado, starting in chapter three was one of my favorite places to visit. I took a few familiar experiences of memory and built on that. The Rocky Mountains have always held great mysteries and known stories have been told of secret tunnels hidden by our government. Who knows what's actually out there, but it makes you think if there's a world like this so bizarre, so outlandish, what could happen to our world with so much going on at the same time? Many people become more alert when faced with challenges that mean the end of life. What will people go through to save their families, the ones they love? If you had to live in a world like this, how would you survive?

Humanity, at times, I believe, has this incessant ability to draw courage from us when we least expect it. A story told, reanimated through the imaginations of writers and story tellers across the globe, do tend to have their purpose. Their purpose is to draw from each of us emotion that pulls us through the story. That way, from the writer's perspective, he or she might sell more books.

What gave me the idea to draft this novel were the many influences of other superheroes as slightly mentioned throughout. I had to find a hero created from a scientific effort from a greater mind like in the character of Dr. Alfred Geneses, usually as believable compared to a Marvel comic hero, which have been quite popular so many times over. As seen in this imaginary world, we might come to believe that this could be possible in a real-world scenario as long as our imagination is willing to take us there. Dually noted, the boundaries of the human heart will surprise us when we're put into a dire situation. Who knows what we will do at the moment we're tested?

B G Simpson